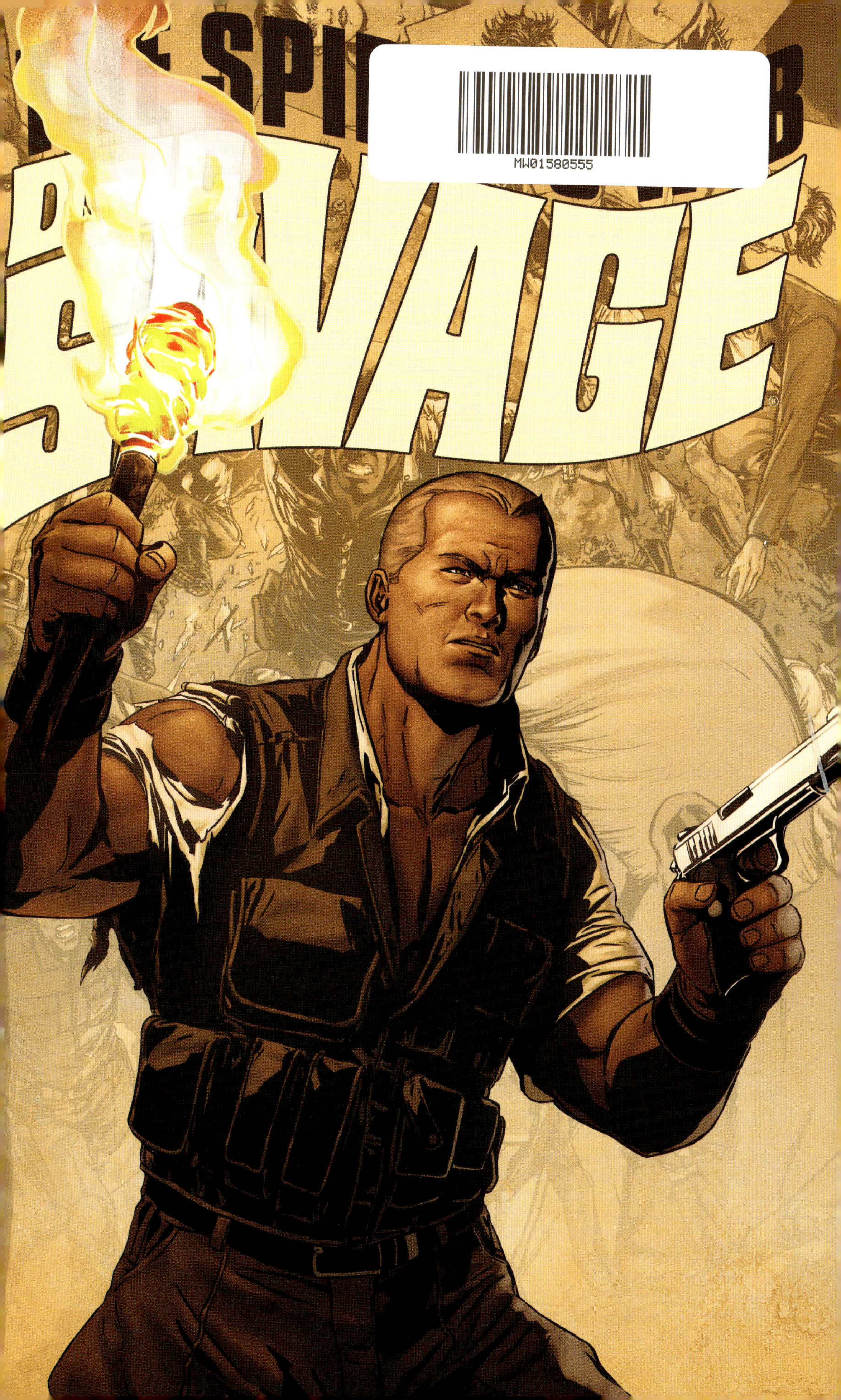

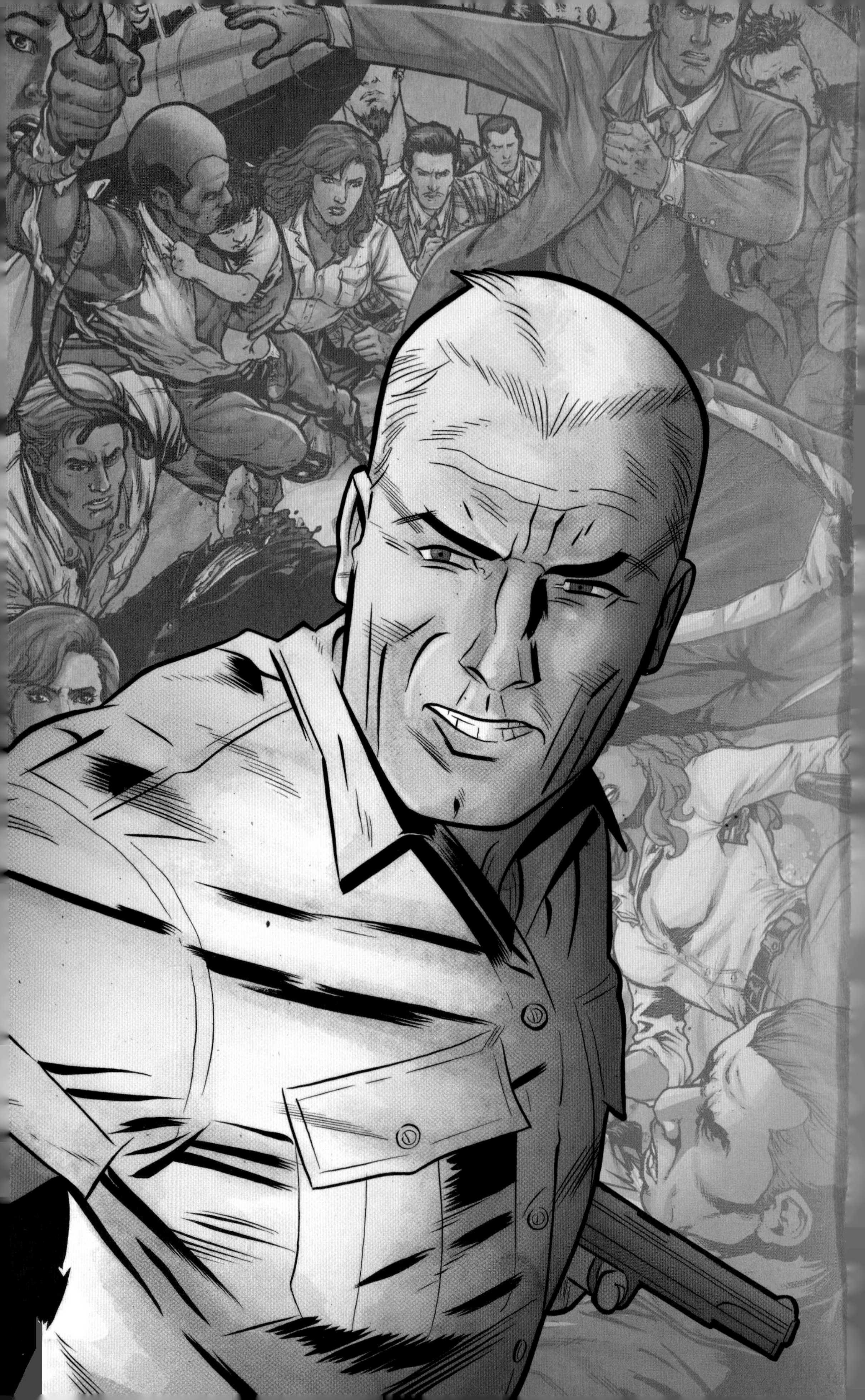

THE SPIDER'S WEB
DOC SAVAGE

WRITTEN BY .... CHRIS ROBERSON

ART BY .... CEZAR RAZEK

COLORS BY .... DIJO LIMA

LETTERS BY .... SIMON BOWLAND

COLLECTION DESIGN BY .... ALEXIS PERSSON

DYNAMITE

Nick Barrucci, CEO / Publisher
Juan Collado, President / COO

Joe Rybandt, Executive Editor
Matt Idelson, Senior Editor
Rachel Pinnelas, Associate Editor
Anthony Marques, Assistant Editor
Kevin Ketner, Editorial Assistant

Jason Ullmeyer, Art Director
Geoff Harkins, Senior Graphic Designer
Cathleen Heard, Graphic Designer
Alexis Persson, Production Artist

Chris Caniano, Digital Associate
Rachel Kilbury, Digital Assistant

Brandon Dante Primavera, V.P. of IT and Operations
Rich Young, Director of Business Development

Alan Payne, V.P. of Sales and Marketing
Keith Davidsen, Marketing Director
Pat O'Connell, Sales Manager

Online at www.DYNAMITE.com On Tumblr dynamitecomics.tumblr.com
On Facebook /Dynamitecomics On Twitter @dynamitecomics
Instagram /Dynamitecomics On YouTube /dynamitecomics

First Printing   ISBN-10: 1-5241-0056-0      ISBN-13: 978-1-5241-0056-8   10 9 8 7 6 5 4 3 2 1

DOC SAVAGE: THE SPIDER'S WEB®, VOLUME 1, First printing. Contains materials originally published in DOC SAVAGE: THE SPIDER'S WEB®, VOLUME 1, #1-5. Published by Dynamite Entertainment. 113 Gaither Dr., STE 205, Mt. Laurel, NJ 08054. Seduction of the Innocent is ™ & © 2016 Dynamite Characters, llc. DYNAMITE, DYNAMITE ENTERTAINMENT and its logo are ® & © 2016 Dynamite. All rights reserved. All names, characters, events, and locales in this publication are entirely fictional. Any resemblance to actual persons (living or dead), events or places, without satiric intent, is coincidental. No portion of this book may be reproduced by any means (digital or print) without the written permission of Dynamite Entertainment except for review purposes. The scanning, uploading and distribution of this book via the Internet or via any other means without the permission of the publisher is illegal and punishable by law. Please purchase only authorized electronic editions, and do not participate in or encourage electronic piracy of copyrighted materials. Printed in China.

For media rights, foreign rights, promotions, licensing, and advertising: marketing@dynamite.com

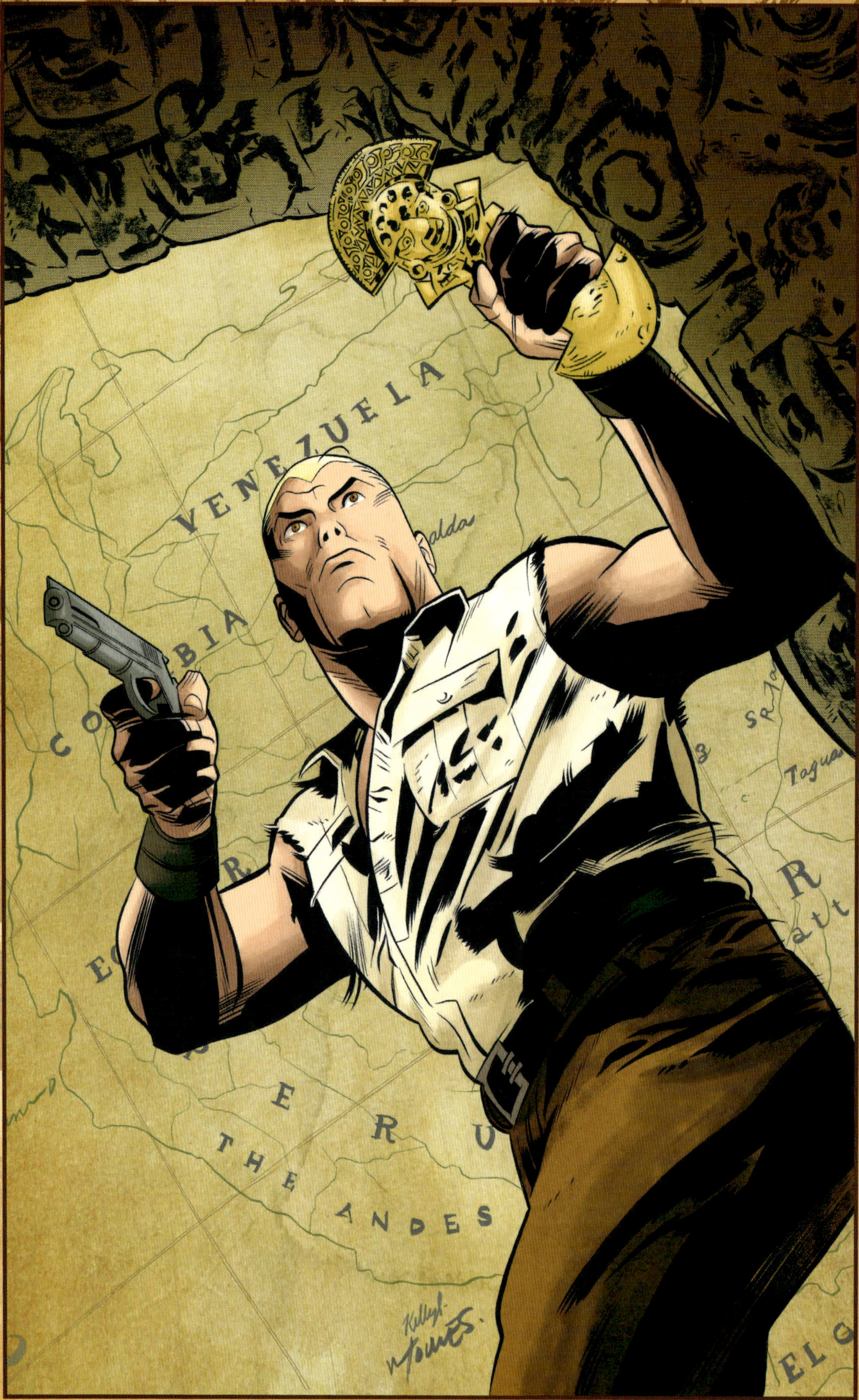
VENEZUELA
THE ANDES

ISSUE #1 COVER
art by **WILFREDO TORRES** colors by **KELLY FITZPATRICK**

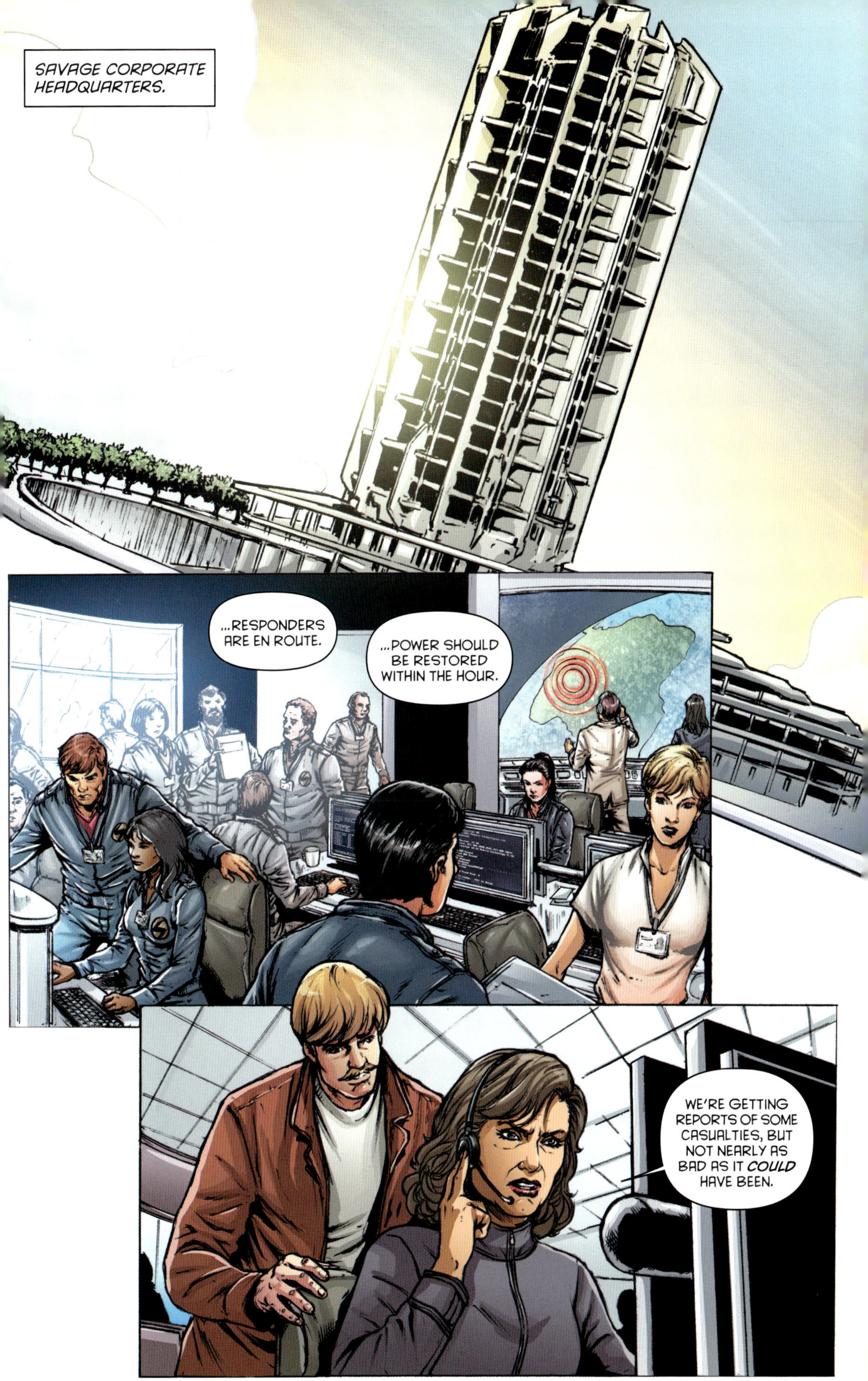
SAVAGE CORPORATE HEADQUARTERS.
...RESPONDERS ARE EN ROUTE.
...POWER SHOULD BE RESTORED WITHIN THE HOUR.
WE'RE GETTING REPORTS OF SOME CASUALTIES, BUT NOT NEARLY AS BAD AS IT *COULD* HAVE BEEN.

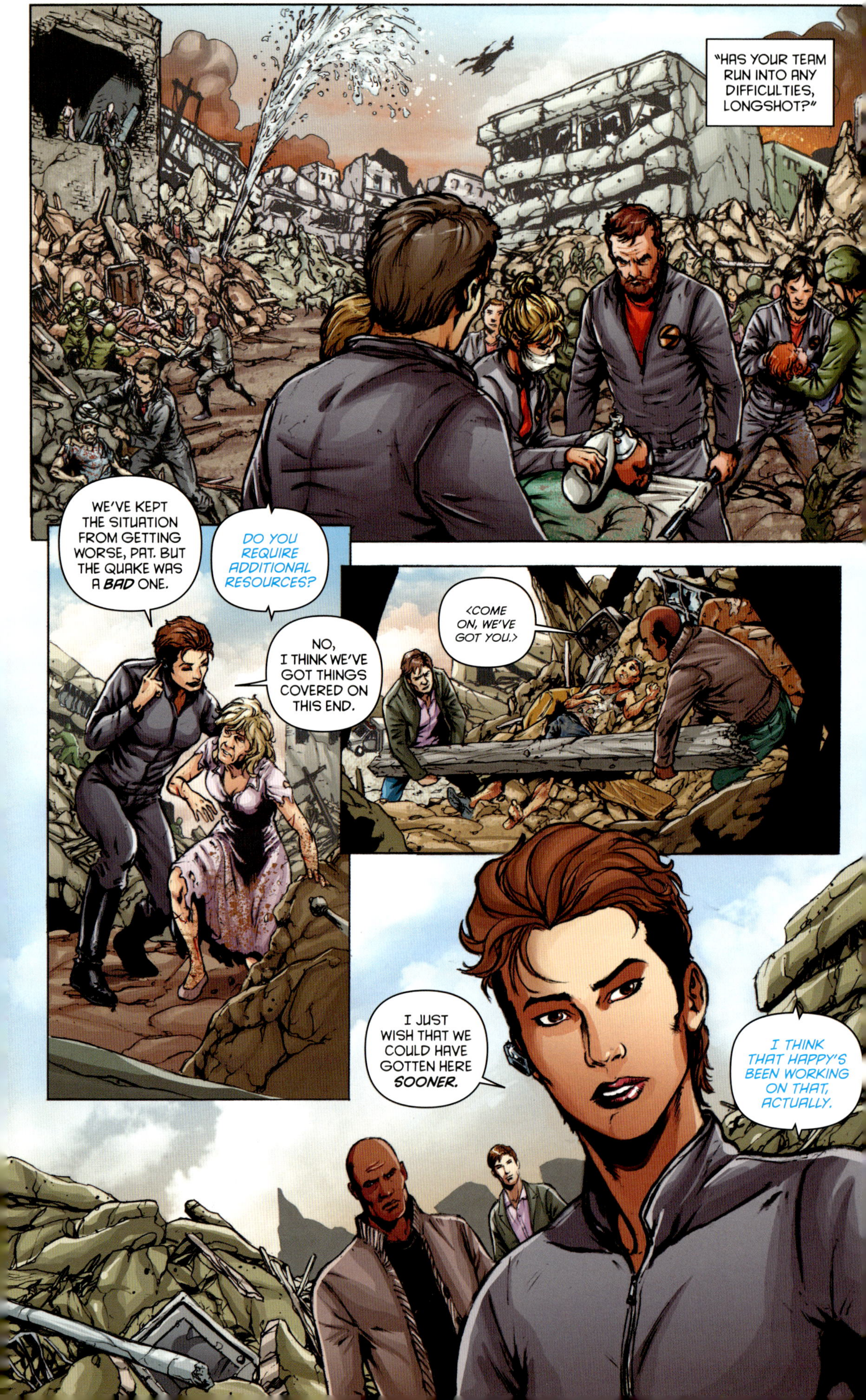
"HAS YOUR TEAM RUN INTO ANY DIFFICULTIES, LONGSHOT?"
WE'VE KEPT THE SITUATION FROM GETTING WORSE, PAT. BUT THE QUAKE WAS A *BAD* ONE.
DO YOU REQUIRE ADDITIONAL RESOURCES?
NO, I THINK WE'VE GOT THINGS COVERED ON THIS END.
<COME ON, WE'VE GOT YOU.>
I JUST WISH THAT WE COULD HAVE GOTTEN HERE *SOONER.*
I THINK THAT HAPPY'S BEEN WORKING ON THAT, ACTUALLY.

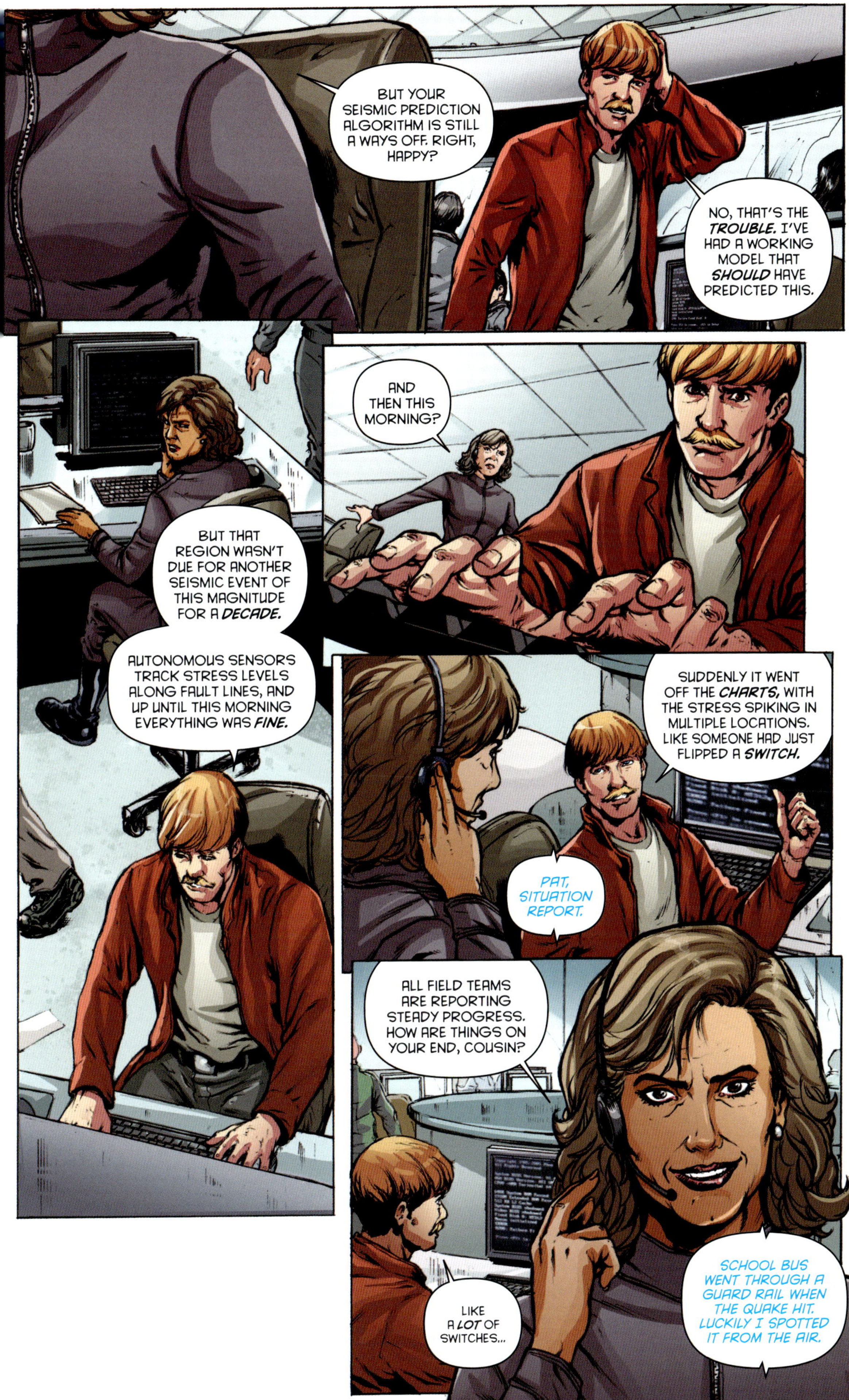
BUT YOUR SEISMIC PREDICTION ALGORITHM IS STILL A WAYS OFF. RIGHT, HAPPY?
NO, THAT'S THE *TROUBLE.* I'VE HAD A WORKING MODEL THAT *SHOULD* HAVE PREDICTED THIS.
AND THEN THIS MORNING?
BUT THAT REGION WASN'T DUE FOR ANOTHER SEISMIC EVENT OF THIS MAGNITUDE FOR A *DECADE.*
AUTONOMOUS SENSORS TRACK STRESS LEVELS ALONG FAULT LINES, AND UP UNTIL THIS MORNING EVERYTHING WAS *FINE.*
SUDDENLY IT WENT OFF THE *CHARTS,* WITH THE STRESS SPIKING IN MULTIPLE LOCATIONS. LIKE SOMEONE HAD JUST FLIPPED A *SWITCH.*
PAT, SITUATION REPORT.
ALL FIELD TEAMS ARE REPORTING STEADY PROGRESS. HOW ARE THINGS ON YOUR END, COUSIN?
SCHOOL BUS WENT THROUGH A GUARD RAIL WHEN THE QUAKE HIT. LUCKILY I SPOTTED IT FROM THE AIR.
LIKE A *LOT* OF SWITCHES...

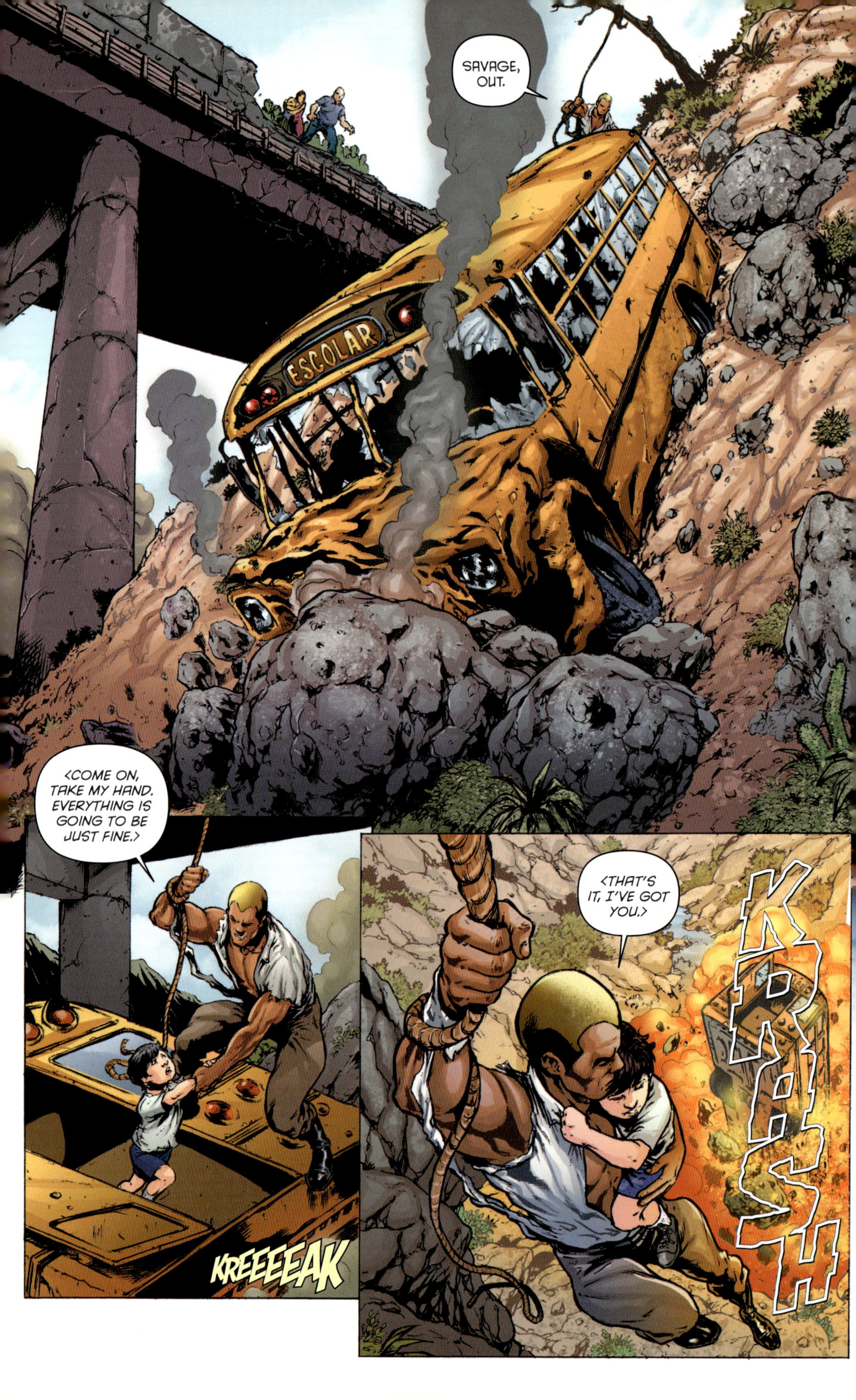
SAVAGE, OUT.
ESCOLAR
<COME ON, TAKE MY HAND. EVERYTHING IS GOING TO BE JUST FINE.>
KREEEEAK
<THAT'S IT, I'VE GOT YOU.>
KRASH

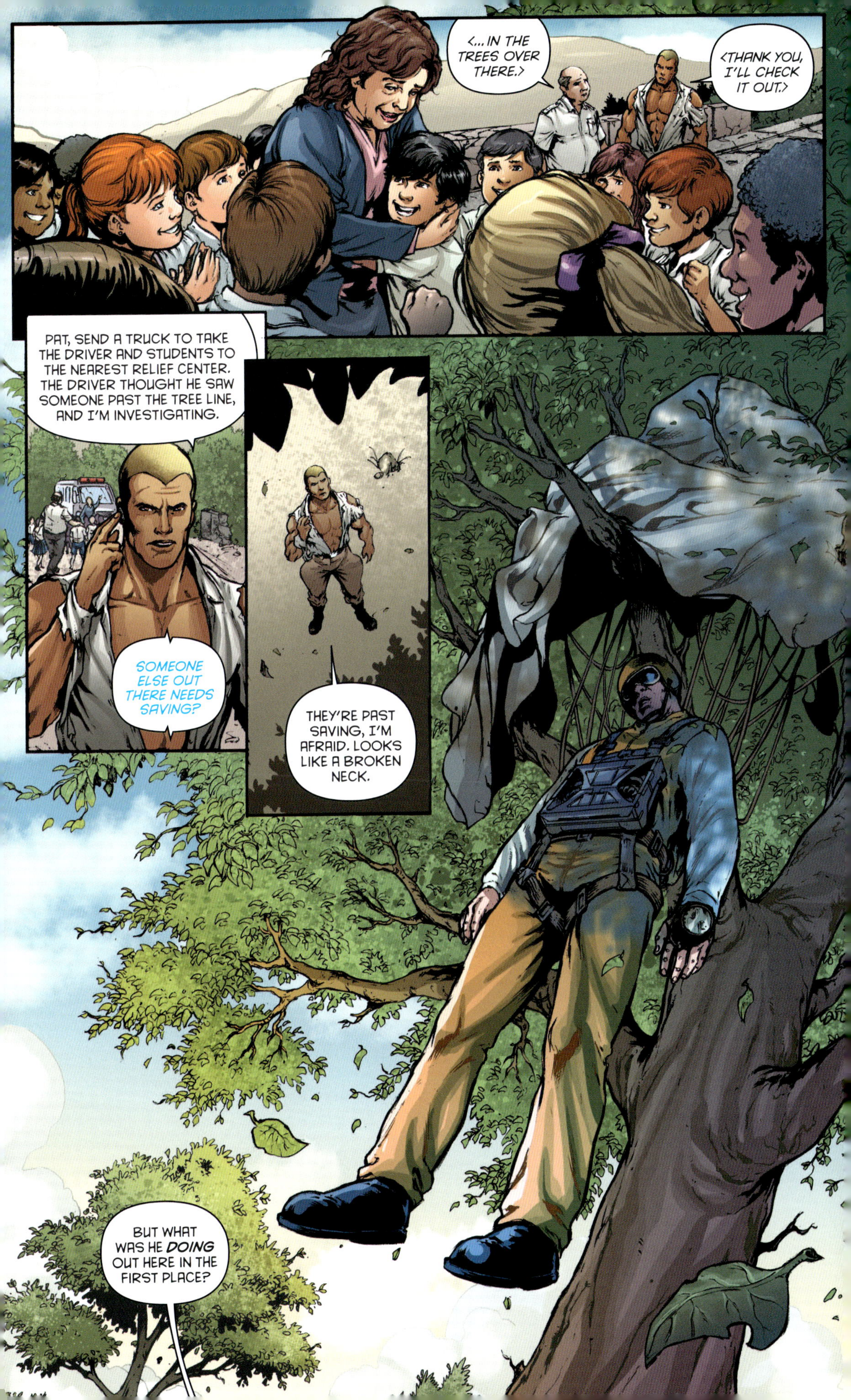

<...IN THE TREES OVER THERE.>
<THANK YOU, I'LL CHECK IT OUT.>
PAT, SEND A TRUCK TO TAKE THE DRIVER AND STUDENTS TO THE NEAREST RELIEF CENTER. THE DRIVER THOUGHT HE SAW SOMEONE PAST THE TREE LINE, AND I'M INVESTIGATING.
SOMEONE ELSE OUT THERE NEEDS SAVING?
THEY'RE PAST SAVING, I'M AFRAID. LOOKS LIKE A BROKEN NECK.
BUT WHAT WAS HE *DOING* OUT HERE IN THE FIRST PLACE?

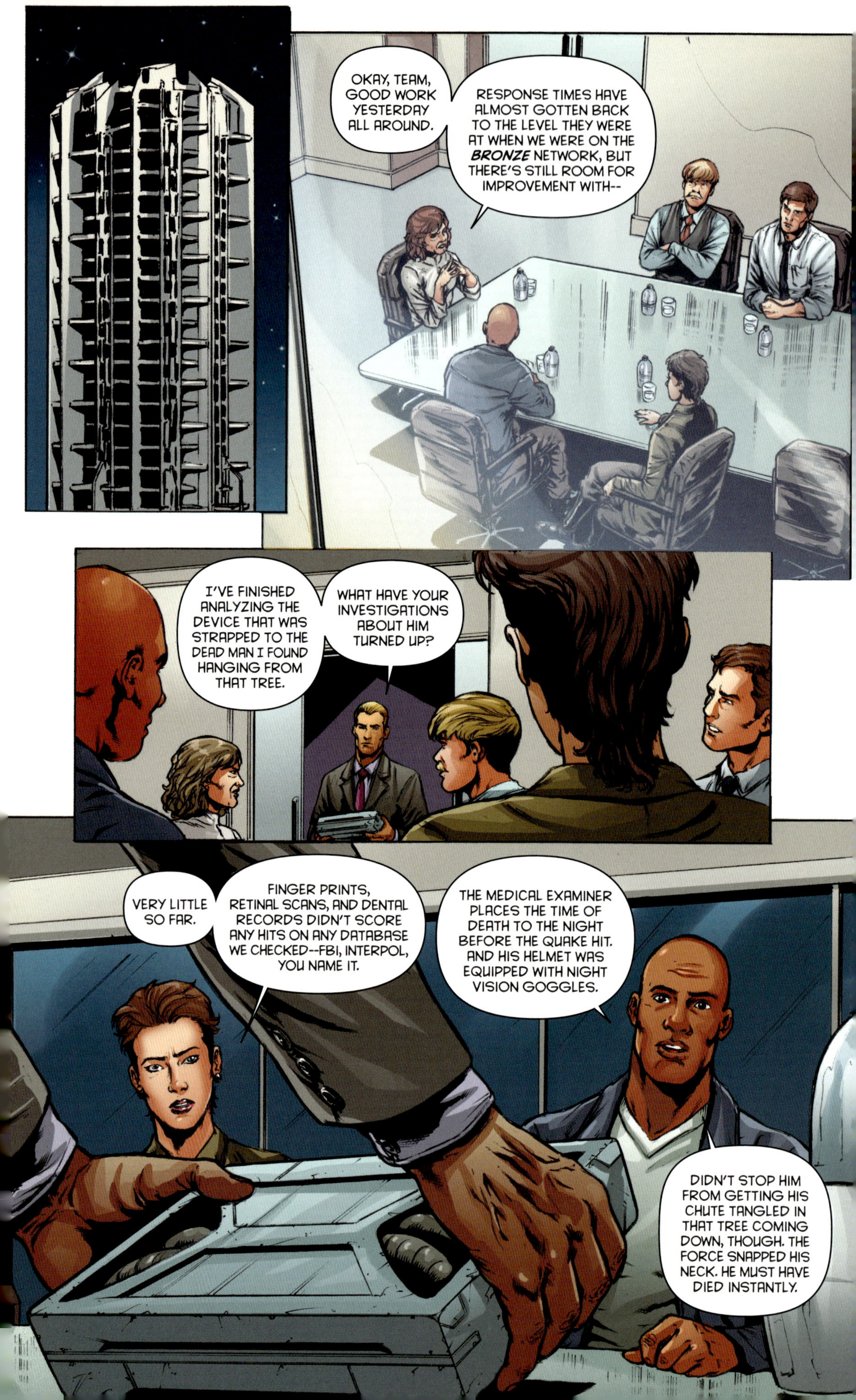
OKAY, TEAM, GOOD WORK YESTERDAY ALL AROUND.
RESPONSE TIMES HAVE ALMOST GOTTEN BACK TO THE LEVEL THEY WERE AT WHEN WE WERE ON THE *BRONZE* NETWORK, BUT THERE'S STILL ROOM FOR IMPROVEMENT WITH--
I'VE FINISHED ANALYZING THE DEVICE THAT WAS STRAPPED TO THE DEAD MAN I FOUND HANGING FROM THAT TREE.
WHAT HAVE YOUR INVESTIGATIONS ABOUT HIM TURNED UP?
VERY LITTLE SO FAR.
FINGER PRINTS, RETINAL SCANS, AND DENTAL RECORDS DIDN'T SCORE ANY HITS ON ANY DATABASE WE CHECKED--FBI, INTERPOL, YOU NAME IT.
THE MEDICAL EXAMINER PLACES THE TIME OF DEATH TO THE NIGHT BEFORE THE QUAKE HIT. AND HIS HELMET WAS EQUIPPED WITH NIGHT VISION GOGGLES.
DIDN'T STOP HIM FROM GETTING HIS CHUTE TANGLED IN THAT TREE COMING DOWN, THOUGH. THE FORCE SNAPPED HIS NECK. HE MUST HAVE DIED INSTANTLY.

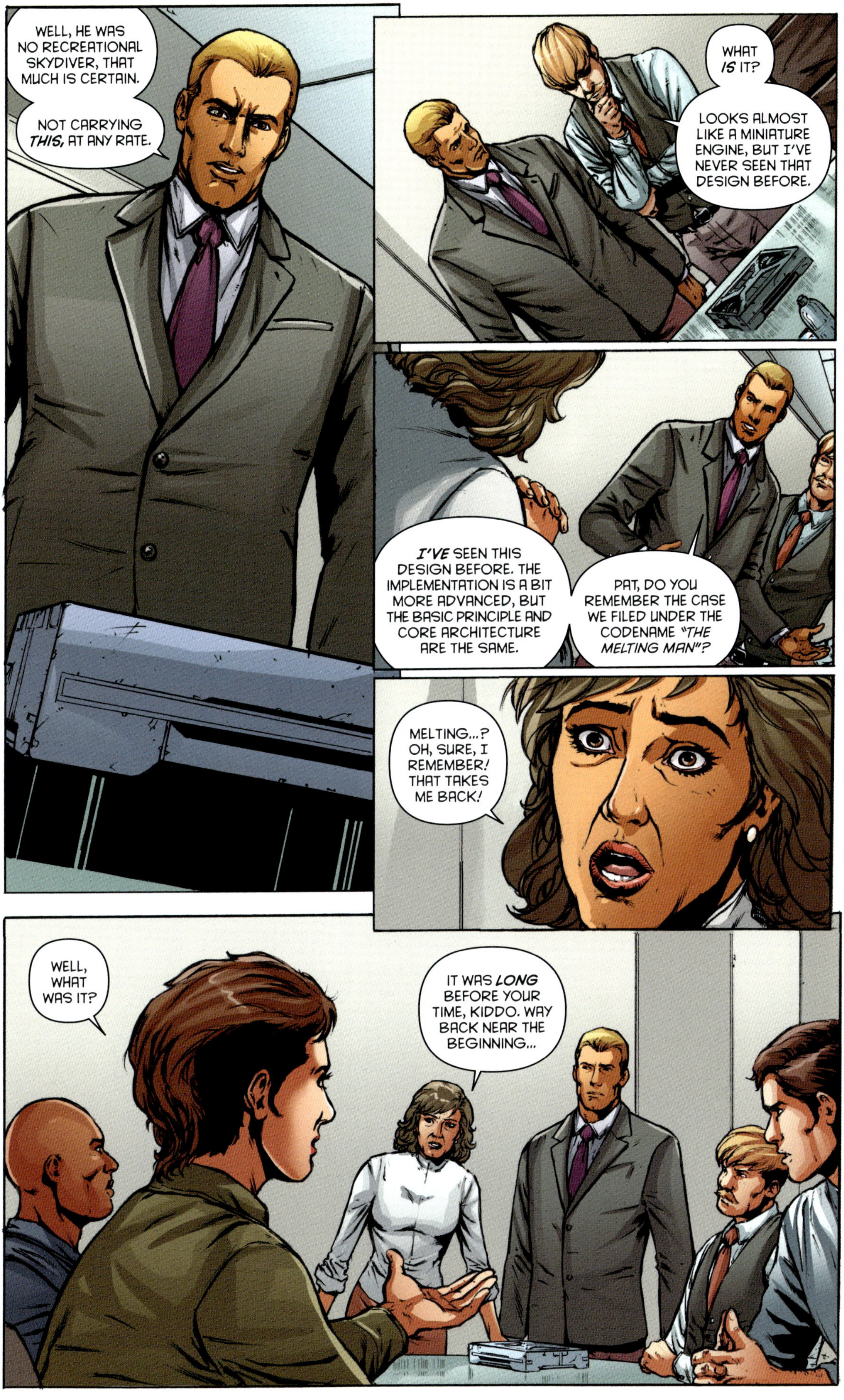
WELL, HE WAS NO RECREATIONAL SKYDIVER, THAT MUCH IS CERTAIN.
NOT CARRYING *THIS,* AT ANY RATE.
WHAT *IS* IT?
LOOKS ALMOST LIKE A MINIATURE ENGINE, BUT I'VE NEVER SEEN THAT DESIGN BEFORE.
I'VE SEEN THIS DESIGN BEFORE. THE IMPLEMENTATION IS A BIT MORE ADVANCED, BUT THE BASIC PRINCIPLE AND CORE ARCHITECTURE ARE THE SAME.
PAT, DO YOU REMEMBER THE CASE WE FILED UNDER THE CODENAME *"THE MELTING MAN"*?
MELTING...? OH, SURE, I REMEMBER! THAT TAKES ME BACK!
WELL, WHAT WAS IT?
IT WAS *LONG* BEFORE YOUR TIME, KIDDO. WAY BACK NEAR THE BEGINNING...

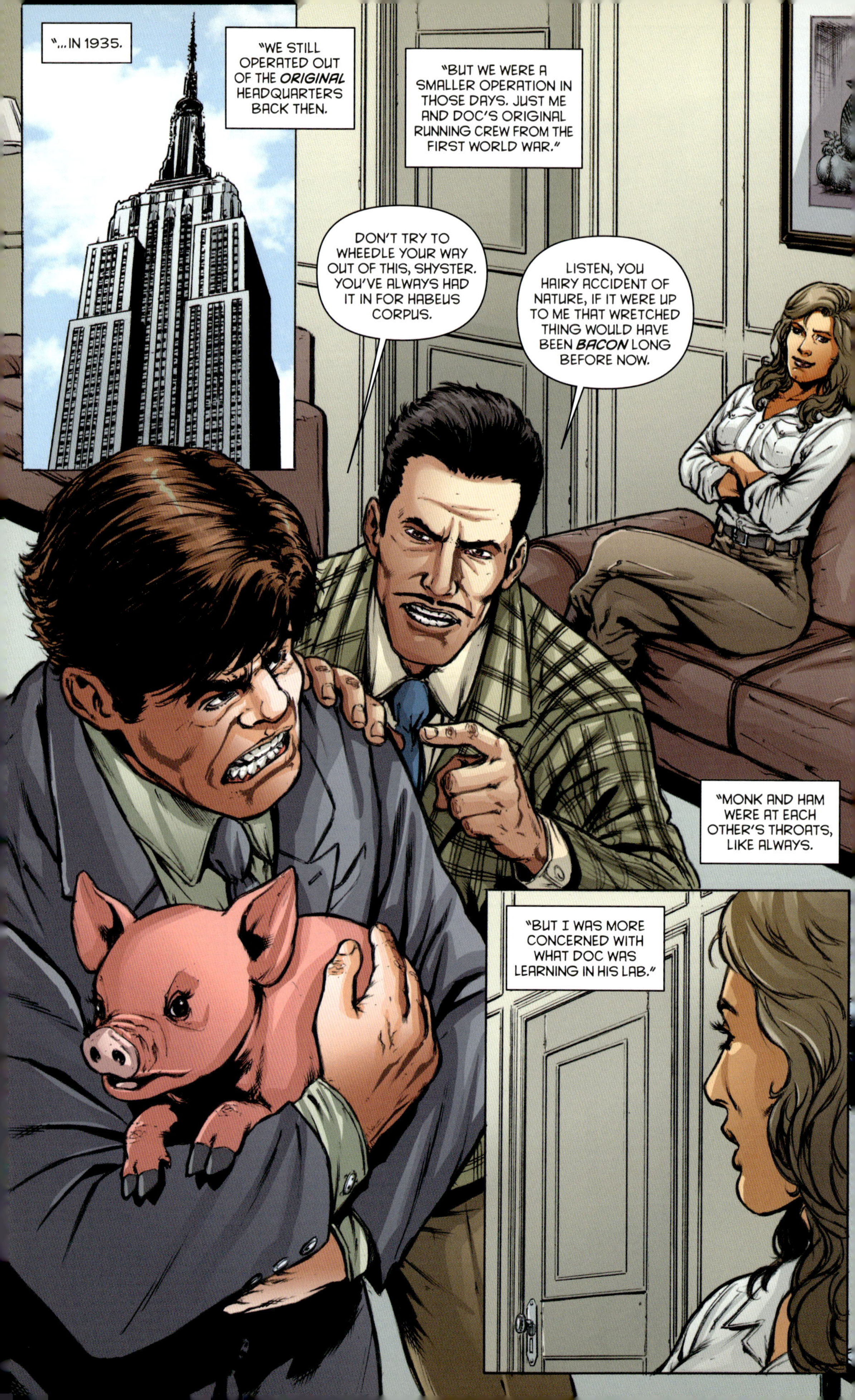
"...IN 1935.
"WE STILL OPERATED OUT OF THE *ORIGINAL* HEADQUARTERS BACK THEN.
"BUT WE WERE A SMALLER OPERATION IN THOSE DAYS. JUST ME AND DOC'S ORIGINAL RUNNING CREW FROM THE FIRST WORLD WAR."
DON'T TRY TO WHEEDLE YOUR WAY OUT OF THIS, SHYSTER. YOU'VE ALWAYS HAD IT IN FOR HABEUS CORPUS.
LISTEN, YOU HAIRY ACCIDENT OF NATURE, IF IT WERE UP TO ME THAT WRETCHED THING WOULD HAVE BEEN *BACON* LONG BEFORE NOW.
"MONK AND HAM WERE AT EACH OTHER'S THROATS, LIKE ALWAYS.
"BUT I WAS MORE CONCERNED WITH WHAT DOC WAS LEARNING IN HIS LAB."

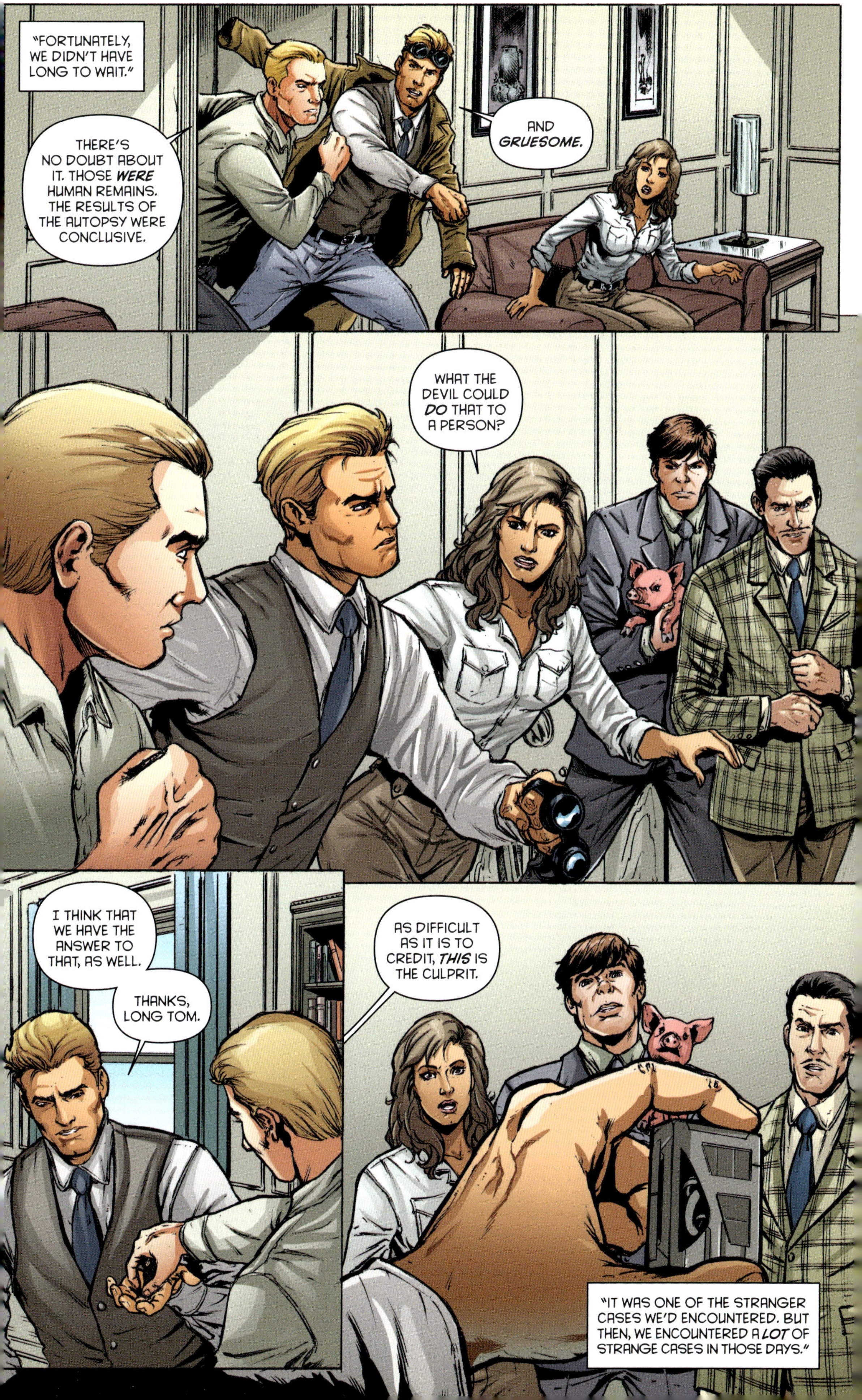
"FORTUNATELY, WE DIDN'T HAVE LONG TO WAIT."
THERE'S NO DOUBT ABOUT IT. THOSE *WERE* HUMAN REMAINS. THE RESULTS OF THE AUTOPSY WERE CONCLUSIVE.
AND *GRUESOME.*
WHAT THE DEVIL COULD *DO* THAT TO A PERSON?
I THINK THAT WE HAVE THE ANSWER TO THAT, AS WELL.
THANKS, LONG TOM.
AS DIFFICULT AS IT IS TO CREDIT, *THIS* IS THE CULPRIT.
"IT WAS ONE OF THE STRANGER CASES WE'D ENCOUNTERED. BUT THEN, WE ENCOUNTERED A *LOT* OF STRANGE CASES IN THOSE DAYS."

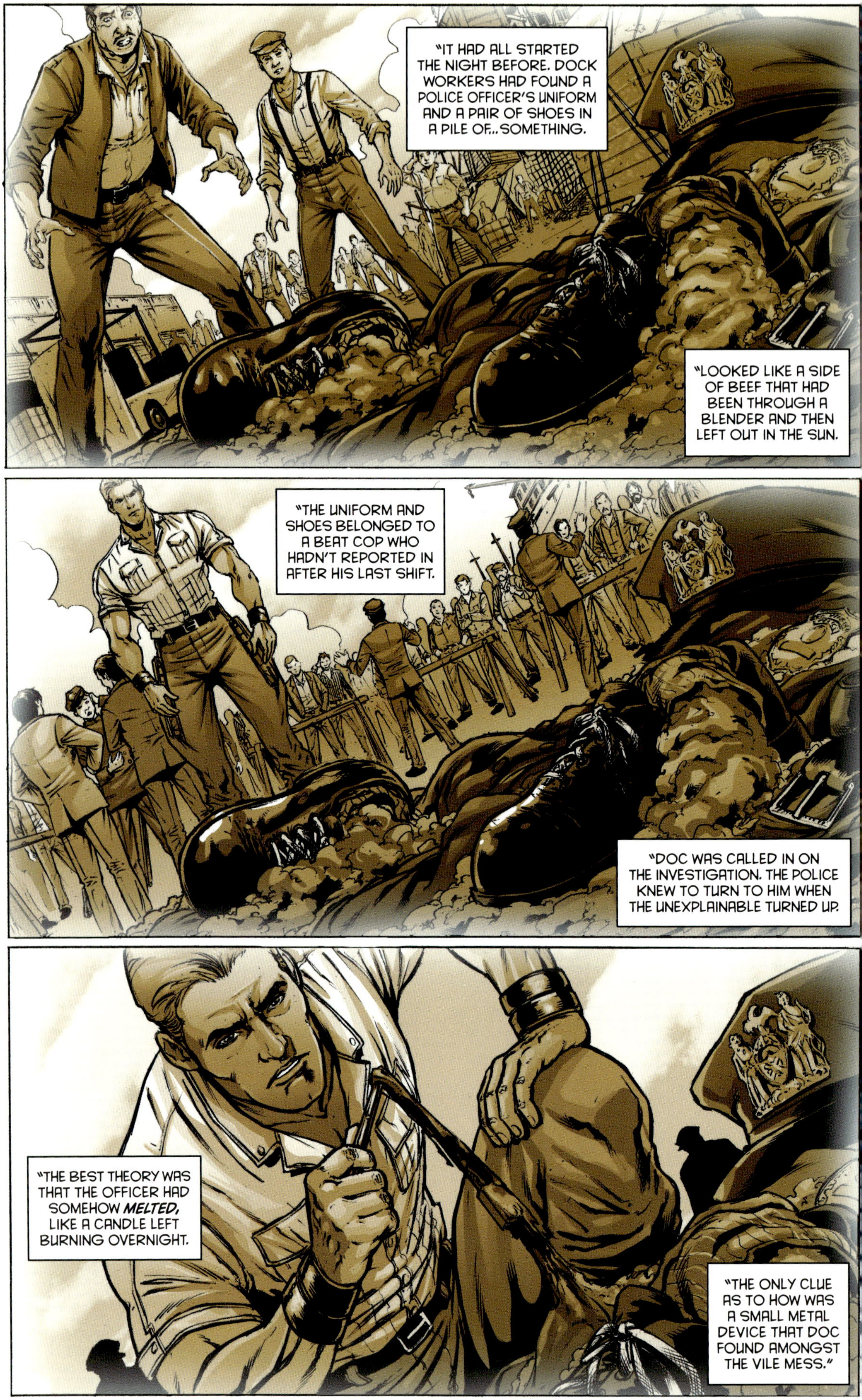
"IT HAD ALL STARTED THE NIGHT BEFORE. DOCK WORKERS HAD FOUND A POLICE OFFICER'S UNIFORM AND A PAIR OF SHOES IN A PILE OF... SOMETHING.
"LOOKED LIKE A SIDE OF BEEF THAT HAD BEEN THROUGH A BLENDER AND THEN LEFT OUT IN THE SUN.
"THE UNIFORM AND SHOES BELONGED TO A BEAT COP WHO HADN'T REPORTED IN AFTER HIS LAST SHIFT.
"DOC WAS CALLED IN ON THE INVESTIGATION. THE POLICE KNEW TO TURN TO HIM WHEN THE UNEXPLAINABLE TURNED UP.
"THE BEST THEORY WAS THAT THE OFFICER HAD SOMEHOW *MELTED,* LIKE A CANDLE LEFT BURNING OVERNIGHT.
"THE ONLY CLUE AS TO HOW WAS A SMALL METAL DEVICE THAT DOC FOUND AMONGST THE VILE MESS."

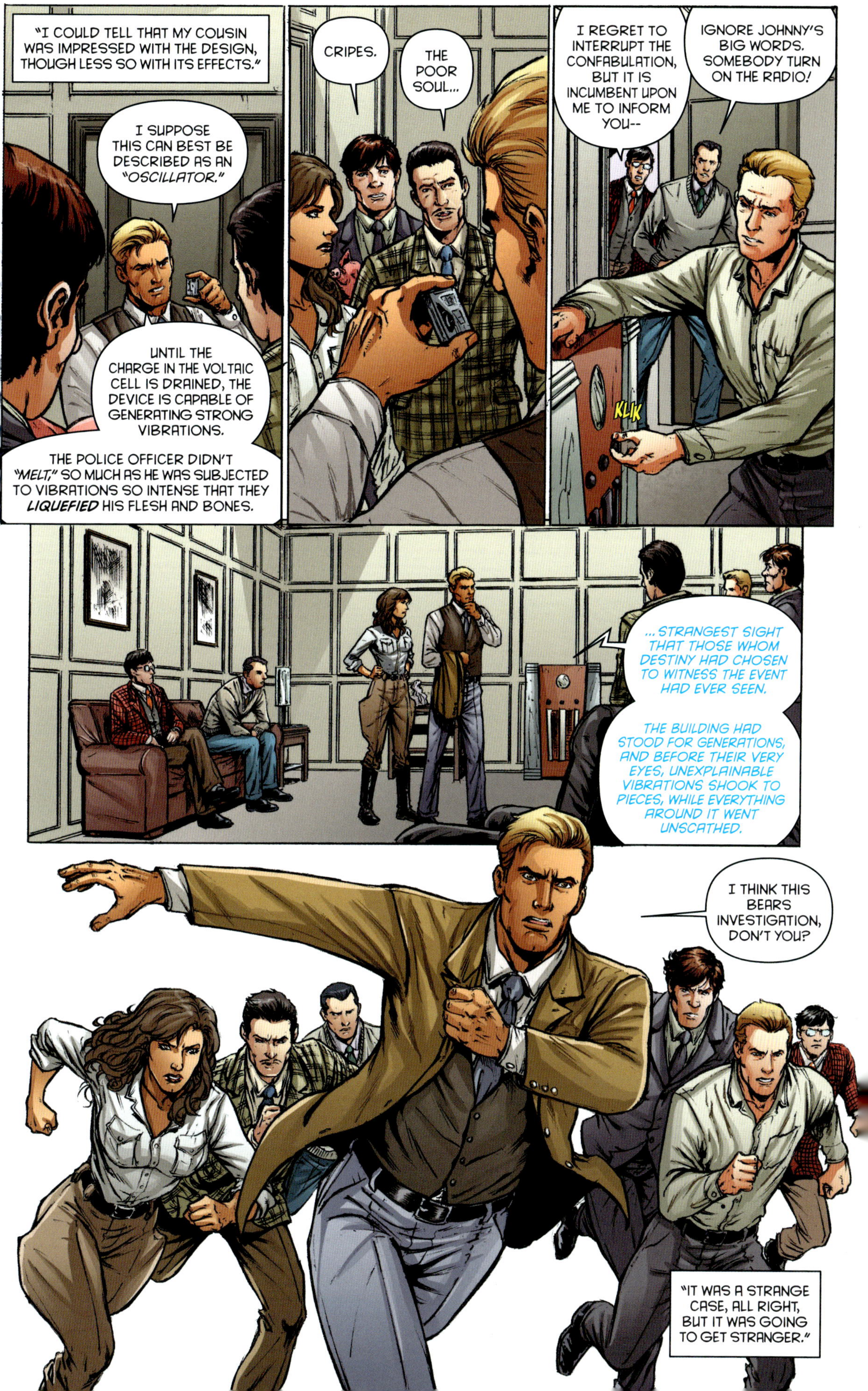
"I COULD TELL THAT MY COUSIN WAS IMPRESSED WITH THE DESIGN, THOUGH LESS SO WITH ITS EFFECTS."
I SUPPOSE THIS CAN BEST BE DESCRIBED AS AN "OSCILLATOR."
UNTIL THE CHARGE IN THE VOLTAIC CELL IS DRAINED, THE DEVICE IS CAPABLE OF GENERATING STRONG VIBRATIONS.
THE POLICE OFFICER DIDN'T "MELT," SO MUCH AS HE WAS SUBJECTED TO VIBRATIONS SO INTENSE THAT THEY LIQUEFIED HIS FLESH AND BONES.
CRIPES.
THE POOR SOUL...
I REGRET TO INTERRUPT THE CONFABULATION, BUT IT IS INCUMBENT UPON ME TO INFORM YOU--
IGNORE JOHNNY'S BIG WORDS. SOMEBODY TURN ON THE RADIO!
KLIK
...STRANGEST SIGHT THAT THOSE WHOM DESTINY HAD CHOSEN TO WITNESS THE EVENT HAD EVER SEEN.
THE BUILDING HAD STOOD FOR GENERATIONS, AND BEFORE THEIR VERY EYES, UNEXPLAINABLE VIBRATIONS SHOOK TO PIECES, WHILE EVERYTHING AROUND IT WENT UNSCATHED.
I THINK THIS BEARS INVESTIGATION, DON'T YOU?
"IT WAS A STRANGE CASE, ALL RIGHT, BUT IT WAS GOING TO GET STRANGER."

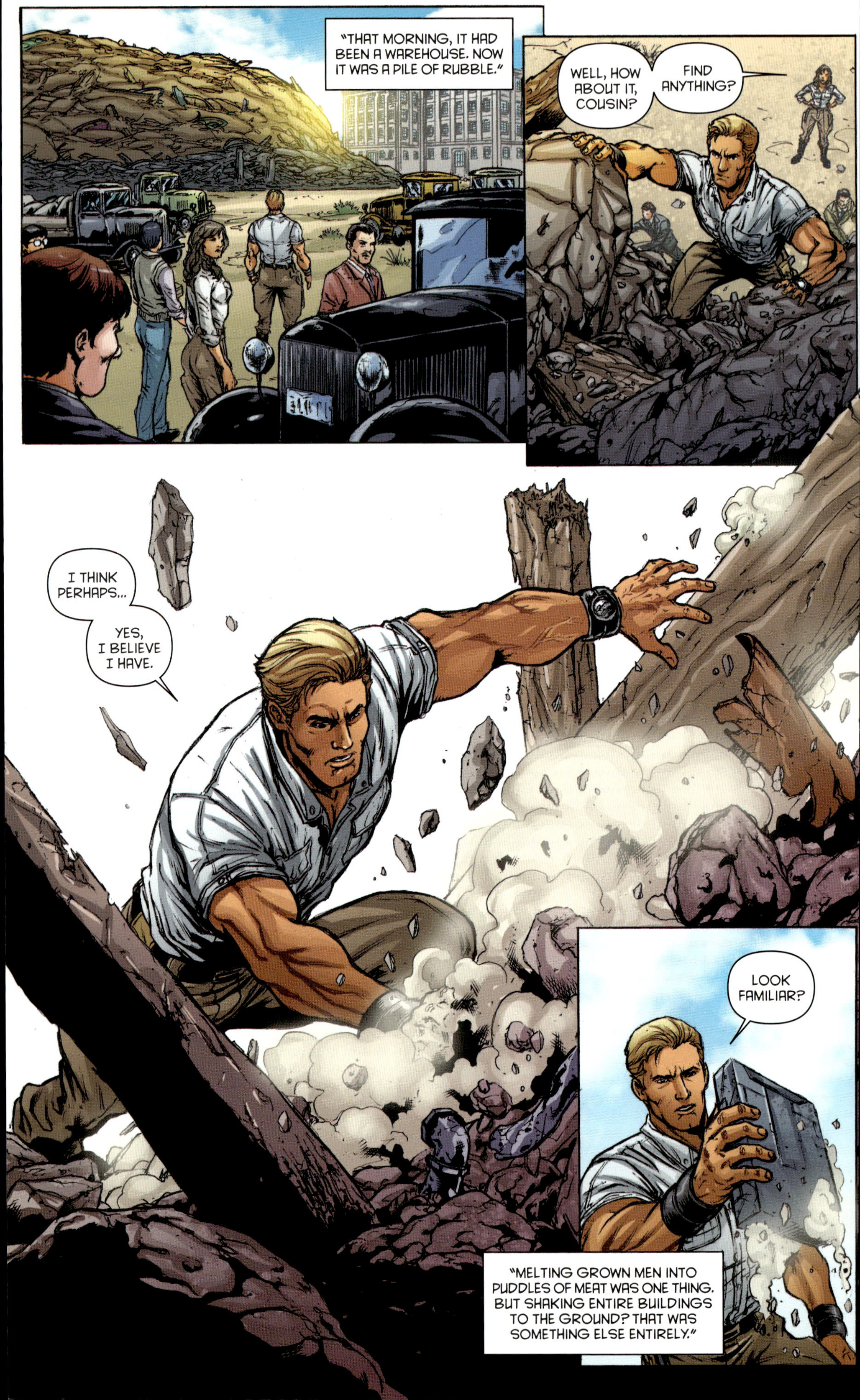
"THAT MORNING, IT HAD BEEN A WAREHOUSE. NOW IT WAS A PILE OF RUBBLE."
WELL, HOW ABOUT IT, COUSIN?
FIND ANYTHING?
I THINK PERHAPS...
YES, I BELIEVE I HAVE.
LOOK FAMILIAR?
"MELTING GROWN MEN INTO PUDDLES OF MEAT WAS ONE THING. BUT SHAKING ENTIRE BUILDINGS TO THE GROUND? THAT WAS SOMETHING ELSE ENTIRELY."

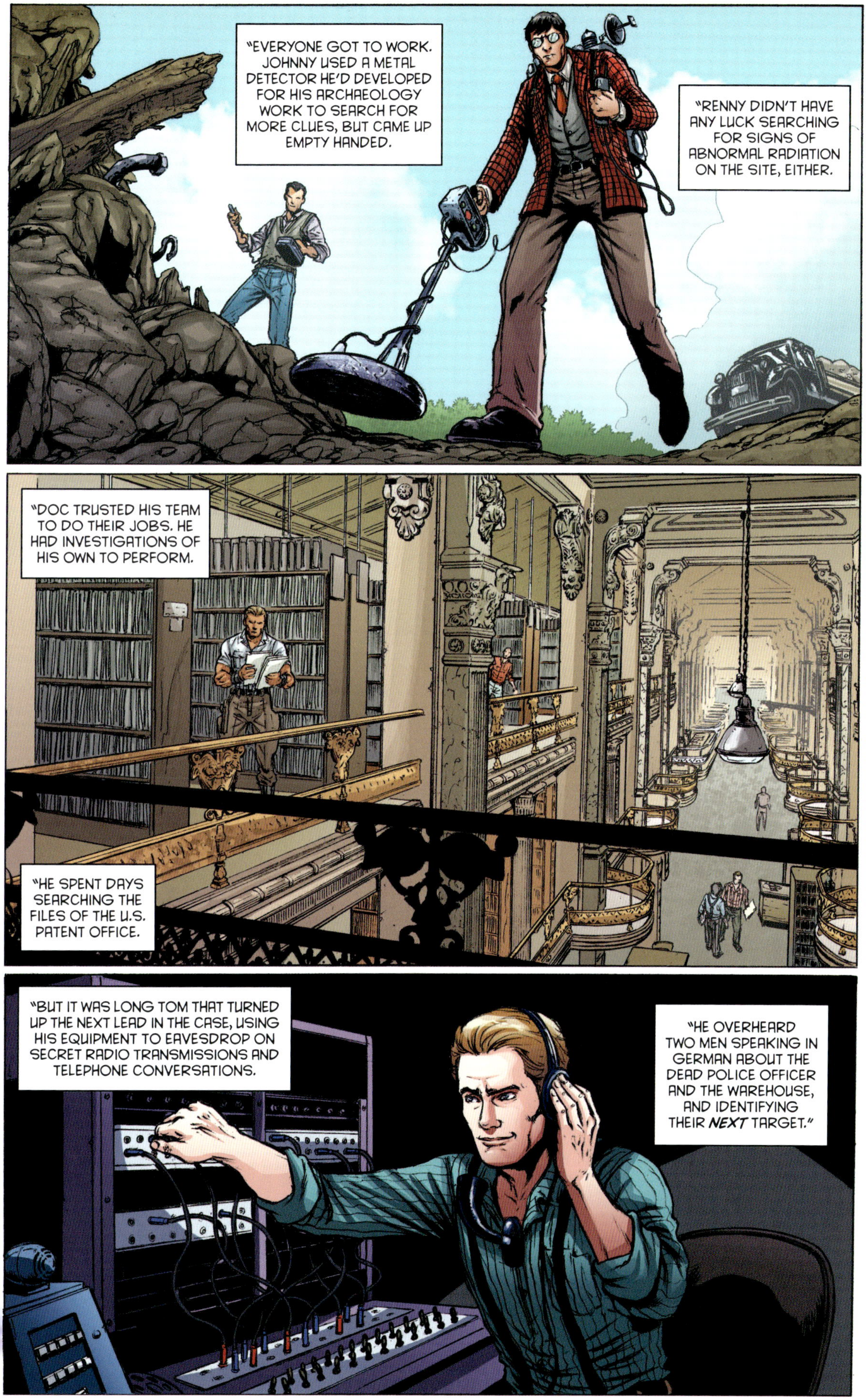
"EVERYONE GOT TO WORK. JOHNNY USED A METAL DETECTOR HE'D DEVELOPED FOR HIS ARCHAEOLOGY WORK TO SEARCH FOR MORE CLUES, BUT CAME UP EMPTY HANDED.
"RENNY DIDN'T HAVE ANY LUCK SEARCHING FOR SIGNS OF ABNORMAL RADIATION ON THE SITE, EITHER.
"DOC TRUSTED HIS TEAM TO DO THEIR JOBS. HE HAD INVESTIGATIONS OF HIS OWN TO PERFORM.
"HE SPENT DAYS SEARCHING THE FILES OF THE U.S. PATENT OFFICE.
"BUT IT WAS LONG TOM THAT TURNED UP THE NEXT LEAD IN THE CASE, USING HIS EQUIPMENT TO EAVESDROP ON SECRET RADIO TRANSMISSIONS AND TELEPHONE CONVERSATIONS.
"HE OVERHEARD TWO MEN SPEAKING IN GERMAN ABOUT THE DEAD POLICE OFFICER AND THE WAREHOUSE, AND IDENTIFYING THEIR ***NEXT*** TARGET."

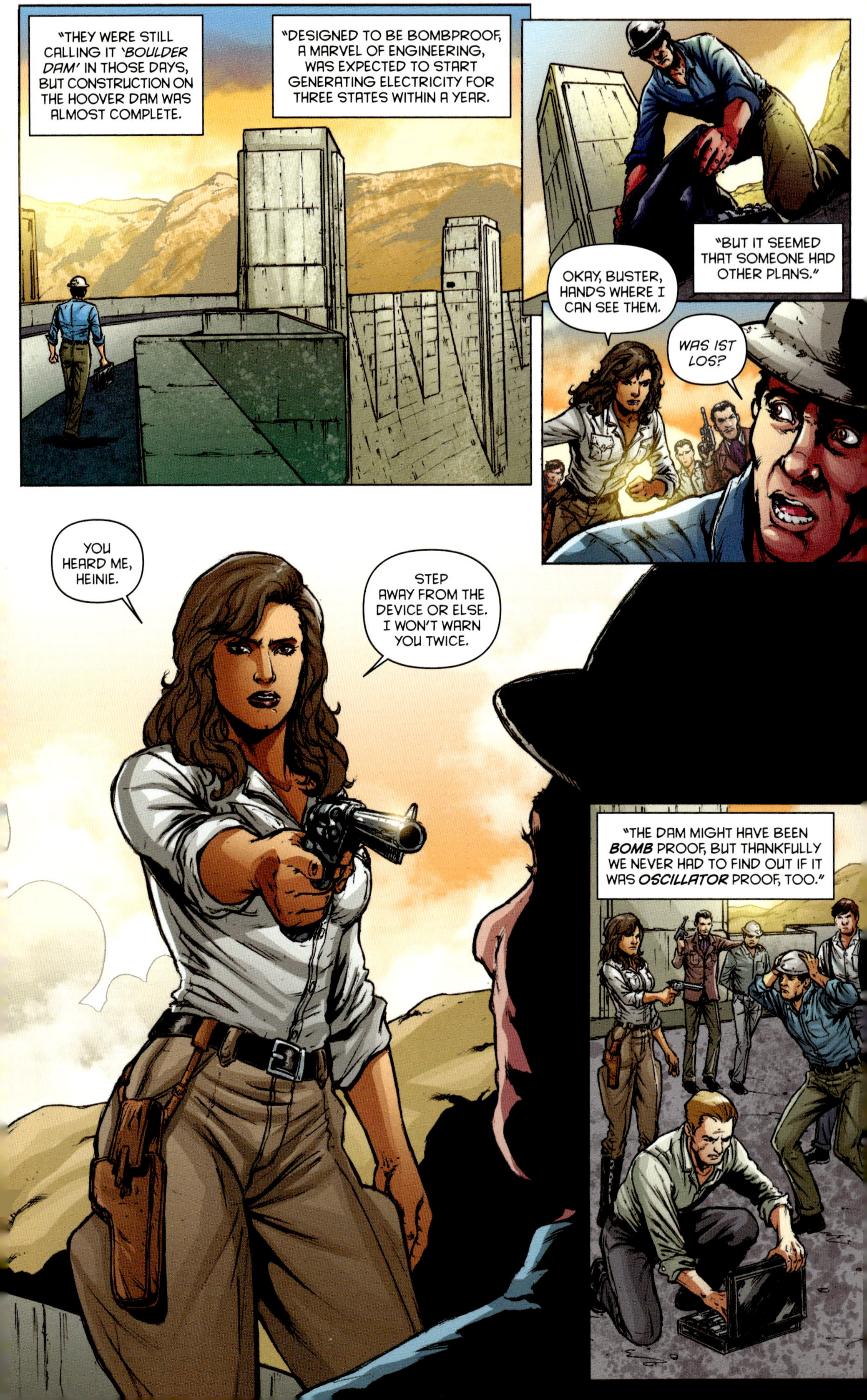
"THEY WERE STILL CALLING IT 'BOULDER DAM' IN THOSE DAYS, BUT CONSTRUCTION ON THE HOOVER DAM WAS ALMOST COMPLETE.
"DESIGNED TO BE BOMBPROOF, A MARVEL OF ENGINEERING, WAS EXPECTED TO START GENERATING ELECTRICITY FOR THREE STATES WITHIN A YEAR.
"BUT IT SEEMED THAT SOMEONE HAD OTHER PLANS."
OKAY, BUSTER, HANDS WHERE I CAN SEE THEM.
WAS IST LOS?
YOU HEARD ME, HEINIE.
STEP AWAY FROM THE DEVICE OR ELSE. I WON'T WARN YOU TWICE.
"THE DAM MIGHT HAVE BEEN BOMB PROOF, BUT THANKFULLY WE NEVER HAD TO FIND OUT IF IT WAS OSCILLATOR PROOF, TOO."

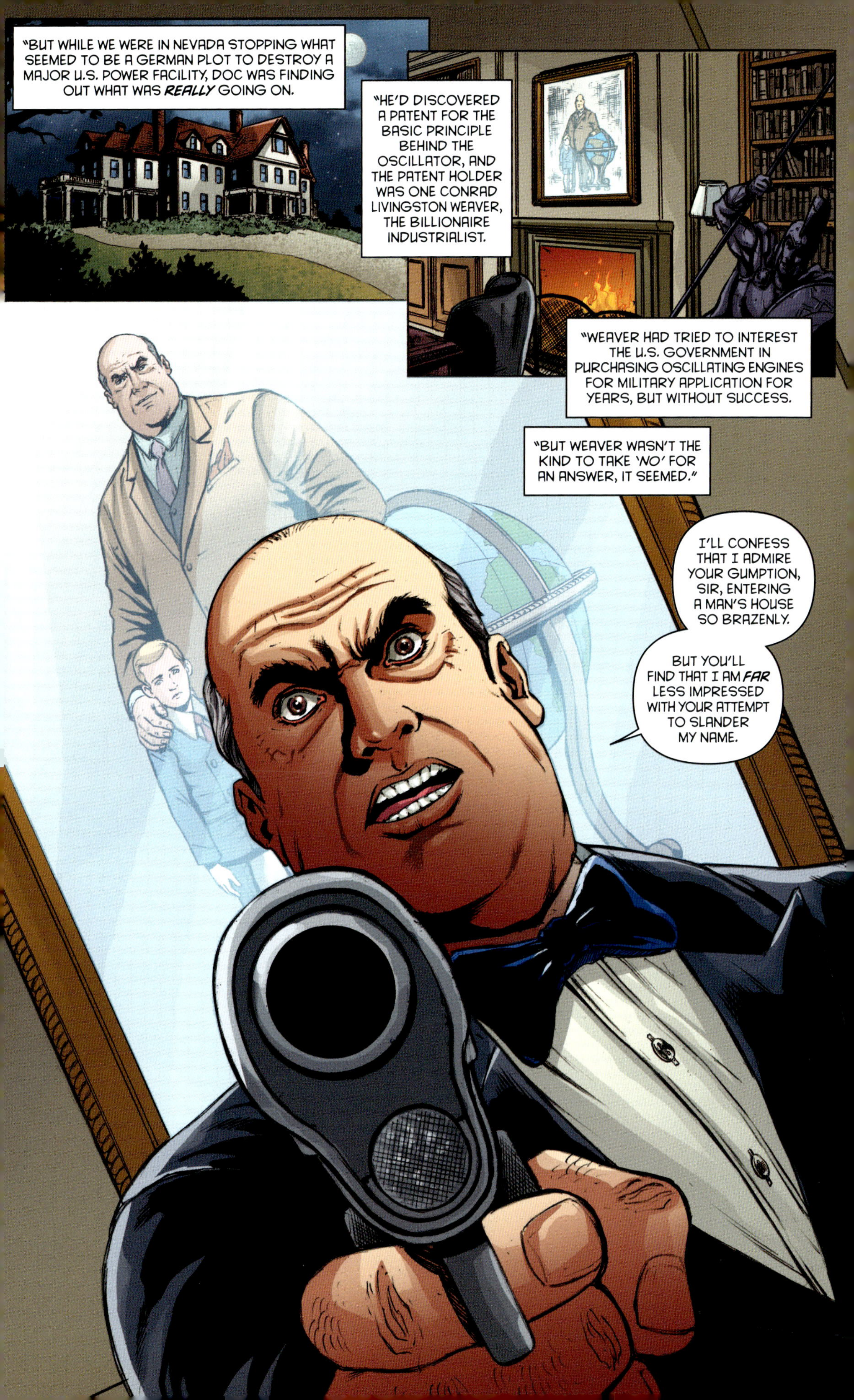
"BUT WHILE WE WERE IN NEVADA STOPPING WHAT SEEMED TO BE A GERMAN PLOT TO DESTROY A MAJOR U.S. POWER FACILITY, DOC WAS FINDING OUT WHAT WAS *REALLY* GOING ON.
"HE'D DISCOVERED A PATENT FOR THE BASIC PRINCIPLE BEHIND THE OSCILLATOR, AND THE PATENT HOLDER WAS ONE CONRAD LIVINGSTON WEAVER, THE BILLIONAIRE INDUSTRIALIST.
"WEAVER HAD TRIED TO INTEREST THE U.S. GOVERNMENT IN PURCHASING OSCILLATING ENGINES FOR MILITARY APPLICATION FOR YEARS, BUT WITHOUT SUCCESS.
"BUT WEAVER WASN'T THE KIND TO TAKE '*NO*' FOR AN ANSWER, IT SEEMED."
I'LL CONFESS THAT I ADMIRE YOUR GUMPTION, SIR, ENTERING A MAN'S HOUSE SO BRAZENLY.
BUT YOU'LL FIND THAT I AM *FAR* LESS IMPRESSED WITH YOUR ATTEMPT TO SLANDER MY NAME.

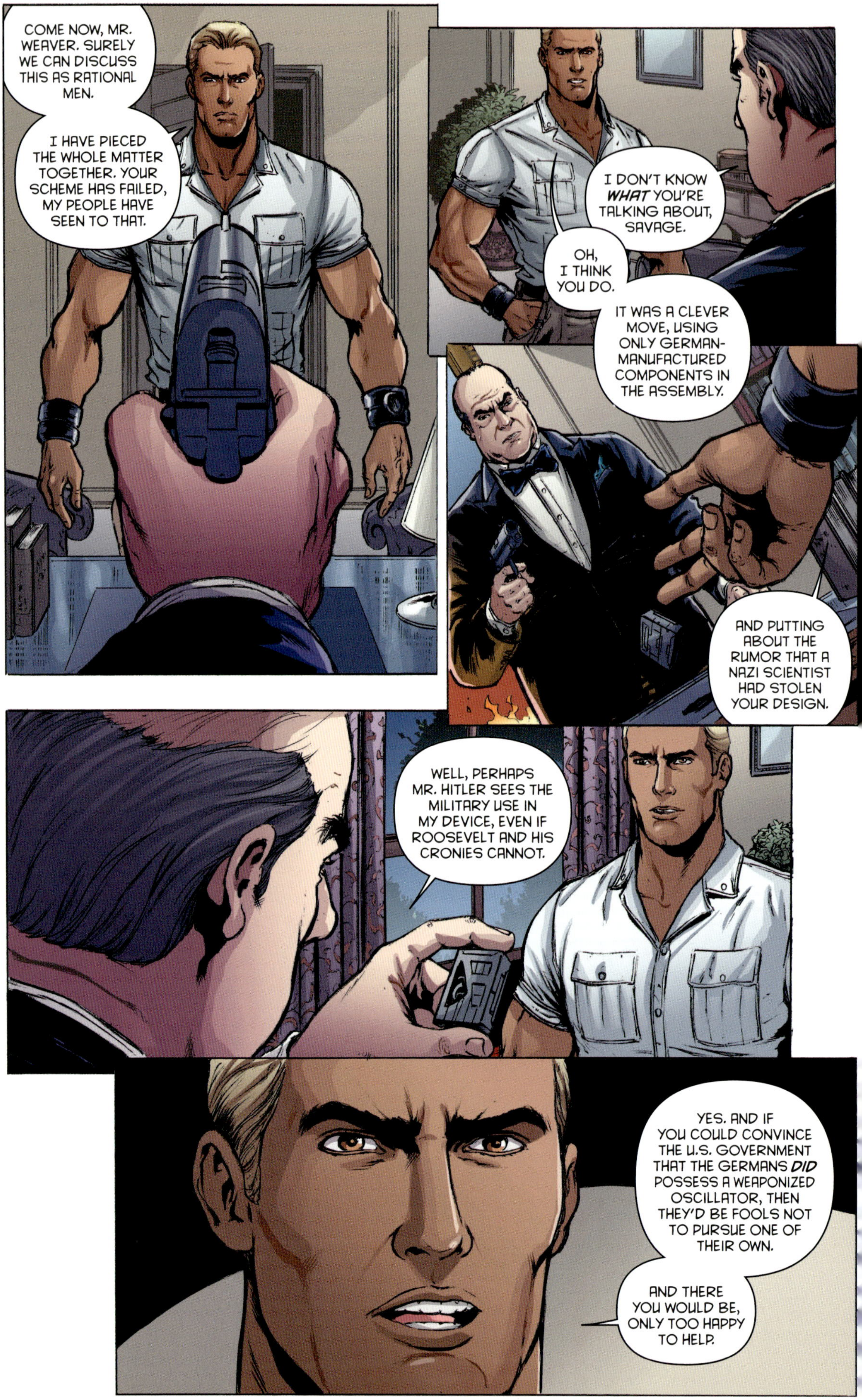
COME NOW, MR. WEAVER. SURELY WE CAN DISCUSS THIS AS RATIONAL MEN.
I HAVE PIECED THE WHOLE MATTER TOGETHER. YOUR SCHEME HAS FAILED, MY PEOPLE HAVE SEEN TO THAT.
I DON'T KNOW ***WHAT*** YOU'RE TALKING ABOUT, SAVAGE.
OH, I THINK YOU DO.
IT WAS A CLEVER MOVE, USING ONLY GERMAN-MANUFACTURED COMPONENTS IN THE ASSEMBLY.
AND PUTTING ABOUT THE RUMOR THAT A NAZI SCIENTIST HAD STOLEN YOUR DESIGN.
WELL, PERHAPS MR. HITLER SEES THE MILITARY USE IN MY DEVICE, EVEN IF ROOSEVELT AND HIS CRONIES CANNOT.
YES. AND IF YOU COULD CONVINCE THE U.S. GOVERNMENT THAT THE GERMANS ***DID*** POSSESS A WEAPONIZED OSCILLATOR, THEN THEY'D BE FOOLS NOT TO PURSUE ONE OF THEIR OWN.
AND THERE YOU WOULD BE, ONLY TOO HAPPY TO HELP.

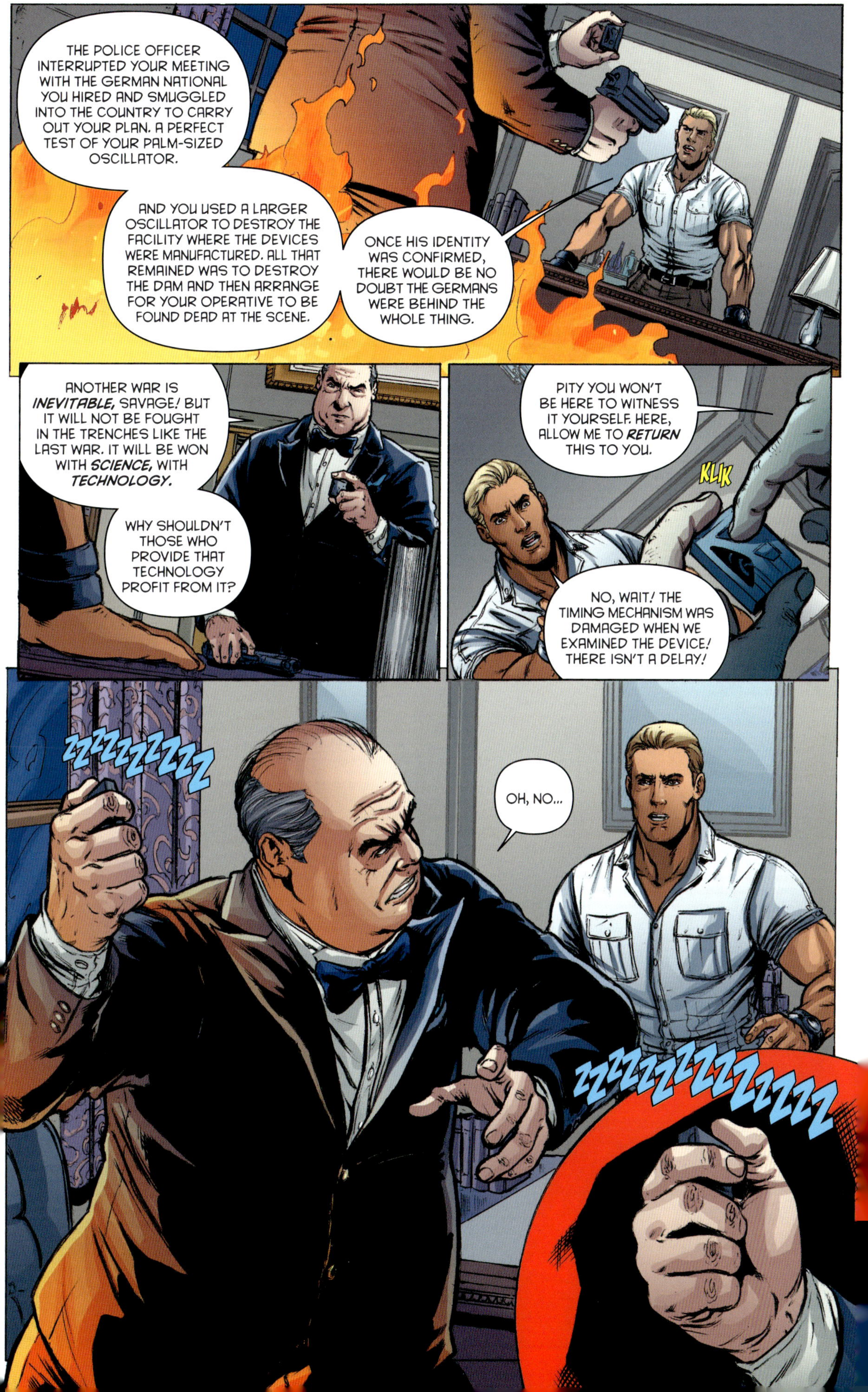
THE POLICE OFFICER INTERRUPTED YOUR MEETING WITH THE GERMAN NATIONAL YOU HIRED AND SMUGGLED INTO THE COUNTRY TO CARRY OUT YOUR PLAN. A PERFECT TEST OF YOUR PALM-SIZED OSCILLATOR.
AND YOU USED A LARGER OSCILLATOR TO DESTROY THE FACILITY WHERE THE DEVICES WERE MANUFACTURED. ALL THAT REMAINED WAS TO DESTROY THE DAM AND THEN ARRANGE FOR YOUR OPERATIVE TO BE FOUND DEAD AT THE SCENE.
ONCE HIS IDENTITY WAS CONFIRMED, THERE WOULD BE NO DOUBT THE GERMANS WERE BEHIND THE WHOLE THING.
ANOTHER WAR IS *INEVITABLE,* SAVAGE! BUT IT WILL NOT BE FOUGHT IN THE TRENCHES LIKE THE LAST WAR. IT WILL BE WON WITH *SCIENCE,* WITH *TECHNOLOGY.*
WHY SHOULDN'T THOSE WHO PROVIDE THAT TECHNOLOGY PROFIT FROM IT?
PITY YOU WON'T BE HERE TO WITNESS IT YOURSELF. HERE, ALLOW ME TO *RETURN* THIS TO YOU.
KLIK
NO, WAIT! THE TIMING MECHANISM WAS DAMAGED WHEN WE EXAMINED THE DEVICE! THERE ISN'T A DELAY!
ZZZZZZZZZZ
OH, NO...
ZZZZZZZZZZZZZZZ

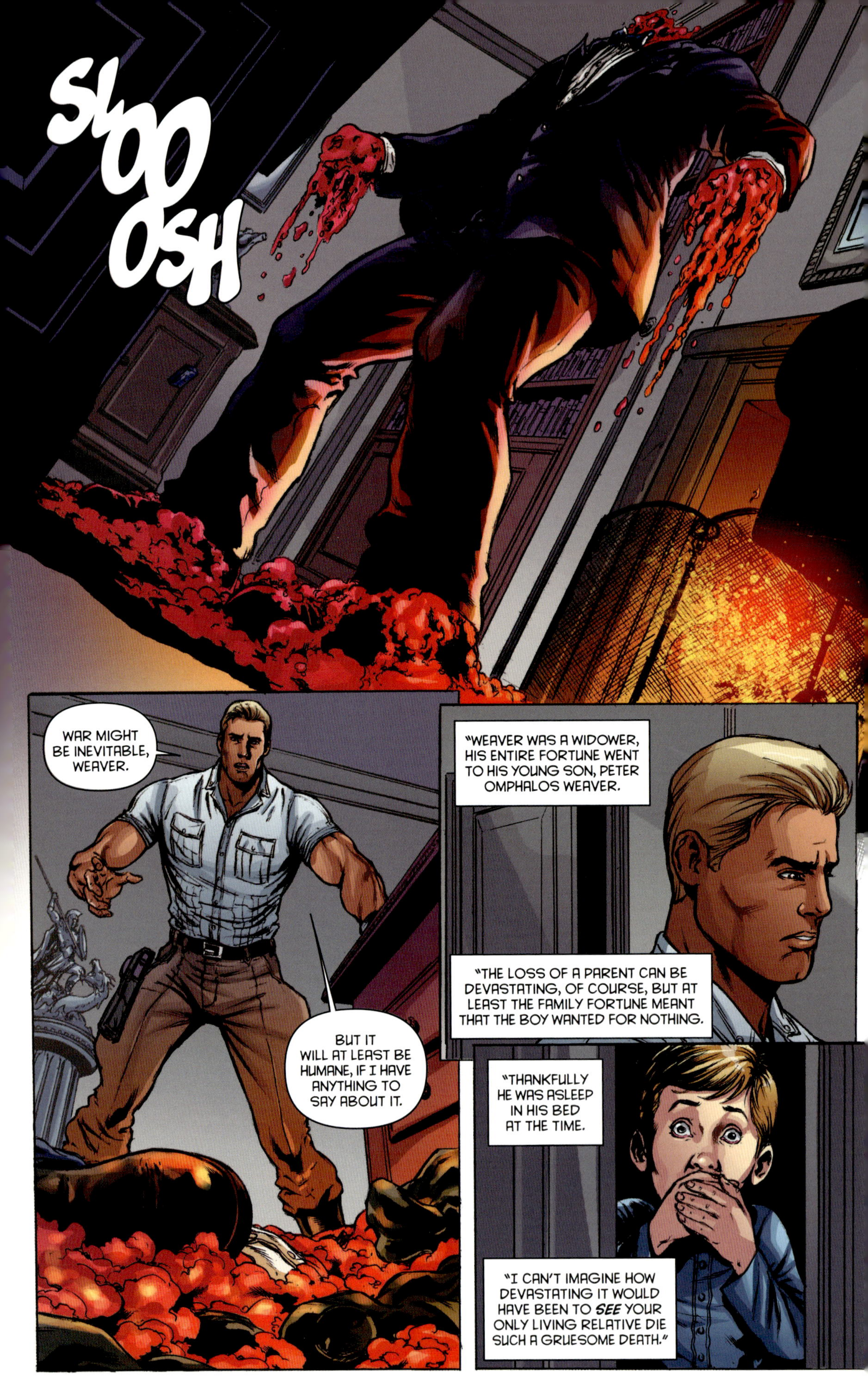
SHLOOOSH
WAR MIGHT BE INEVITABLE, WEAVER.
BUT IT WILL AT LEAST BE HUMANE, IF I HAVE ANYTHING TO SAY ABOUT IT.
"WEAVER WAS A WIDOWER, HIS ENTIRE FORTUNE WENT TO HIS YOUNG SON, PETER OMPHALOS WEAVER.
"THE LOSS OF A PARENT CAN BE DEVASTATING, OF COURSE, BUT AT LEAST THE FAMILY FORTUNE MEANT THAT THE BOY WANTED FOR NOTHING.
"THANKFULLY HE WAS ASLEEP IN HIS BED AT THE TIME.
"I CAN'T IMAGINE HOW DEVASTATING IT WOULD HAVE BEEN TO *SEE* YOUR ONLY LIVING RELATIVE DIE SUCH A GRUESOME DEATH."

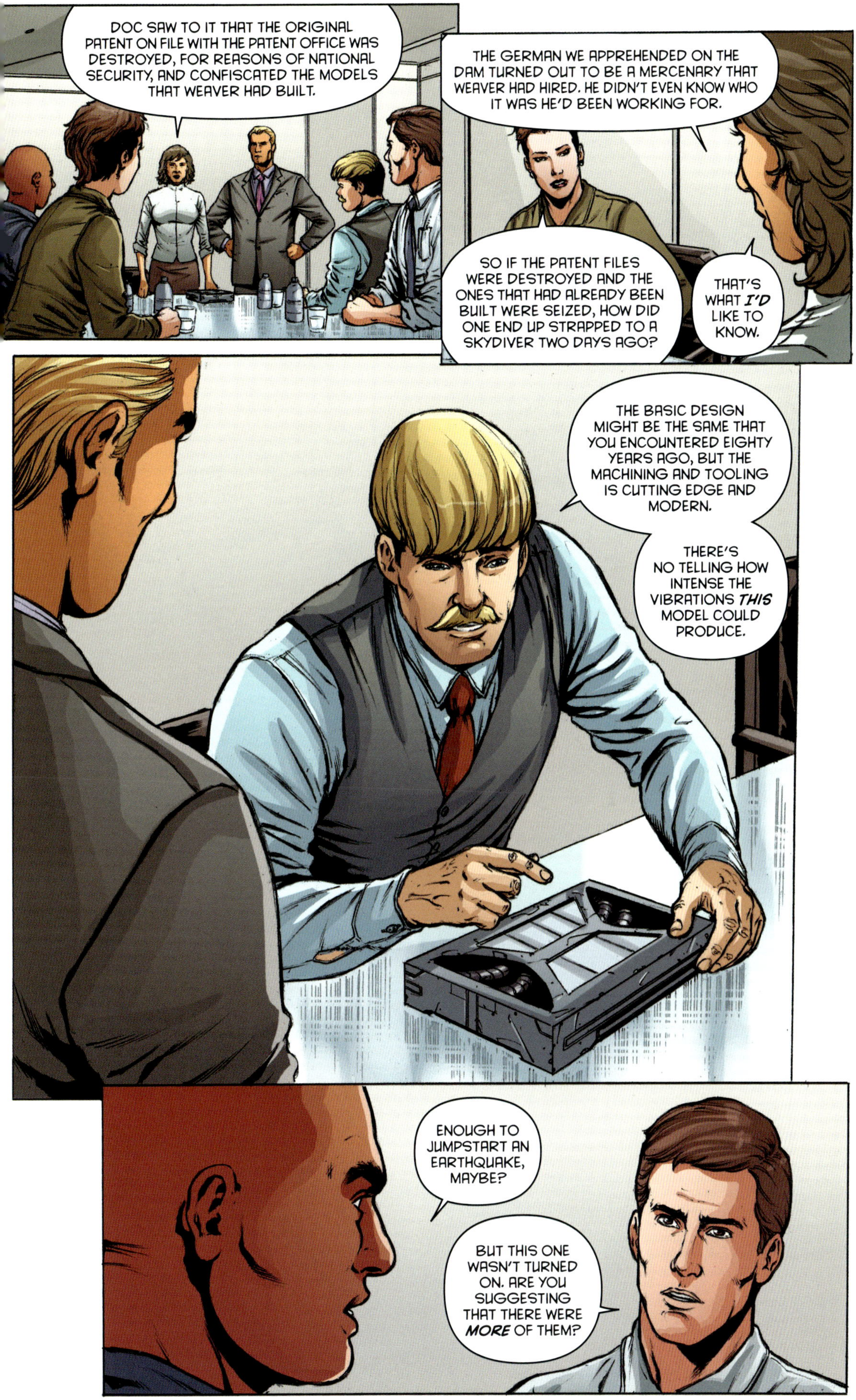
DOC SAW TO IT THAT THE ORIGINAL PATENT ON FILE WITH THE PATENT OFFICE WAS DESTROYED, FOR REASONS OF NATIONAL SECURITY, AND CONFISCATED THE MODELS THAT WEAVER HAD BUILT.
THE GERMAN WE APPREHENDED ON THE DAM TURNED OUT TO BE A MERCENARY THAT WEAVER HAD HIRED. HE DIDN'T EVEN KNOW WHO IT WAS HE'D BEEN WORKING FOR.
SO IF THE PATENT FILES WERE DESTROYED AND THE ONES THAT HAD ALREADY BEEN BUILT WERE SEIZED, HOW DID ONE END UP STRAPPED TO A SKYDIVER TWO DAYS AGO?
THAT'S WHAT *I'D* LIKE TO KNOW.
THE BASIC DESIGN MIGHT BE THE SAME THAT YOU ENCOUNTERED EIGHTY YEARS AGO, BUT THE MACHINING AND TOOLING IS CUTTING EDGE AND MODERN.
THERE'S NO TELLING HOW INTENSE THE VIBRATIONS *THIS* MODEL COULD PRODUCE.
ENOUGH TO JUMPSTART AN EARTHQUAKE, MAYBE?
BUT THIS ONE WASN'T TURNED ON. ARE YOU SUGGESTING THAT THERE WERE *MORE* OF THEM?

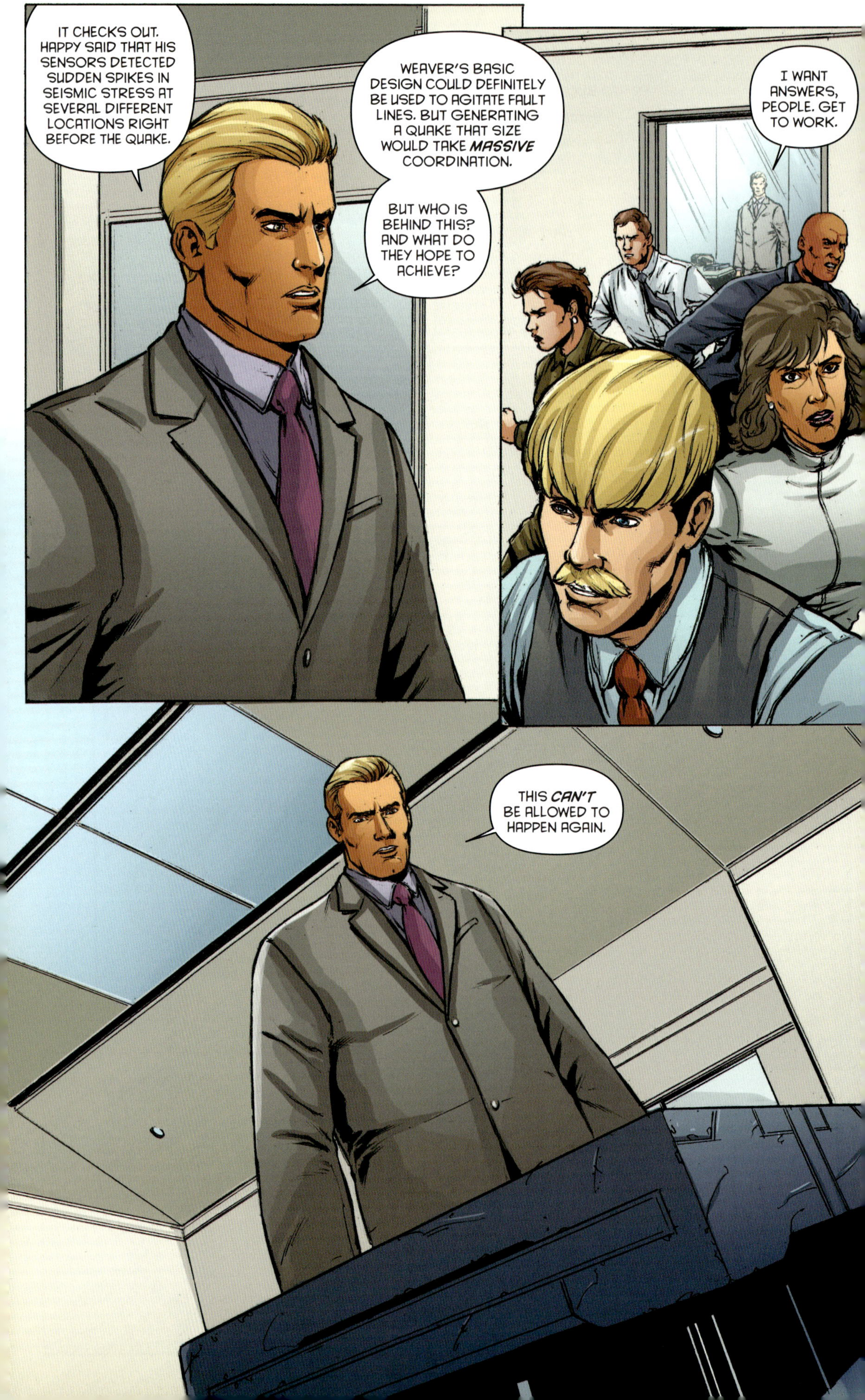
IT CHECKS OUT. HAPPY SAID THAT HIS SENSORS DETECTED SUDDEN SPIKES IN SEISMIC STRESS AT SEVERAL DIFFERENT LOCATIONS RIGHT BEFORE THE QUAKE.
WEAVER'S BASIC DESIGN COULD DEFINITELY BE USED TO AGITATE FAULT LINES. BUT GENERATING A QUAKE THAT SIZE WOULD TAKE *MASSIVE* COORDINATION.
BUT WHO IS BEHIND THIS? AND WHAT DO THEY HOPE TO ACHIEVE?
I WANT ANSWERS, PEOPLE. GET TO WORK.
THIS *CAN'T* BE ALLOWED TO HAPPEN AGAIN.

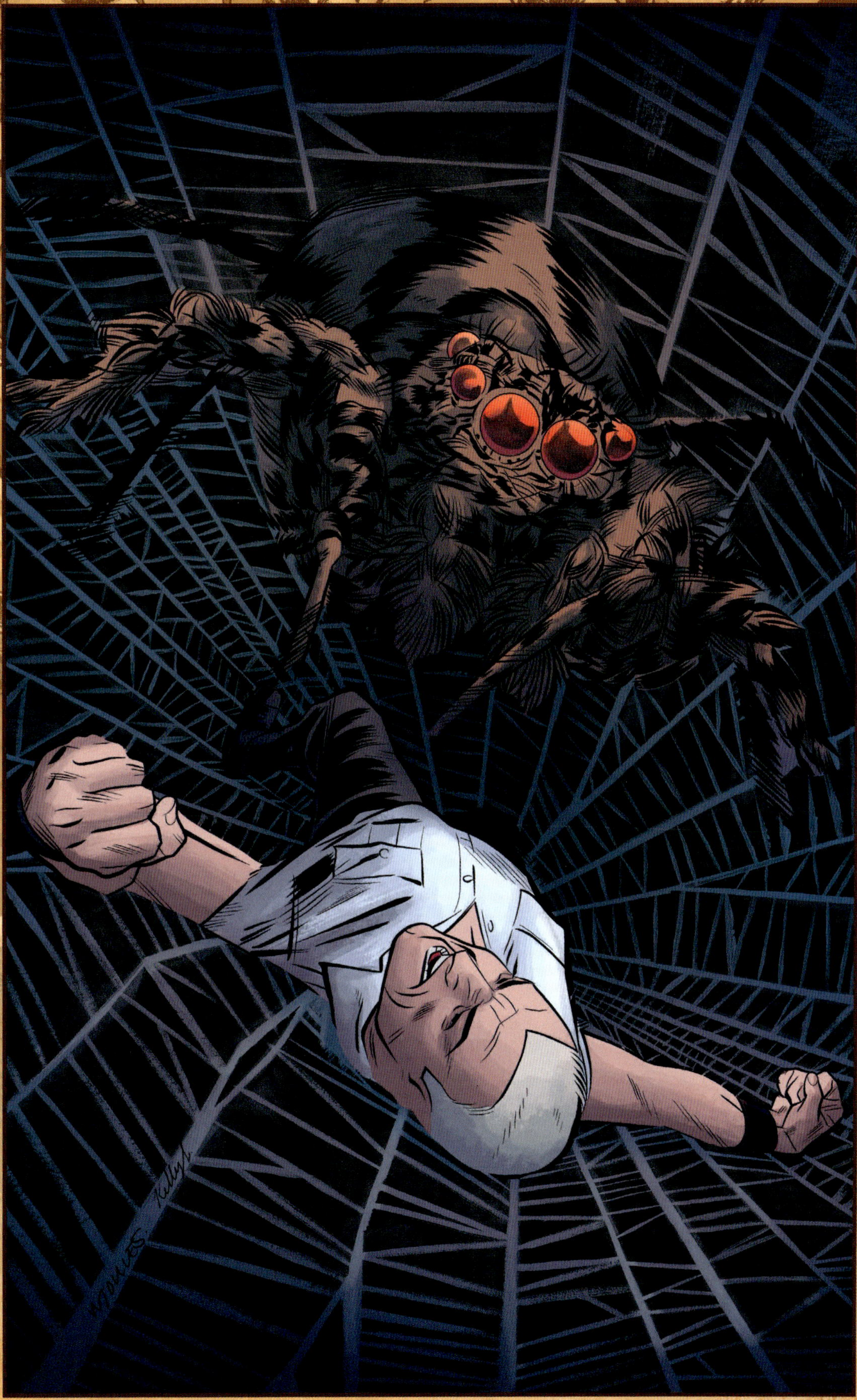

ISSUE **#2** COVER
art by **WILFREDO TORRES** colors by **KELLY FITZPATRICK**

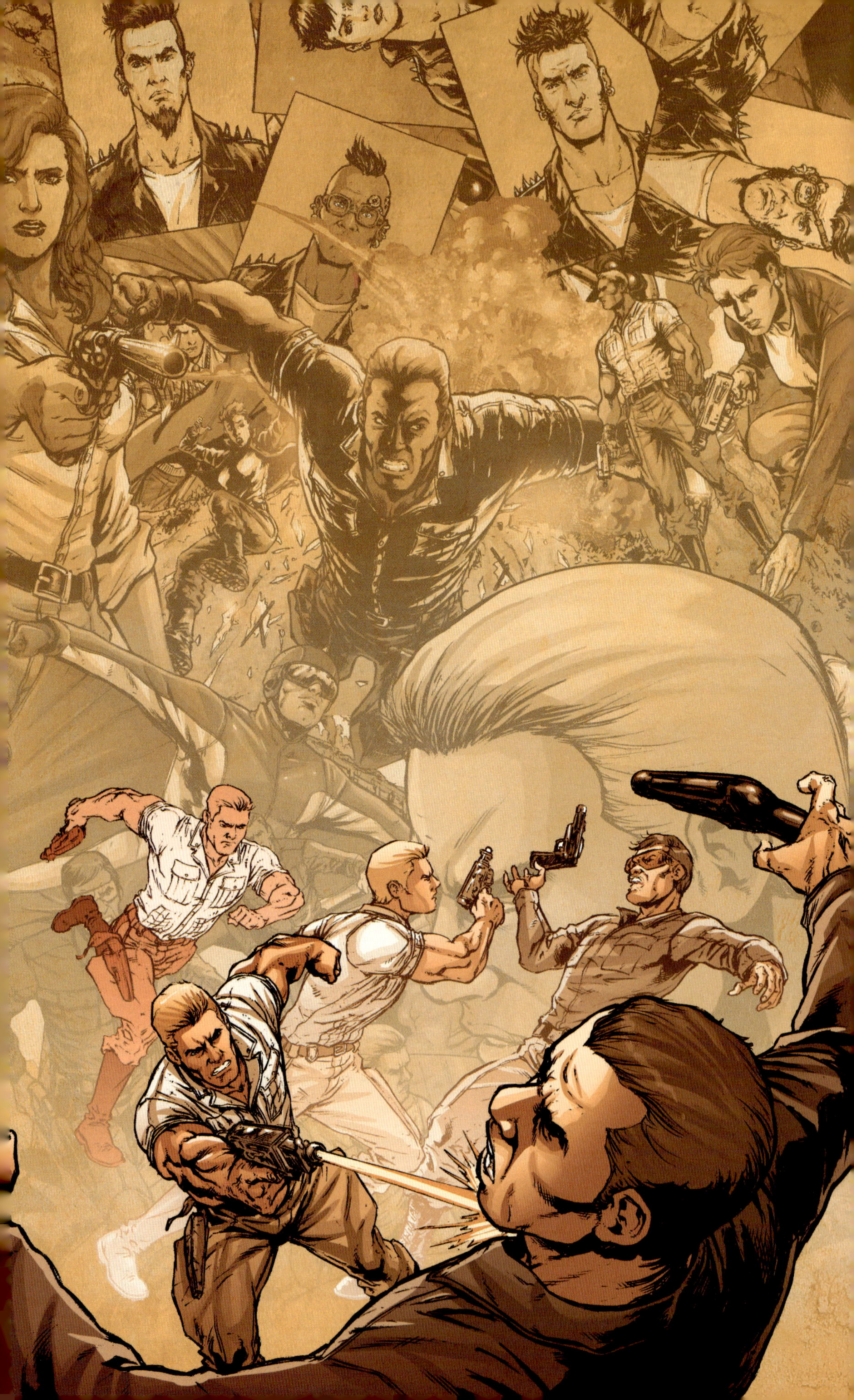

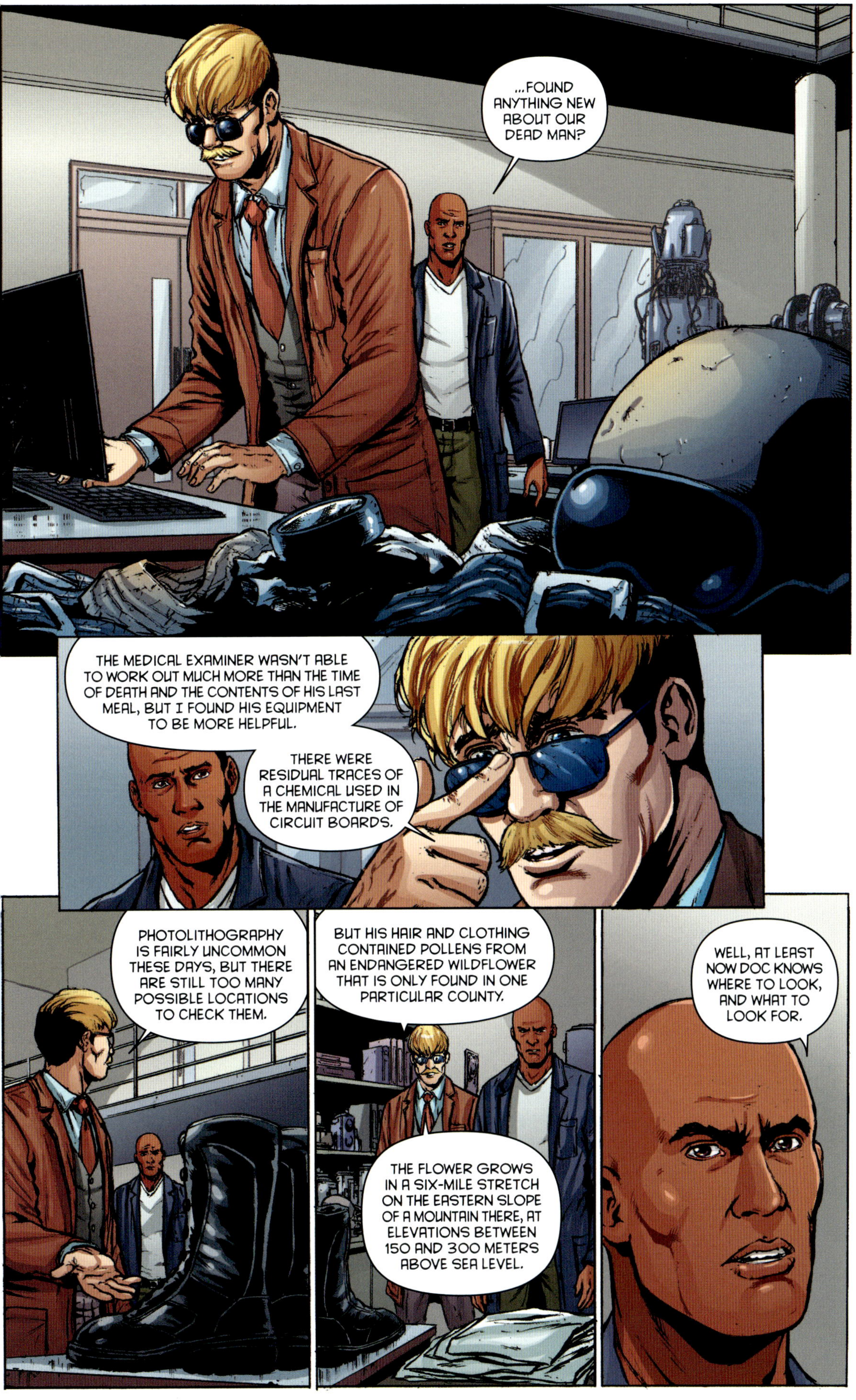
...FOUND ANYTHING NEW ABOUT OUR DEAD MAN?
THE MEDICAL EXAMINER WASN'T ABLE TO WORK OUT MUCH MORE THAN THE TIME OF DEATH AND THE CONTENTS OF HIS LAST MEAL, BUT I FOUND HIS EQUIPMENT TO BE MORE HELPFUL.
THERE WERE RESIDUAL TRACES OF A CHEMICAL USED IN THE MANUFACTURE OF CIRCUIT BOARDS.
PHOTOLITHOGRAPHY IS FAIRLY UNCOMMON THESE DAYS, BUT THERE ARE STILL TOO MANY POSSIBLE LOCATIONS TO CHECK THEM.
BUT HIS HAIR AND CLOTHING CONTAINED POLLENS FROM AN ENDANGERED WILDFLOWER THAT IS ONLY FOUND IN ONE PARTICULAR COUNTY.
THE FLOWER GROWS IN A SIX-MILE STRETCH ON THE EASTERN SLOPE OF A MOUNTAIN THERE, AT ELEVATIONS BETWEEN 150 AND 300 METERS ABOVE SEA LEVEL.
WELL, AT LEAST NOW DOC KNOWS WHERE TO LOOK, AND WHAT TO LOOK FOR.

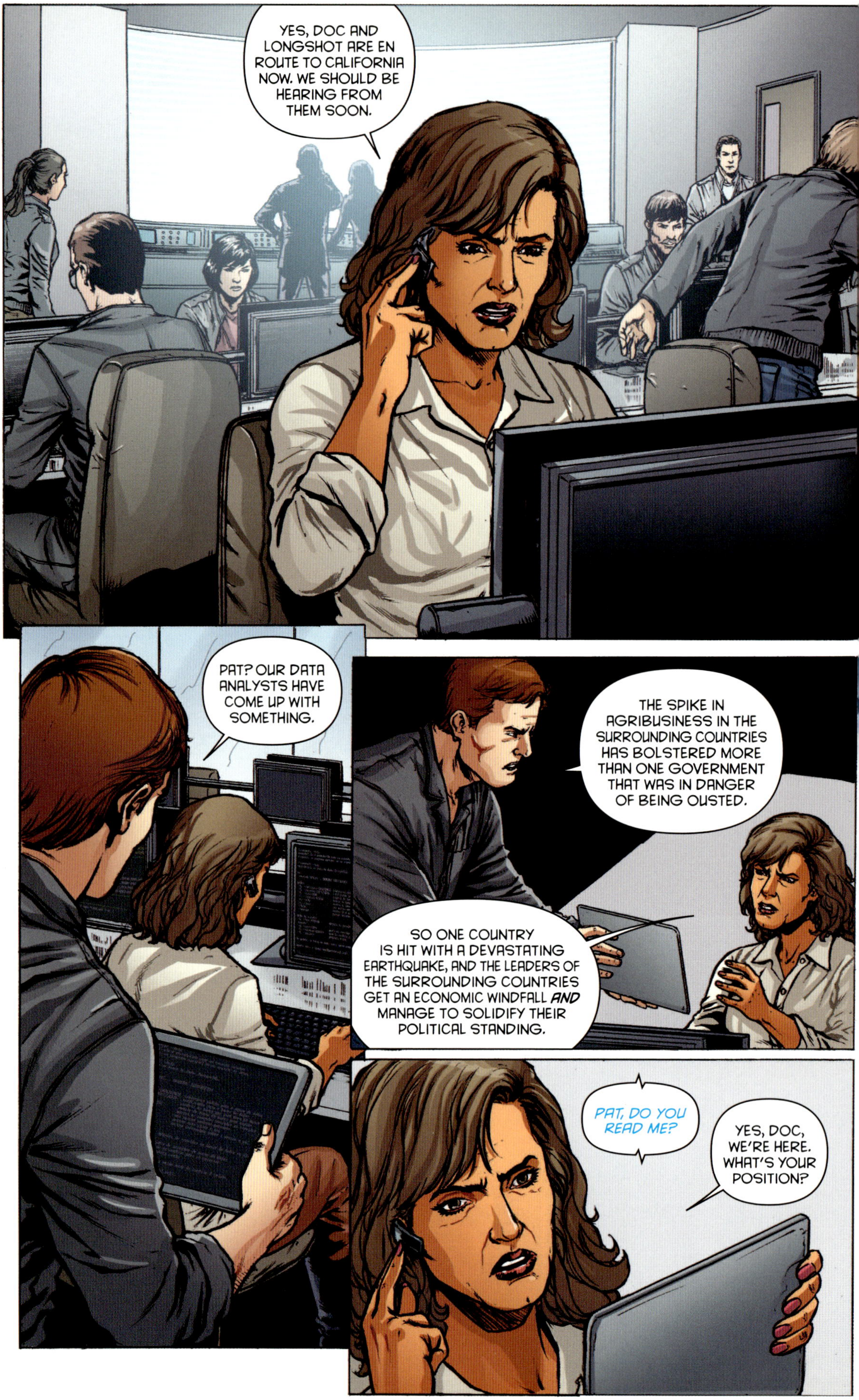
YES, DOC AND LONGSHOT ARE EN ROUTE TO CALIFORNIA NOW. WE SHOULD BE HEARING FROM THEM SOON.
PAT? OUR DATA ANALYSTS HAVE COME UP WITH SOMETHING.
THE SPIKE IN AGRIBUSINESS IN THE SURROUNDING COUNTRIES HAS BOLSTERED MORE THAN ONE GOVERNMENT THAT WAS IN DANGER OF BEING OUSTED.
SO ONE COUNTRY IS HIT WITH A DEVASTATING EARTHQUAKE, AND THE LEADERS OF THE SURROUNDING COUNTRIES GET AN ECONOMIC WINDFALL AND MANAGE TO SOLIDIFY THEIR POLITICAL STANDING.
PAT, DO YOU READ ME?
YES, DOC, WE'RE HERE. WHAT'S YOUR POSITION?

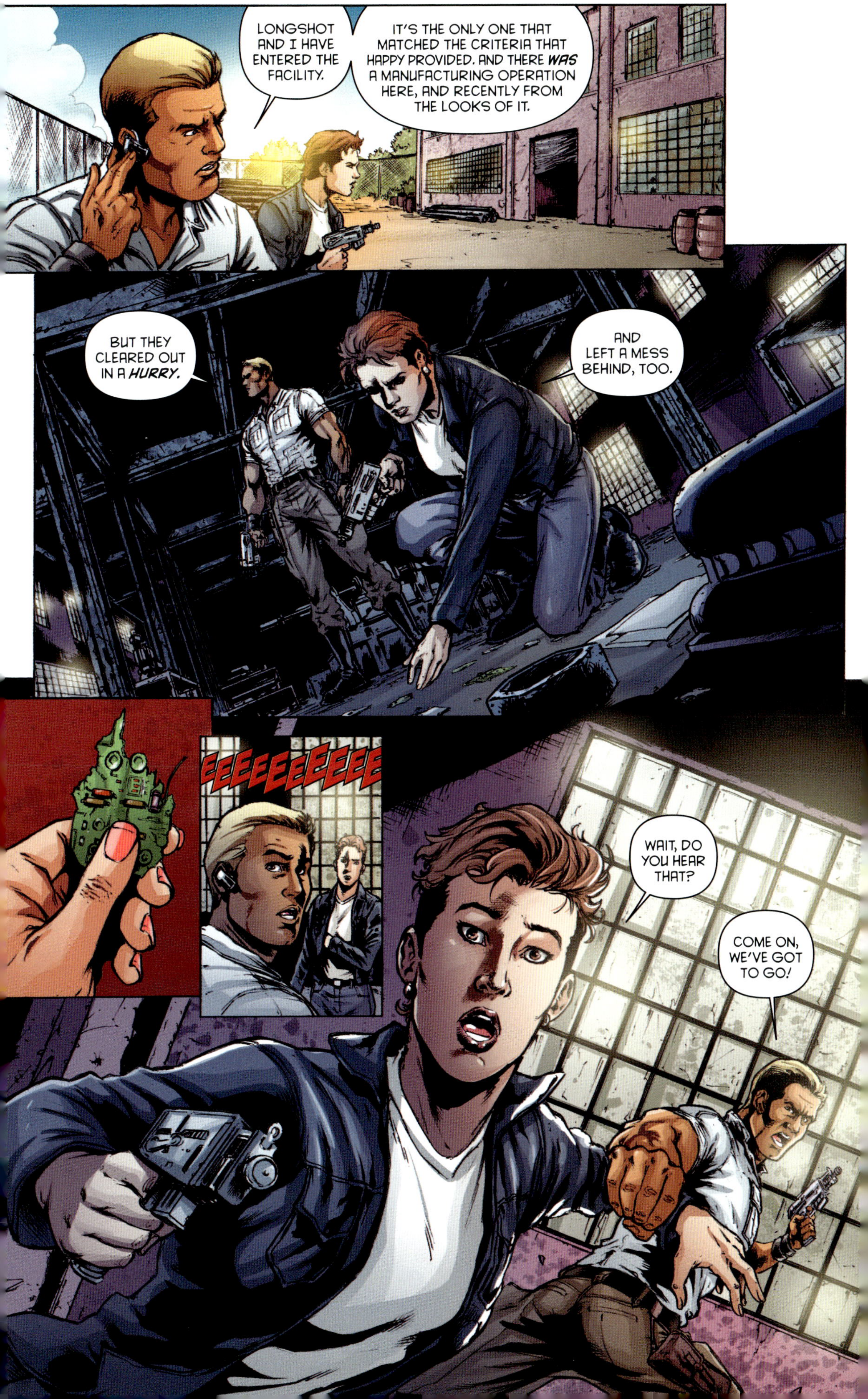
LONGSHOT AND I HAVE ENTERED THE FACILITY.
IT'S THE ONLY ONE THAT MATCHED THE CRITERIA THAT HAPPY PROVIDED. AND THERE *WAS* A MANUFACTURING OPERATION HERE, AND RECENTLY FROM THE LOOKS OF IT.
BUT THEY CLEARED OUT IN A *HURRY.*
AND LEFT A MESS BEHIND, TOO.
EEEEEEEEEE
WAIT, DO YOU HEAR THAT?
COME ON, WE'VE GOT TO GO!

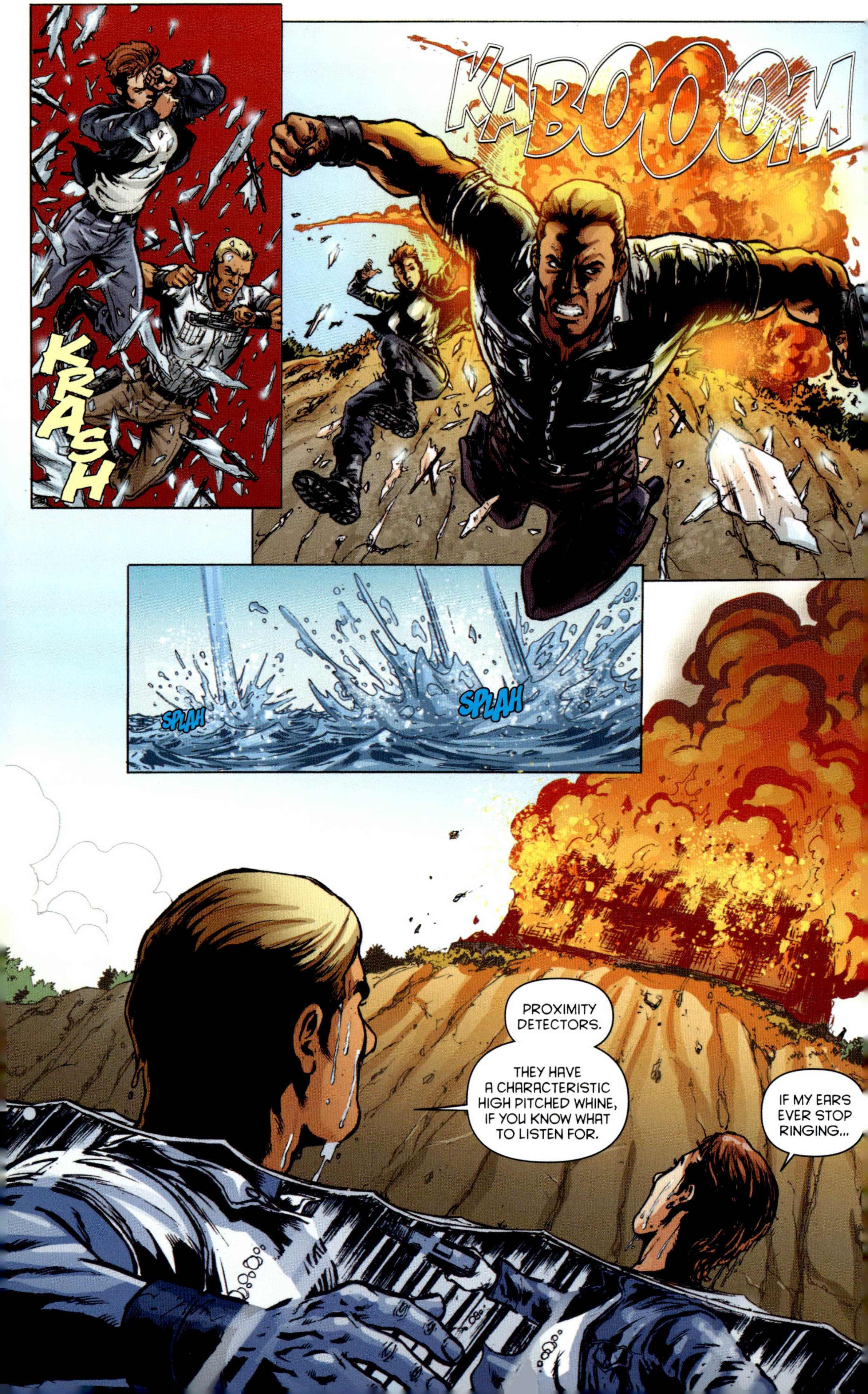
KRASH
KABOOOM
SPLAH
SPLAH
PROXIMITY DETECTORS.
THEY HAVE A CHARACTERISTIC HIGH PITCHED WHINE, IF YOU KNOW WHAT TO LISTEN FOR.
IF MY EARS EVER STOP RINGING...

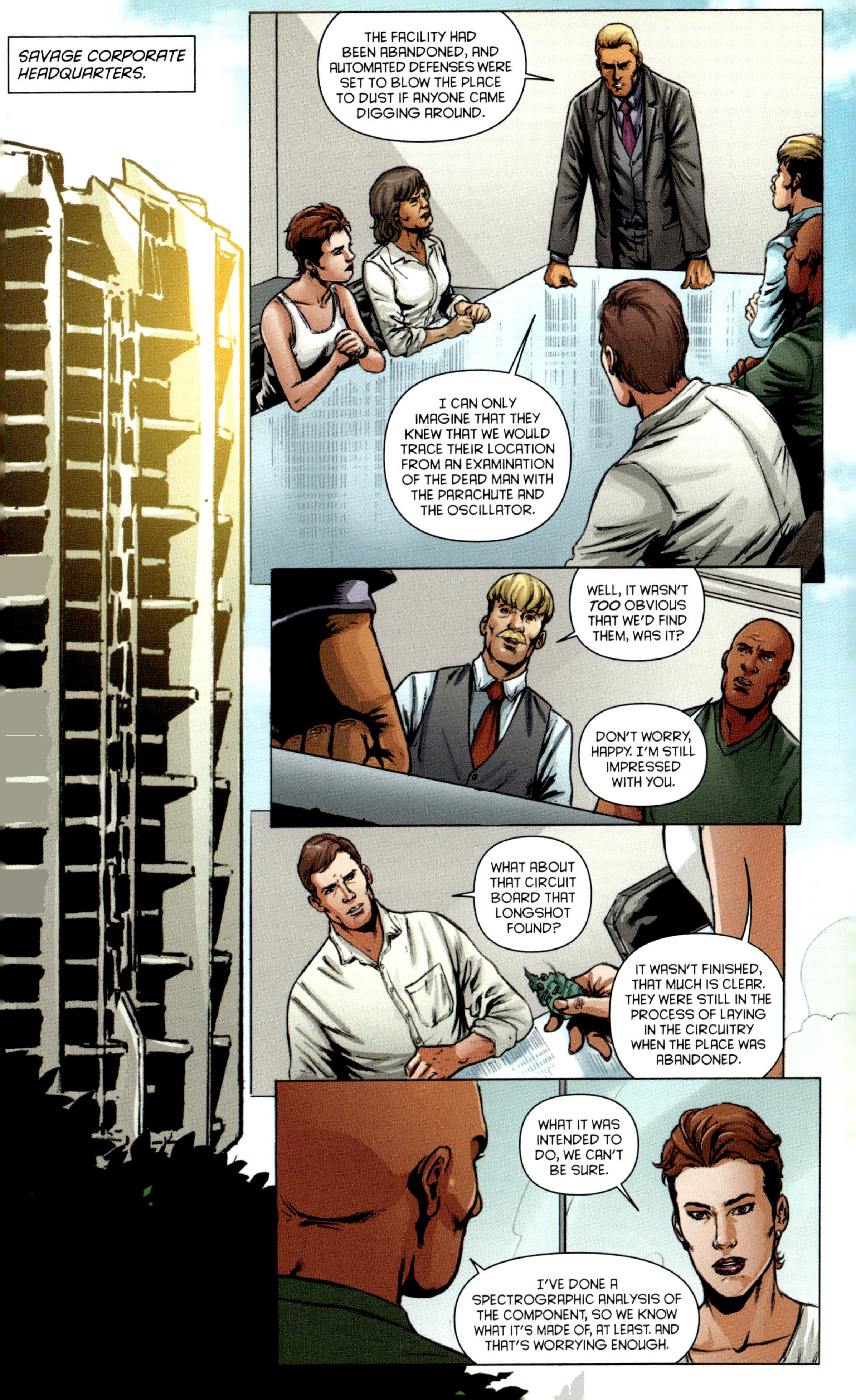
SAVAGE CORPORATE HEADQUARTERS.
THE FACILITY HAD BEEN ABANDONED, AND AUTOMATED DEFENSES WERE SET TO BLOW THE PLACE TO DUST IF ANYONE CAME DIGGING AROUND.
I CAN ONLY IMAGINE THAT THEY KNEW THAT WE WOULD TRACE THEIR LOCATION FROM AN EXAMINATION OF THE DEAD MAN WITH THE PARACHUTE AND THE OSCILLATOR.
WELL, IT WASN'T TOO OBVIOUS THAT WE'D FIND THEM, WAS IT?
DON'T WORRY, HAPPY. I'M STILL IMPRESSED WITH YOU.
WHAT ABOUT THAT CIRCUIT BOARD THAT LONGSHOT FOUND?
IT WASN'T FINISHED, THAT MUCH IS CLEAR. THEY WERE STILL IN THE PROCESS OF LAYING IN THE CIRCUITRY WHEN THE PLACE WAS ABANDONED.
WHAT IT WAS INTENDED TO DO, WE CAN'T BE SURE.
I'VE DONE A SPECTROGRAPHIC ANALYSIS OF THE COMPONENT, SO WE KNOW WHAT IT'S MADE OF, AT LEAST. AND THAT'S WORRYING ENOUGH.

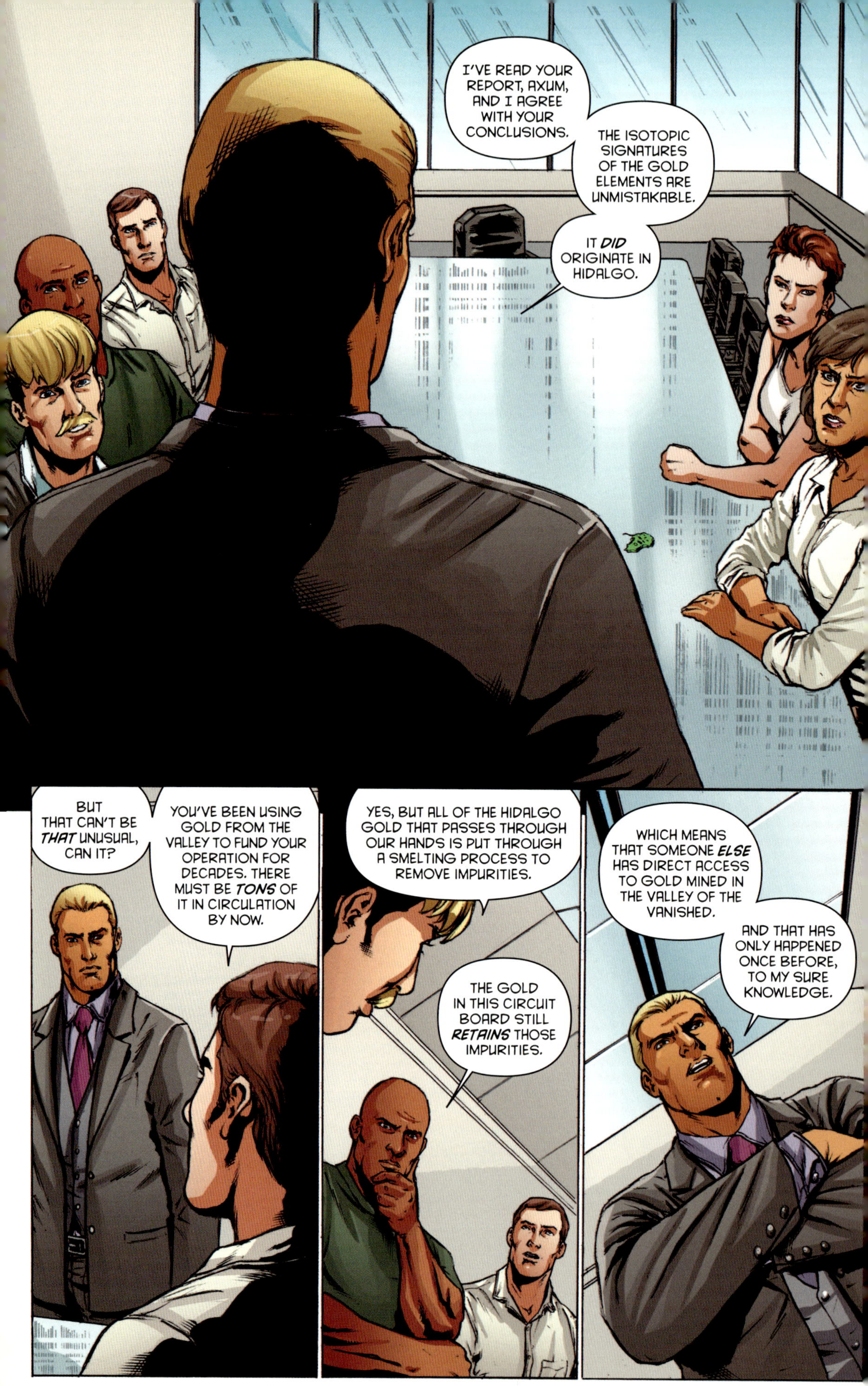
I'VE READ YOUR REPORT, AXUM, AND I AGREE WITH YOUR CONCLUSIONS.
THE ISOTOPIC SIGNATURES OF THE GOLD ELEMENTS ARE UNMISTAKABLE.
IT *DID* ORIGINATE IN HIDALGO.
BUT THAT CAN'T BE *THAT* UNUSUAL, CAN IT?
YOU'VE BEEN USING GOLD FROM THE VALLEY TO FUND YOUR OPERATION FOR DECADES. THERE MUST BE *TONS* OF IT IN CIRCULATION BY NOW.
YES, BUT ALL OF THE HIDALGO GOLD THAT PASSES THROUGH OUR HANDS IS PUT THROUGH A SMELTING PROCESS TO REMOVE IMPURITIES.
THE GOLD IN THIS CIRCUIT BOARD STILL *RETAINS* THOSE IMPURITIES.
WHICH MEANS THAT SOMEONE *ELSE* HAS DIRECT ACCESS TO GOLD MINED IN THE VALLEY OF THE VANISHED.
AND THAT HAS ONLY HAPPENED ONCE BEFORE, TO MY SURE KNOWLEDGE.

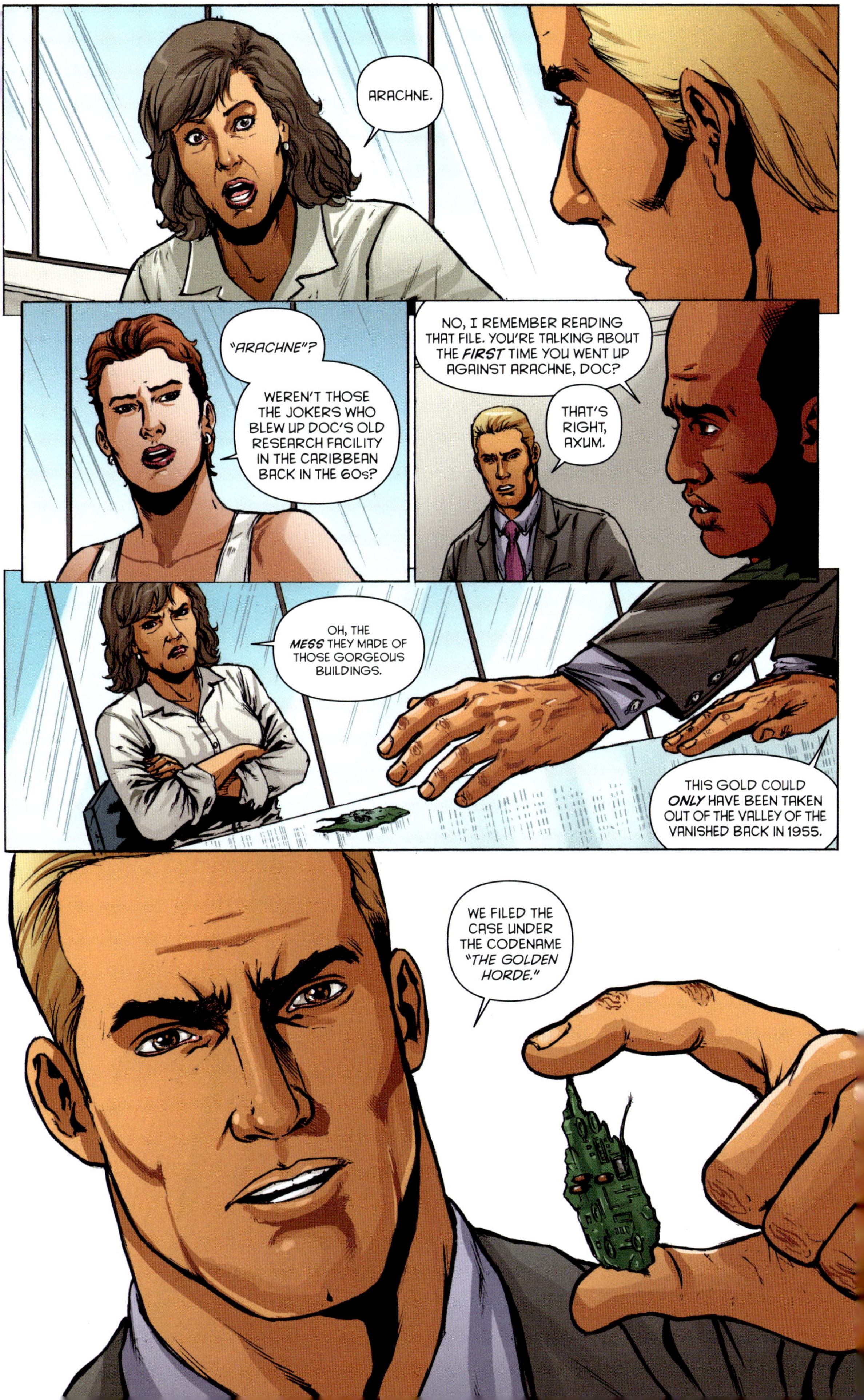
ARACHNE.
"ARACHNE"?
WEREN'T THOSE THE JOKERS WHO BLEW UP DOC'S OLD RESEARCH FACILITY IN THE CARIBBEAN BACK IN THE 60s?
NO, I REMEMBER READING THAT FILE. YOU'RE TALKING ABOUT THE *FIRST* TIME YOU WENT UP AGAINST ARACHNE, DOC?
THAT'S RIGHT, AXUM.
OH, THE *MESS* THEY MADE OF THOSE GORGEOUS BUILDINGS.
THIS GOLD COULD *ONLY* HAVE BEEN TAKEN OUT OF THE VALLEY OF THE VANISHED BACK IN 1955.
WE FILED THE CASE UNDER THE CODENAME *"THE GOLDEN HORDE."*

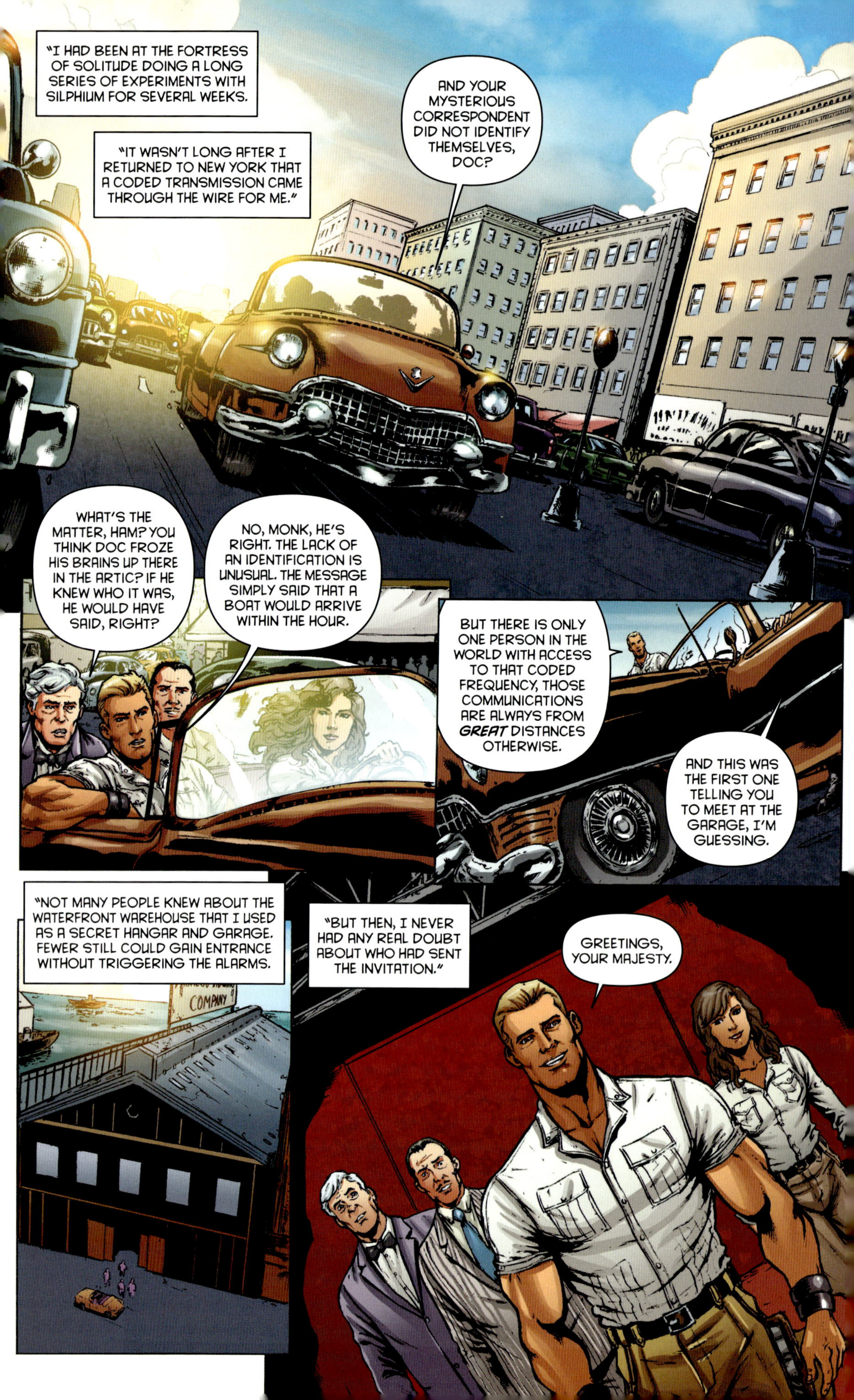
"I HAD BEEN AT THE FORTRESS OF SOLITUDE DOING A LONG SERIES OF EXPERIMENTS WITH SILPHIUM FOR SEVERAL WEEKS.
"IT WASN'T LONG AFTER I RETURNED TO NEW YORK THAT A CODED TRANSMISSION CAME THROUGH THE WIRE FOR ME."
AND YOUR MYSTERIOUS CORRESPONDENT DID NOT IDENTIFY THEMSELVES, DOC?
WHAT'S THE MATTER, HAM? YOU THINK DOC FROZE HIS BRAINS UP THERE IN THE ARTIC? IF HE KNEW WHO IT WAS, HE WOULD HAVE SAID, RIGHT?
NO, MONK, HE'S RIGHT. THE LACK OF AN IDENTIFICATION IS UNUSUAL. THE MESSAGE SIMPLY SAID THAT A BOAT WOULD ARRIVE WITHIN THE HOUR.
BUT THERE IS ONLY ONE PERSON IN THE WORLD WITH ACCESS TO THAT CODED FREQUENCY, THOSE COMMUNICATIONS ARE ALWAYS FROM *GREAT* DISTANCES OTHERWISE.
AND THIS WAS THE FIRST ONE TELLING YOU TO MEET AT THE GARAGE, I'M GUESSING.
"NOT MANY PEOPLE KNEW ABOUT THE WATERFRONT WAREHOUSE THAT I USED AS A SECRET HANGAR AND GARAGE. FEWER STILL COULD GAIN ENTRANCE WITHOUT TRIGGERING THE ALARMS.
COMPANY
"BUT THEN, I NEVER HAD ANY REAL DOUBT ABOUT WHO HAD SENT THE INVITATION."
GREETINGS, YOUR MAJESTY.

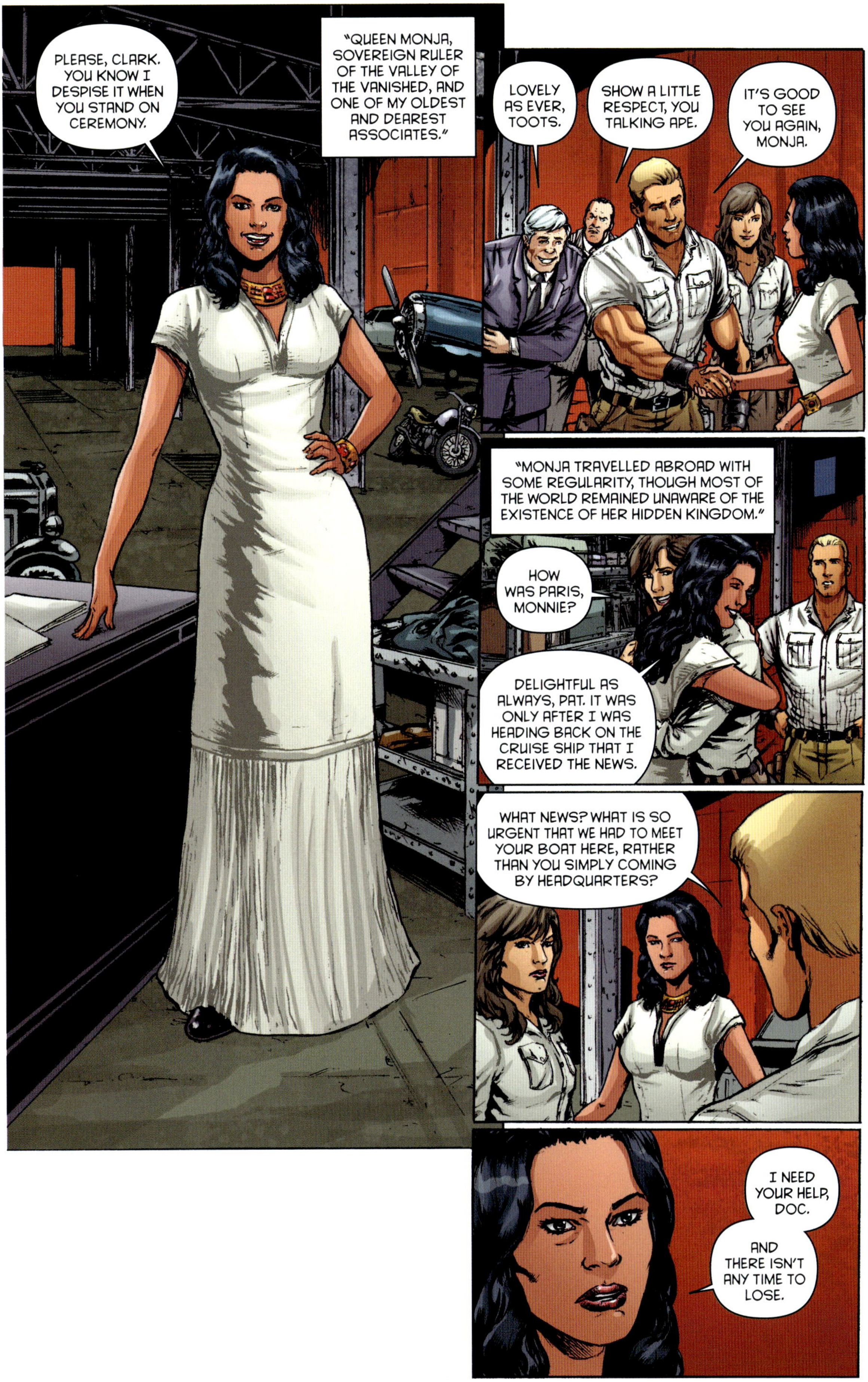
PLEASE, CLARK. YOU KNOW I DESPISE IT WHEN YOU STAND ON CEREMONY.
"QUEEN MONJA, SOVEREIGN RULER OF THE VALLEY OF THE VANISHED, AND ONE OF MY OLDEST AND DEAREST ASSOCIATES."
LOVELY AS EVER, TOOTS.
SHOW A LITTLE RESPECT, YOU TALKING APE.
IT'S GOOD TO SEE YOU AGAIN, MONJA.
"MONJA TRAVELLED ABROAD WITH SOME REGULARITY, THOUGH MOST OF THE WORLD REMAINED UNAWARE OF THE EXISTENCE OF HER HIDDEN KINGDOM."
HOW WAS PARIS, MONNIE?
DELIGHTFUL AS ALWAYS, PAT. IT WAS ONLY AFTER I WAS HEADING BACK ON THE CRUISE SHIP THAT I RECEIVED THE NEWS.
WHAT NEWS? WHAT IS SO URGENT THAT WE HAD TO MEET YOUR BOAT HERE, RATHER THAN YOU SIMPLY COMING BY HEADQUARTERS?
I NEED YOUR HELP, DOC.
AND THERE ISN'T ANY TIME TO LOSE.

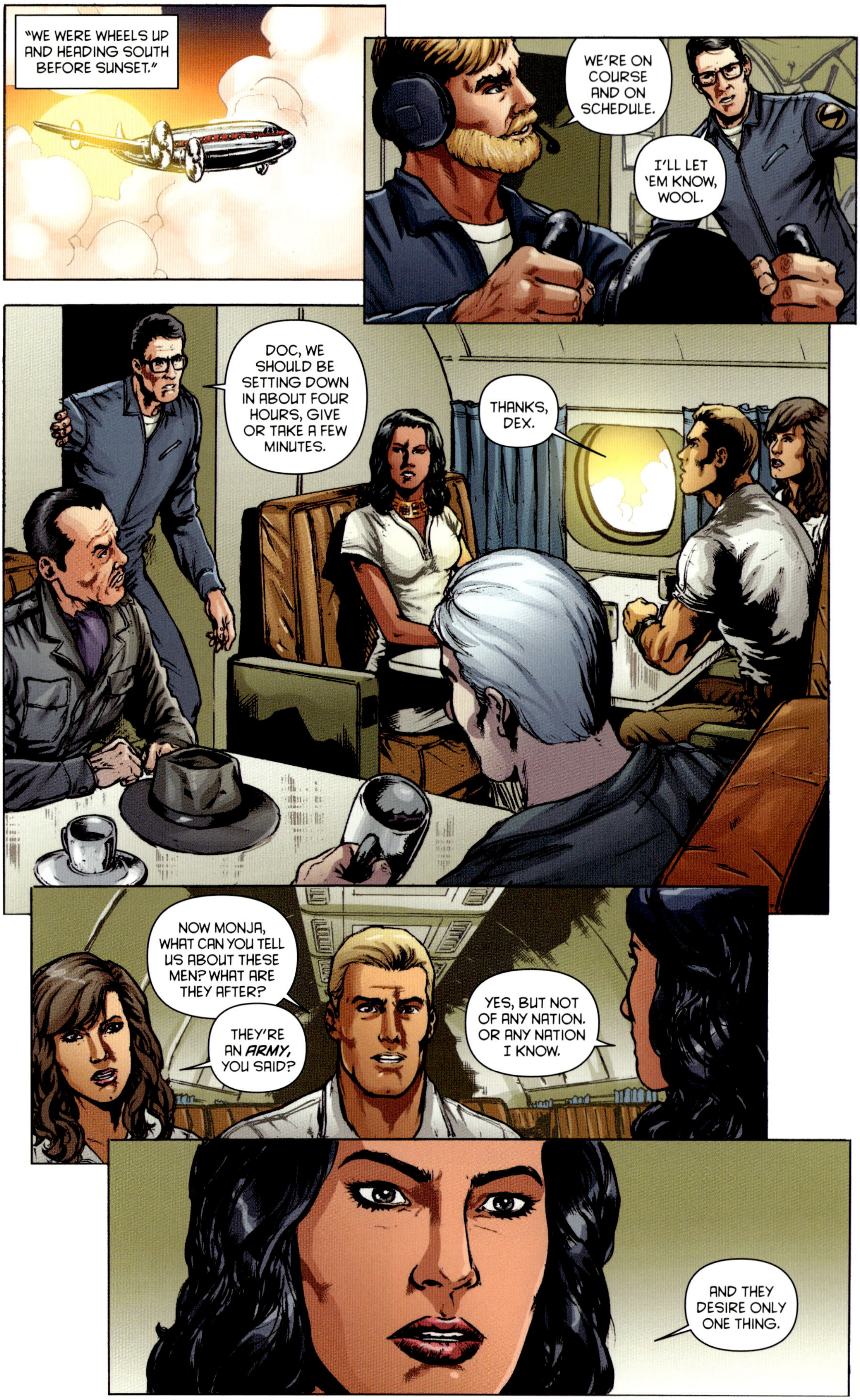
"WE WERE WHEELS UP AND HEADING SOUTH BEFORE SUNSET."
WE'RE ON COURSE AND ON SCHEDULE.
I'LL LET 'EM KNOW, WOOL.
DOC, WE SHOULD BE SETTING DOWN IN ABOUT FOUR HOURS, GIVE OR TAKE A FEW MINUTES.
THANKS, DEX.
NOW MONJA, WHAT CAN YOU TELL US ABOUT THESE MEN? WHAT ARE THEY AFTER?
THEY'RE AN *ARMY,* YOU SAID?
YES, BUT NOT OF ANY NATION. OR ANY NATION I KNOW.
AND THEY DESIRE ONLY ONE THING.

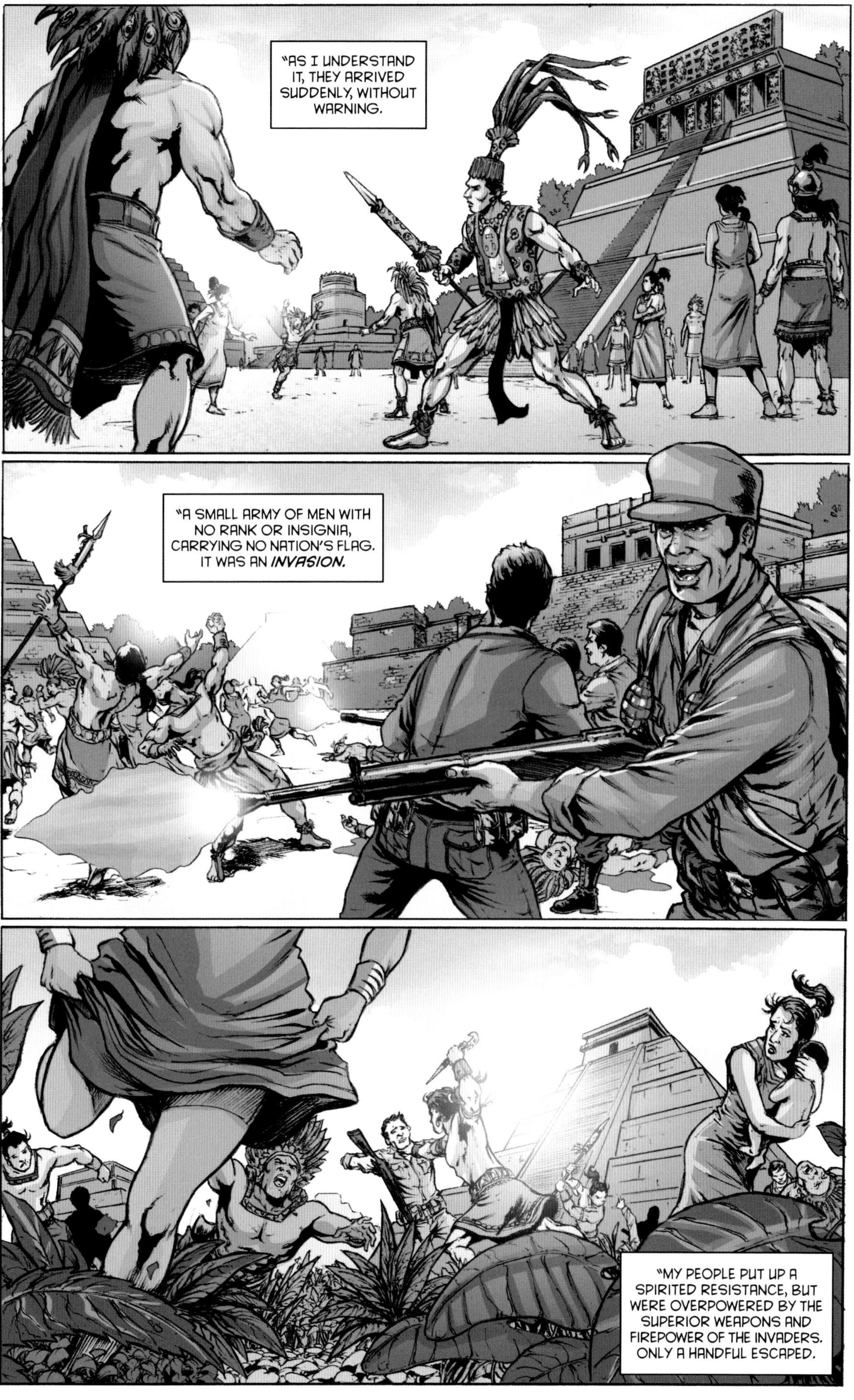
"AS I UNDERSTAND IT, THEY ARRIVED SUDDENLY, WITHOUT WARNING.
"A SMALL ARMY OF MEN WITH NO RANK OR INSIGNIA, CARRYING NO NATION'S FLAG. IT WAS AN *INVASION.*
"MY PEOPLE PUT UP A SPIRITED RESISTANCE, BUT WERE OVERPOWERED BY THE SUPERIOR WEAPONS AND FIREPOWER OF THE INVADERS. ONLY A HANDFUL ESCAPED.

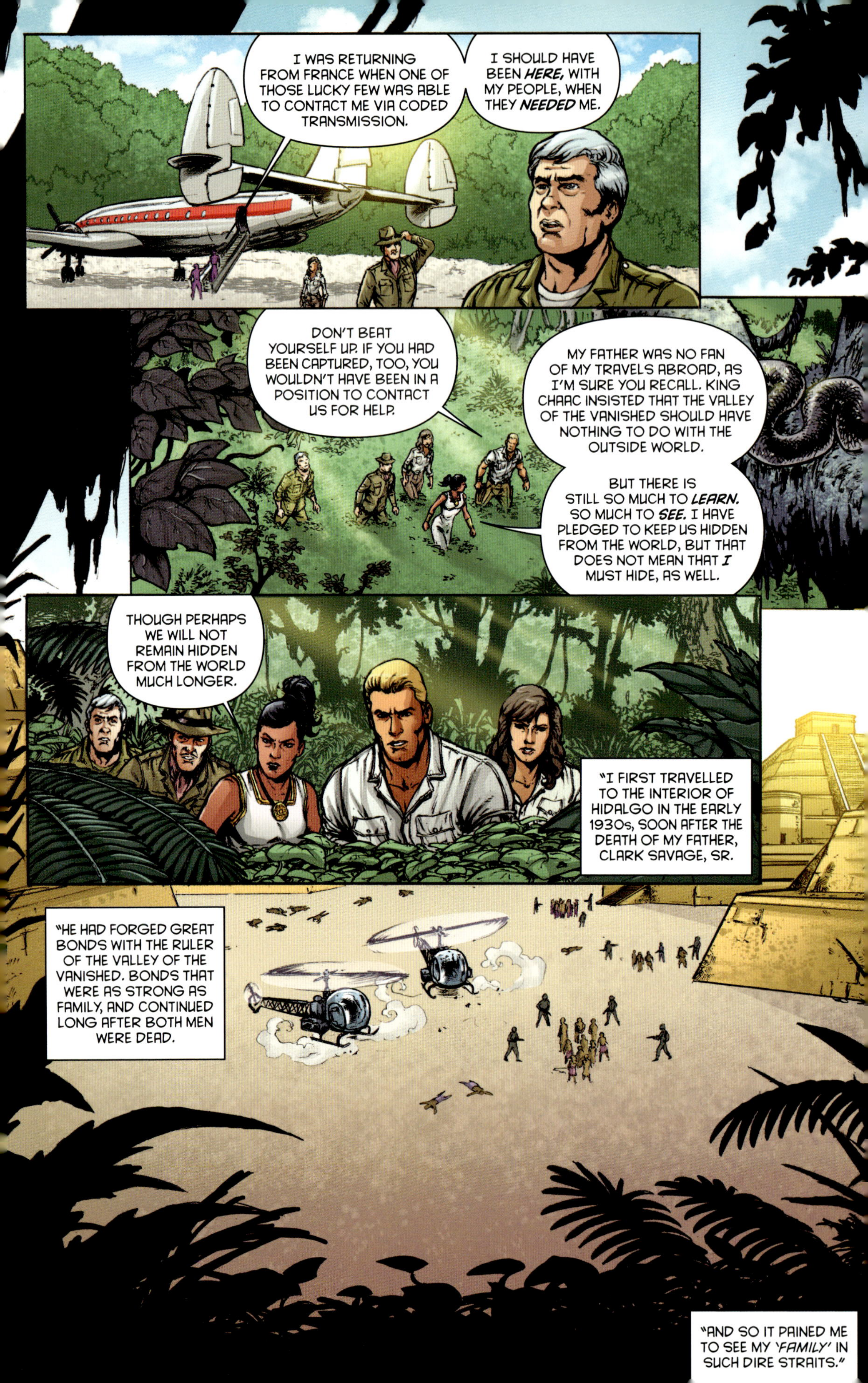
I WAS RETURNING FROM FRANCE WHEN ONE OF THOSE LUCKY FEW WAS ABLE TO CONTACT ME VIA CODED TRANSMISSION.
I SHOULD HAVE BEEN *HERE,* WITH MY PEOPLE, WHEN THEY *NEEDED* ME.
DON'T BEAT YOURSELF UP. IF YOU HAD BEEN CAPTURED, TOO, YOU WOULDN'T HAVE BEEN IN A POSITION TO CONTACT US FOR HELP.
MY FATHER WAS NO FAN OF MY TRAVELS ABROAD, AS I'M SURE YOU RECALL. KING CHAAC INSISTED THAT THE VALLEY OF THE VANISHED SHOULD HAVE NOTHING TO DO WITH THE OUTSIDE WORLD.
BUT THERE IS STILL SO MUCH TO *LEARN.* SO MUCH TO *SEE.* I HAVE PLEDGED TO KEEP US HIDDEN FROM THE WORLD, BUT THAT DOES NOT MEAN THAT *I* MUST HIDE, AS WELL.
THOUGH PERHAPS WE WILL NOT REMAIN HIDDEN FROM THE WORLD MUCH LONGER.
"I FIRST TRAVELLED TO THE INTERIOR OF HIDALGO IN THE EARLY 1930s, SOON AFTER THE DEATH OF MY FATHER, CLARK SAVAGE, SR.
"HE HAD FORGED GREAT BONDS WITH THE RULER OF THE VALLEY OF THE VANISHED. BONDS THAT WERE AS STRONG AS FAMILY, AND CONTINUED LONG AFTER BOTH MEN WERE DEAD.
"AND SO IT PAINED ME TO SEE MY *'FAMILY'* IN SUCH DIRE STRAITS."

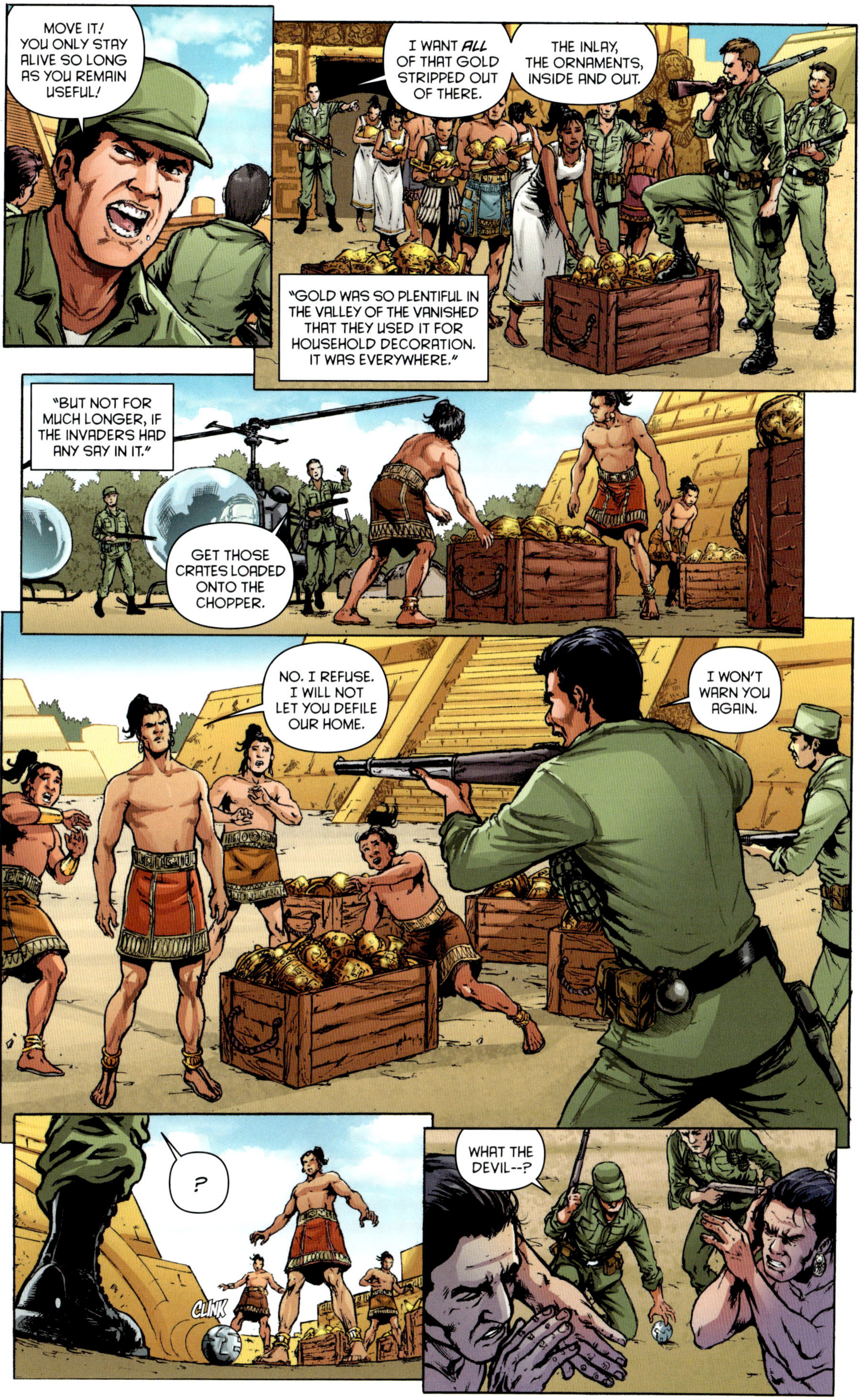
MOVE IT! YOU ONLY STAY ALIVE SO LONG AS YOU REMAIN USEFUL!
I WANT ALL OF THAT GOLD STRIPPED OUT OF THERE.
THE INLAY, THE ORNAMENTS, INSIDE AND OUT.
"GOLD WAS SO PLENTIFUL IN THE VALLEY OF THE VANISHED THAT THEY USED IT FOR HOUSEHOLD DECORATION. IT WAS EVERYWHERE."
"BUT NOT FOR MUCH LONGER, IF THE INVADERS HAD ANY SAY IN IT."
GET THOSE CRATES LOADED ONTO THE CHOPPER.
NO. I REFUSE. I WILL NOT LET YOU DEFILE OUR HOME.
I WON'T WARN YOU AGAIN.
?
CLINK
WHAT THE DEVIL--?

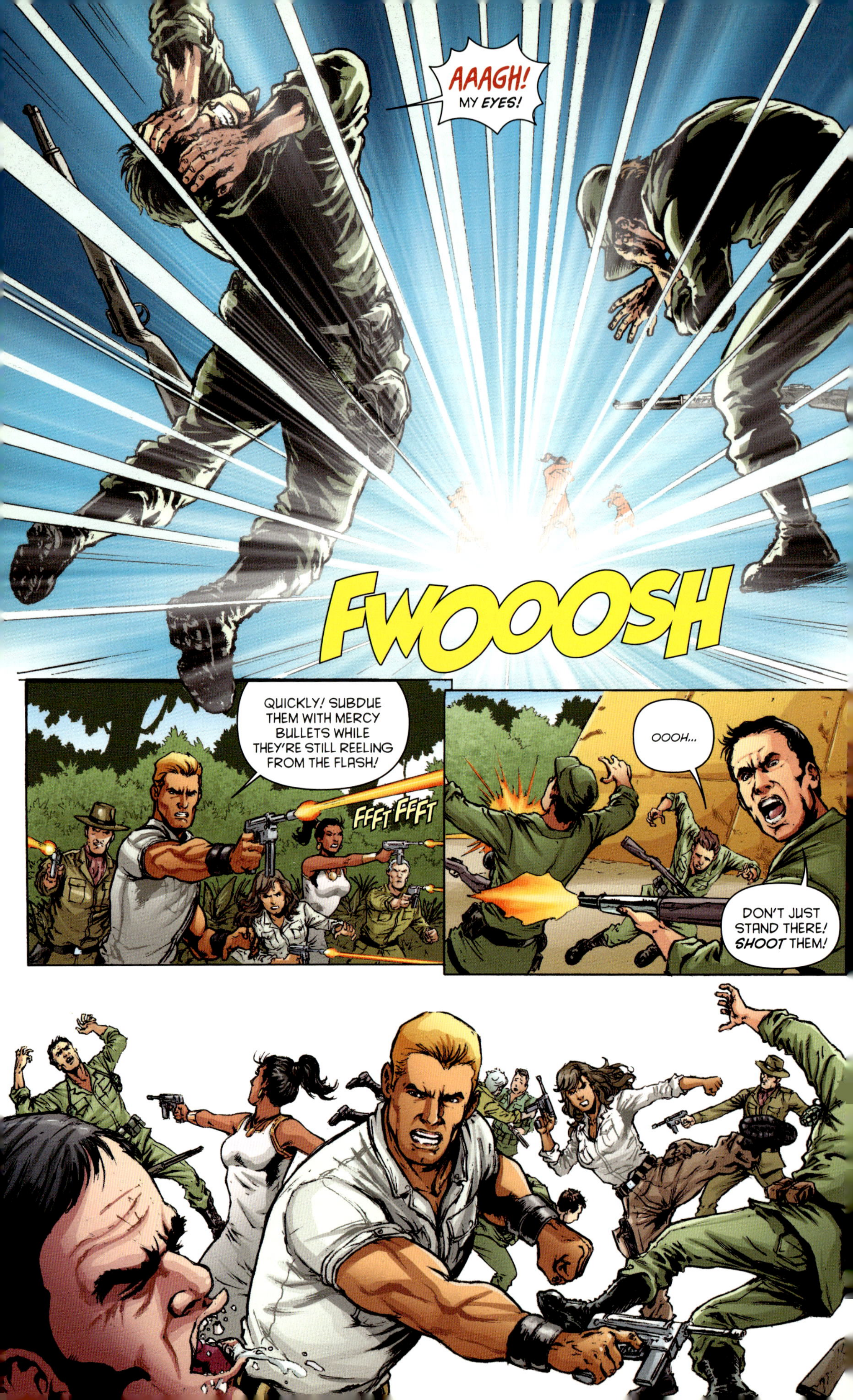
AAAGH! MY EYES!
FWOOOSH
QUICKLY! SUBDUE THEM WITH MERCY BULLETS WHILE THEY'RE STILL REELING FROM THE FLASH!
FFFT FFFT
OOOH...
DON'T JUST STAND THERE! SHOOT THEM!

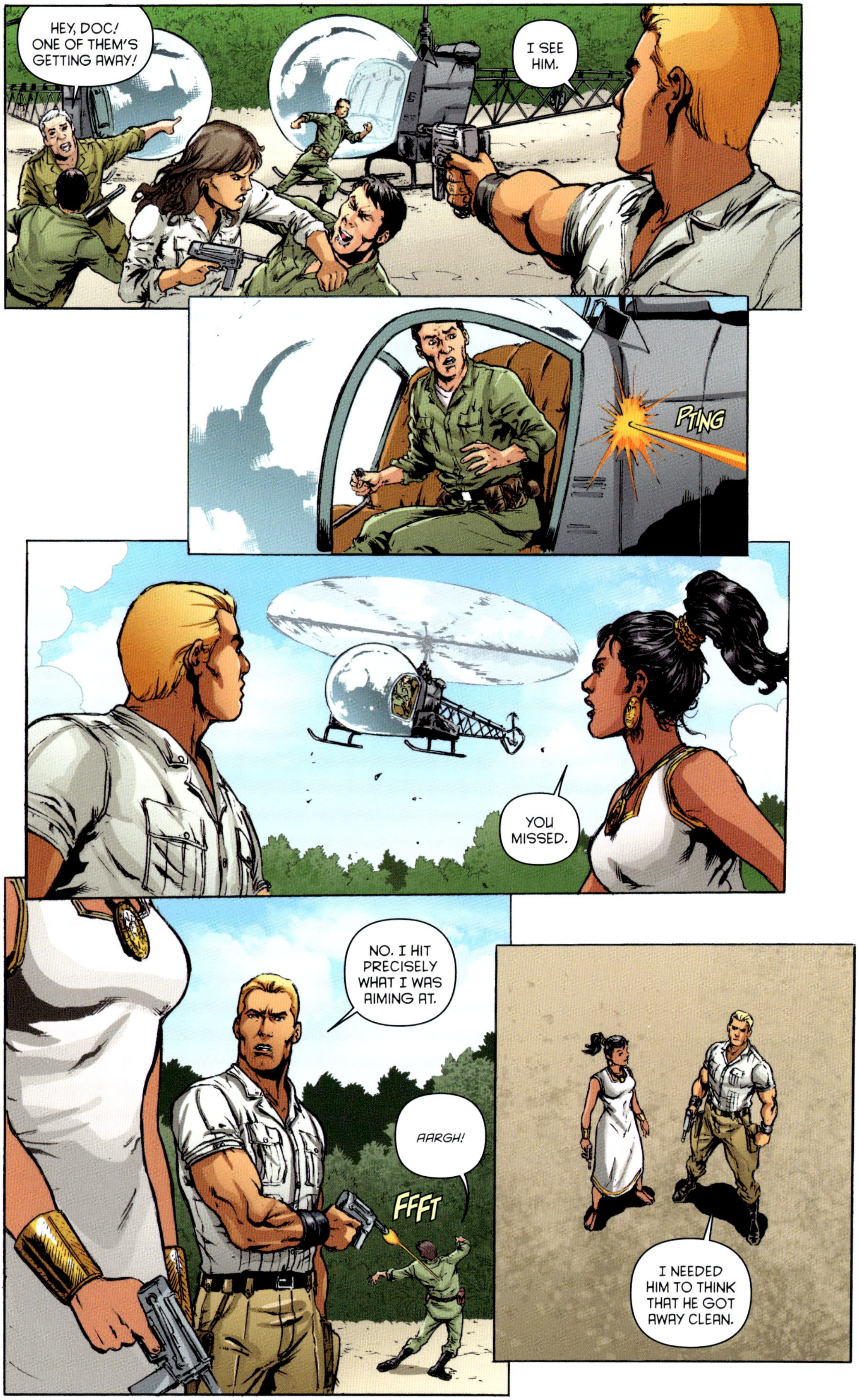
HEY, DOC! ONE OF THEM'S GETTING AWAY!
I SEE HIM.
PTING
YOU MISSED.
NO. I HIT PRECISELY WHAT I WAS AIMING AT.
AARGH!
FFFT
I NEEDED HIM TO THINK THAT HE GOT AWAY CLEAN.

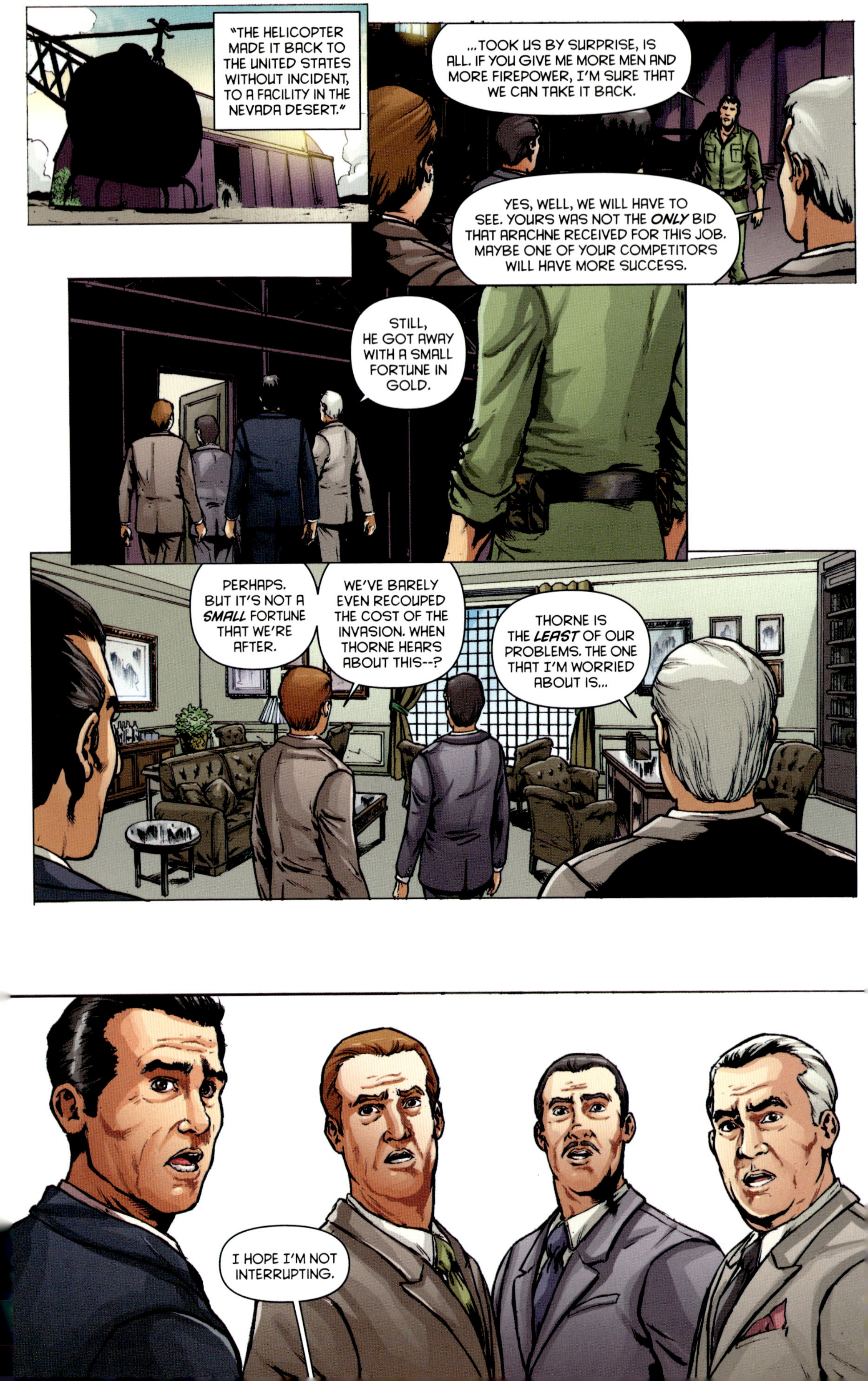
"THE HELICOPTER MADE IT BACK TO THE UNITED STATES WITHOUT INCIDENT, TO A FACILITY IN THE NEVADA DESERT."
...TOOK US BY SURPRISE, IS ALL. IF YOU GIVE ME MORE MEN AND MORE FIREPOWER, I'M SURE THAT WE CAN TAKE IT BACK.
YES, WELL, WE WILL HAVE TO SEE. YOURS WAS NOT THE ONLY BID THAT ARACHNE RECEIVED FOR THIS JOB. MAYBE ONE OF YOUR COMPETITORS WILL HAVE MORE SUCCESS.
STILL, HE GOT AWAY WITH A SMALL FORTUNE IN GOLD.
PERHAPS. BUT IT'S NOT A SMALL FORTUNE THAT WE'RE AFTER.
WE'VE BARELY EVEN RECOUPED THE COST OF THE INVASION. WHEN THORNE HEARS ABOUT THIS--?
THORNE IS THE LEAST OF OUR PROBLEMS. THE ONE THAT I'M WORRIED ABOUT IS...
I HOPE I'M NOT INTERRUPTING.

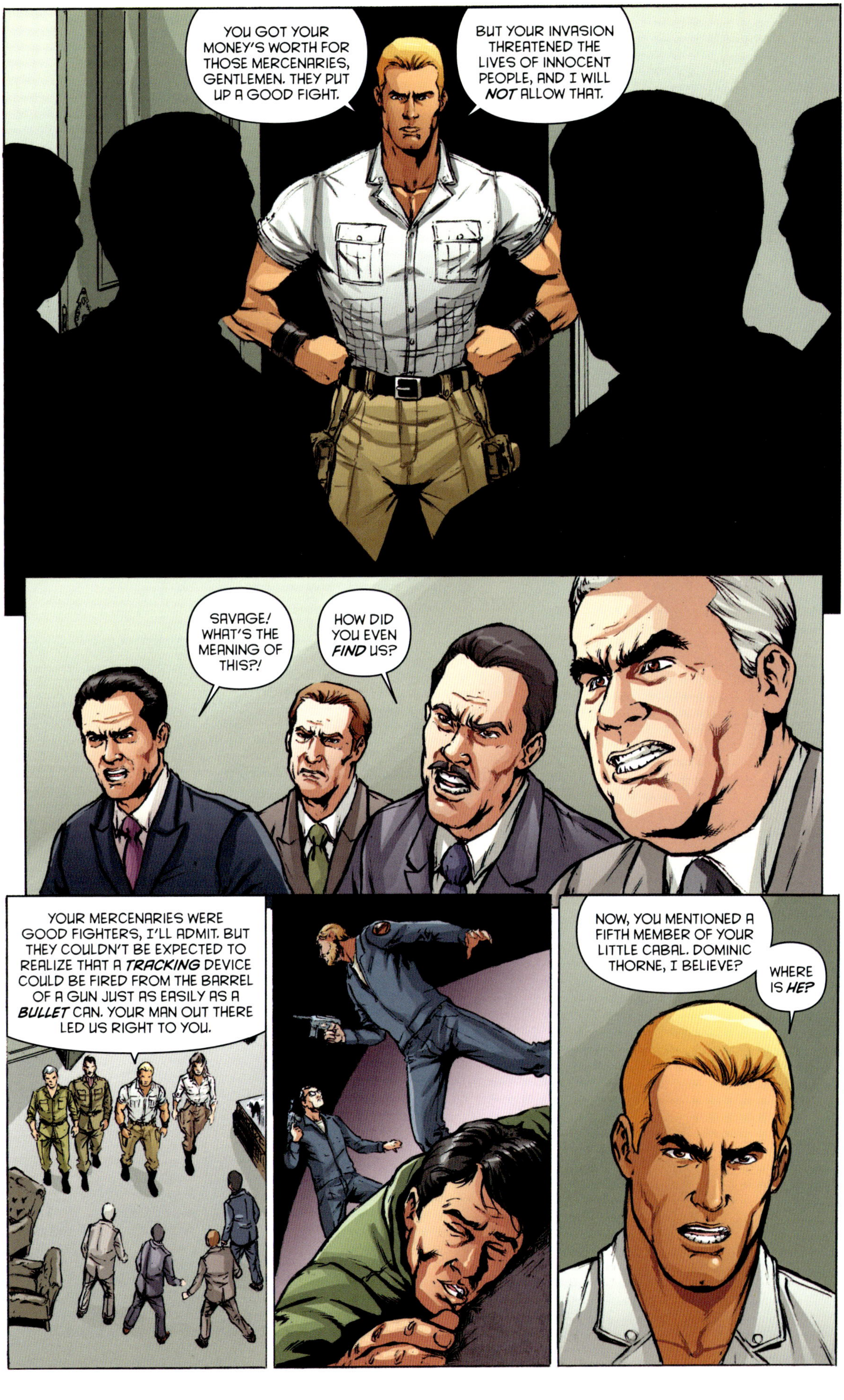

YOU GOT YOUR MONEY'S WORTH FOR THOSE MERCENARIES, GENTLEMEN. THEY PUT UP A GOOD FIGHT.
BUT YOUR INVASION THREATENED THE LIVES OF INNOCENT PEOPLE, AND I WILL *NOT* ALLOW THAT.
SAVAGE! WHAT'S THE MEANING OF THIS?!
HOW DID YOU EVEN *FIND* US?
YOUR MERCENARIES WERE GOOD FIGHTERS, I'LL ADMIT. BUT THEY COULDN'T BE EXPECTED TO REALIZE THAT A *TRACKING* DEVICE COULD BE FIRED FROM THE BARREL OF A GUN JUST AS EASILY AS A *BULLET* CAN. YOUR MAN OUT THERE LED US RIGHT TO YOU.
NOW, YOU MENTIONED A FIFTH MEMBER OF YOUR LITTLE CABAL. DOMINIC THORNE, I BELIEVE?
WHERE IS *HE?*

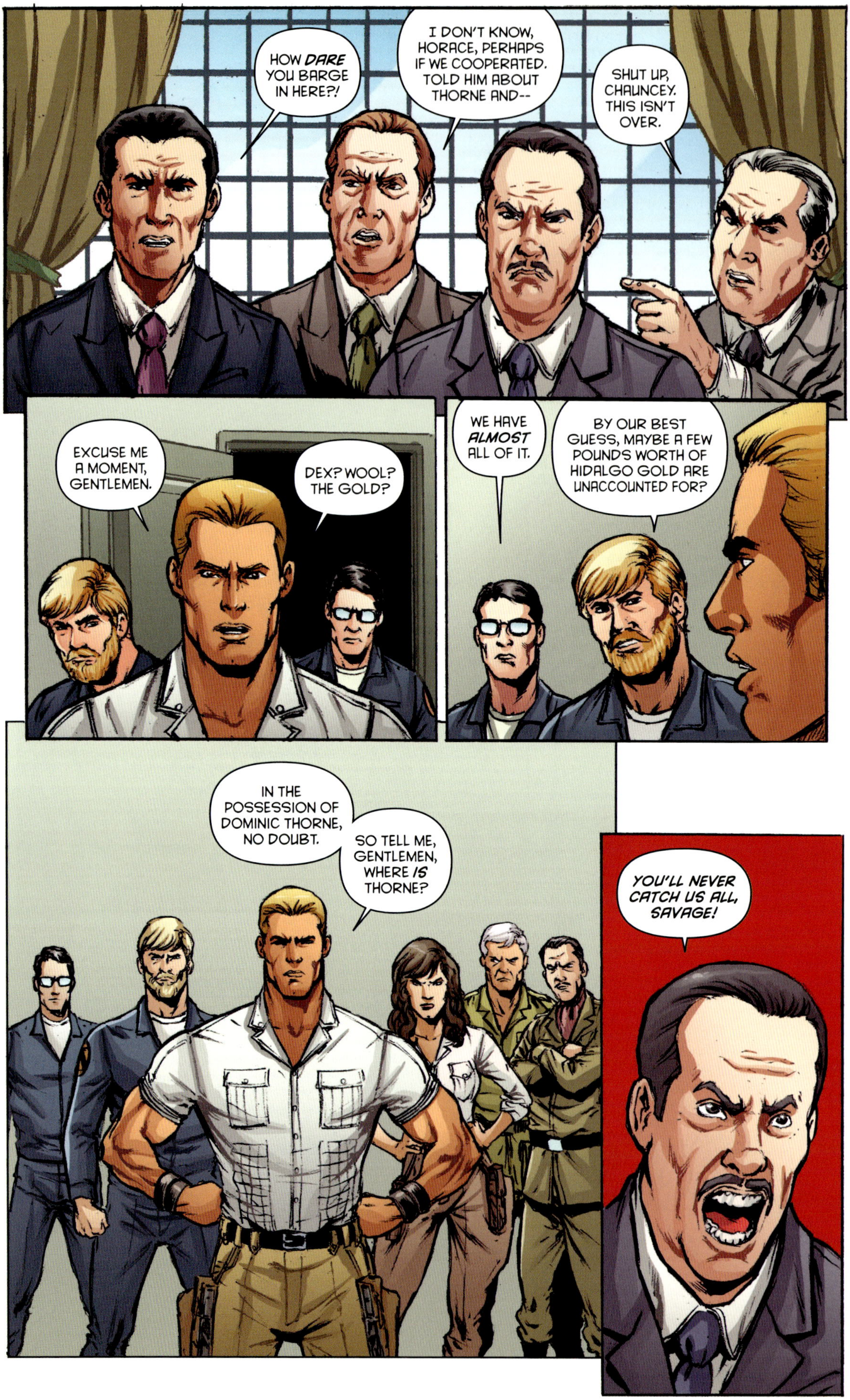
HOW *DARE* YOU BARGE IN HERE?!
I DON'T KNOW, HORACE, PERHAPS IF WE COOPERATED. TOLD HIM ABOUT THORNE AND--
SHUT UP, CHAUNCEY. THIS ISN'T OVER.
EXCUSE ME A MOMENT, GENTLEMEN.
DEX? WOOL? THE GOLD?
WE HAVE *ALMOST* ALL OF IT.
BY OUR BEST GUESS, MAYBE A FEW POUNDS WORTH OF HIDALGO GOLD ARE UNACCOUNTED FOR?
IN THE POSSESSION OF DOMINIC THORNE, NO DOUBT.
SO TELL ME, GENTLEMEN, WHERE *IS* THORNE?
YOU'LL NEVER CATCH US ALL, SAVAGE!

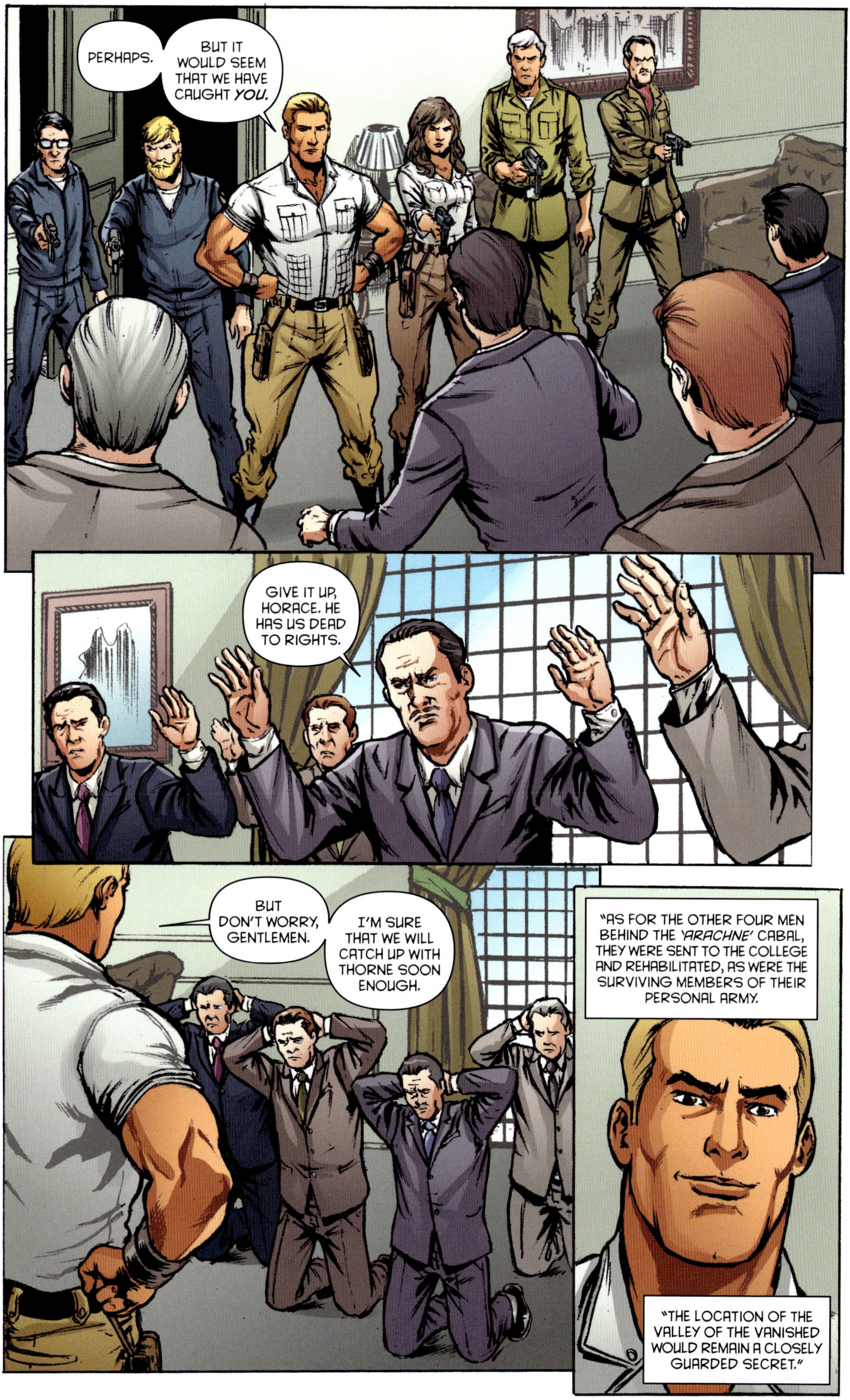

PERHAPS.
BUT IT WOULD SEEM THAT WE HAVE CAUGHT *YOU.*
GIVE IT UP, HORACE. HE HAS US DEAD TO RIGHTS.
BUT DON'T WORRY, GENTLEMEN.
I'M SURE THAT WE WILL CATCH UP WITH THORNE SOON ENOUGH.
"AS FOR THE OTHER FOUR MEN BEHIND THE *'ARACHNE'* CABAL, THEY WERE SENT TO THE COLLEGE AND REHABILITATED, AS WERE THE SURVIVING MEMBERS OF THEIR PERSONAL ARMY.
"THE LOCATION OF THE VALLEY OF THE VANISHED WOULD REMAIN A CLOSELY GUARDED SECRET."

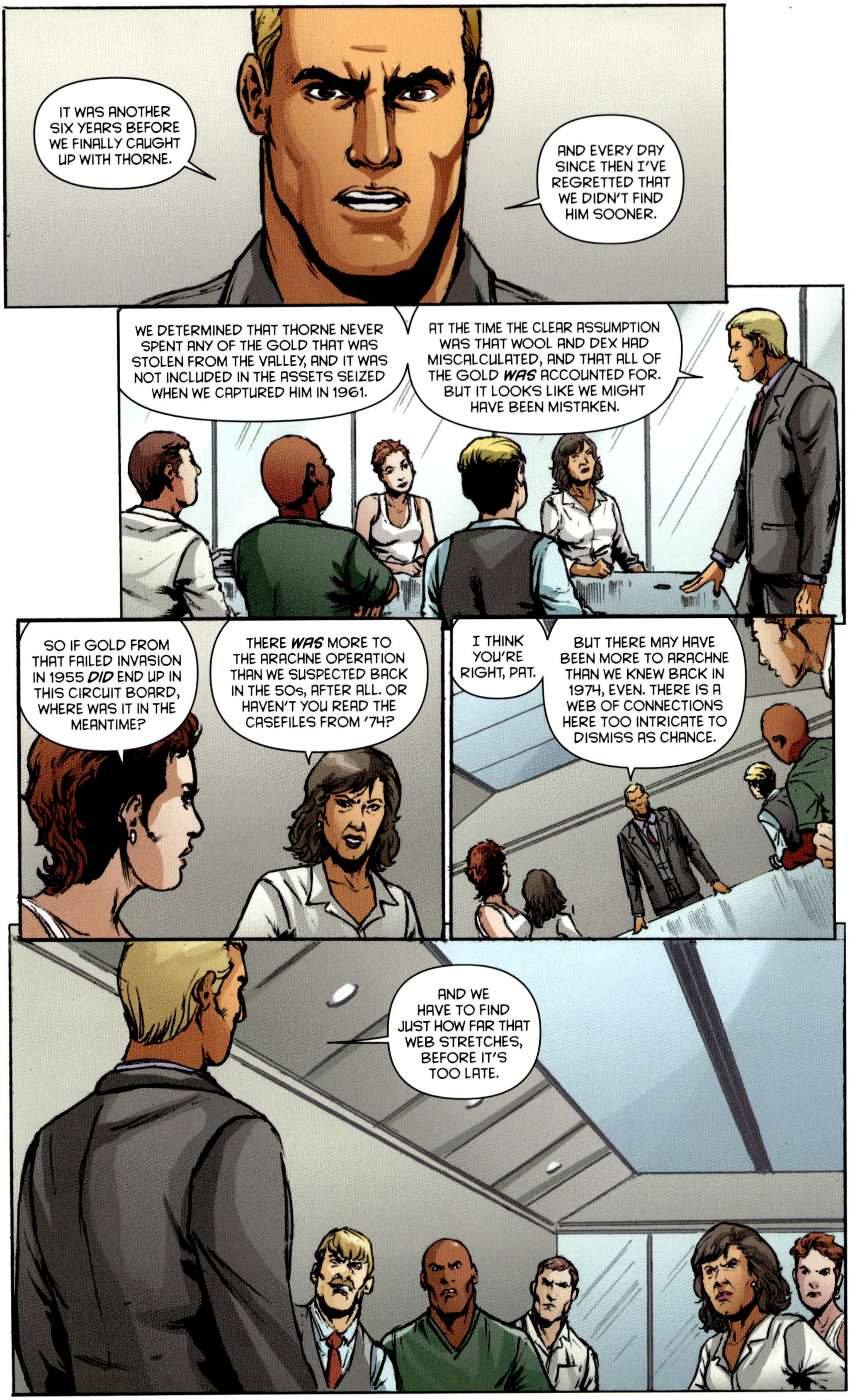
IT WAS ANOTHER SIX YEARS BEFORE WE FINALLY CAUGHT UP WITH THORNE.
AND EVERY DAY SINCE THEN I'VE REGRETTED THAT WE DIDN'T FIND HIM SOONER.
WE DETERMINED THAT THORNE NEVER SPENT ANY OF THE GOLD THAT WAS STOLEN FROM THE VALLEY, AND IT WAS NOT INCLUDED IN THE ASSETS SEIZED WHEN WE CAPTURED HIM IN 1961.
AT THE TIME THE CLEAR ASSUMPTION WAS THAT WOOL AND DEX HAD MISCALCULATED, AND THAT ALL OF THE GOLD *WAS* ACCOUNTED FOR. BUT IT LOOKS LIKE WE MIGHT HAVE BEEN MISTAKEN.
SO IF GOLD FROM THAT FAILED INVASION IN 1955 *DID* END UP IN THIS CIRCUIT BOARD, WHERE WAS IT IN THE MEANTIME?
THERE *WAS* MORE TO THE ARACHNE OPERATION THAN WE SUSPECTED BACK IN THE 50s, AFTER ALL. OR HAVEN'T YOU READ THE CASEFILES FROM '74?
I THINK YOU'RE RIGHT, PAT.
BUT THERE MAY HAVE BEEN MORE TO ARACHNE THAN WE KNEW BACK IN 1974, EVEN. THERE IS A WEB OF CONNECTIONS HERE TOO INTRICATE TO DISMISS AS CHANCE.
AND WE HAVE TO FIND JUST HOW FAR THAT WEB STRETCHES, BEFORE IT'S TOO LATE.

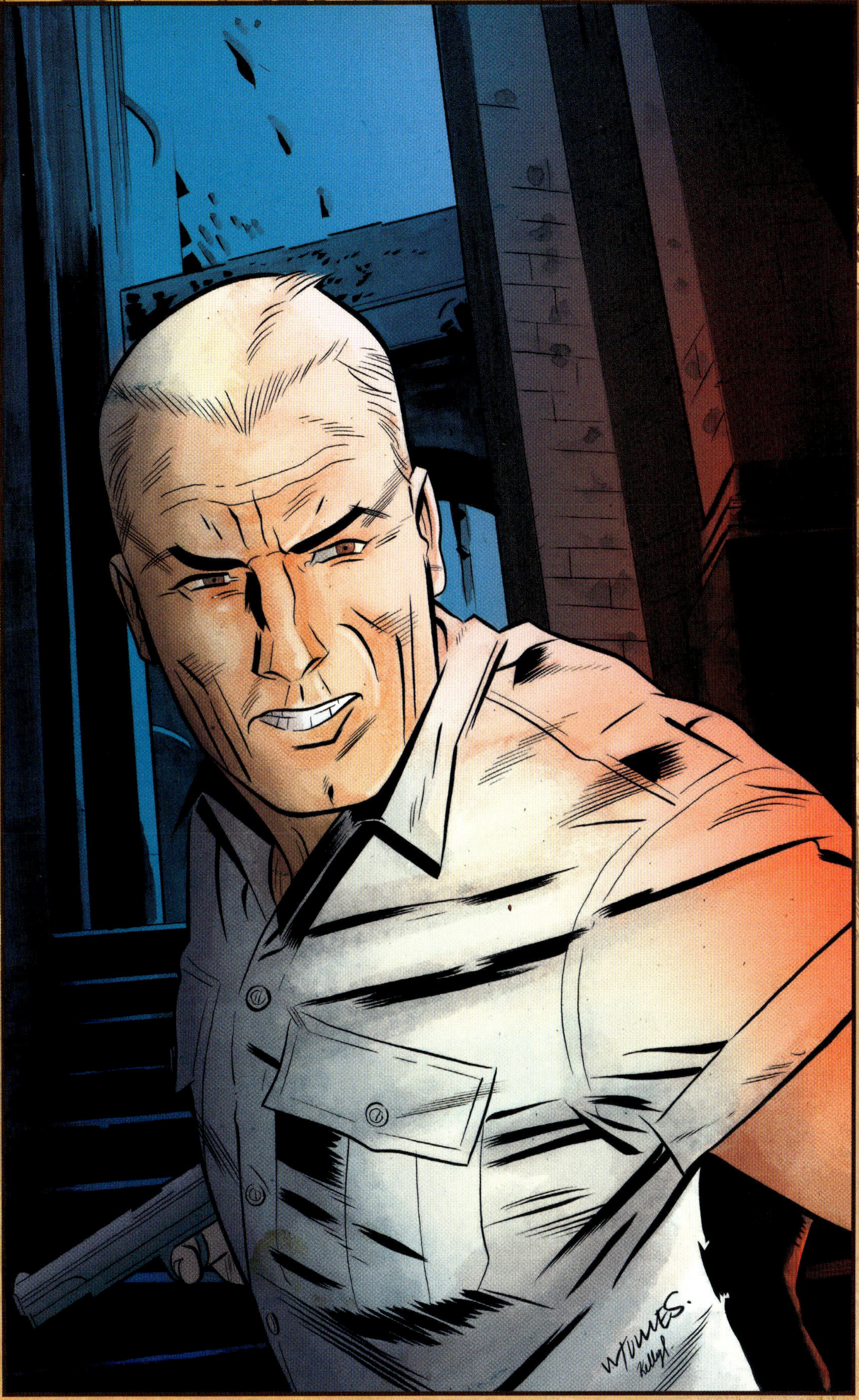

ISSUE **#3** COVER

art by **WILFREDO TORRES** colors by **KELLY FITZPATRICK**

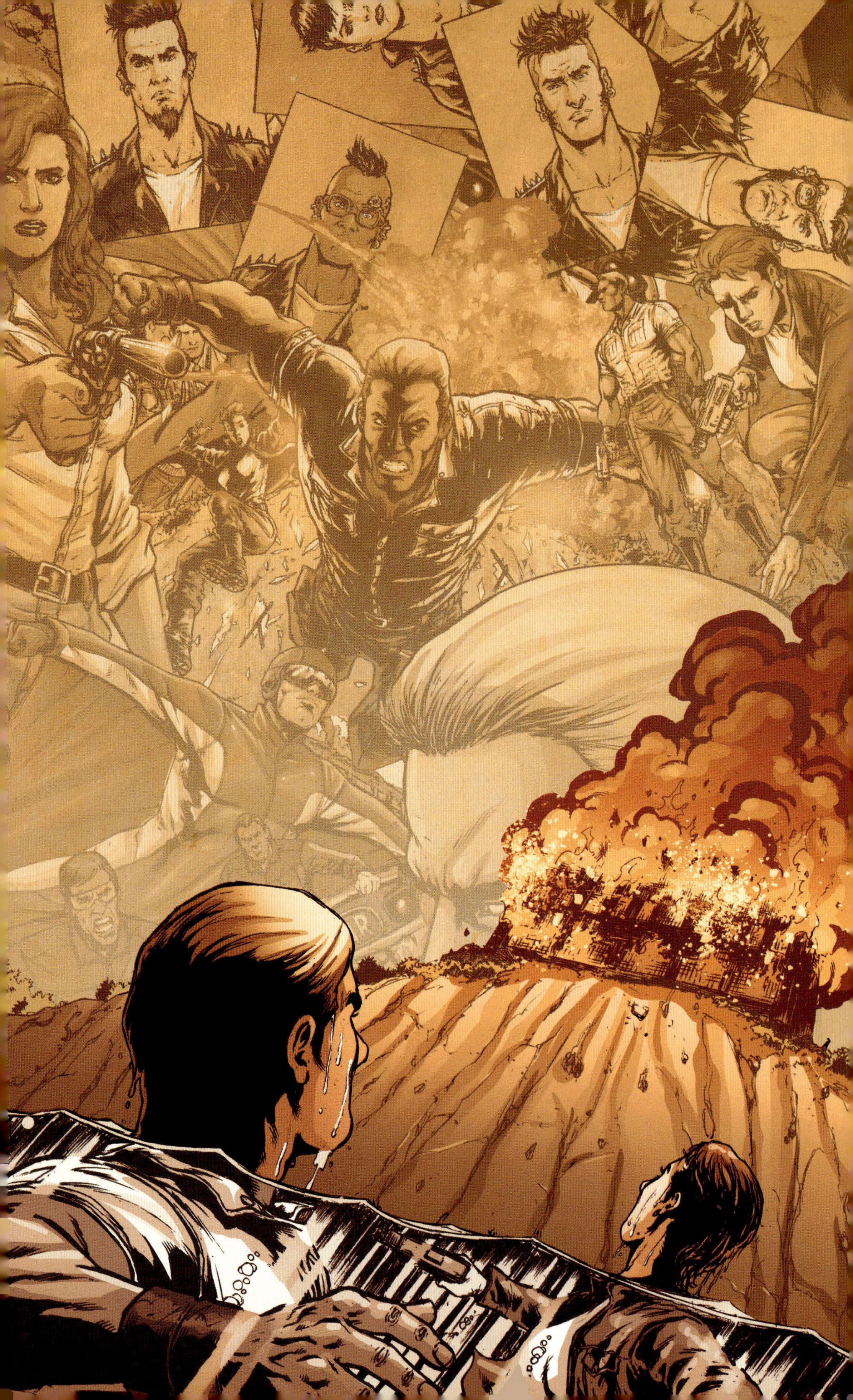

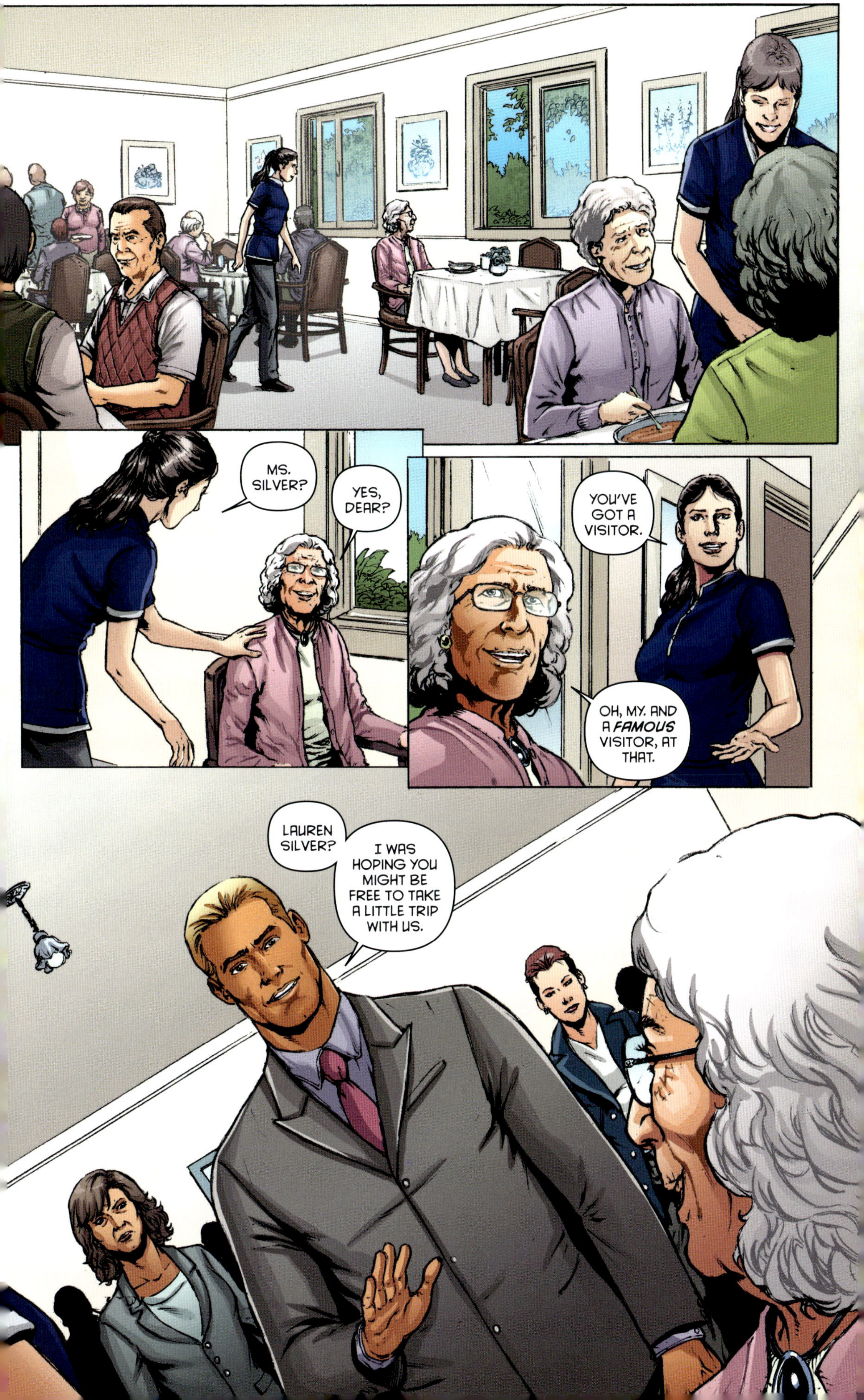
MS. SILVER?
YES, DEAR?
YOU'VE GOT A VISITOR.
OH, MY. AND A *FAMOUS* VISITOR, AT THAT.
LAUREN SILVER?
I WAS HOPING YOU MIGHT BE FREE TO TAKE A LITTLE TRIP WITH US.

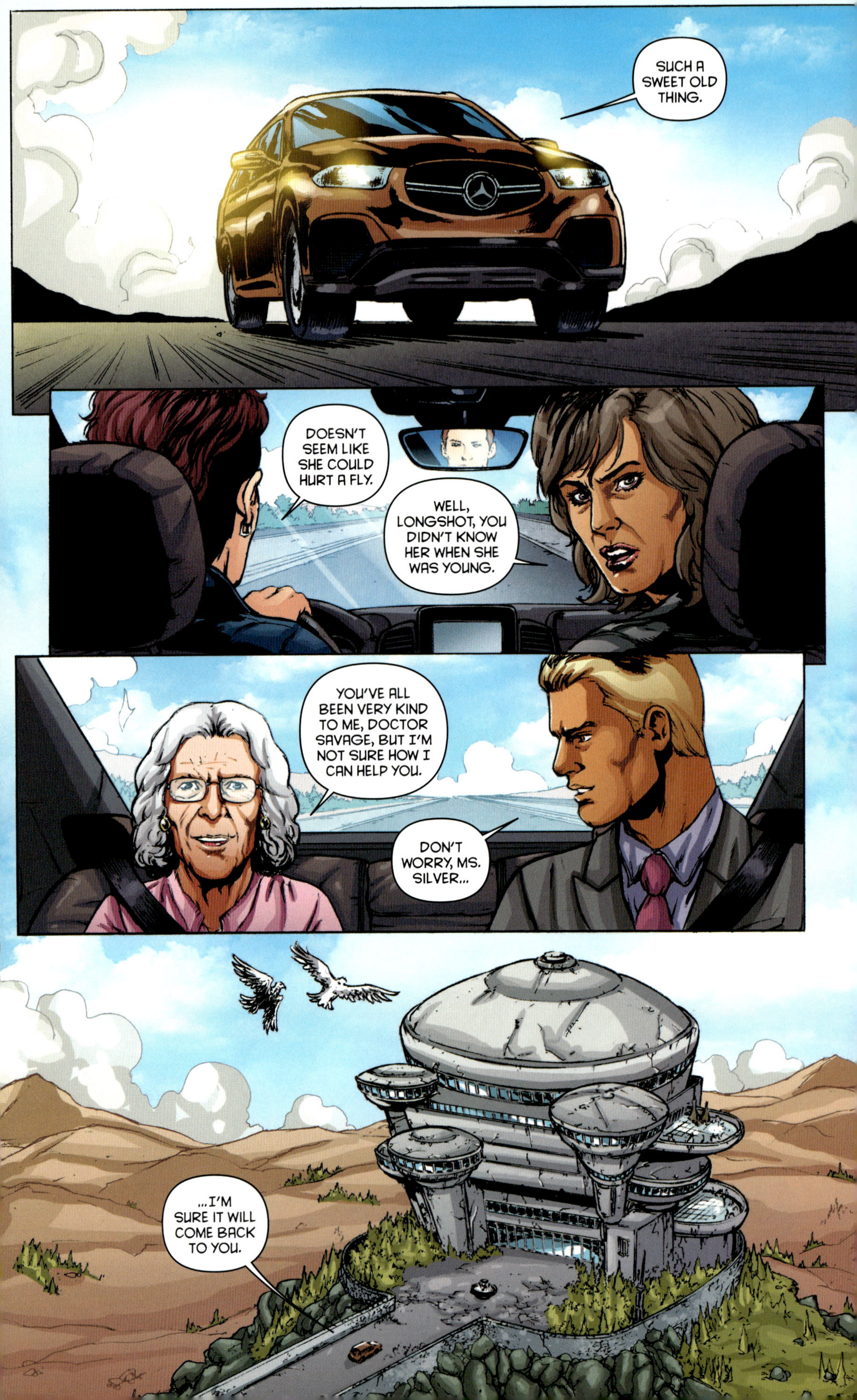
SUCH A SWEET OLD THING.
DOESN'T SEEM LIKE SHE COULD HURT A FLY.
WELL, LONGSHOT, YOU DIDN'T KNOW HER WHEN SHE WAS YOUNG.
YOU'VE ALL BEEN VERY KIND TO ME, DOCTOR SAVAGE, BUT I'M NOT SURE HOW I CAN HELP YOU.
DON'T WORRY, MS. SILVER...
...I'M SURE IT WILL COME BACK TO YOU.

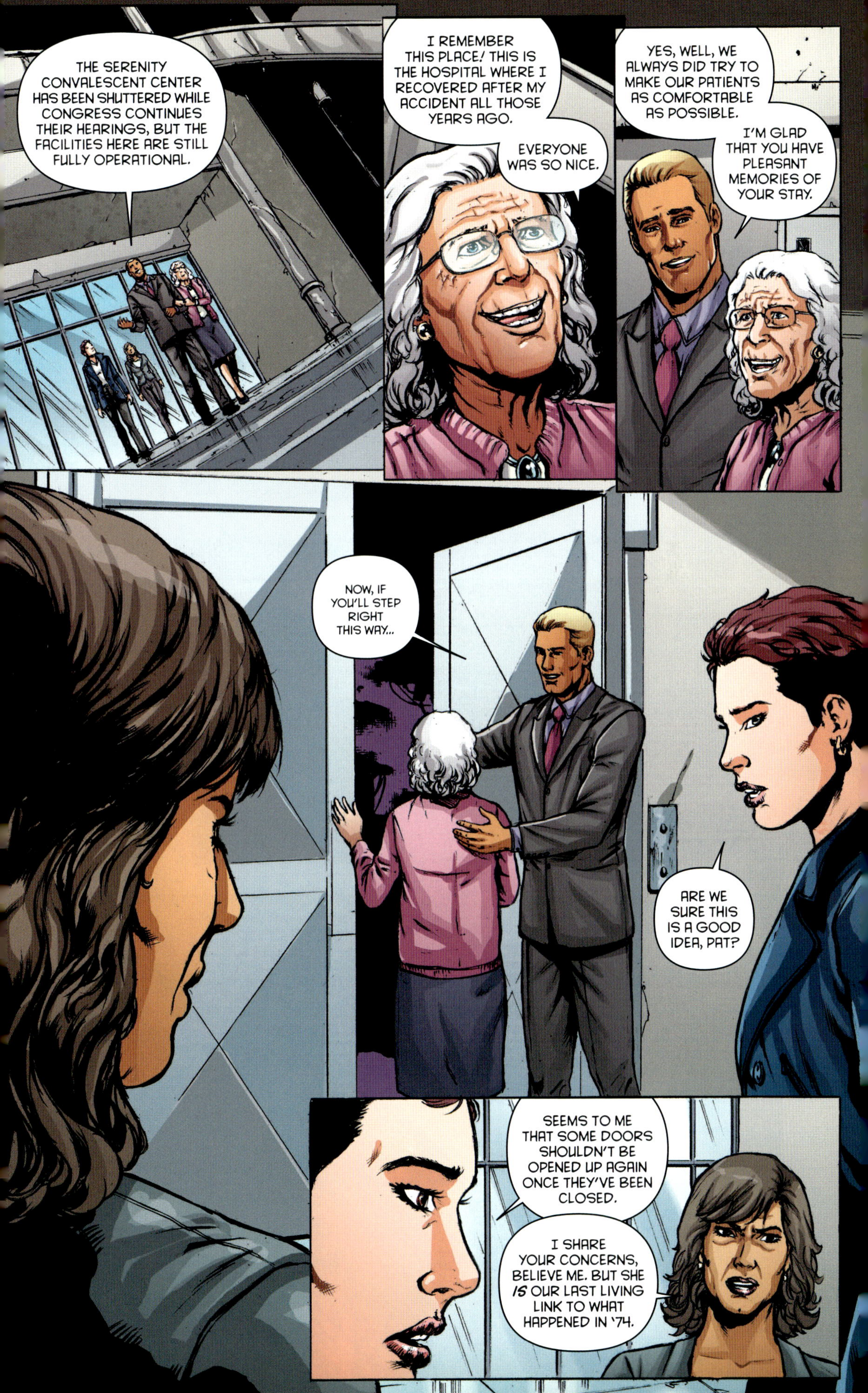
THE SERENITY CONVALESCENT CENTER HAS BEEN SHUTTERED WHILE CONGRESS CONTINUES THEIR HEARINGS, BUT THE FACILITIES HERE ARE STILL FULLY OPERATIONAL.
I REMEMBER THIS PLACE! THIS IS THE HOSPITAL WHERE I RECOVERED AFTER MY ACCIDENT ALL THOSE YEARS AGO.
EVERYONE WAS SO NICE.
YES, WELL, WE ALWAYS DID TRY TO MAKE OUR PATIENTS AS COMFORTABLE AS POSSIBLE.
I'M GLAD THAT YOU HAVE PLEASANT MEMORIES OF YOUR STAY.
NOW, IF YOU'LL STEP RIGHT THIS WAY...
ARE WE SURE THIS IS A GOOD IDEA, PAT?
SEEMS TO ME THAT SOME DOORS SHOULDN'T BE OPENED UP AGAIN ONCE THEY'VE BEEN CLOSED.
I SHARE YOUR CONCERNS, BELIEVE ME. BUT SHE *IS* OUR LAST LIVING LINK TO WHAT HAPPENED IN '74.

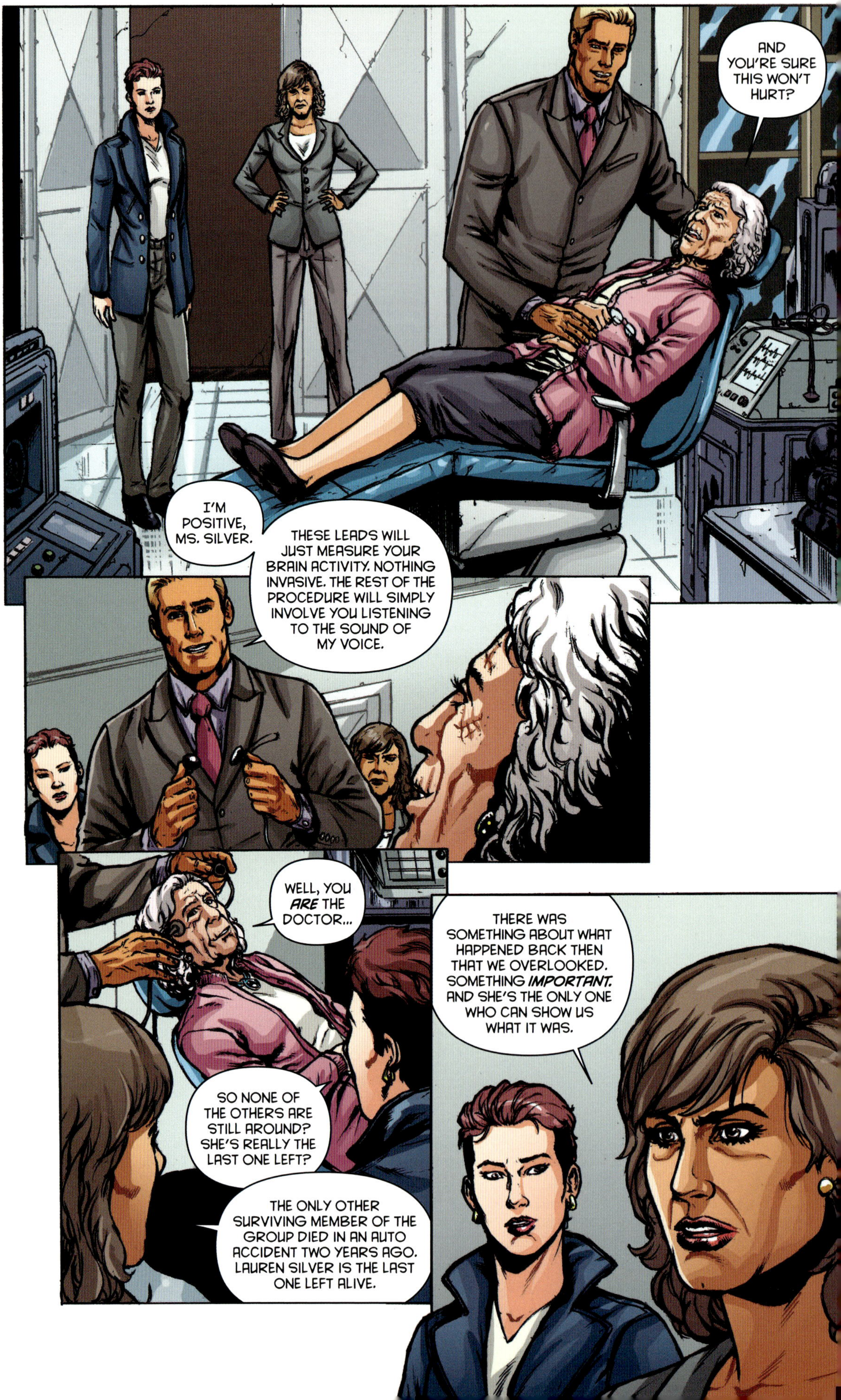
AND YOU'RE SURE THIS WON'T HURT?
I'M POSITIVE, MS. SILVER.
THESE LEADS WILL JUST MEASURE YOUR BRAIN ACTIVITY. NOTHING INVASIVE. THE REST OF THE PROCEDURE WILL SIMPLY INVOLVE YOU LISTENING TO THE SOUND OF MY VOICE.
WELL, YOU *ARE* THE DOCTOR...
SO NONE OF THE OTHERS ARE STILL AROUND? SHE'S REALLY THE LAST ONE LEFT?
THE ONLY OTHER SURVIVING MEMBER OF THE GROUP DIED IN AN AUTO ACCIDENT TWO YEARS AGO. LAUREN SILVER IS THE LAST ONE LEFT ALIVE.
THERE WAS SOMETHING ABOUT WHAT HAPPENED BACK THEN THAT WE OVERLOOKED. SOMETHING *IMPORTANT.* AND SHE'S THE ONLY ONE WHO CAN SHOW US WHAT IT WAS.

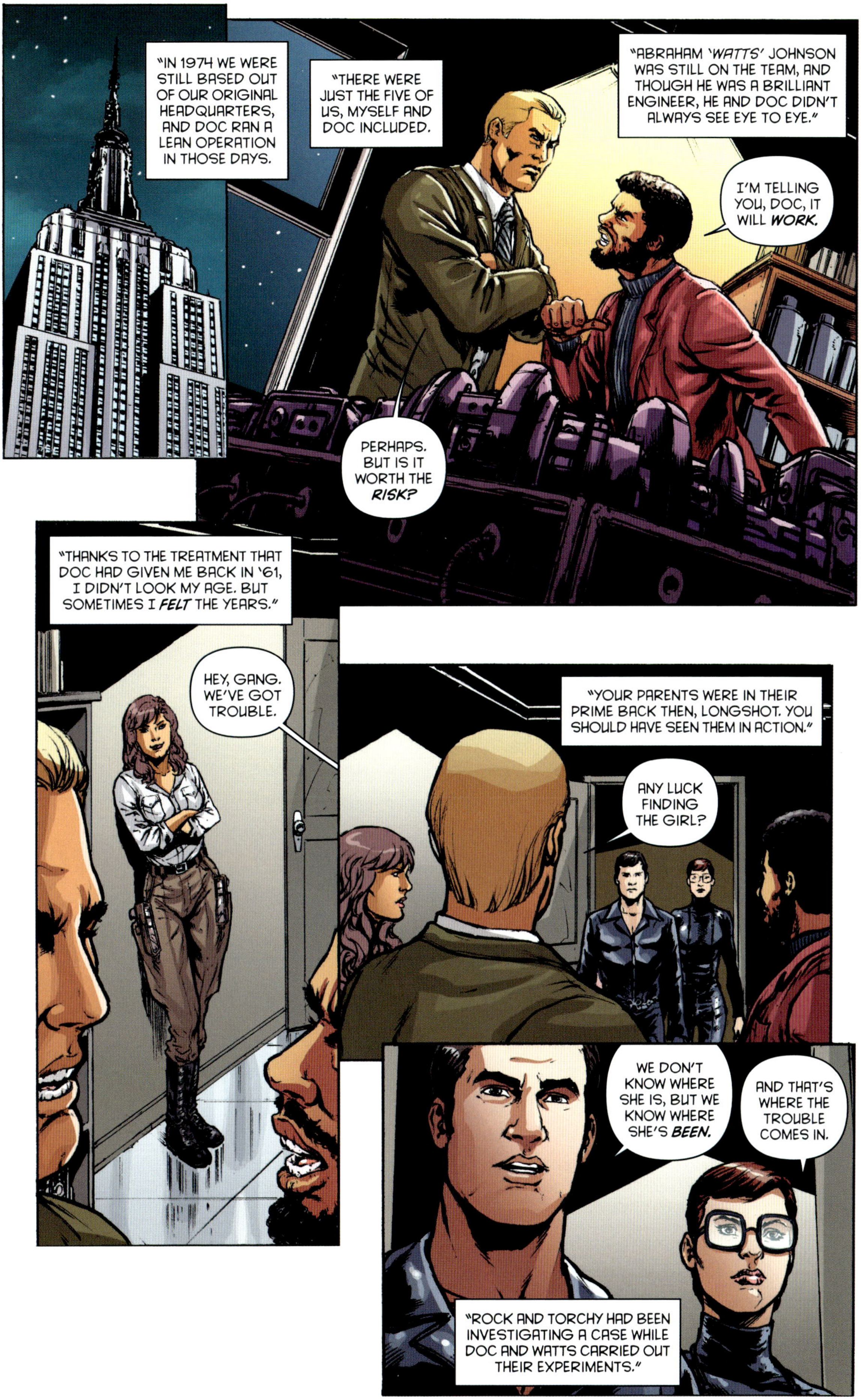
"IN 1974 WE WERE STILL BASED OUT OF OUR ORIGINAL HEADQUARTERS, AND DOC RAN A LEAN OPERATION IN THOSE DAYS.
"THERE WERE JUST THE FIVE OF US, MYSELF AND DOC INCLUDED.
"ABRAHAM '*WATTS*' JOHNSON WAS STILL ON THE TEAM, AND THOUGH HE WAS A BRILLIANT ENGINEER, HE AND DOC DIDN'T ALWAYS SEE EYE TO EYE."
I'M TELLING YOU, DOC, IT WILL *WORK.*
PERHAPS. BUT IS IT WORTH THE *RISK?*
"THANKS TO THE TREATMENT THAT DOC HAD GIVEN ME BACK IN '61, I DIDN'T LOOK MY AGE. BUT SOMETIMES I *FELT* THE YEARS."
HEY, GANG. WE'VE GOT TROUBLE.
"YOUR PARENTS WERE IN THEIR PRIME BACK THEN, LONGSHOT. YOU SHOULD HAVE SEEN THEM IN ACTION."
ANY LUCK FINDING THE GIRL?
WE DON'T KNOW WHERE SHE IS, BUT WE KNOW WHERE SHE'S *BEEN.*
AND THAT'S WHERE THE TROUBLE COMES IN.
"ROCK AND TORCHY HAD BEEN INVESTIGATING A CASE WHILE DOC AND WATTS CARRIED OUT THEIR EXPERIMENTS."

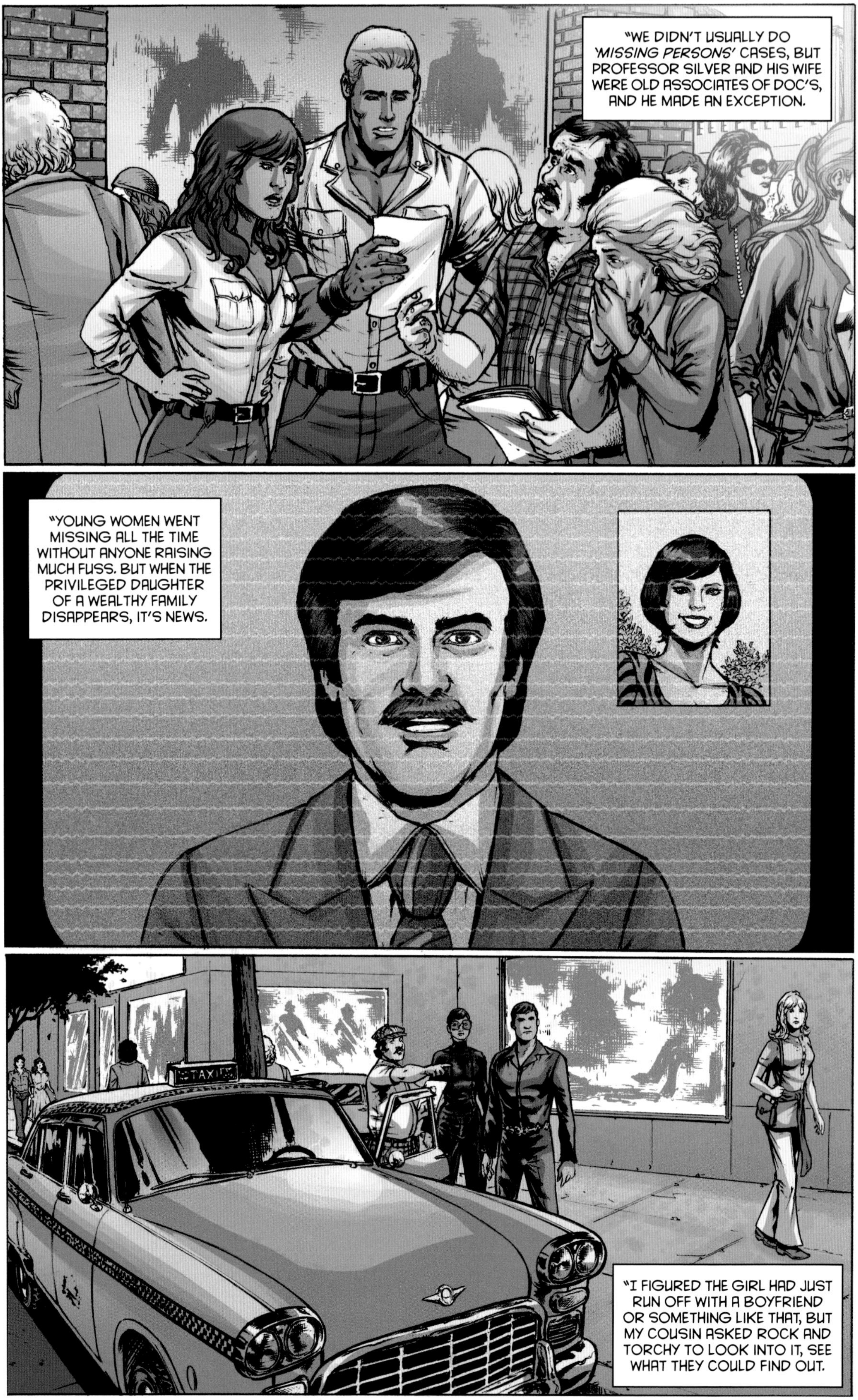

"WE DIDN'T USUALLY DO 'MISSING PERSONS' CASES, BUT PROFESSOR SILVER AND HIS WIFE WERE OLD ASSOCIATES OF DOC'S, AND HE MADE AN EXCEPTION.
"YOUNG WOMEN WENT MISSING ALL THE TIME WITHOUT ANYONE RAISING MUCH FUSS. BUT WHEN THE PRIVILEGED DAUGHTER OF A WEALTHY FAMILY DISAPPEARS, IT'S NEWS.
TAXI
"I FIGURED THE GIRL HAD JUST RUN OFF WITH A BOYFRIEND OR SOMETHING LIKE THAT, BUT MY COUSIN ASKED ROCK AND TORCHY TO LOOK INTO IT, SEE WHAT THEY COULD FIND OUT.

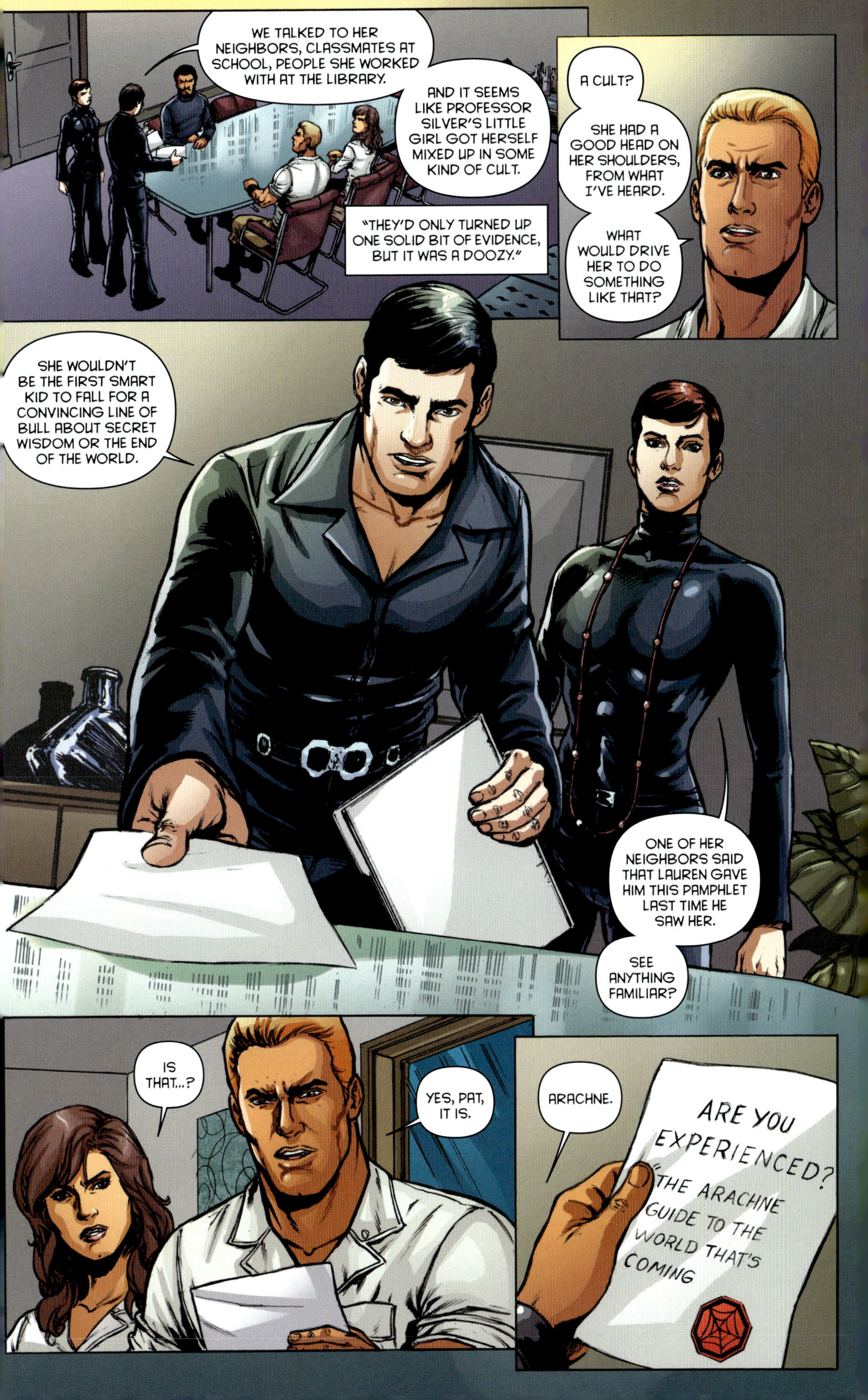
WE TALKED TO HER NEIGHBORS, CLASSMATES AT SCHOOL, PEOPLE SHE WORKED WITH AT THE LIBRARY.
AND IT SEEMS LIKE PROFESSOR SILVER'S LITTLE GIRL GOT HERSELF MIXED UP IN SOME KIND OF CULT.
"THEY'D ONLY TURNED UP ONE SOLID BIT OF EVIDENCE, BUT IT WAS A DOOZY."
A CULT?
SHE HAD A GOOD HEAD ON HER SHOULDERS, FROM WHAT I'VE HEARD.
WHAT WOULD DRIVE HER TO DO SOMETHING LIKE THAT?
SHE WOULDN'T BE THE FIRST SMART KID TO FALL FOR A CONVINCING LINE OF BULL ABOUT SECRET WISDOM OR THE END OF THE WORLD.
ONE OF HER NEIGHBORS SAID THAT LAUREN GAVE HIM THIS PAMPHLET LAST TIME HE SAW HER.
SEE ANYTHING FAMILIAR?
IS THAT...?
YES, PAT, IT IS.
ARACHNE.
ARE YOU EXPERIENCED?
"THE ARACHNE GUIDE TO THE WORLD THAT'S COMING

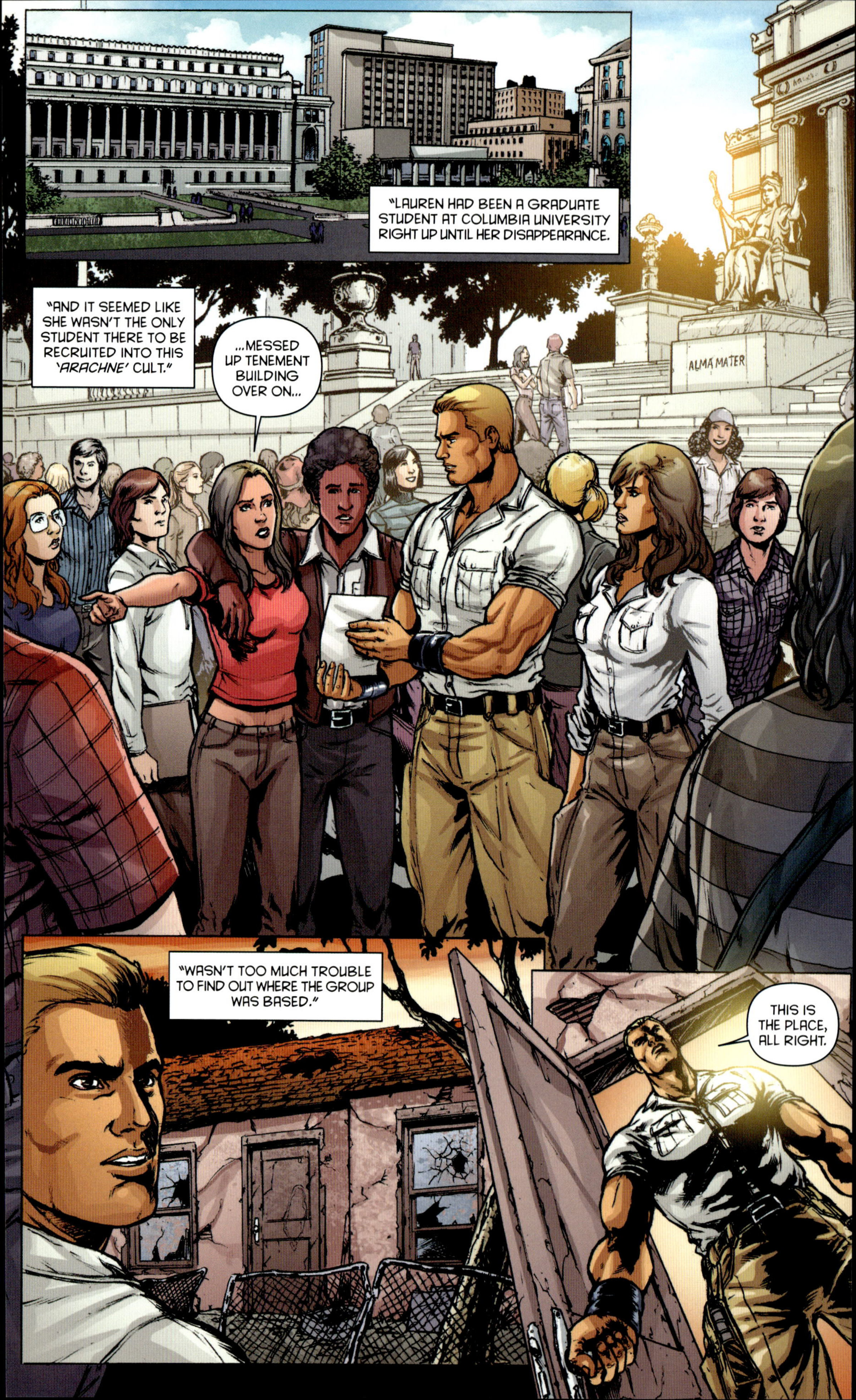
"LAUREN HAD BEEN A GRADUATE STUDENT AT COLUMBIA UNIVERSITY RIGHT UP UNTIL HER DISAPPEARANCE.
"AND IT SEEMED LIKE SHE WASN'T THE ONLY STUDENT THERE TO BE RECRUITED INTO THIS 'ARACHNE' CULT."
...MESSED UP TENEMENT BUILDING OVER ON...
ALMA MATER
"WASN'T TOO MUCH TROUBLE TO FIND OUT WHERE THE GROUP WAS BASED."
THIS IS THE PLACE, ALL RIGHT.

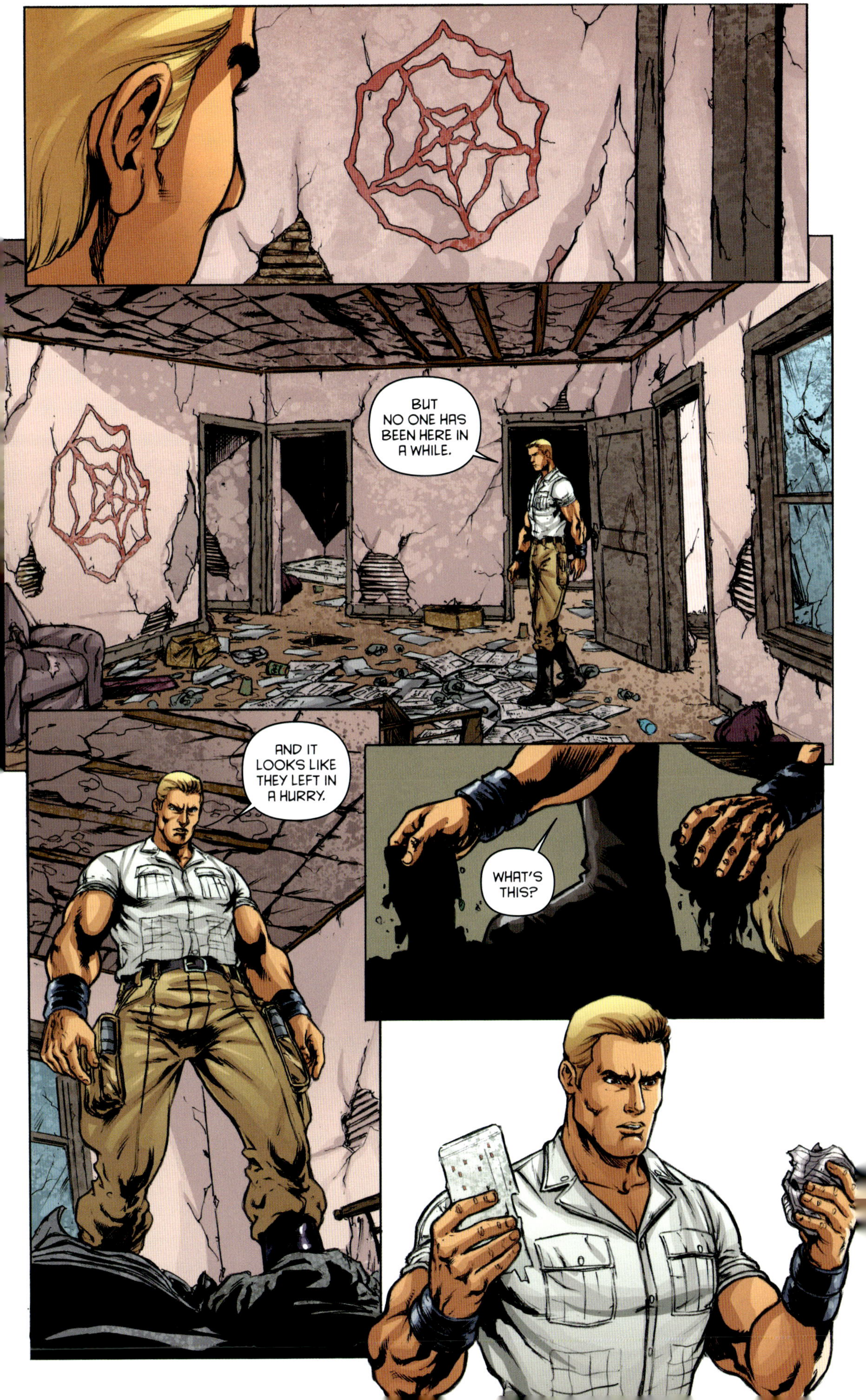
BUT NO ONE HAS BEEN HERE IN A WHILE.
AND IT LOOKS LIKE THEY LEFT IN A HURRY.
WHAT'S THIS?

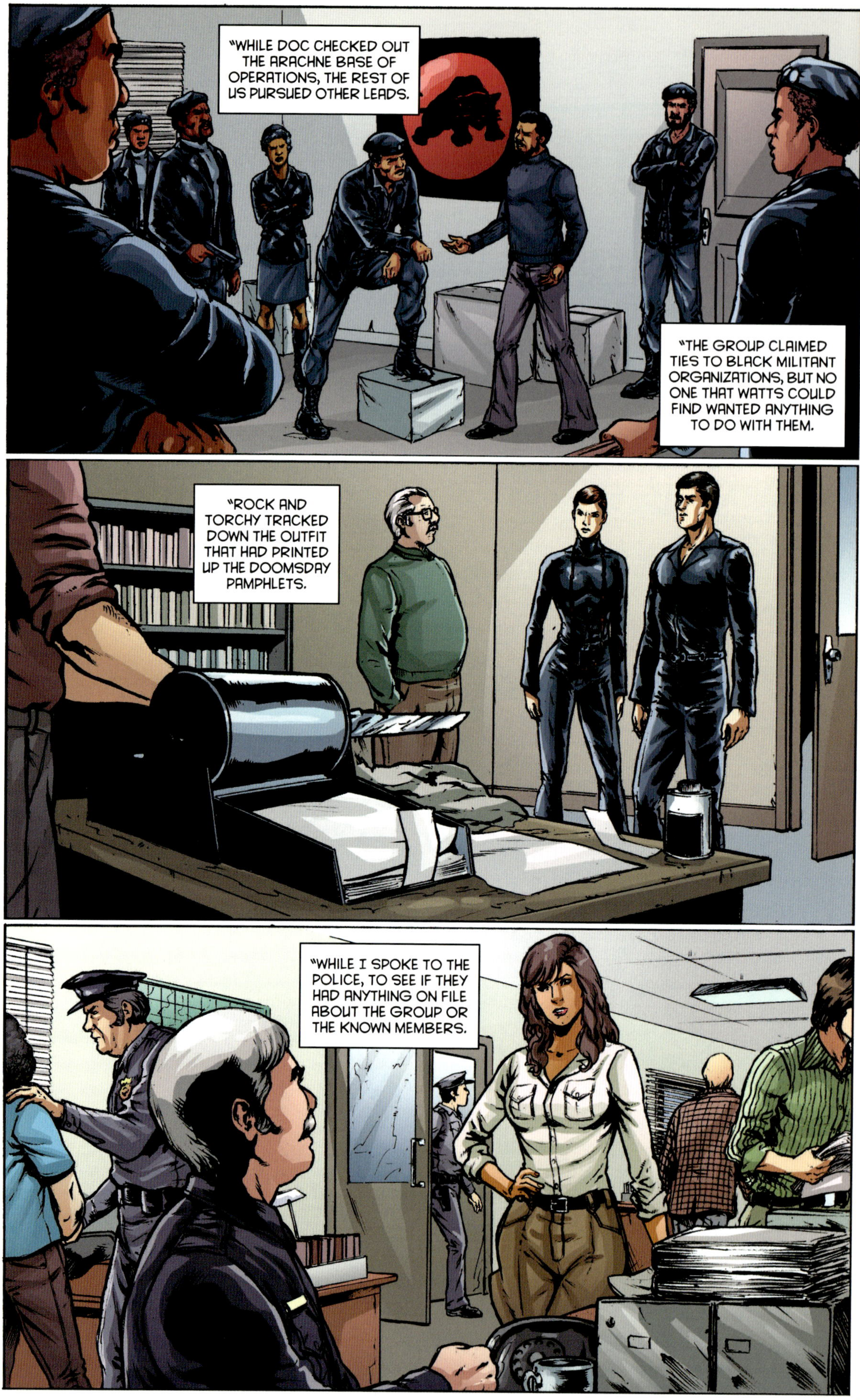
"WHILE DOC CHECKED OUT THE ARACHNE BASE OF OPERATIONS, THE REST OF US PURSUED OTHER LEADS.
"THE GROUP CLAIMED TIES TO BLACK MILITANT ORGANIZATIONS, BUT NO ONE THAT WATTS COULD FIND WANTED ANYTHING TO DO WITH THEM.
"ROCK AND TORCHY TRACKED DOWN THE OUTFIT THAT HAD PRINTED UP THE DOOMSDAY PAMPHLETS.
"WHILE I SPOKE TO THE POLICE, TO SEE IF THEY HAD ANYTHING ON FILE ABOUT THE GROUP OR THE KNOWN MEMBERS.

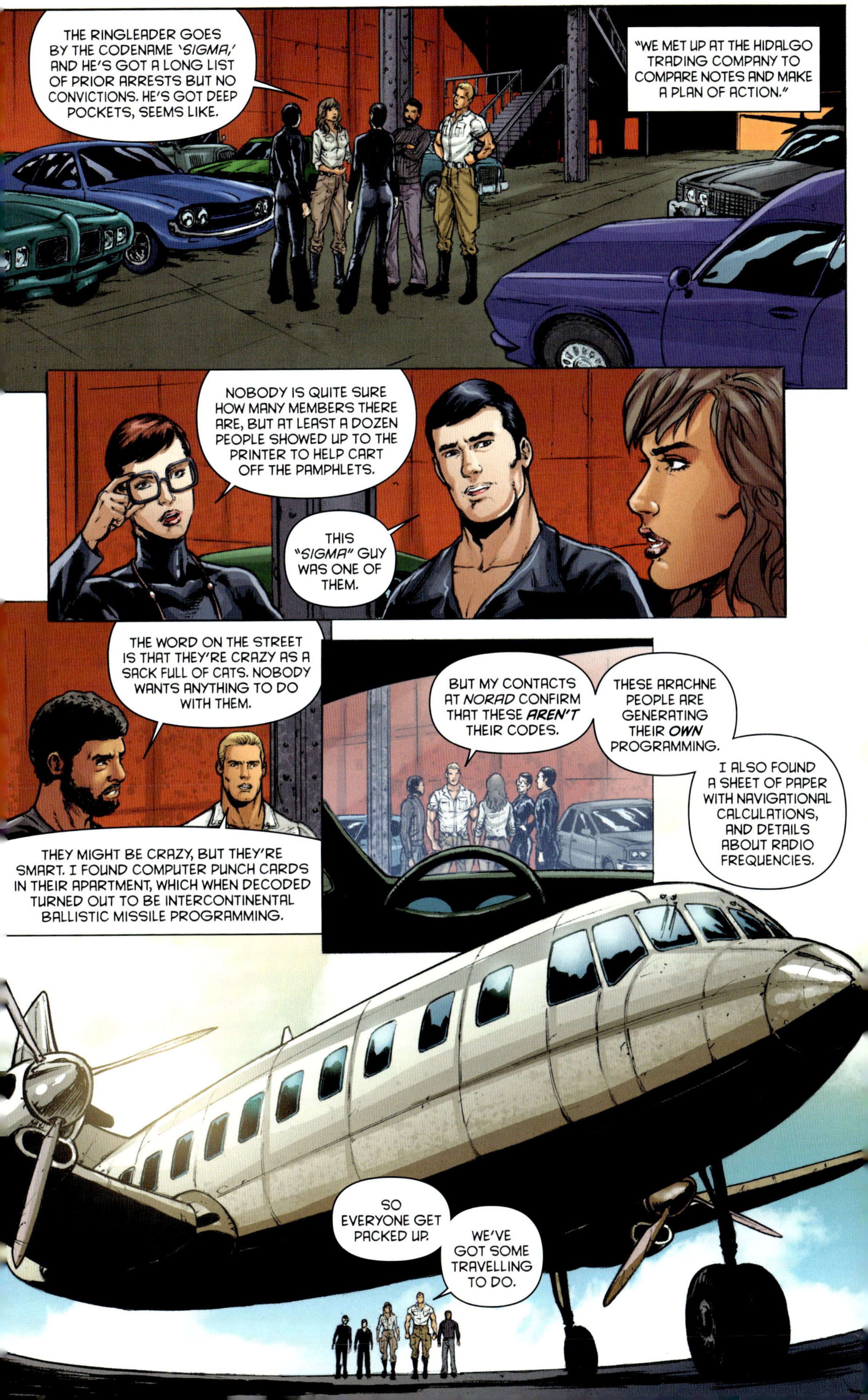
THE RINGLEADER GOES BY THE CODENAME 'SIGMA,' AND HE'S GOT A LONG LIST OF PRIOR ARRESTS BUT NO CONVICTIONS. HE'S GOT DEEP POCKETS, SEEMS LIKE.
"WE MET UP AT THE HIDALGO TRADING COMPANY TO COMPARE NOTES AND MAKE A PLAN OF ACTION."
NOBODY IS QUITE SURE HOW MANY MEMBERS THERE ARE, BUT AT LEAST A DOZEN PEOPLE SHOWED UP TO THE PRINTER TO HELP CART OFF THE PAMPHLETS.
THIS "SIGMA" GUY WAS ONE OF THEM.
THE WORD ON THE STREET IS THAT THEY'RE CRAZY AS A SACK FULL OF CATS. NOBODY WANTS ANYTHING TO DO WITH THEM.
THEY MIGHT BE CRAZY, BUT THEY'RE SMART. I FOUND COMPUTER PUNCH CARDS IN THEIR APARTMENT, WHICH WHEN DECODED TURNED OUT TO BE INTERCONTINENTAL BALLISTIC MISSILE PROGRAMMING.
BUT MY CONTACTS AT NORAD CONFIRM THAT THESE AREN'T THEIR CODES.
THESE ARACHNE PEOPLE ARE GENERATING THEIR OWN PROGRAMMING.
I ALSO FOUND A SHEET OF PAPER WITH NAVIGATIONAL CALCULATIONS, AND DETAILS ABOUT RADIO FREQUENCIES.
SO EVERYONE GET PACKED UP.
WE'VE GOT SOME TRAVELLING TO DO.

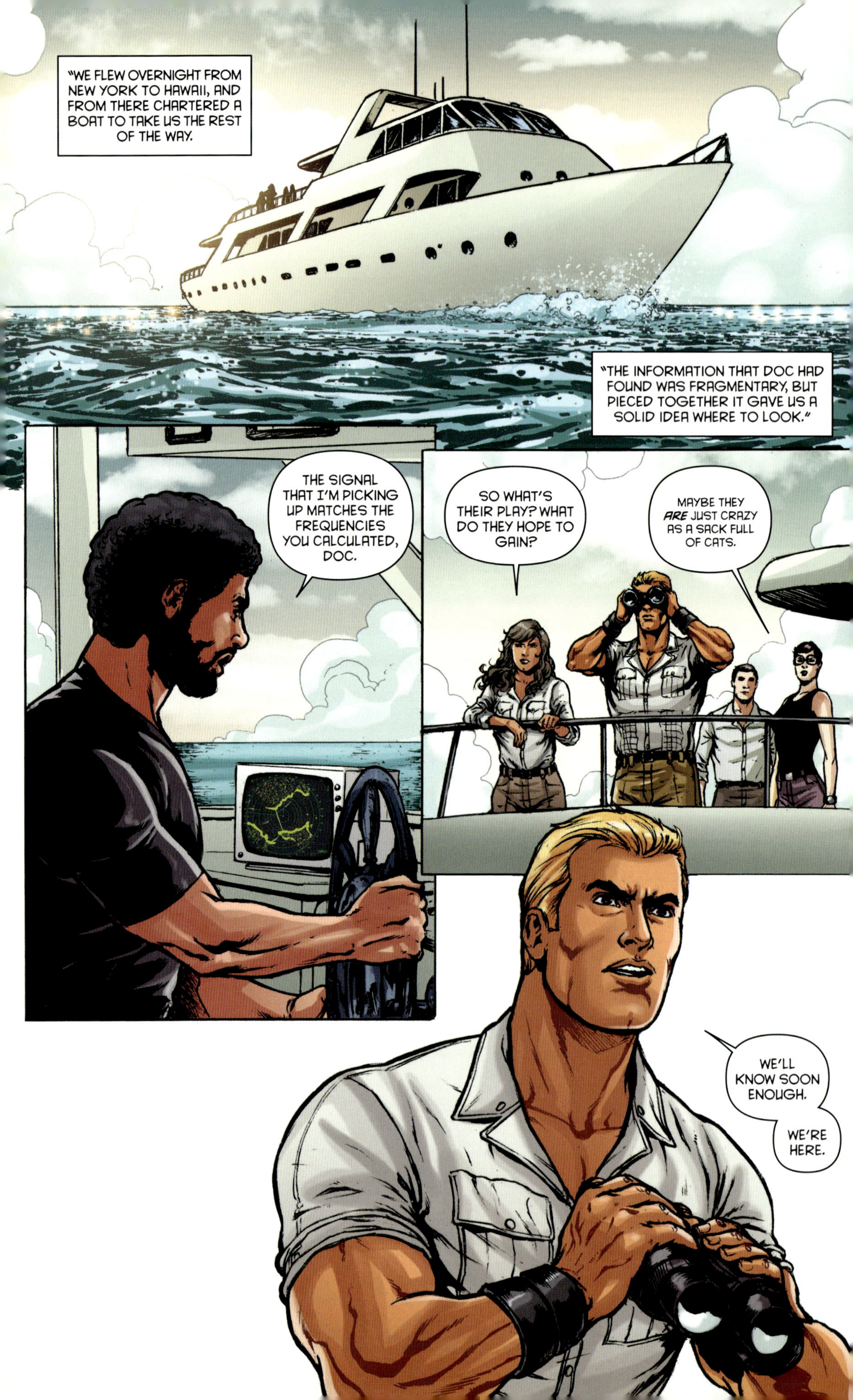
"WE FLEW OVERNIGHT FROM NEW YORK TO HAWAII, AND FROM THERE CHARTERED A BOAT TO TAKE US THE REST OF THE WAY.
"THE INFORMATION THAT DOC HAD FOUND WAS FRAGMENTARY, BUT PIECED TOGETHER IT GAVE US A SOLID IDEA WHERE TO LOOK."
THE SIGNAL THAT I'M PICKING UP MATCHES THE FREQUENCIES YOU CALCULATED, DOC.
SO WHAT'S THEIR PLAY? WHAT DO THEY HOPE TO GAIN?
MAYBE THEY ARE JUST CRAZY AS A SACK FULL OF CATS.
WE'LL KNOW SOON ENOUGH.
WE'RE HERE.

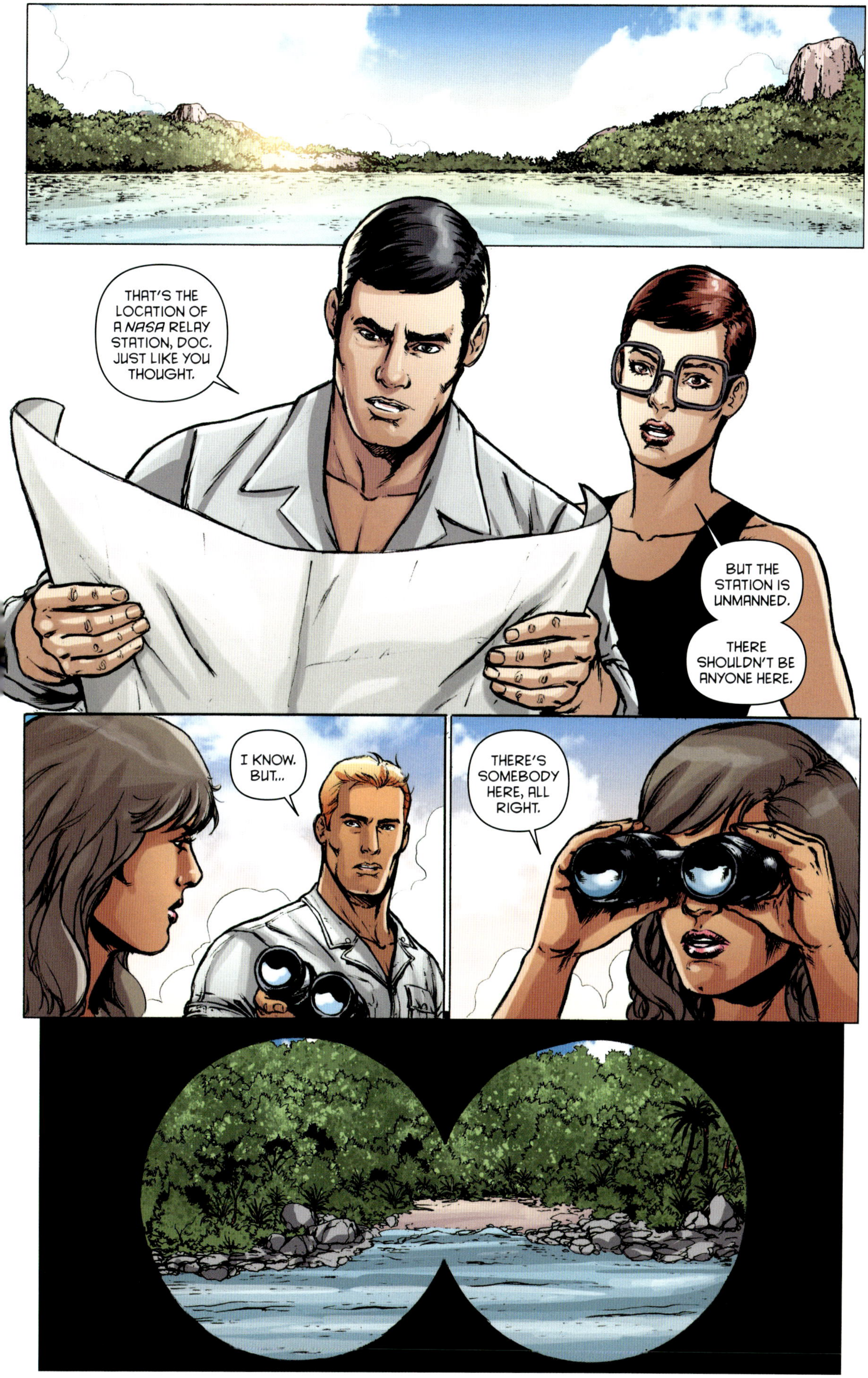
THAT'S THE LOCATION OF A *NASA* RELAY STATION, DOC. JUST LIKE YOU THOUGHT.
BUT THE STATION IS UNMANNED.
THERE SHOULDN'T BE ANYONE HERE.
I KNOW. BUT...
THERE'S SOMEBODY HERE, ALL RIGHT.

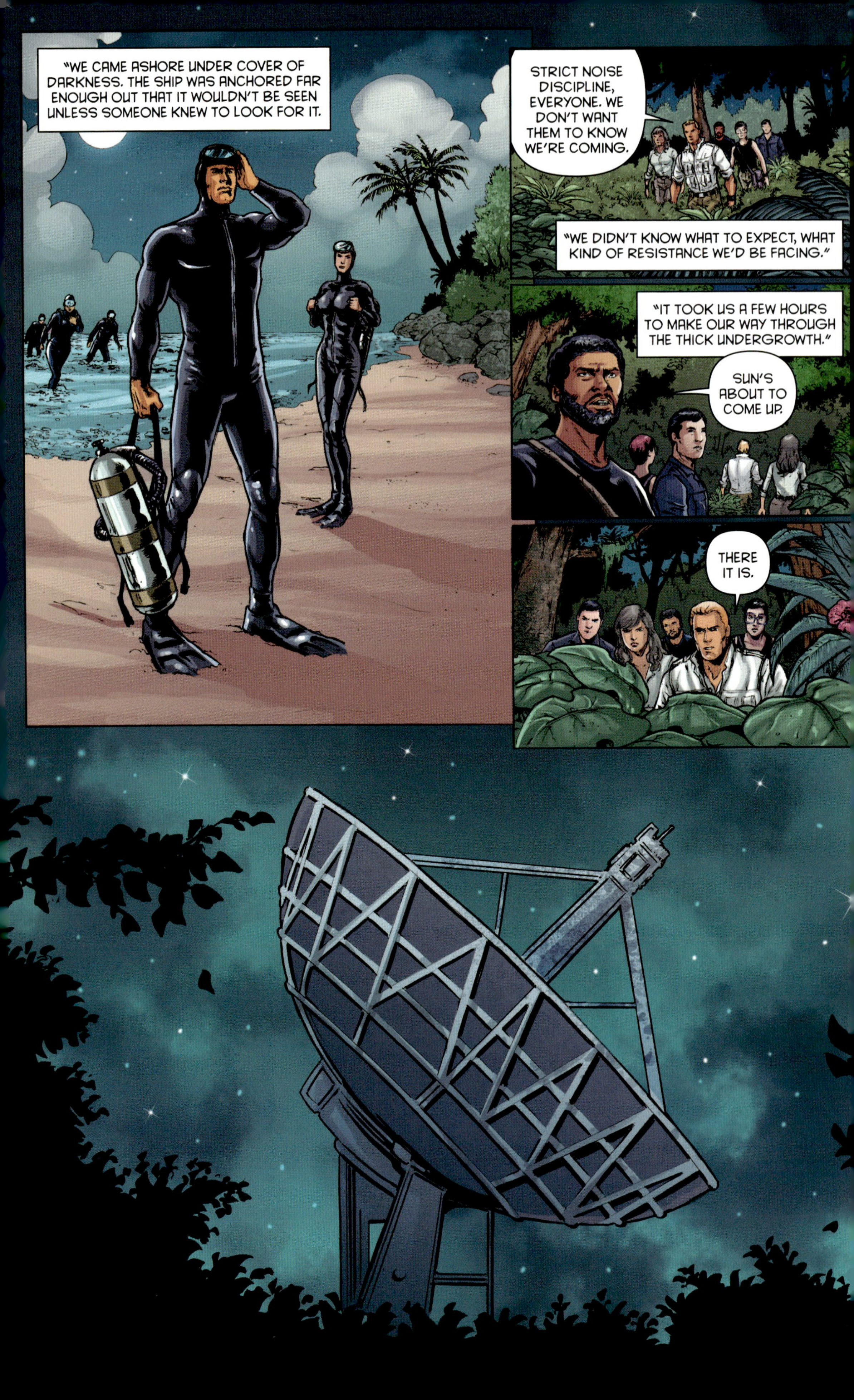
"WE CAME ASHORE UNDER COVER OF DARKNESS. THE SHIP WAS ANCHORED FAR ENOUGH OUT THAT IT WOULDN'T BE SEEN UNLESS SOMEONE KNEW TO LOOK FOR IT.
STRICT NOISE DISCIPLINE, EVERYONE. WE DON'T WANT THEM TO KNOW WE'RE COMING.
"WE DIDN'T KNOW WHAT TO EXPECT, WHAT KIND OF RESISTANCE WE'D BE FACING."
"IT TOOK US A FEW HOURS TO MAKE OUR WAY THROUGH THE THICK UNDERGROWTH."
SUN'S ABOUT TO COME UP.
THERE IT IS.

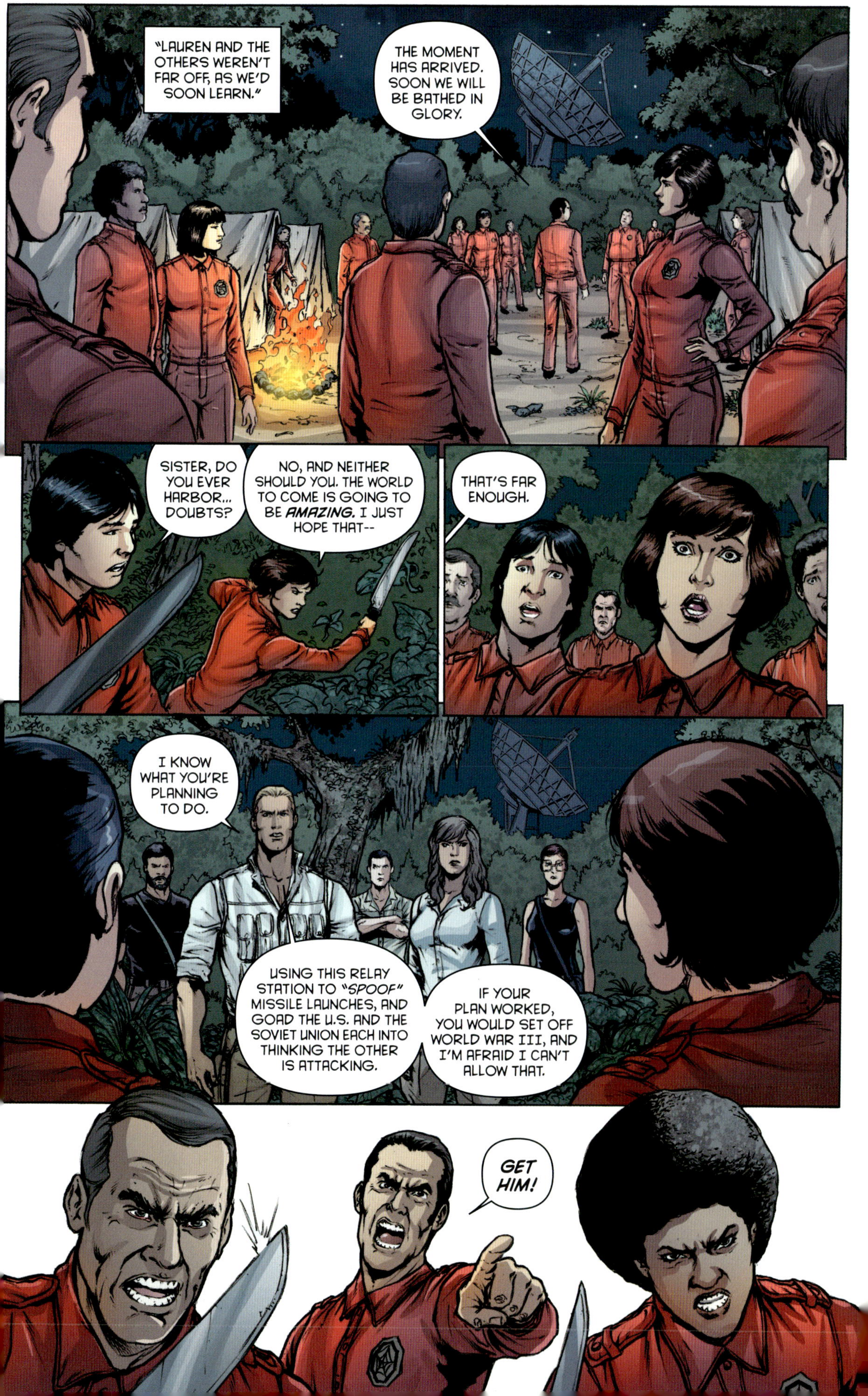
"LAUREN AND THE OTHERS WEREN'T FAR OFF, AS WE'D SOON LEARN."
THE MOMENT HAS ARRIVED. SOON WE WILL BE BATHED IN GLORY.
SISTER, DO YOU EVER HARBOR... DOUBTS?
NO, AND NEITHER SHOULD YOU. THE WORLD TO COME IS GOING TO BE *AMAZING.* I JUST HOPE THAT--
THAT'S FAR ENOUGH.
I KNOW WHAT YOU'RE PLANNING TO DO.
USING THIS RELAY STATION TO *"SPOOF"* MISSILE LAUNCHES, AND GOAD THE U.S. AND THE SOVIET UNION EACH INTO THINKING THE OTHER IS ATTACKING.
IF YOUR PLAN WORKED, YOU WOULD SET OFF WORLD WAR III, AND I'M AFRAID I CAN'T ALLOW THAT.
GET HIM!

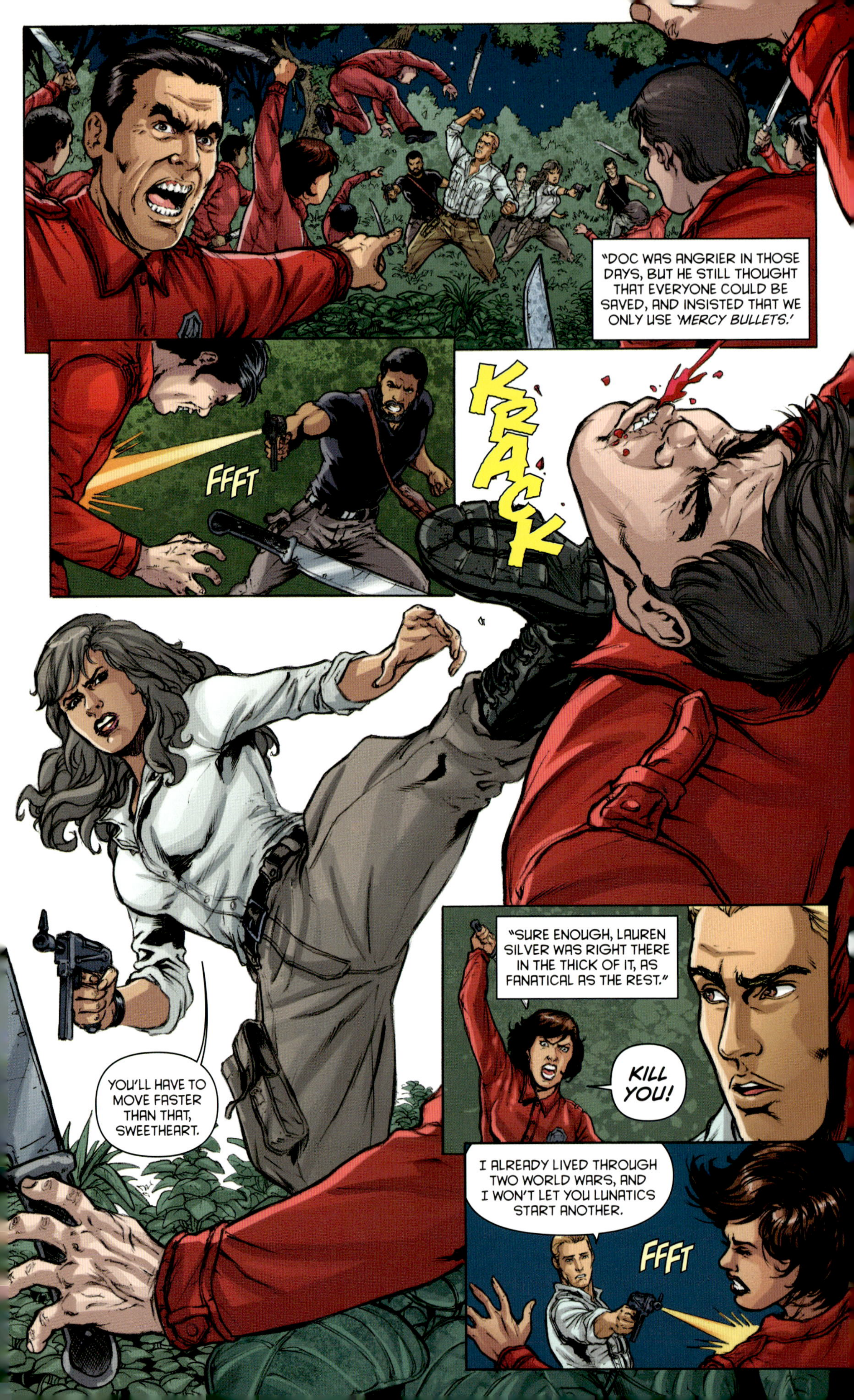
"DOC WAS ANGRIER IN THOSE DAYS, BUT HE STILL THOUGHT THAT EVERYONE COULD BE SAVED, AND INSISTED THAT WE ONLY USE *'MERCY BULLETS.'*
FFFT
KRACK
YOU'LL HAVE TO MOVE FASTER THAN THAT, SWEETHEART.
"SURE ENOUGH, LAUREN SILVER WAS RIGHT THERE IN THE THICK OF IT, AS FANATICAL AS THE REST."
KILL YOU!
I ALREADY LIVED THROUGH TWO WORLD WARS, AND I WON'T LET YOU LUNATICS START ANOTHER.
FFFT

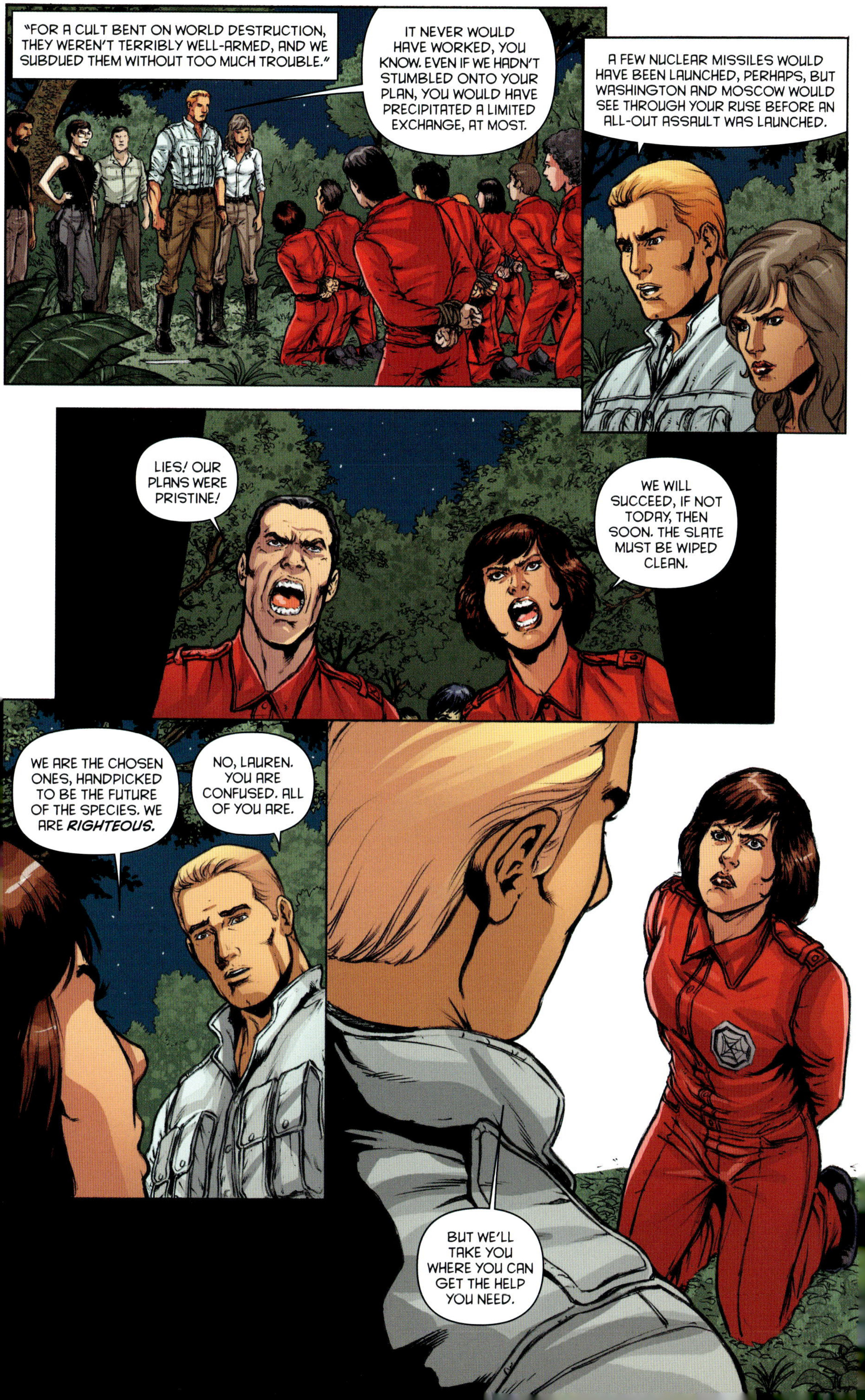
"FOR A CULT BENT ON WORLD DESTRUCTION, THEY WEREN'T TERRIBLY WELL-ARMED, AND WE SUBDUED THEM WITHOUT TOO MUCH TROUBLE."
IT NEVER WOULD HAVE WORKED, YOU KNOW. EVEN IF WE HADN'T STUMBLED ONTO YOUR PLAN, YOU WOULD HAVE PRECIPITATED A LIMITED EXCHANGE, AT MOST.
A FEW NUCLEAR MISSILES WOULD HAVE BEEN LAUNCHED, PERHAPS, BUT WASHINGTON AND MOSCOW WOULD SEE THROUGH YOUR RUSE BEFORE AN ALL-OUT ASSAULT WAS LAUNCHED.
LIES! OUR PLANS WERE PRISTINE!
WE WILL SUCCEED, IF NOT TODAY, THEN SOON. THE SLATE MUST BE WIPED CLEAN.
WE ARE THE CHOSEN ONES, HANDPICKED TO BE THE FUTURE OF THE SPECIES. WE ARE ***RIGHTEOUS.***
NO, LAUREN. YOU ARE CONFUSED. ALL OF YOU ARE.
BUT WE'LL TAKE YOU WHERE YOU CAN GET THE HELP YOU NEED.

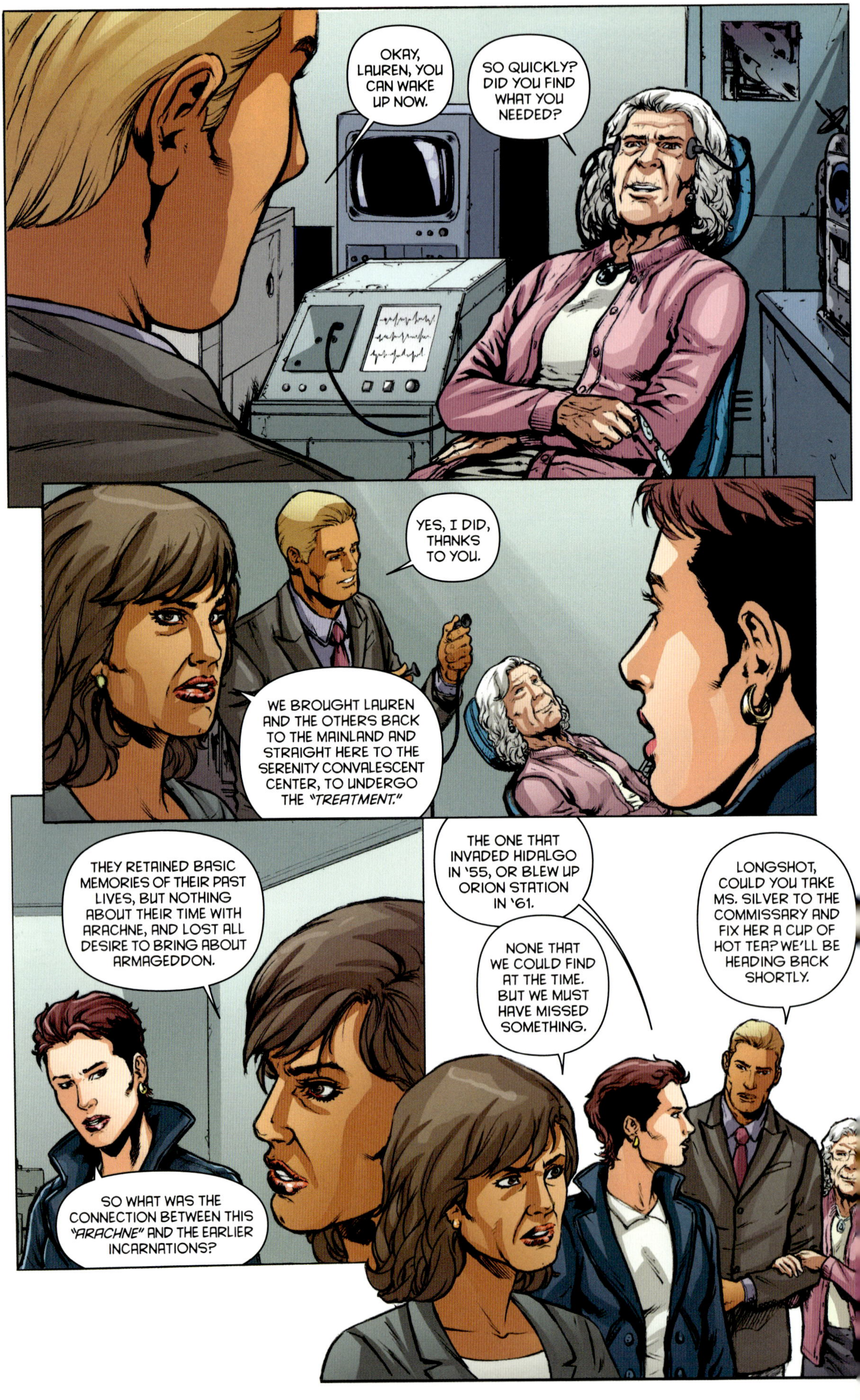
OKAY, LAUREN, YOU CAN WAKE UP NOW.
SO QUICKLY? DID YOU FIND WHAT YOU NEEDED?
YES, I DID, THANKS TO YOU.
WE BROUGHT LAUREN AND THE OTHERS BACK TO THE MAINLAND AND STRAIGHT HERE TO THE SERENITY CONVALESCENT CENTER, TO UNDERGO THE "TREATMENT."
THEY RETAINED BASIC MEMORIES OF THEIR PAST LIVES, BUT NOTHING ABOUT THEIR TIME WITH ARACHNE, AND LOST ALL DESIRE TO BRING ABOUT ARMAGEDDON.
SO WHAT WAS THE CONNECTION BETWEEN THIS "ARACHNE" AND THE EARLIER INCARNATIONS?
THE ONE THAT INVADED HIDALGO IN '55, OR BLEW UP ORION STATION IN '61.
NONE THAT WE COULD FIND AT THE TIME. BUT WE MUST HAVE MISSED SOMETHING.
LONGSHOT, COULD YOU TAKE MS. SILVER TO THE COMMISSARY AND FIX HER A CUP OF HOT TEA? WE'LL BE HEADING BACK SHORTLY.

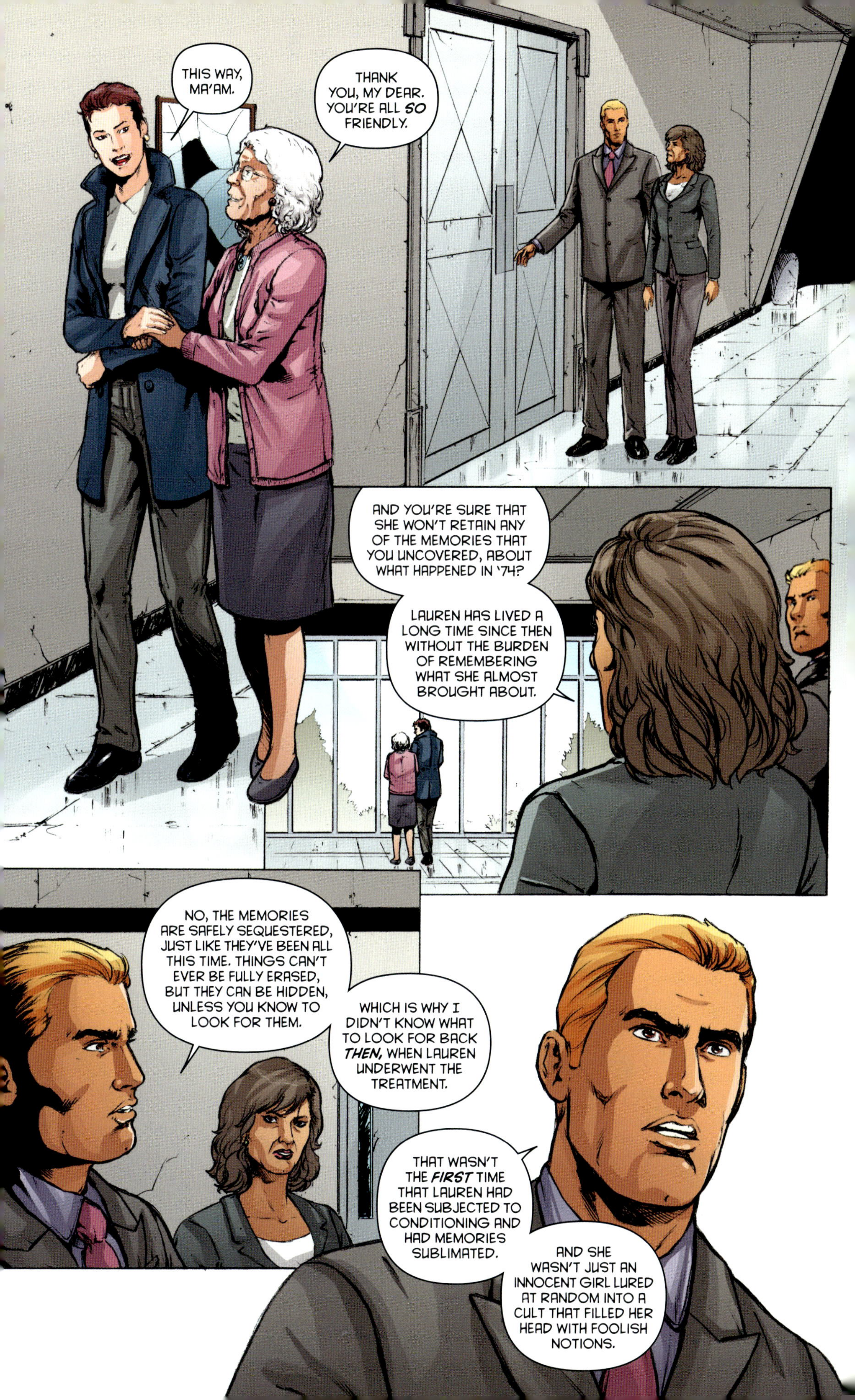
THIS WAY, MA'AM.
THANK YOU, MY DEAR. YOU'RE ALL *SO* FRIENDLY.
AND YOU'RE SURE THAT SHE WON'T RETAIN ANY OF THE MEMORIES THAT YOU UNCOVERED, ABOUT WHAT HAPPENED IN '74?
LAUREN HAS LIVED A LONG TIME SINCE THEN WITHOUT THE BURDEN OF REMEMBERING WHAT SHE ALMOST BROUGHT ABOUT.
NO, THE MEMORIES ARE SAFELY SEQUESTERED, JUST LIKE THEY'VE BEEN ALL THIS TIME. THINGS CAN'T EVER BE FULLY ERASED, BUT THEY CAN BE HIDDEN, UNLESS YOU KNOW TO LOOK FOR THEM.
WHICH IS WHY I DIDN'T KNOW WHAT TO LOOK FOR BACK *THEN,* WHEN LAUREN UNDERWENT THE TREATMENT.
THAT WASN'T THE *FIRST* TIME THAT LAUREN HAD BEEN SUBJECTED TO CONDITIONING AND HAD MEMORIES SUBLIMATED.
AND SHE WASN'T JUST AN INNOCENT GIRL LURED AT RANDOM INTO A CULT THAT FILLED HER HEAD WITH FOOLISH NOTIONS.

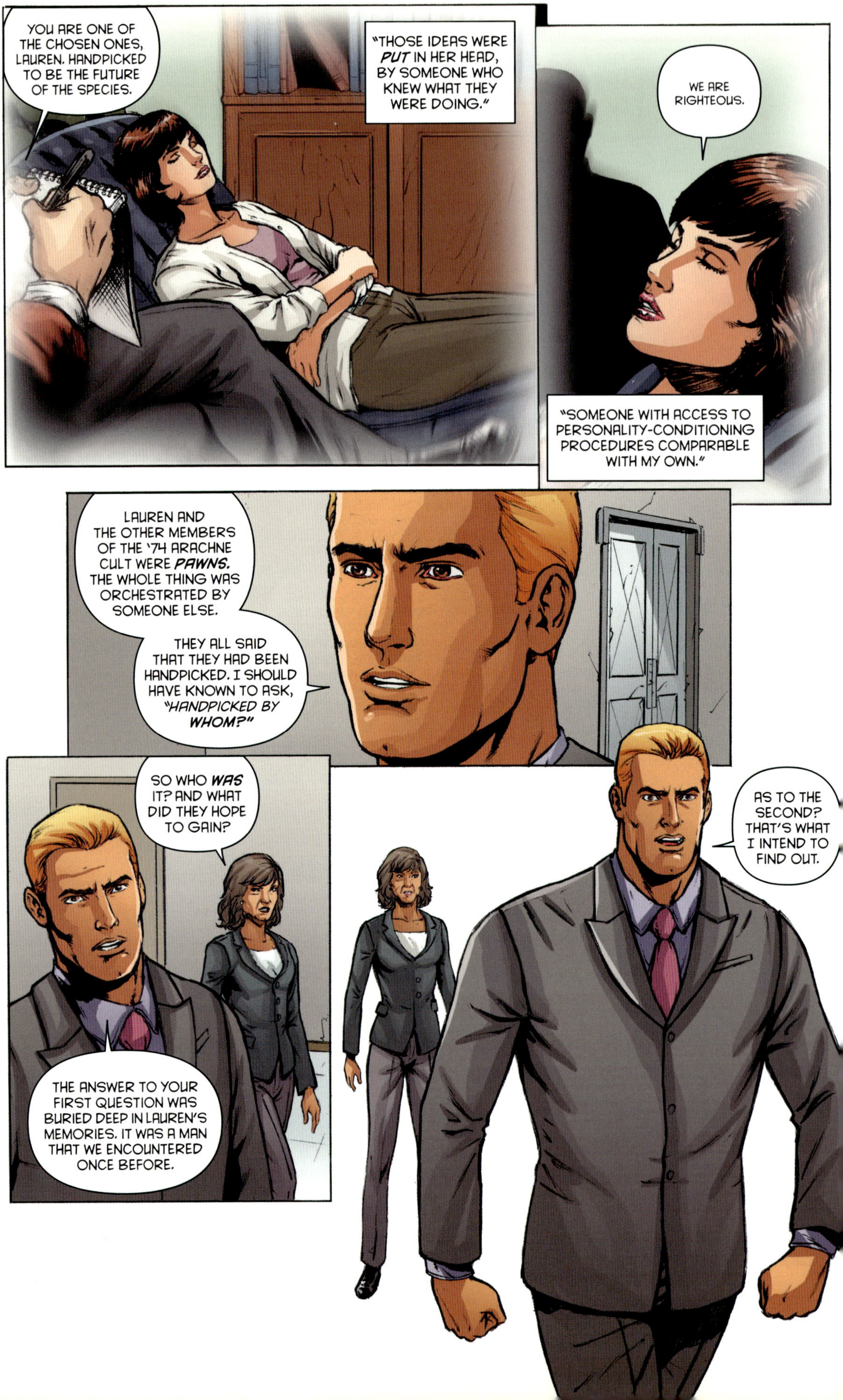

YOU ARE ONE OF THE CHOSEN ONES, LAUREN. HANDPICKED TO BE THE FUTURE OF THE SPECIES.
"THOSE IDEAS WERE *PUT* IN HER HEAD, BY SOMEONE WHO KNEW WHAT THEY WERE DOING."
WE ARE RIGHTEOUS.
"SOMEONE WITH ACCESS TO PERSONALITY-CONDITIONING PROCEDURES COMPARABLE WITH MY OWN."
LAUREN AND THE OTHER MEMBERS OF THE '74 ARACHNE CULT WERE ***PAWNS.*** THE WHOLE THING WAS ORCHESTRATED BY SOMEONE ELSE.
THEY ALL SAID THAT THEY HAD BEEN HANDPICKED. I SHOULD HAVE KNOWN TO ASK, *"HANDPICKED BY **WHOM?**"*
SO WHO ***WAS*** IT? AND WHAT DID THEY HOPE TO GAIN?
THE ANSWER TO YOUR FIRST QUESTION WAS BURIED DEEP IN LAUREN'S MEMORIES. IT WAS A MAN THAT WE ENCOUNTERED ONCE BEFORE.
AS TO THE SECOND? THAT'S WHAT I INTEND TO FIND OUT.

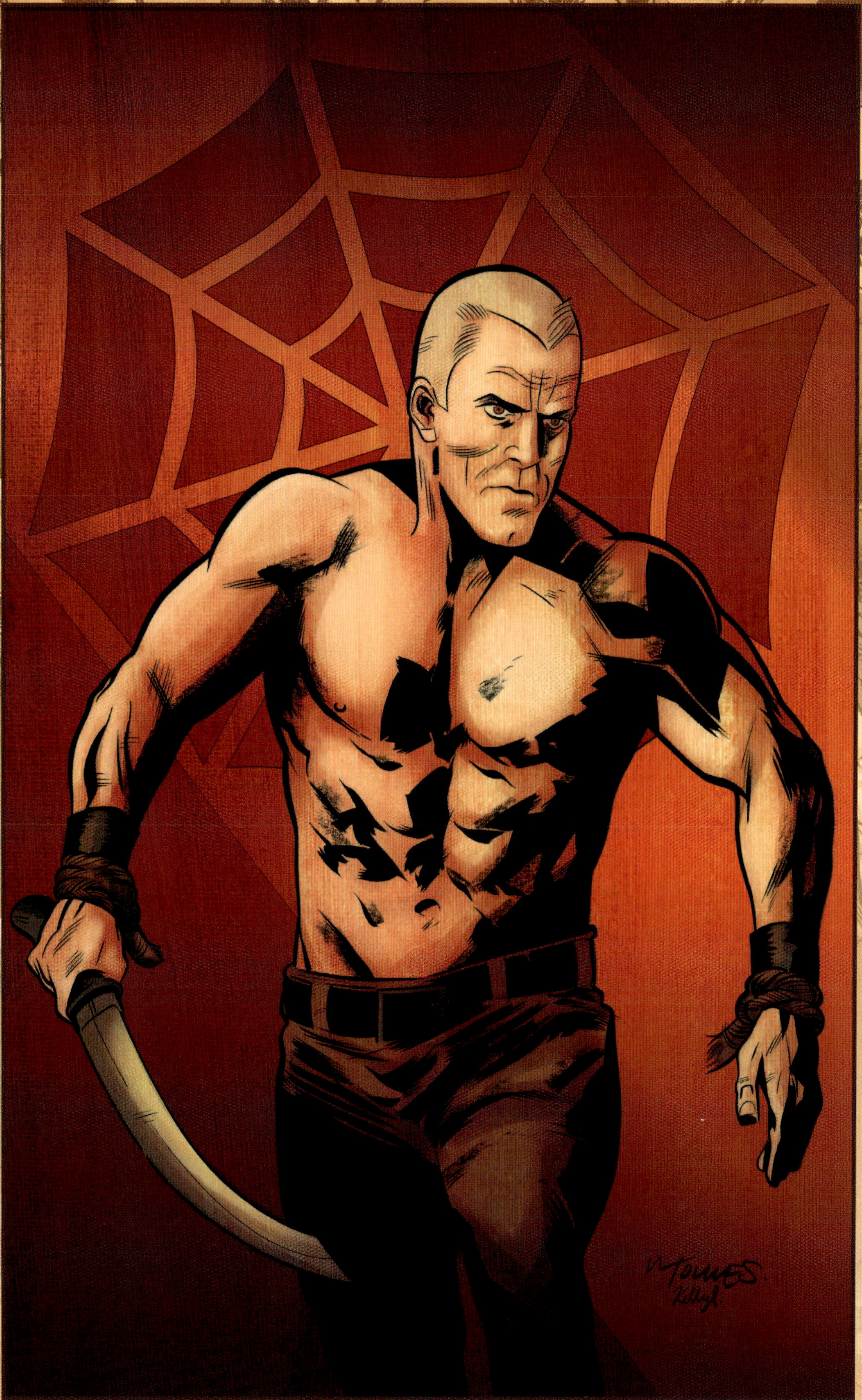

ISSUE #4 COVER
art by **WILFREDO TORRES** colors by **KELLY FITZPATRICK**

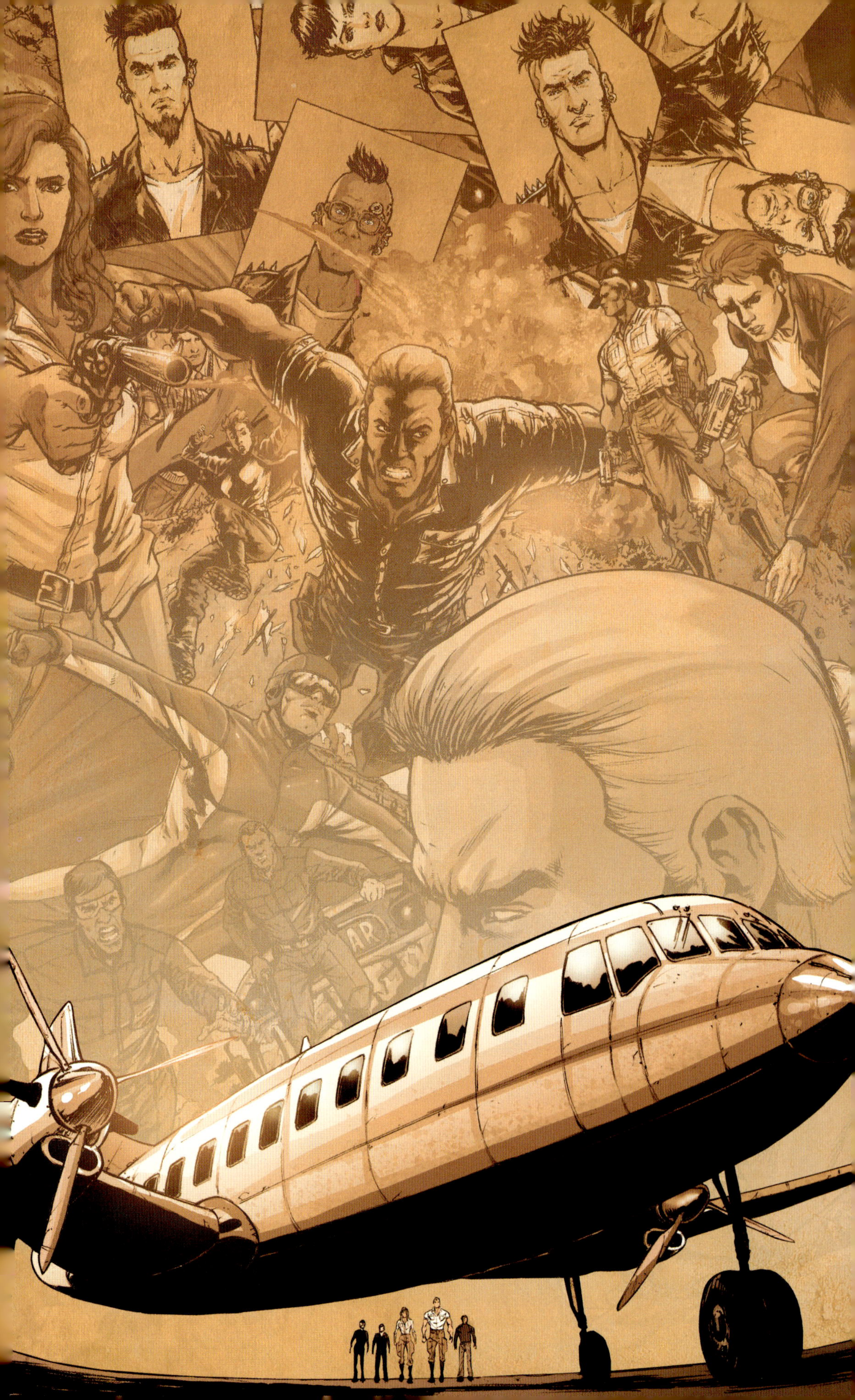

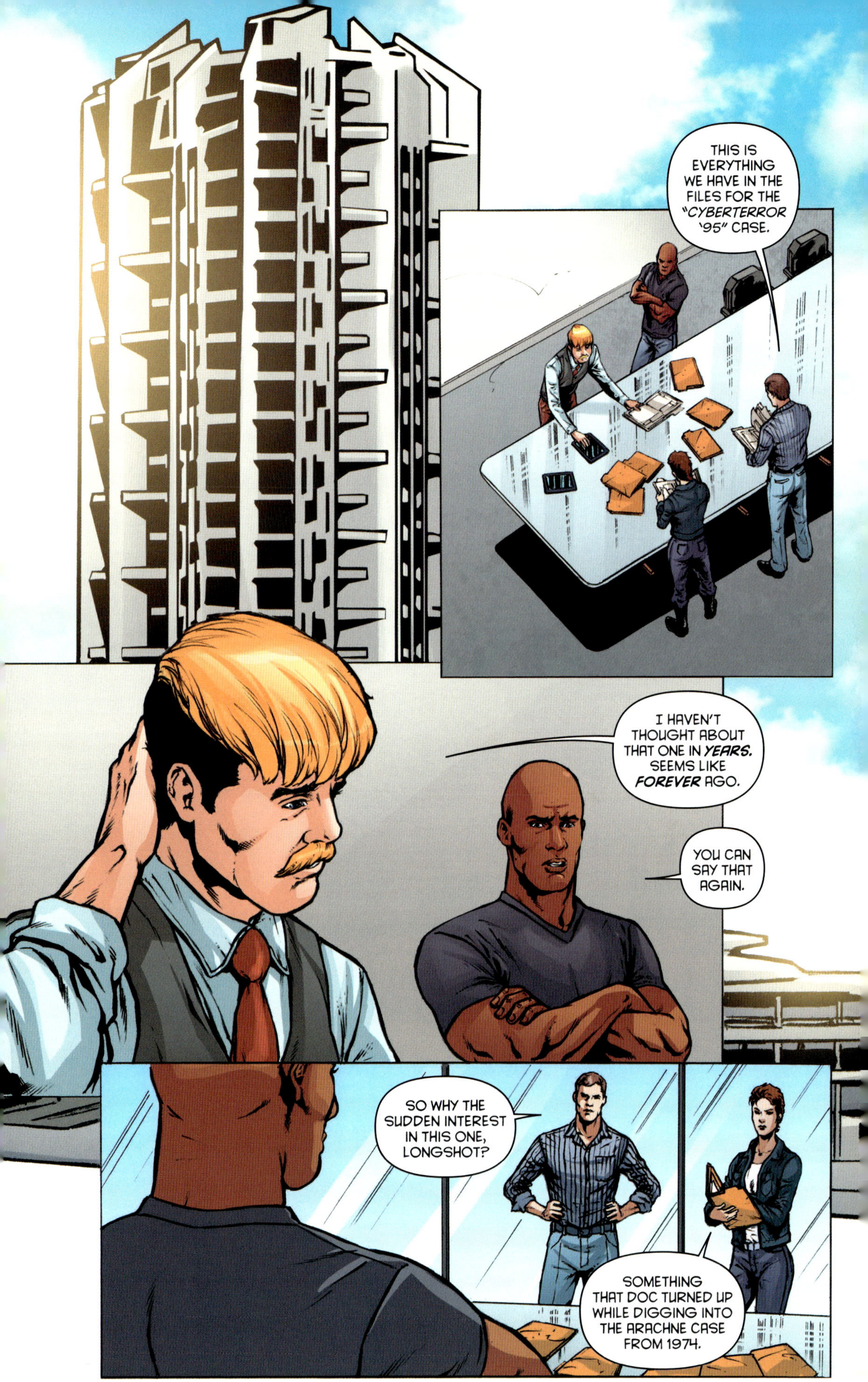
THIS IS EVERYTHING WE HAVE IN THE FILES FOR THE "CYBERTERROR '95" CASE.
I HAVEN'T THOUGHT ABOUT THAT ONE IN YEARS. SEEMS LIKE FOREVER AGO.
YOU CAN SAY THAT AGAIN.
SO WHY THE SUDDEN INTEREST IN THIS ONE, LONGSHOT?
SOMETHING THAT DOC TURNED UP WHILE DIGGING INTO THE ARACHNE CASE FROM 1974.

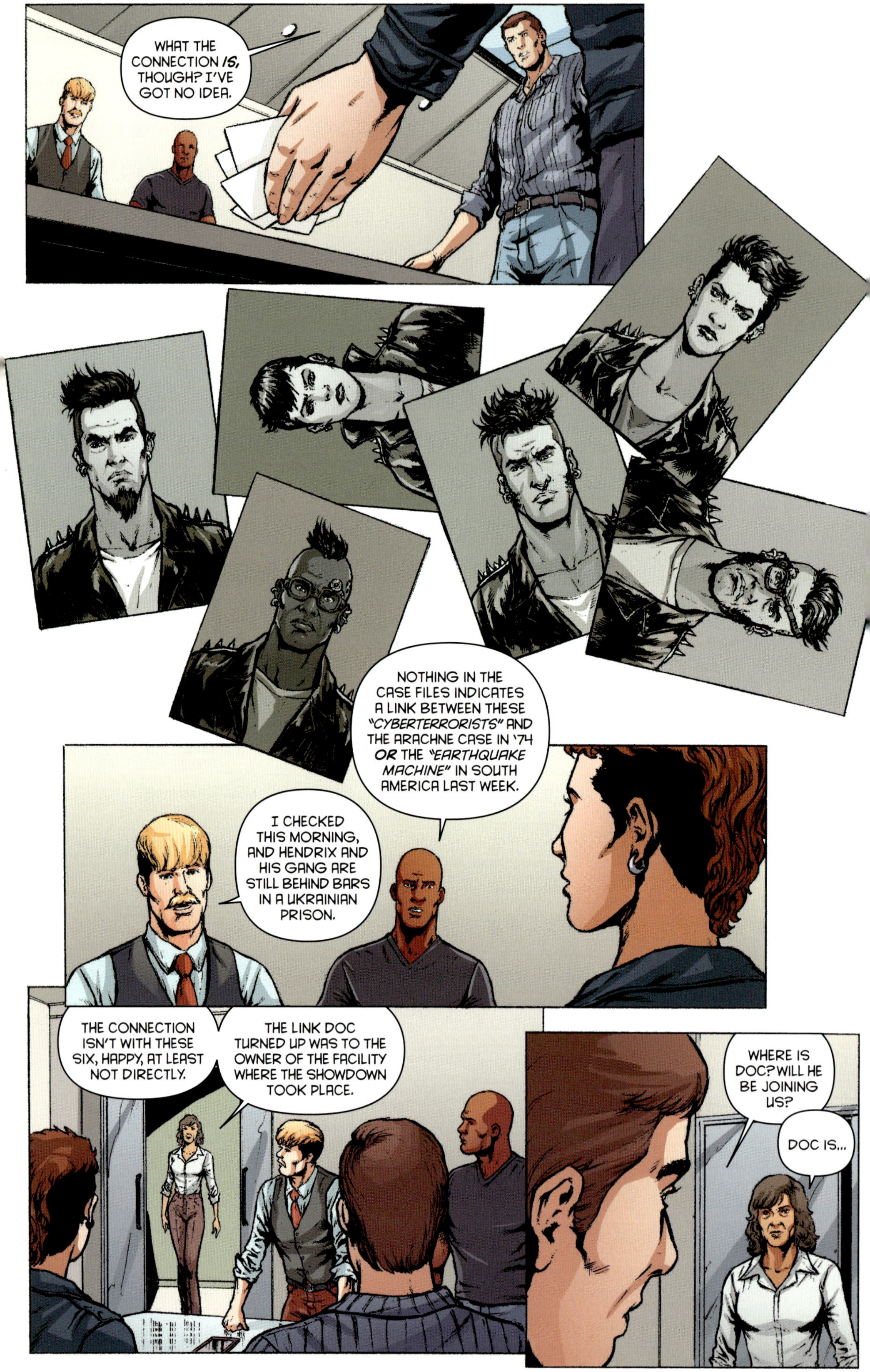
WHAT THE CONNECTION *IS,* THOUGH? I'VE GOT NO IDEA.
NOTHING IN THE CASE FILES INDICATES A LINK BETWEEN THESE *"CYBERTERRORISTS"* AND THE ARACHNE CASE IN '74 ***OR*** THE *"EARTHQUAKE MACHINE"* IN SOUTH AMERICA LAST WEEK.
I CHECKED THIS MORNING, AND HENDRIX AND HIS GANG ARE STILL BEHIND BARS IN A UKRAINIAN PRISON.
THE CONNECTION ISN'T WITH THESE SIX, HAPPY, AT LEAST NOT DIRECTLY.
THE LINK DOC TURNED UP WAS TO THE OWNER OF THE FACILITY WHERE THE SHOWDOWN TOOK PLACE.
WHERE IS DOC? WILL HE BE JOINING US?
DOC IS...

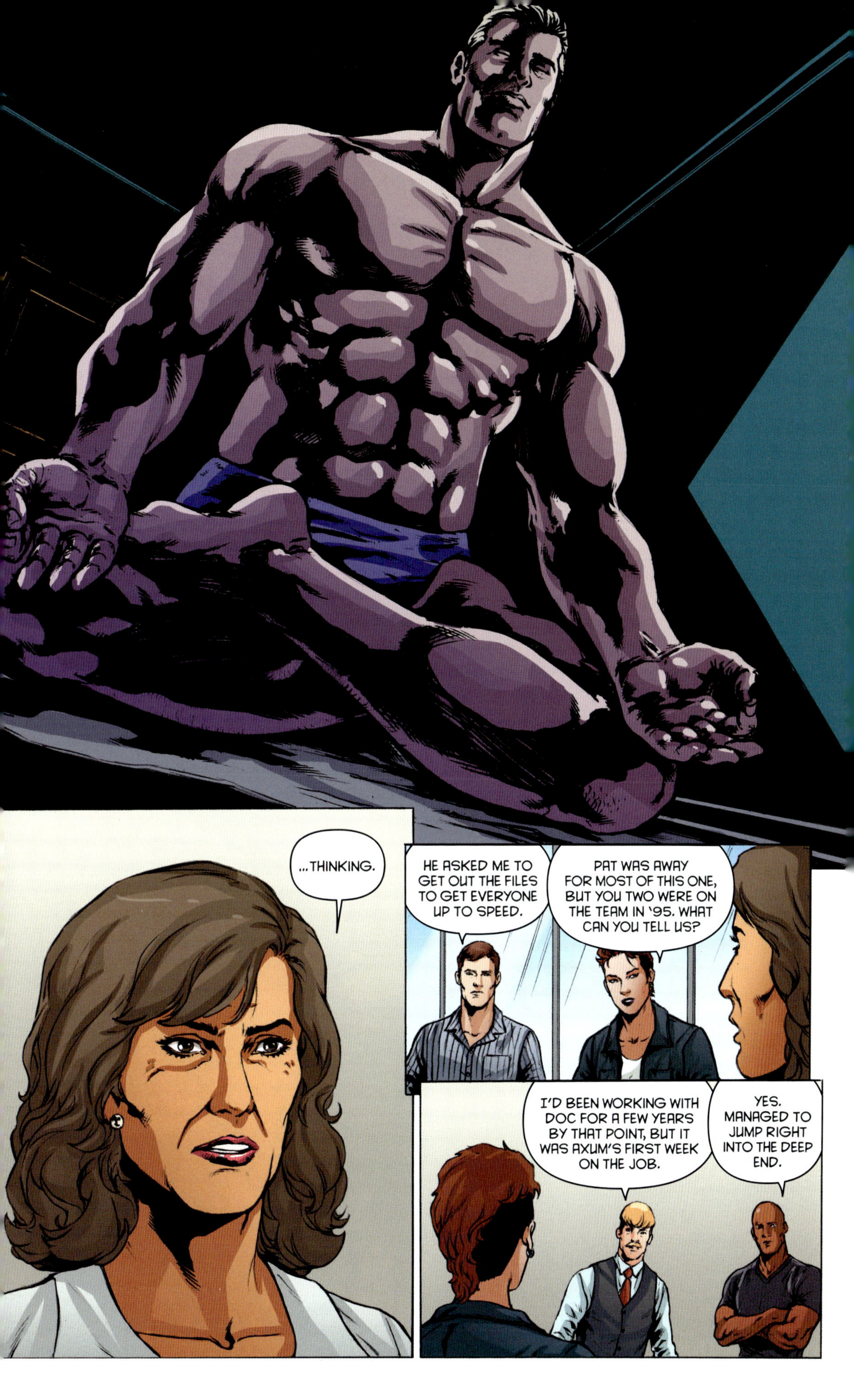
...THINKING.
HE ASKED ME TO GET OUT THE FILES TO GET EVERYONE UP TO SPEED.
PAT WAS AWAY FOR MOST OF THIS ONE, BUT YOU TWO WERE ON THE TEAM IN '95. WHAT CAN YOU TELL US?
I'D BEEN WORKING WITH DOC FOR A FEW YEARS BY THAT POINT, BUT IT WAS AXUM'S FIRST WEEK ON THE JOB.
YES. MANAGED TO JUMP RIGHT INTO THE DEEP END.

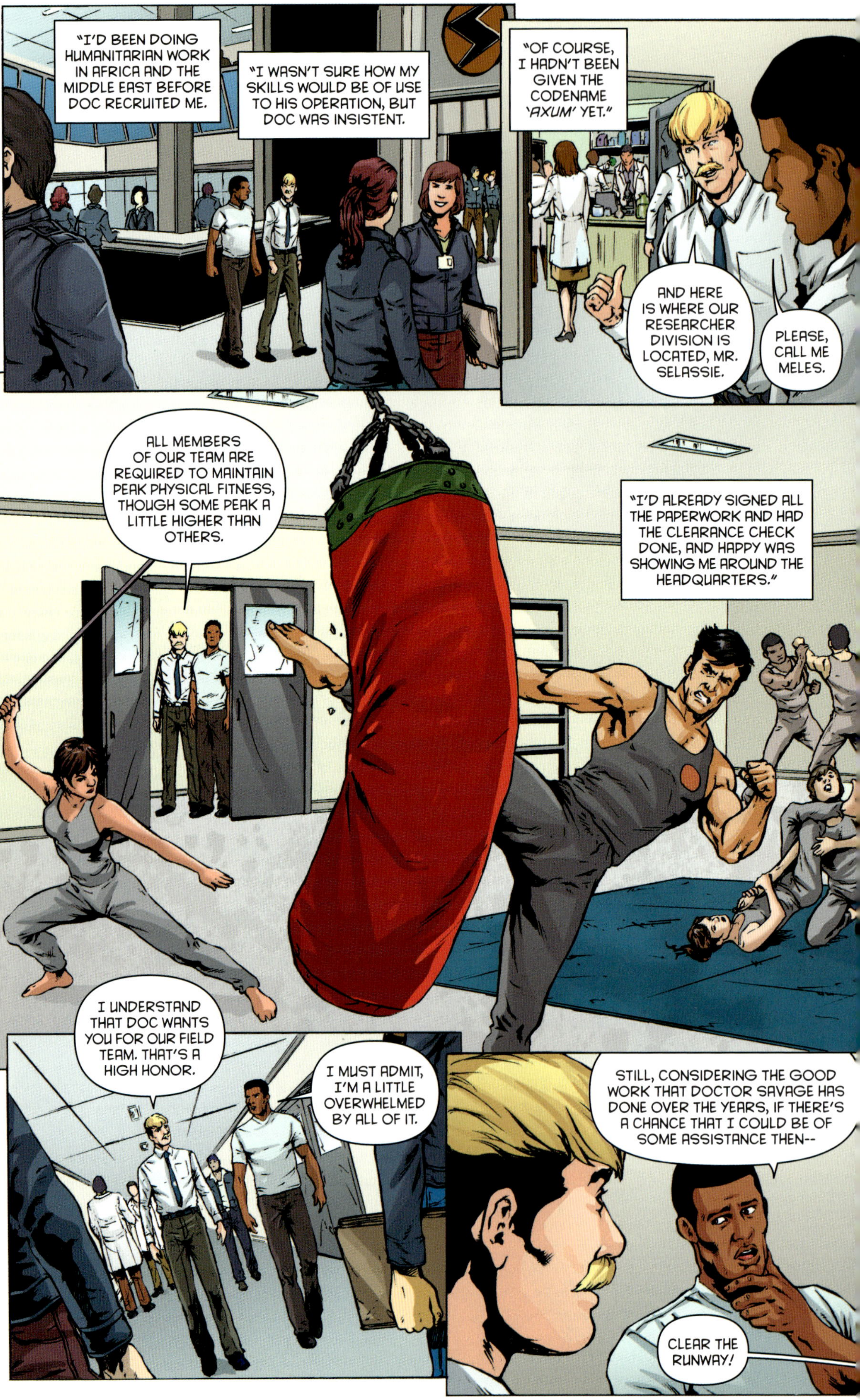
"I'D BEEN DOING HUMANITARIAN WORK IN AFRICA AND THE MIDDLE EAST BEFORE DOC RECRUITED ME.
"I WASN'T SURE HOW MY SKILLS WOULD BE OF USE TO HIS OPERATION, BUT DOC WAS INSISTENT.
"OF COURSE, I HADN'T BEEN GIVEN THE CODENAME 'AXUM' YET."
AND HERE IS WHERE OUR RESEARCHER DIVISION IS LOCATED, MR. SELASSIE.
PLEASE, CALL ME MELES.
ALL MEMBERS OF OUR TEAM ARE REQUIRED TO MAINTAIN PEAK PHYSICAL FITNESS, THOUGH SOME PEAK A LITTLE HIGHER THAN OTHERS.
"I'D ALREADY SIGNED ALL THE PAPERWORK AND HAD THE CLEARANCE CHECK DONE, AND HAPPY WAS SHOWING ME AROUND THE HEADQUARTERS."
I UNDERSTAND THAT DOC WANTS YOU FOR OUR FIELD TEAM. THAT'S A HIGH HONOR.
I MUST ADMIT, I'M A LITTLE OVERWHELMED BY ALL OF IT.
STILL, CONSIDERING THE GOOD WORK THAT DOCTOR SAVAGE HAS DONE OVER THE YEARS, IF THERE'S A CHANCE THAT I COULD BE OF SOME ASSISTANCE THEN--
CLEAR THE RUNWAY!

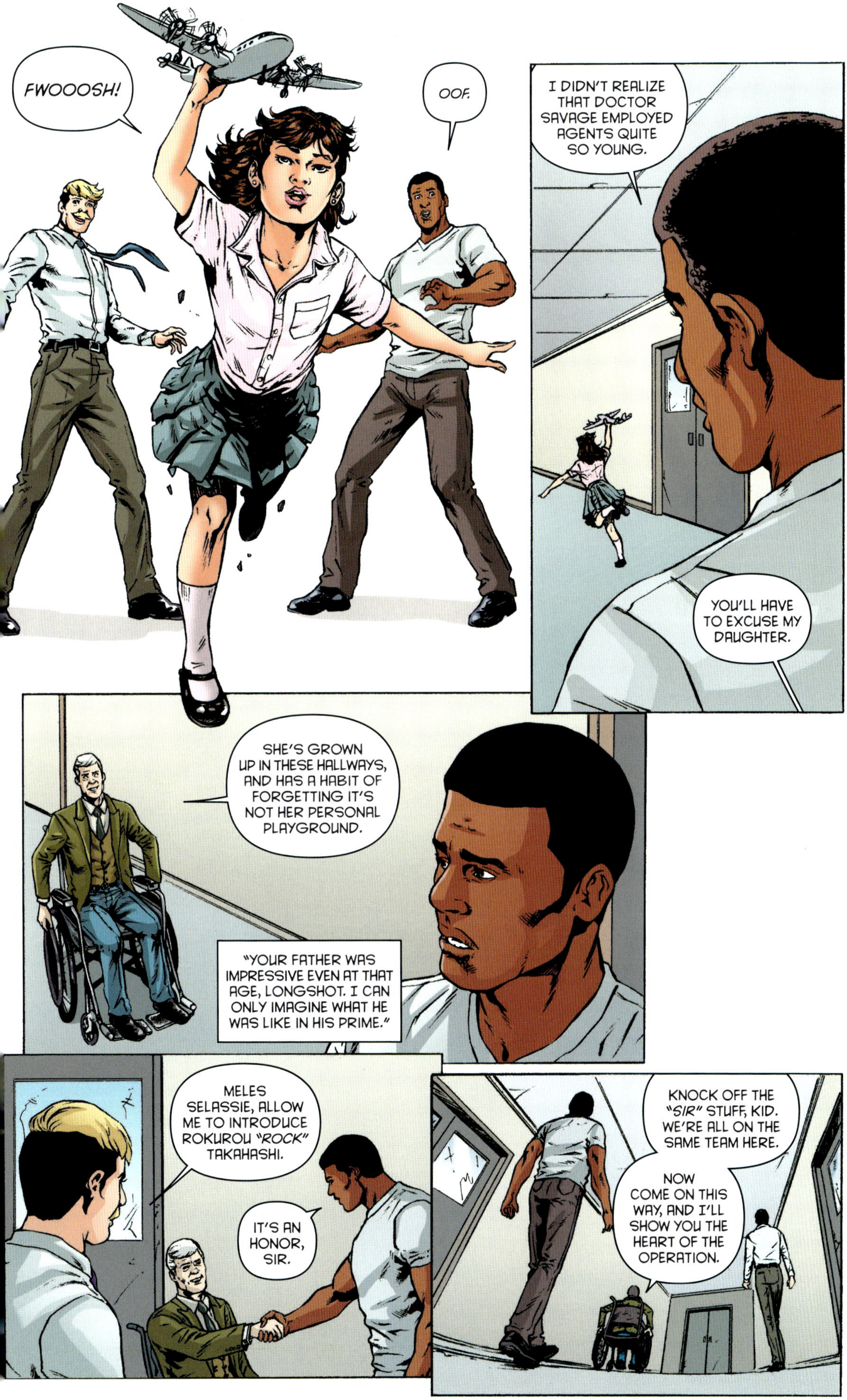
FWOOOSH!
OOF.
I DIDN'T REALIZE THAT DOCTOR SAVAGE EMPLOYED AGENTS QUITE SO YOUNG.
YOU'LL HAVE TO EXCUSE MY DAUGHTER.
SHE'S GROWN UP IN THESE HALLWAYS, AND HAS A HABIT OF FORGETTING IT'S NOT HER PERSONAL PLAYGROUND.
"YOUR FATHER WAS IMPRESSIVE EVEN AT THAT AGE, LONGSHOT. I CAN ONLY IMAGINE WHAT HE WAS LIKE IN HIS PRIME."
MELES SELASSIE, ALLOW ME TO INTRODUCE ROKUROU "ROCK" TAKAHASHI.
IT'S AN HONOR, SIR.
KNOCK OFF THE "SIR" STUFF, KID. WE'RE ALL ON THE SAME TEAM HERE.
NOW COME ON THIS WAY, AND I'LL SHOW YOU THE HEART OF THE OPERATION.

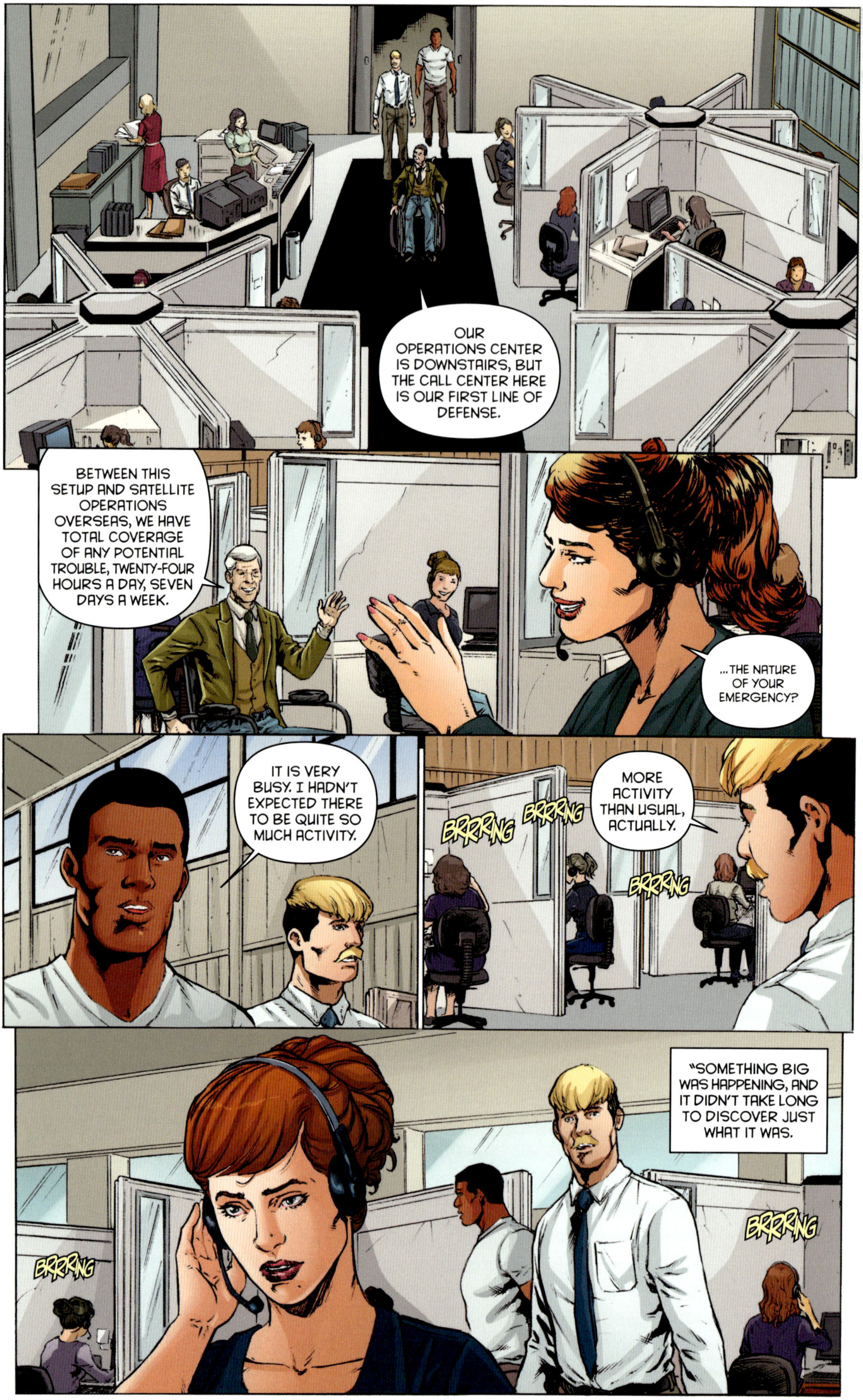
OUR OPERATIONS CENTER IS DOWNSTAIRS, BUT THE CALL CENTER HERE IS OUR FIRST LINE OF DEFENSE.
BETWEEN THIS SETUP AND SATELLITE OPERATIONS OVERSEAS, WE HAVE TOTAL COVERAGE OF ANY POTENTIAL TROUBLE, TWENTY-FOUR HOURS A DAY, SEVEN DAYS A WEEK.
...THE NATURE OF YOUR EMERGENCY?
IT IS VERY BUSY. I HADN'T EXPECTED THERE TO BE QUITE SO MUCH ACTIVITY.
BRRRING
BRRRING
MORE ACTIVITY THAN USUAL, ACTUALLY.
BRRRING
"SOMETHING BIG WAS HAPPENING, AND IT DIDN'T TAKE LONG TO DISCOVER JUST WHAT IT WAS.
BRRRING
BRRRING

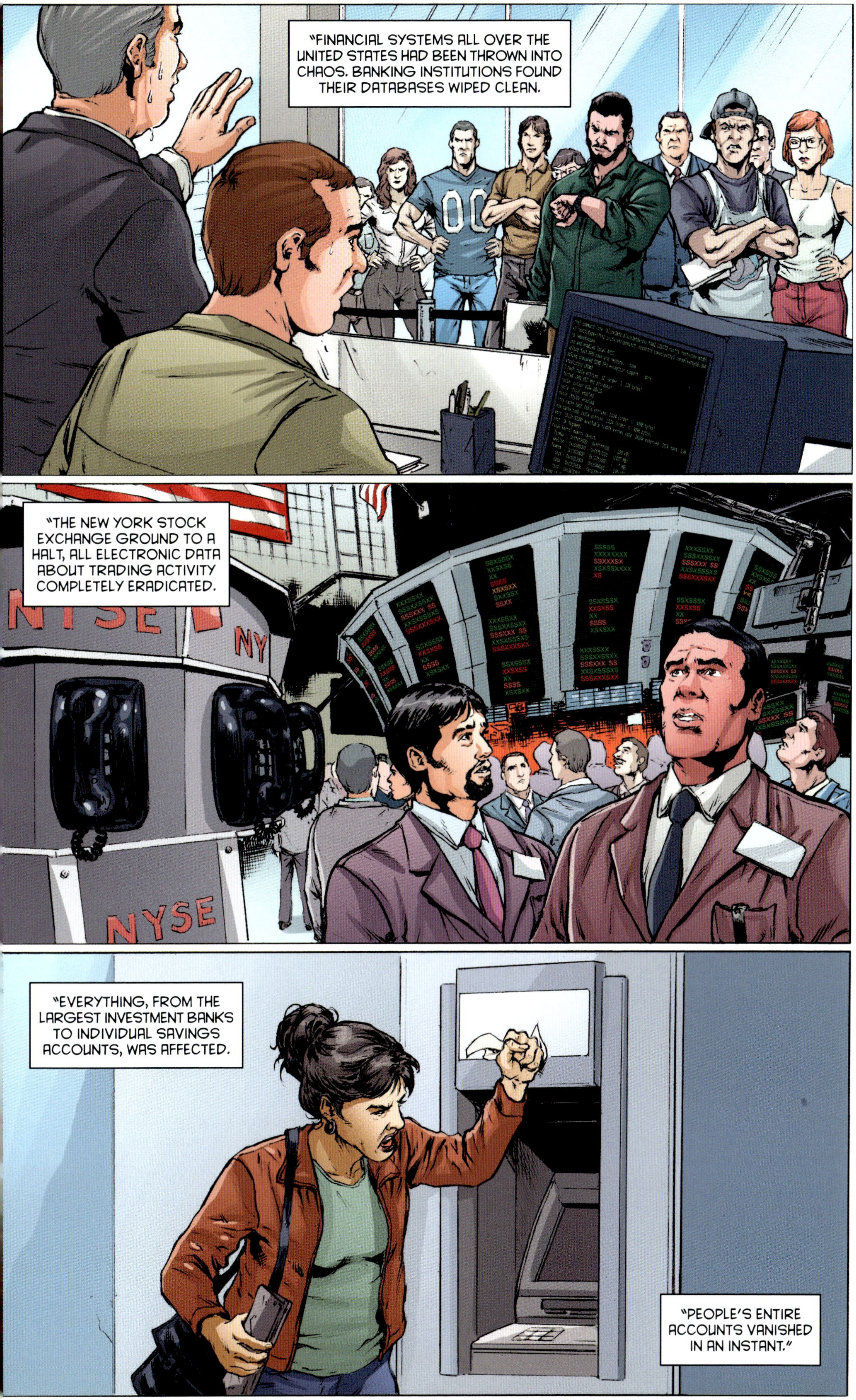
"FINANCIAL SYSTEMS ALL OVER THE UNITED STATES HAD BEEN THROWN INTO CHAOS. BANKING INSTITUTIONS FOUND THEIR DATABASES WIPED CLEAN.
"THE NEW YORK STOCK EXCHANGE GROUND TO A HALT, ALL ELECTRONIC DATA ABOUT TRADING ACTIVITY COMPLETELY ERADICATED.
NYSE
NY
NYSE
"EVERYTHING, FROM THE LARGEST INVESTMENT BANKS TO INDIVIDUAL SAVINGS ACCOUNTS, WAS AFFECTED.
"PEOPLE'S ENTIRE ACCOUNTS VANISHED IN AN INSTANT."

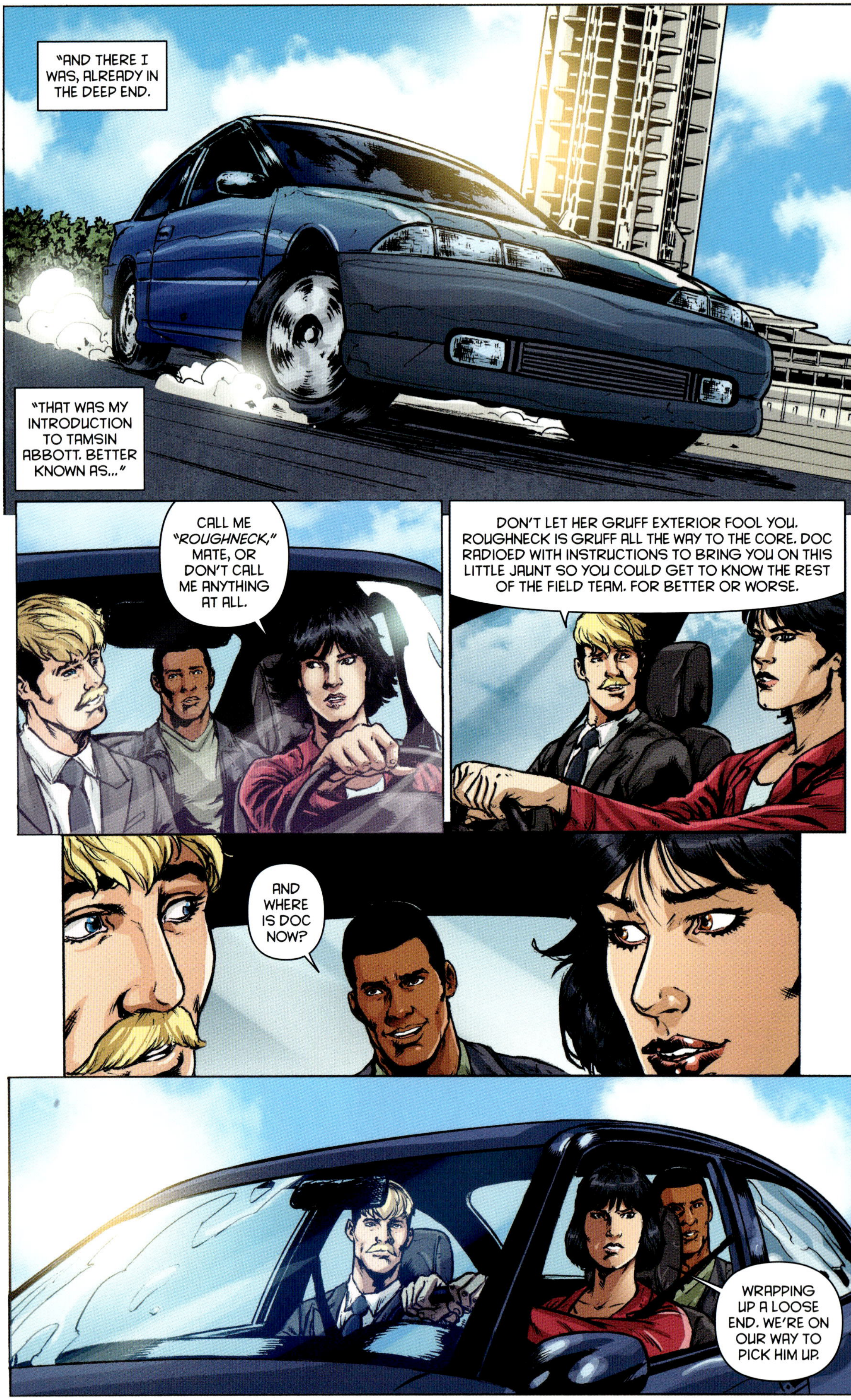
"AND THERE I WAS, ALREADY IN THE DEEP END.
"THAT WAS MY INTRODUCTION TO TAMSIN ABBOTT. BETTER KNOWN AS..."
CALL ME "ROUGHNECK," MATE, OR DON'T CALL ME ANYTHING AT ALL.
DON'T LET HER GRUFF EXTERIOR FOOL YOU. ROUGHNECK IS GRUFF ALL THE WAY TO THE CORE. DOC RADIOED WITH INSTRUCTIONS TO BRING YOU ON THIS LITTLE JAUNT SO YOU COULD GET TO KNOW THE REST OF THE FIELD TEAM. FOR BETTER OR WORSE.
AND WHERE IS DOC NOW?
WRAPPING UP A LOOSE END. WE'RE ON OUR WAY TO PICK HIM UP.

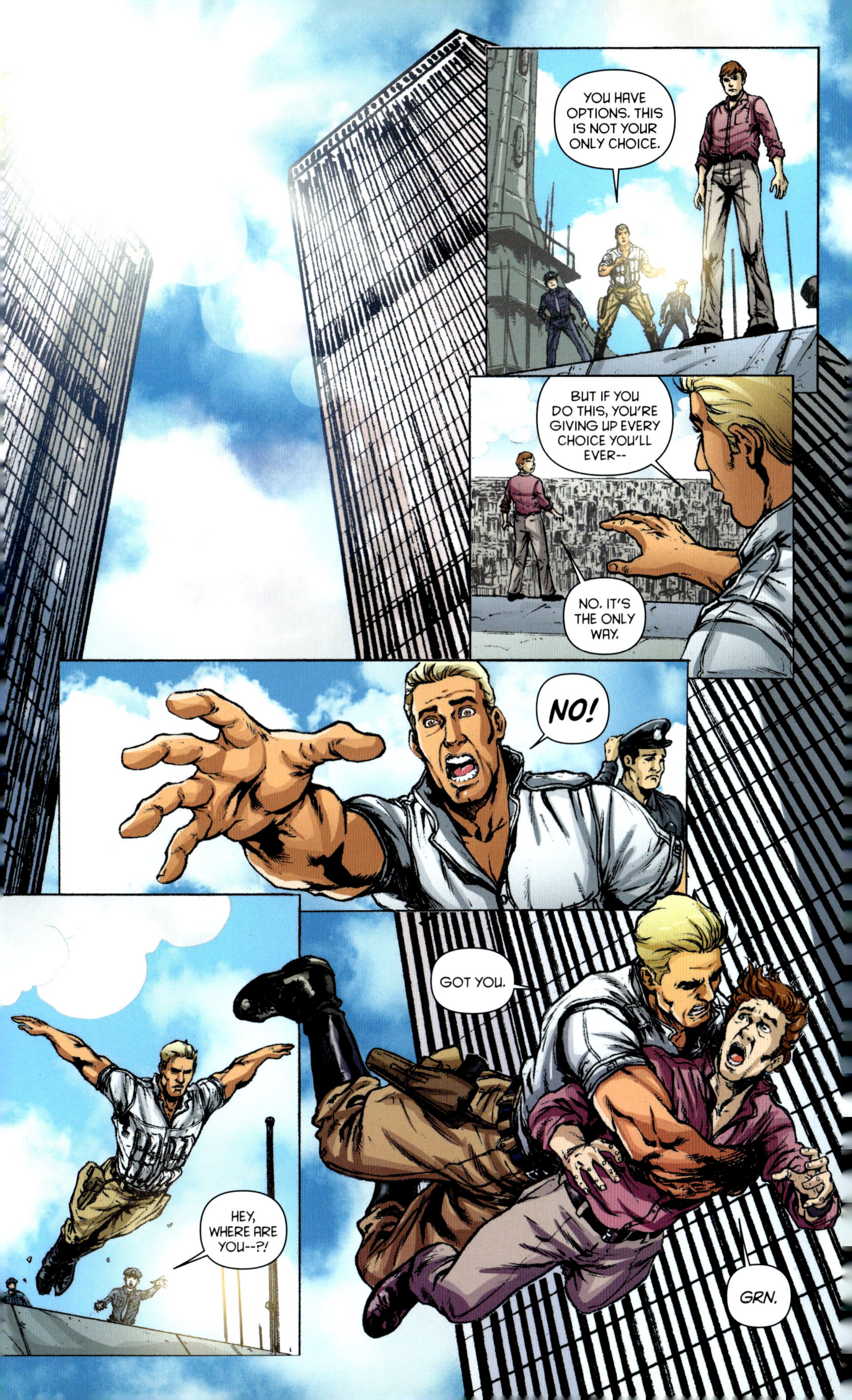
YOU HAVE OPTIONS. THIS IS NOT YOUR ONLY CHOICE.
BUT IF YOU DO THIS, YOU'RE GIVING UP EVERY CHOICE YOU'LL EVER--
NO. IT'S THE ONLY WAY.
NO!
HEY, WHERE ARE YOU--?!
GOT YOU.
GRN.

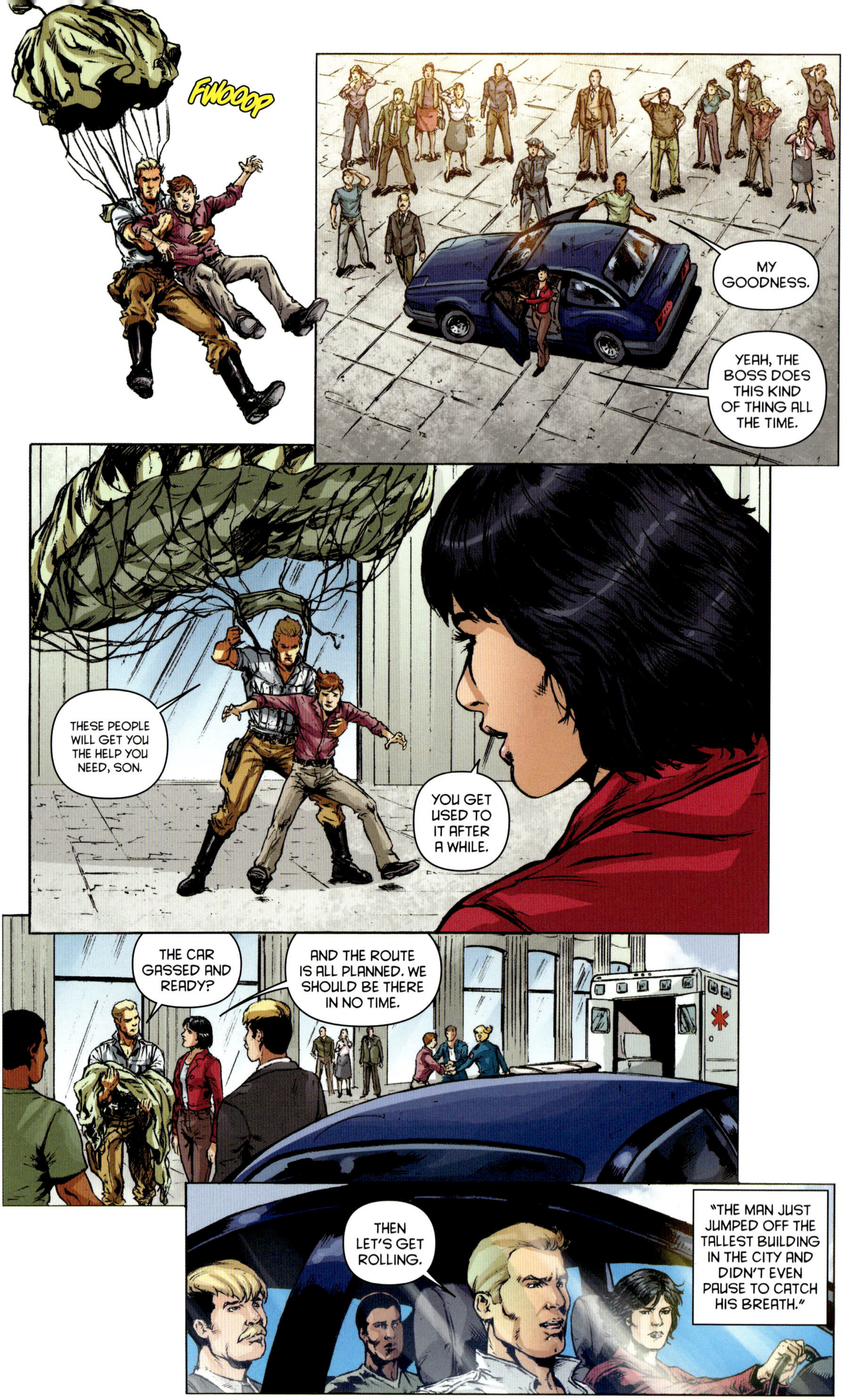
FWOOOP
MY GOODNESS.
YEAH, THE BOSS DOES THIS KIND OF THING ALL THE TIME.
THESE PEOPLE WILL GET YOU THE HELP YOU NEED, SON.
YOU GET USED TO IT AFTER A WHILE.
THE CAR GASSED AND READY?
AND THE ROUTE IS ALL PLANNED. WE SHOULD BE THERE IN NO TIME.
THEN LET'S GET ROLLING.
"THE MAN JUST JUMPED OFF THE TALLEST BUILDING IN THE CITY AND DIDN'T EVEN PAUSE TO CATCH HIS BREATH."

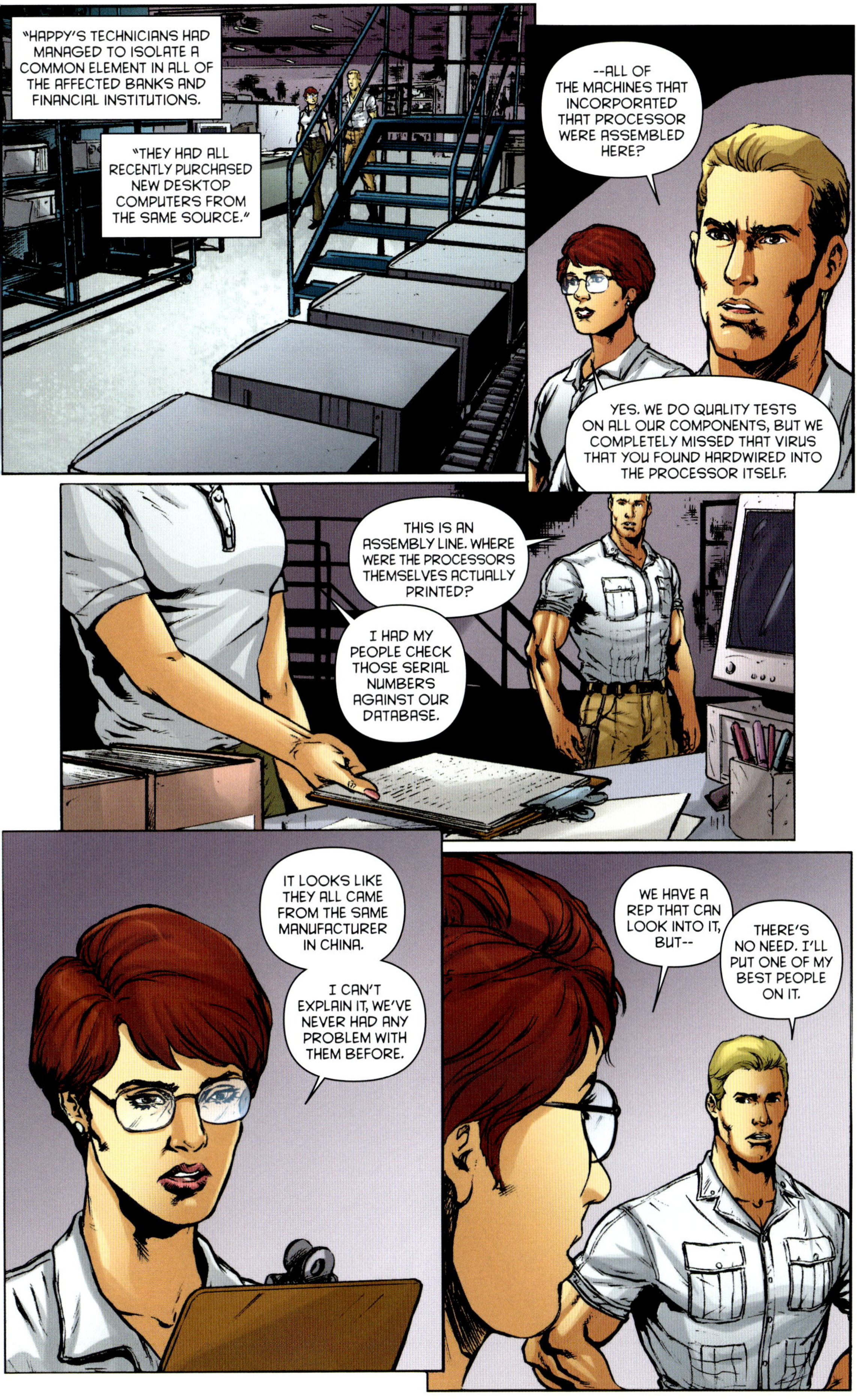
"HAPPY'S TECHNICIANS HAD MANAGED TO ISOLATE A COMMON ELEMENT IN ALL OF THE AFFECTED BANKS AND FINANCIAL INSTITUTIONS.
"THEY HAD ALL RECENTLY PURCHASED NEW DESKTOP COMPUTERS FROM THE SAME SOURCE."
--ALL OF THE MACHINES THAT INCORPORATED THAT PROCESSOR WERE ASSEMBLED HERE?
YES. WE DO QUALITY TESTS ON ALL OUR COMPONENTS, BUT WE COMPLETELY MISSED THAT VIRUS THAT YOU FOUND HARDWIRED INTO THE PROCESSOR ITSELF.
THIS IS AN ASSEMBLY LINE. WHERE WERE THE PROCESSORS THEMSELVES ACTUALLY PRINTED?
I HAD MY PEOPLE CHECK THOSE SERIAL NUMBERS AGAINST OUR DATABASE.
IT LOOKS LIKE THEY ALL CAME FROM THE SAME MANUFACTURER IN CHINA.
I CAN'T EXPLAIN IT, WE'VE NEVER HAD ANY PROBLEM WITH THEM BEFORE.
WE HAVE A REP THAT CAN LOOK INTO IT, BUT--
THERE'S NO NEED. I'LL PUT ONE OF MY BEST PEOPLE ON IT.

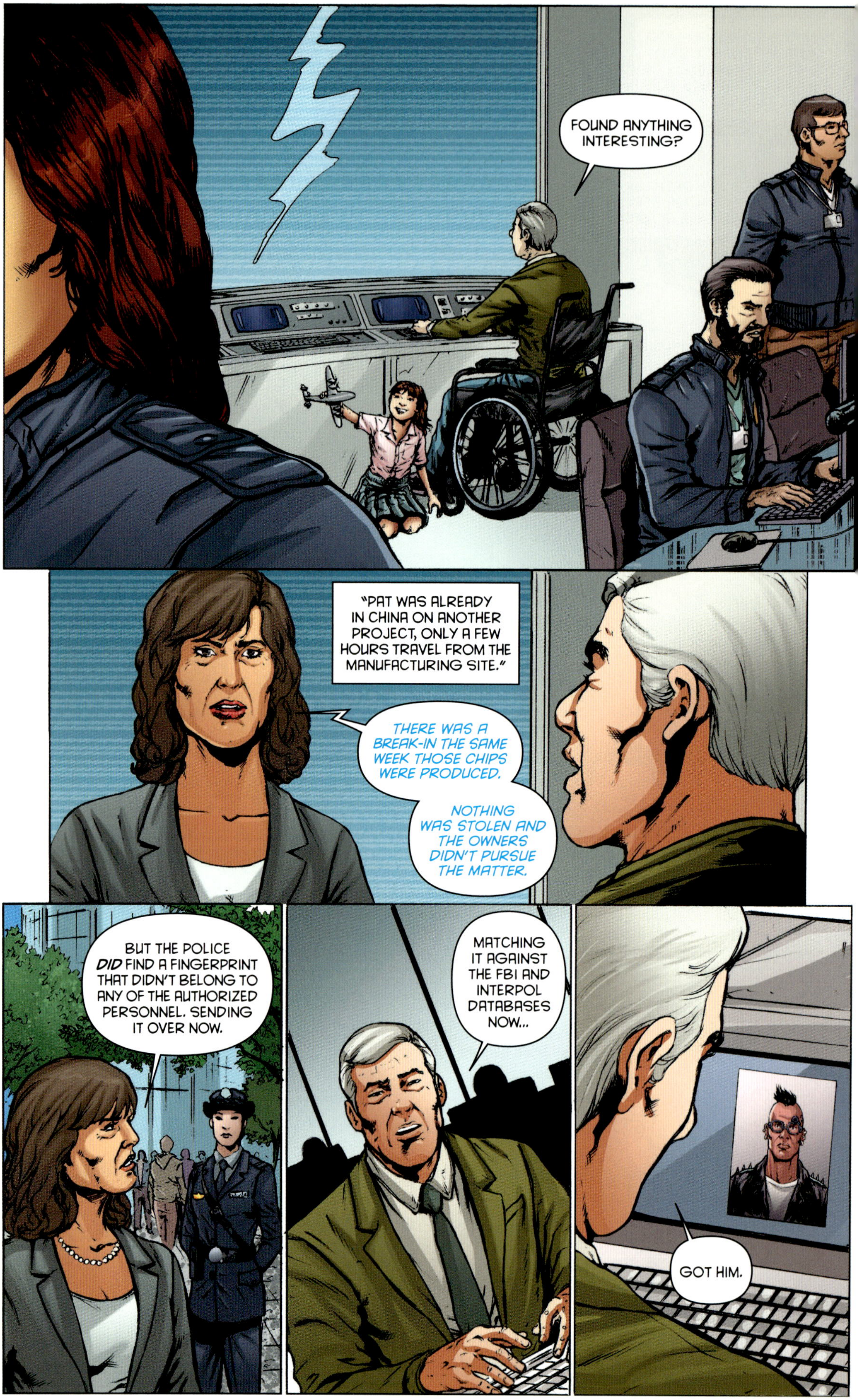
FOUND ANYTHING INTERESTING?
"PAT WAS ALREADY IN CHINA ON ANOTHER PROJECT, ONLY A FEW HOURS TRAVEL FROM THE MANUFACTURING SITE."
THERE WAS A BREAK-IN THE SAME WEEK THOSE CHIPS WERE PRODUCED.
NOTHING WAS STOLEN AND THE OWNERS DIDN'T PURSUE THE MATTER.
BUT THE POLICE *DID* FIND A FINGERPRINT THAT DIDN'T BELONG TO ANY OF THE AUTHORIZED PERSONNEL. SENDING IT OVER NOW.
MATCHING IT AGAINST THE FBI AND INTERPOL DATABASES NOW...
GOT HIM.

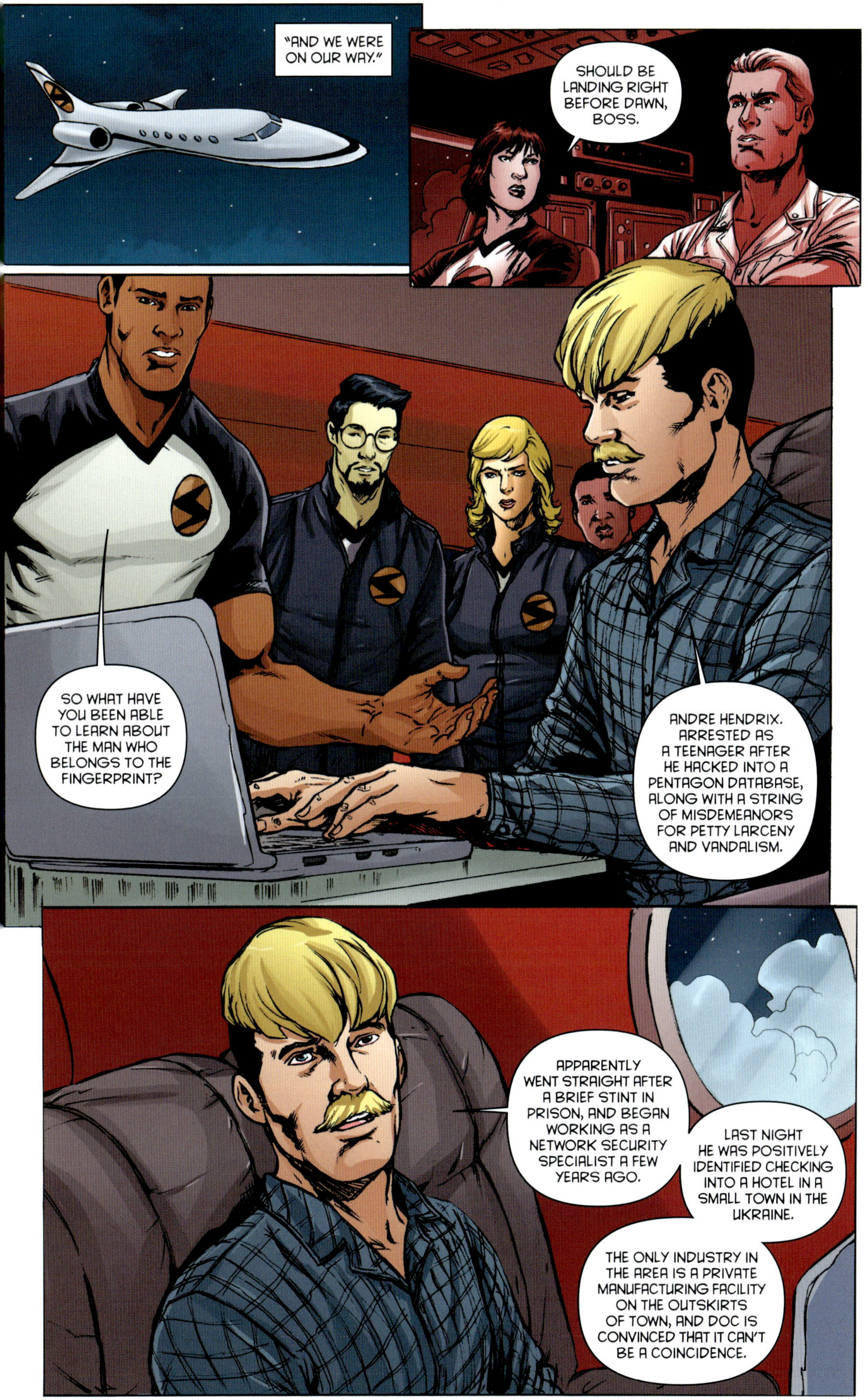
"AND WE WERE ON OUR WAY."
SHOULD BE LANDING RIGHT BEFORE DAWN, BOSS.
SO WHAT HAVE YOU BEEN ABLE TO LEARN ABOUT THE MAN WHO BELONGS TO THE FINGERPRINT?
ANDRE HENDRIX. ARRESTED AS A TEENAGER AFTER HE HACKED INTO A PENTAGON DATABASE, ALONG WITH A STRING OF MISDEMEANORS FOR PETTY LARCENY AND VANDALISM.
APPARENTLY WENT STRAIGHT AFTER A BRIEF STINT IN PRISON, AND BEGAN WORKING AS A NETWORK SECURITY SPECIALIST A FEW YEARS AGO.
LAST NIGHT HE WAS POSITIVELY IDENTIFIED CHECKING INTO A HOTEL IN A SMALL TOWN IN THE UKRAINE.
THE ONLY INDUSTRY IN THE AREA IS A PRIVATE MANUFACTURING FACILITY ON THE OUTSKIRTS OF TOWN, AND DOC IS CONVINCED THAT IT CAN'T BE A COINCIDENCE.

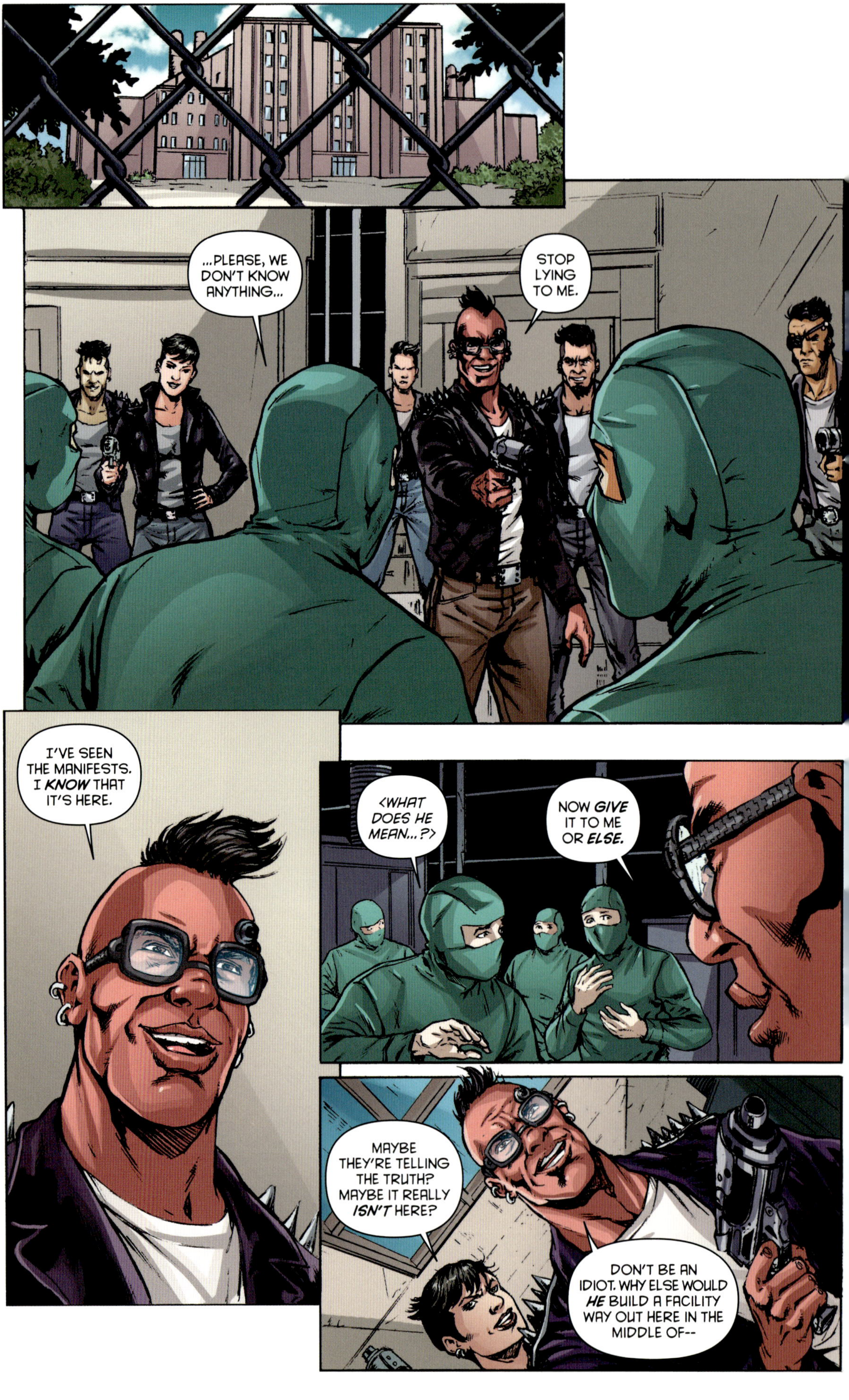
...PLEASE, WE DON'T KNOW ANYTHING...
STOP LYING TO ME.
I'VE SEEN THE MANIFESTS. I *KNOW* THAT IT'S HERE.
<WHAT DOES HE MEAN...?>
NOW *GIVE* IT TO ME OR *ELSE.*
MAYBE THEY'RE TELLING THE TRUTH? MAYBE IT REALLY *ISN'T* HERE?
DON'T BE AN IDIOT. WHY ELSE WOULD *HE* BUILD A FACILITY WAY OUT HERE IN THE MIDDLE OF--

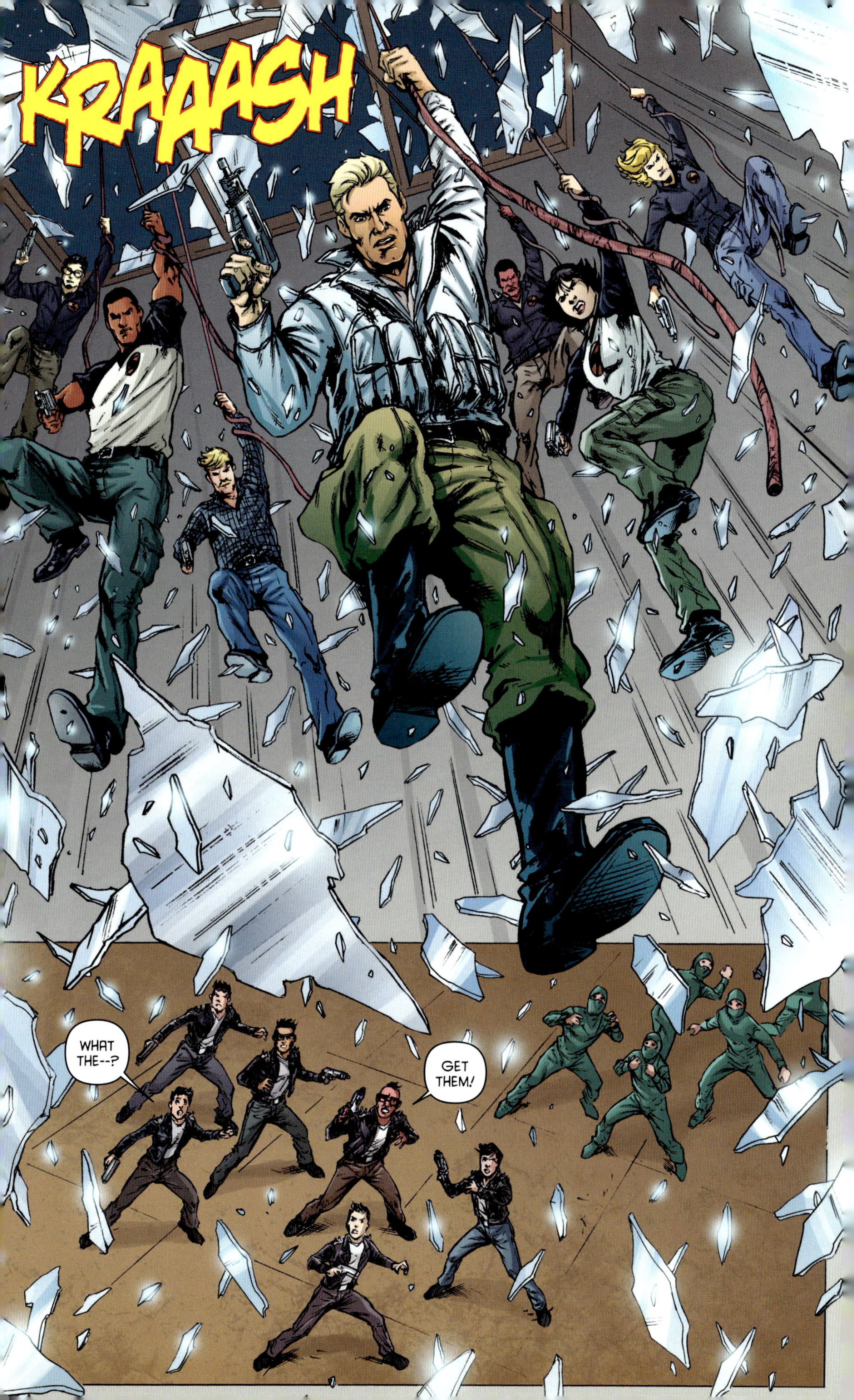
KRAAASH
WHAT THE--?
GET THEM!

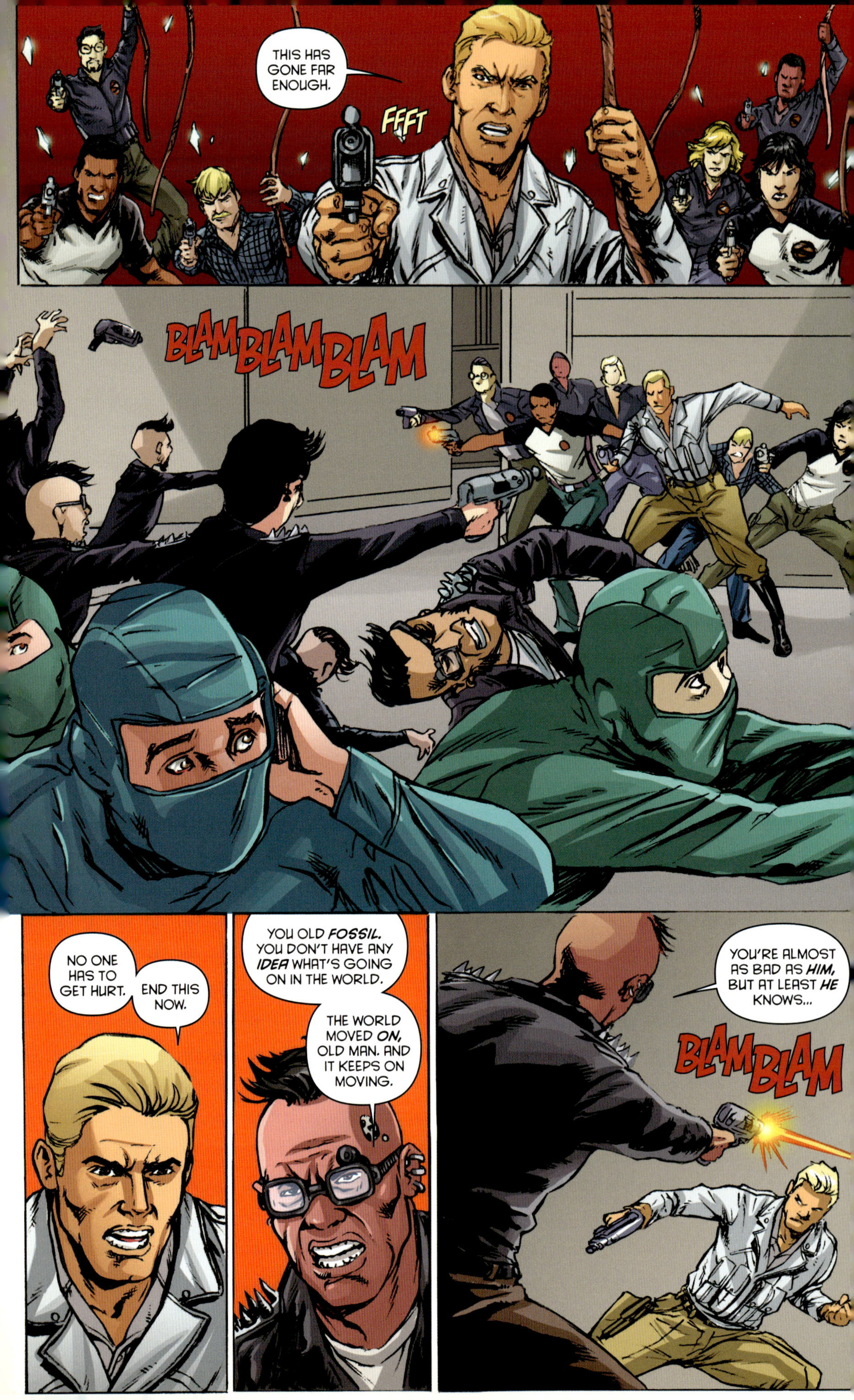
THIS HAS GONE FAR ENOUGH.
FFFT
BLAMBLAMBLAM
NO ONE HAS TO GET HURT.
END THIS NOW.
YOU OLD *FOSSIL.* YOU DON'T HAVE ANY *IDEA* WHAT'S GOING ON IN THE WORLD.
THE WORLD MOVED *ON,* OLD MAN. AND IT KEEPS ON MOVING.
YOU'RE ALMOST AS BAD AS *HIM,* BUT AT LEAST *HE* KNOWS...
BLAMBLAM

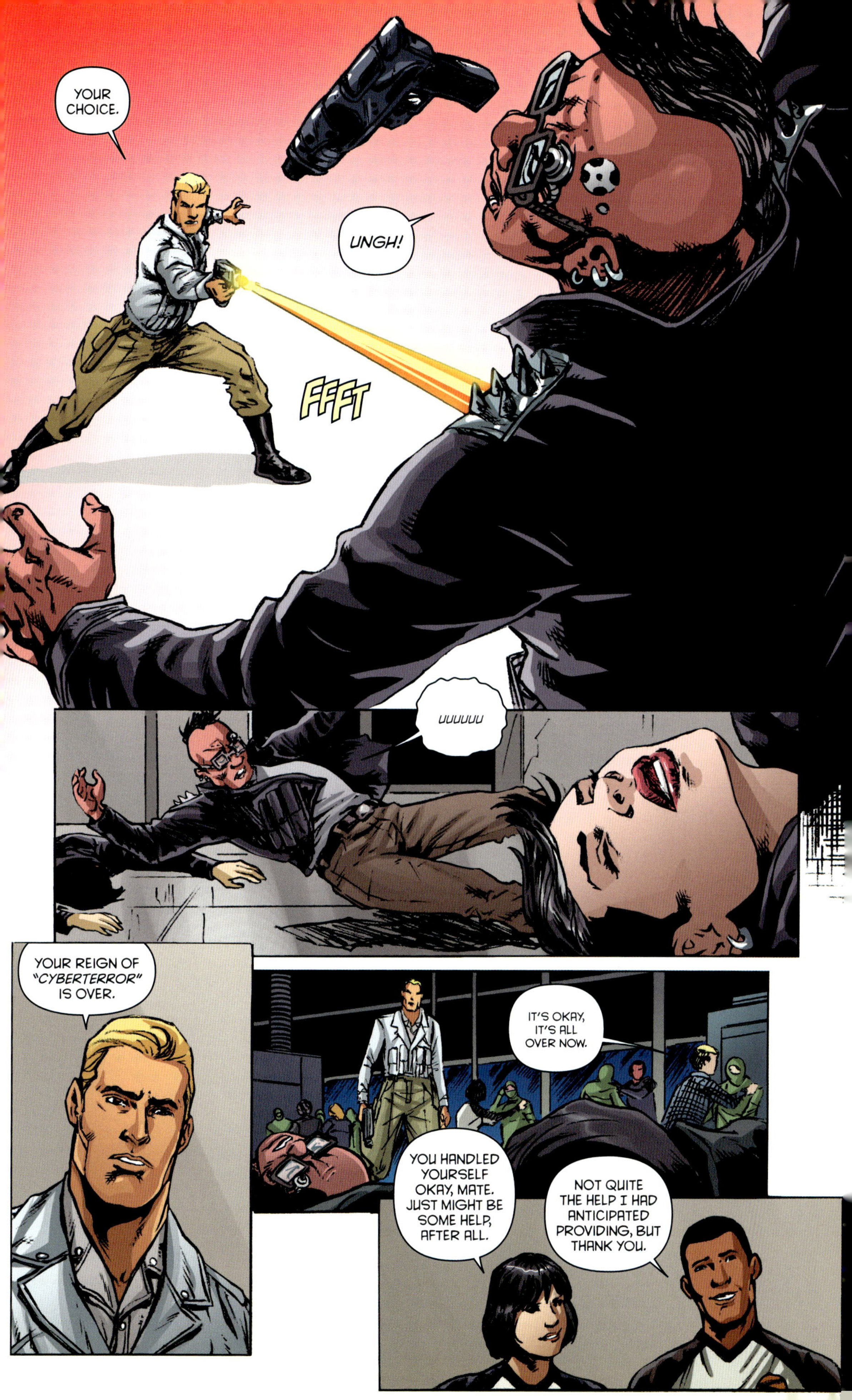
YOUR CHOICE.
UNGH!
FFFT
UUUUUU
YOUR REIGN OF "CYBERTERROR" IS OVER.
IT'S OKAY, IT'S ALL OVER NOW.
YOU HANDLED YOURSELF OKAY, MATE. JUST MIGHT BE SOME HELP, AFTER ALL.
NOT QUITE THE HELP I HAD ANTICIPATED PROVIDING, BUT THANK YOU.

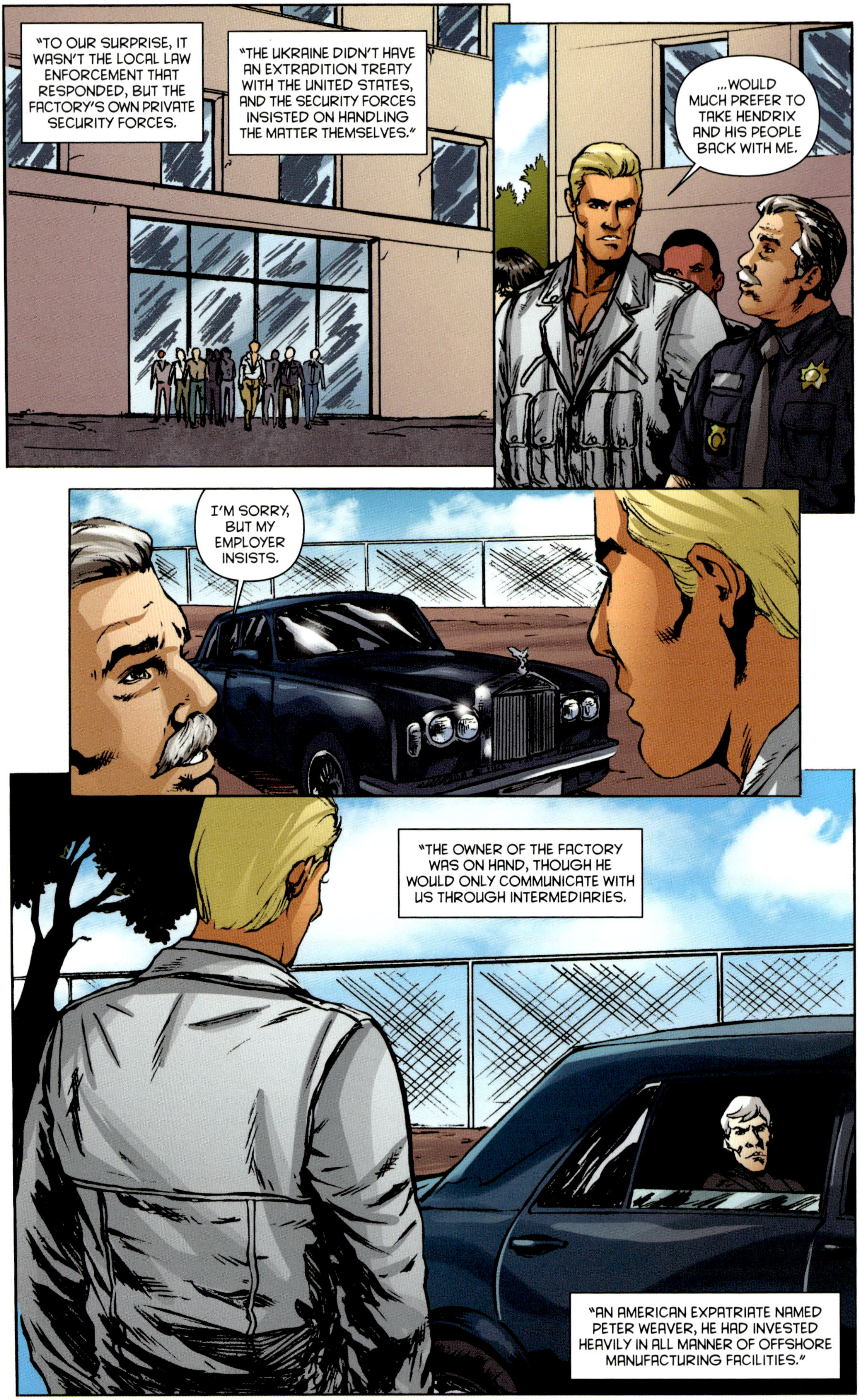
"TO OUR SURPRISE, IT WASN'T THE LOCAL LAW ENFORCEMENT THAT RESPONDED, BUT THE FACTORY'S OWN PRIVATE SECURITY FORCES.
"THE UKRAINE DIDN'T HAVE AN EXTRADITION TREATY WITH THE UNITED STATES, AND THE SECURITY FORCES INSISTED ON HANDLING THE MATTER THEMSELVES."
...WOULD MUCH PREFER TO TAKE HENDRIX AND HIS PEOPLE BACK WITH ME.
I'M SORRY, BUT MY EMPLOYER INSISTS.
"THE OWNER OF THE FACTORY WAS ON HAND, THOUGH HE WOULD ONLY COMMUNICATE WITH US THROUGH INTERMEDIARIES.
"AN AMERICAN EXPATRIATE NAMED PETER WEAVER, HE HAD INVESTED HEAVILY IN ALL MANNER OF OFFSHORE MANUFACTURING FACILITIES."

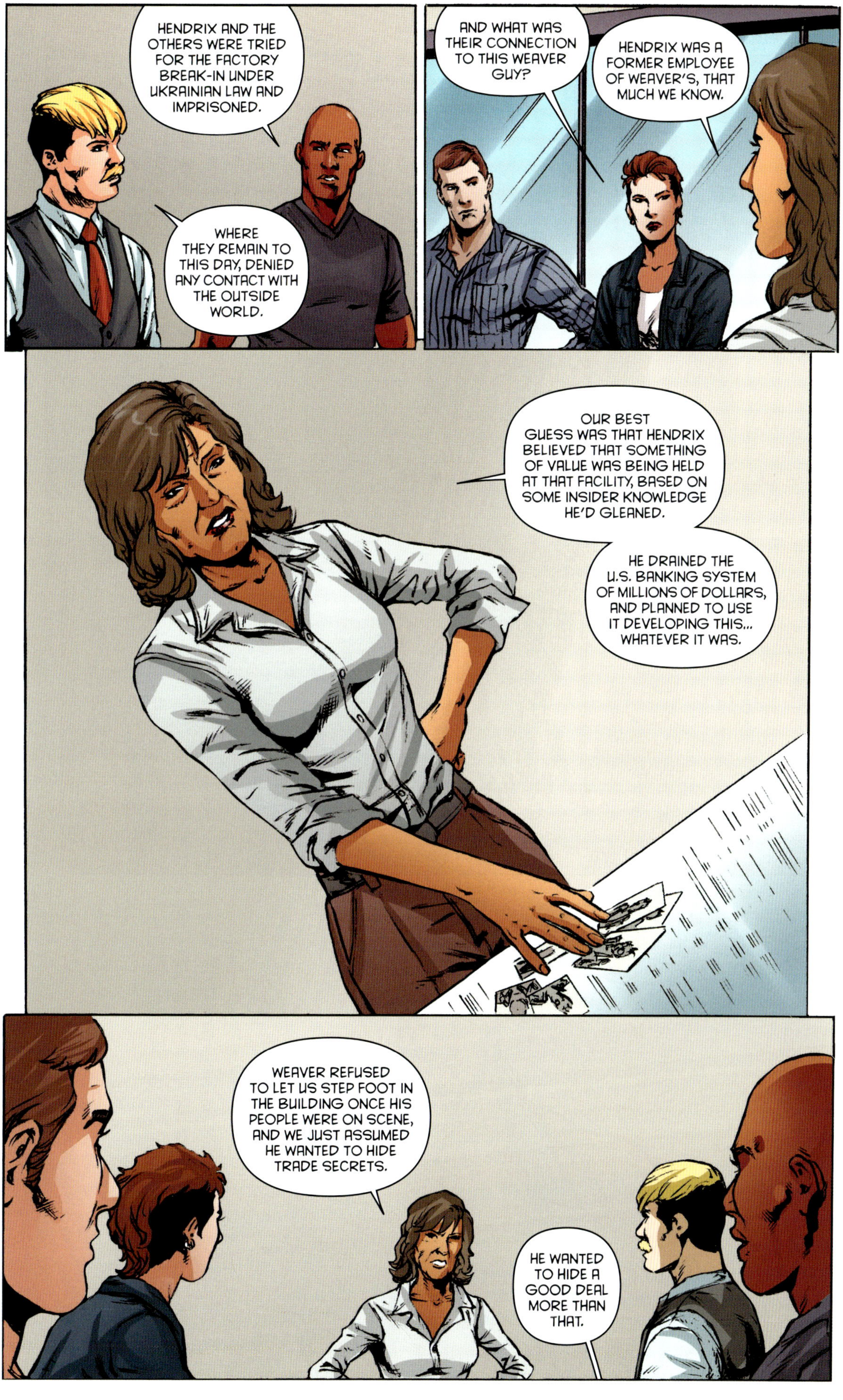
HENDRIX AND THE OTHERS WERE TRIED FOR THE FACTORY BREAK-IN UNDER UKRAINIAN LAW AND IMPRISONED.
WHERE THEY REMAIN TO THIS DAY, DENIED ANY CONTACT WITH THE OUTSIDE WORLD.
AND WHAT WAS THEIR CONNECTION TO THIS WEAVER GUY?
HENDRIX WAS A FORMER EMPLOYEE OF WEAVER'S, THAT MUCH WE KNOW.
OUR BEST GUESS WAS THAT HENDRIX BELIEVED THAT SOMETHING OF VALUE WAS BEING HELD AT THAT FACILITY, BASED ON SOME INSIDER KNOWLEDGE HE'D GLEANED.
HE DRAINED THE U.S. BANKING SYSTEM OF MILLIONS OF DOLLARS, AND PLANNED TO USE IT DEVELOPING THIS... WHATEVER IT WAS.
WEAVER REFUSED TO LET US STEP FOOT IN THE BUILDING ONCE HIS PEOPLE WERE ON SCENE, AND WE JUST ASSUMED HE WANTED TO HIDE TRADE SECRETS.
HE WANTED TO HIDE A GOOD DEAL MORE THAN THAT.

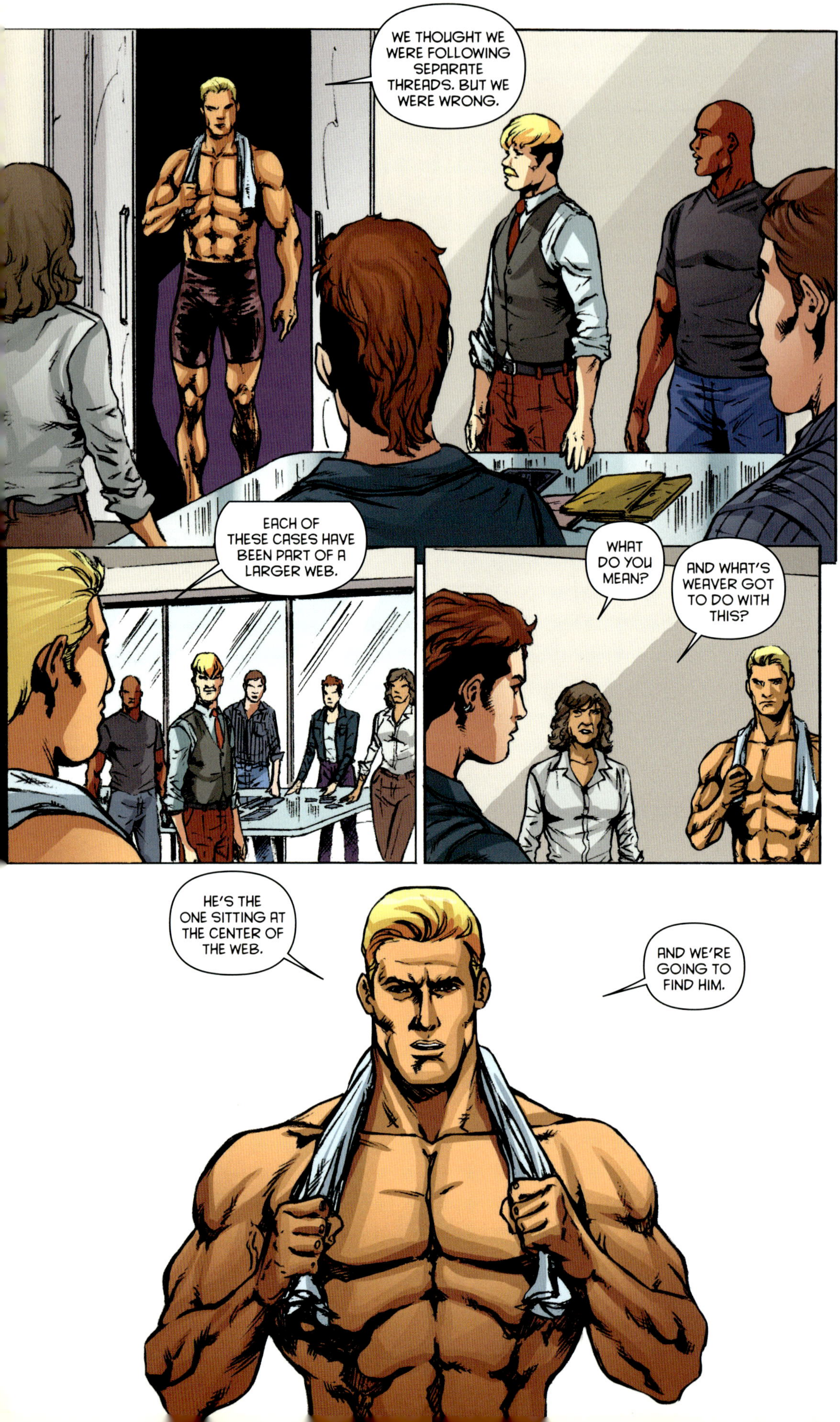
WE THOUGHT WE WERE FOLLOWING SEPARATE THREADS. BUT WE WERE WRONG.
EACH OF THESE CASES HAVE BEEN PART OF A LARGER WEB.
WHAT DO YOU MEAN?
AND WHAT'S WEAVER GOT TO DO WITH THIS?
HE'S THE ONE SITTING AT THE CENTER OF THE WEB.
AND WE'RE GOING TO FIND HIM.

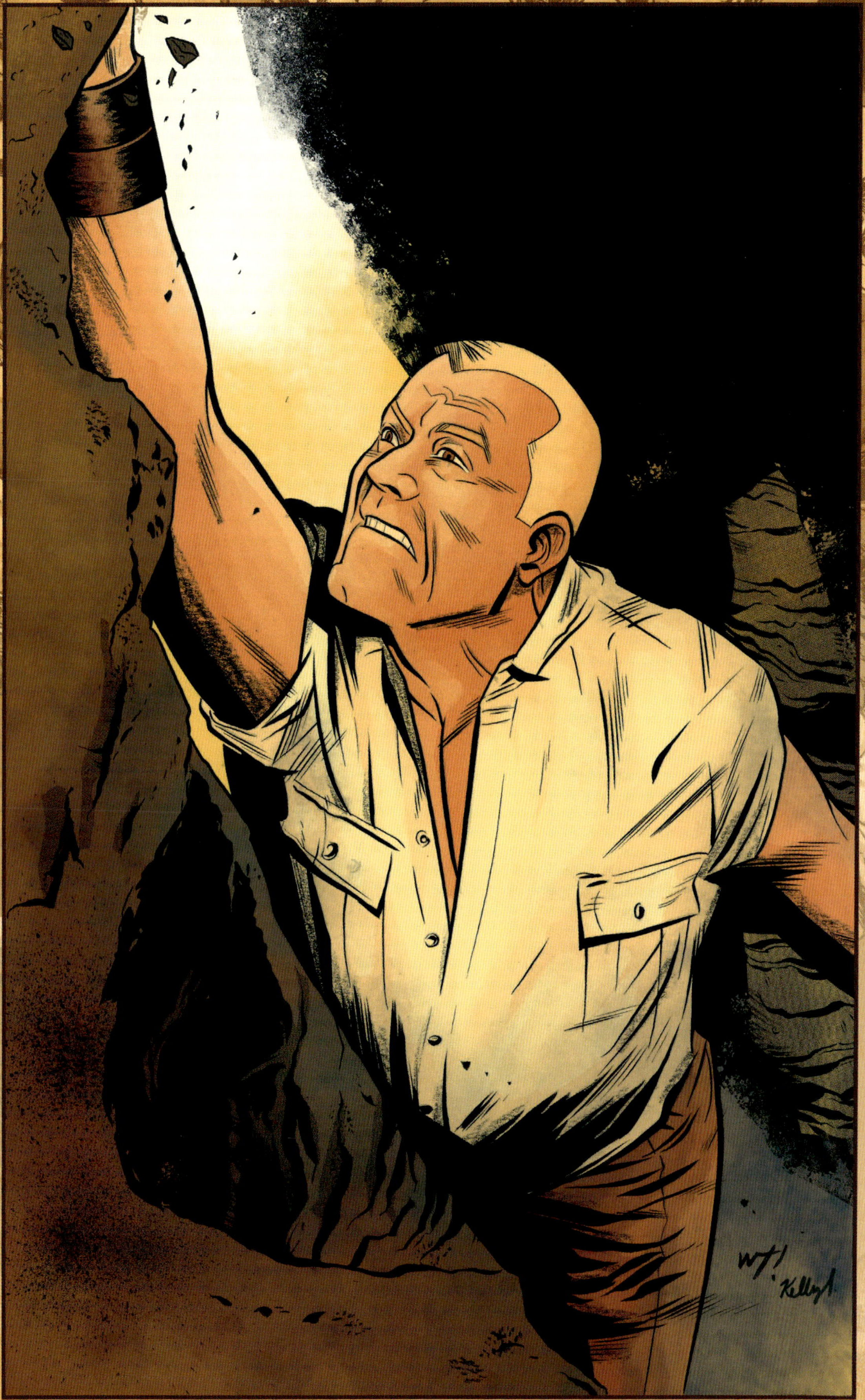
WT!
Kelly!

ISSUE #5 COVER
art by **WILFREDO TORRES** colors by **KELLY FITZPATRICK**

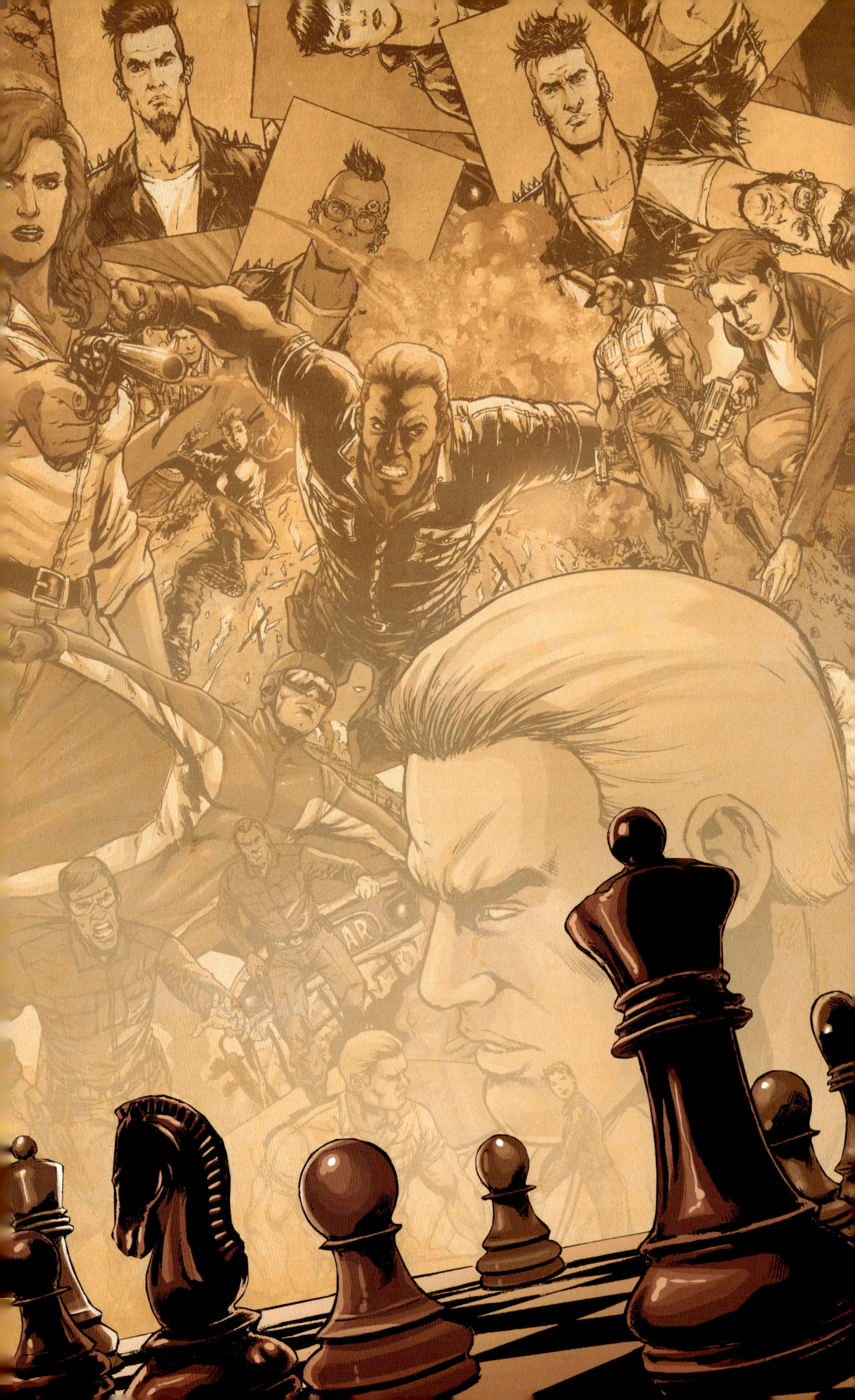

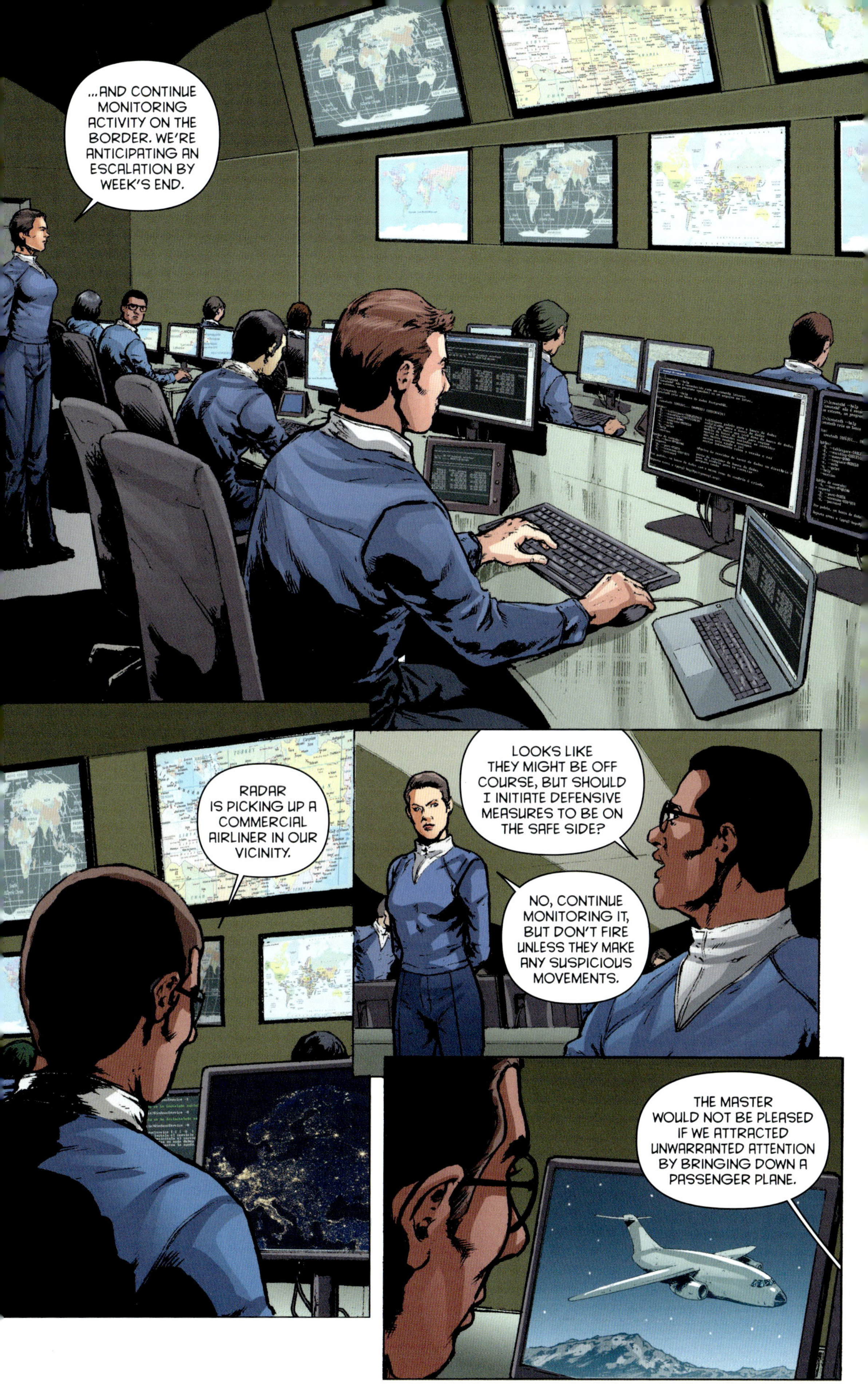
...AND CONTINUE MONITORING ACTIVITY ON THE BORDER. WE'RE ANTICIPATING AN ESCALATION BY WEEK'S END.
RADAR IS PICKING UP A COMMERCIAL AIRLINER IN OUR VICINITY.
LOOKS LIKE THEY MIGHT BE OFF COURSE, BUT SHOULD I INITIATE DEFENSIVE MEASURES TO BE ON THE SAFE SIDE?
NO, CONTINUE MONITORING IT, BUT DON'T FIRE UNLESS THEY MAKE ANY SUSPICIOUS MOVEMENTS.
THE MASTER WOULD NOT BE PLEASED IF WE ATTRACTED UNWARRANTED ATTENTION BY BRINGING DOWN A PASSENGER PLANE.

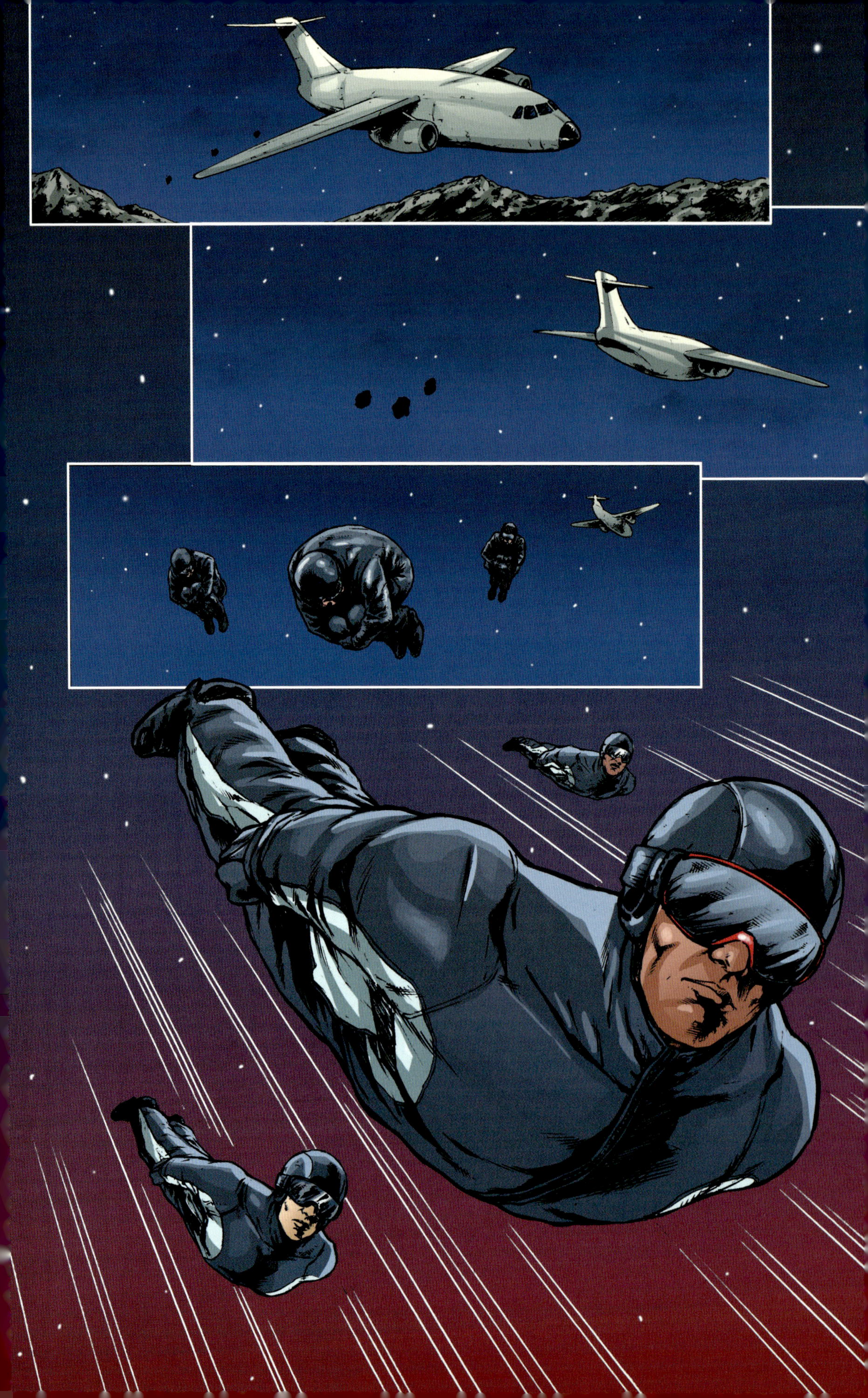

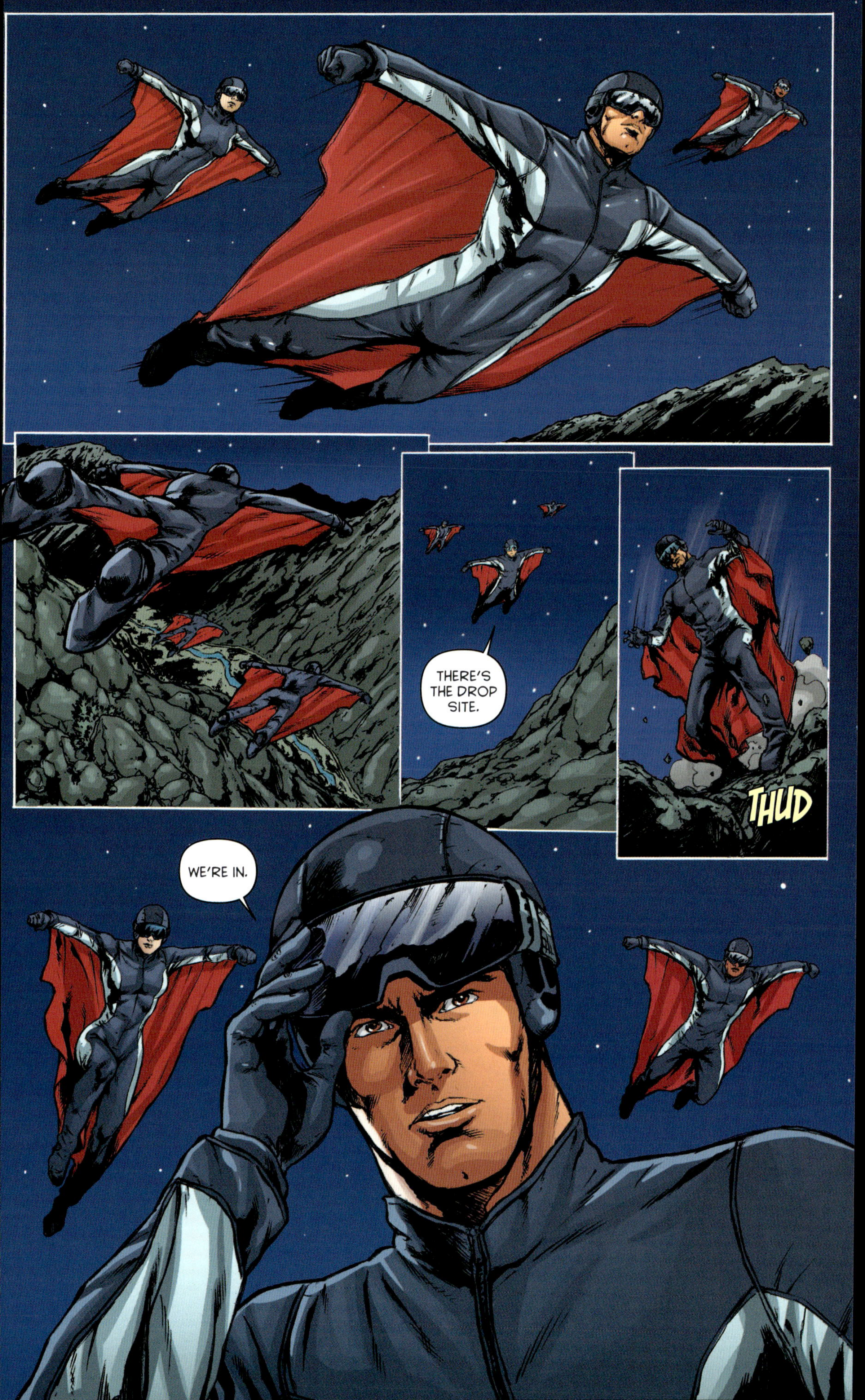
THERE'S THE DROP SITE.
THUD
WE'RE IN.

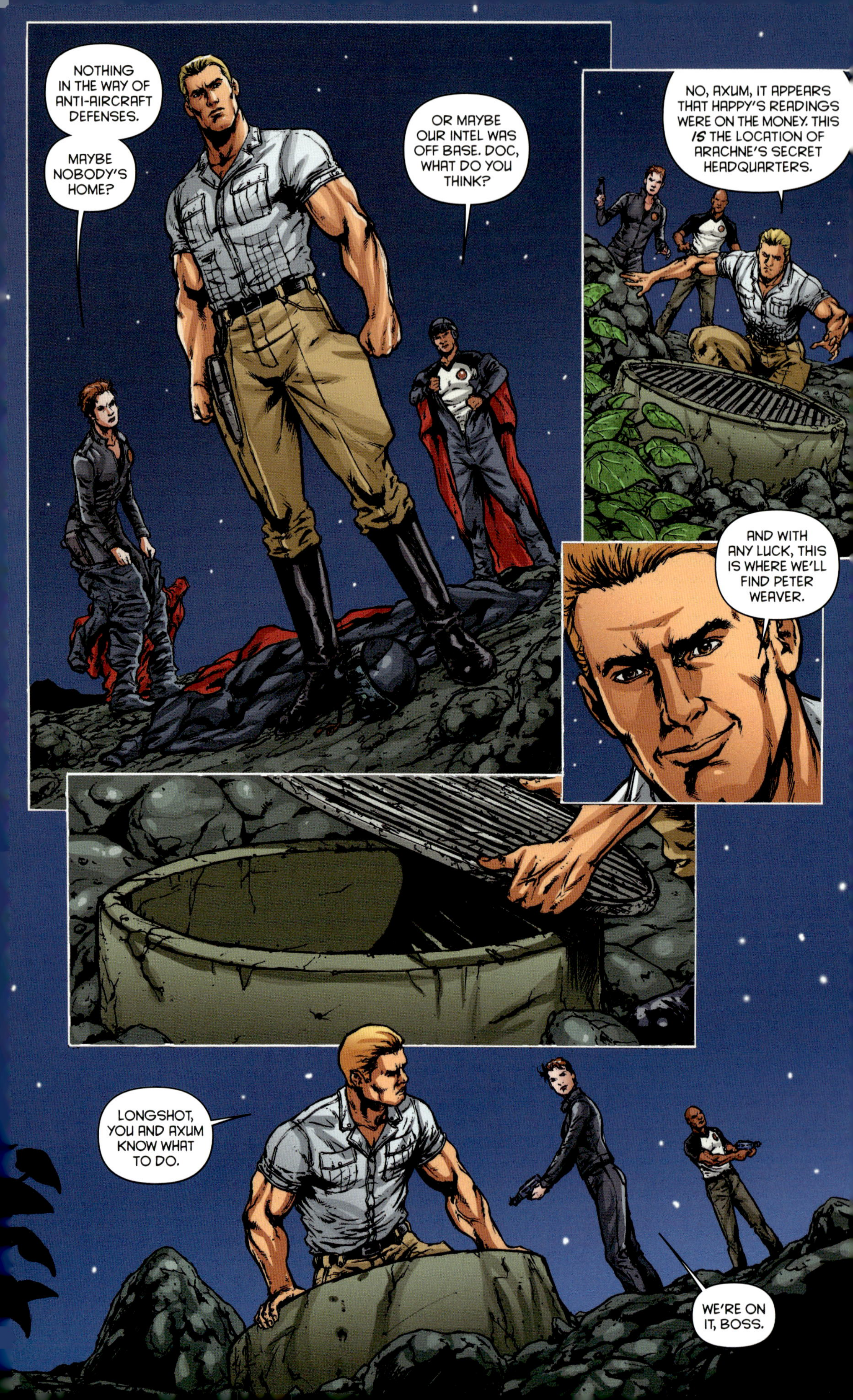
NOTHING IN THE WAY OF ANTI-AIRCRAFT DEFENSES.
MAYBE NOBODY'S HOME?
OR MAYBE OUR INTEL WAS OFF BASE. DOC, WHAT DO YOU THINK?
NO, AXUM, IT APPEARS THAT HAPPY'S READINGS WERE ON THE MONEY. THIS *IS* THE LOCATION OF ARACHNE'S SECRET HEADQUARTERS.
AND WITH ANY LUCK, THIS IS WHERE WE'LL FIND PETER WEAVER.
LONGSHOT, YOU AND AXUM KNOW WHAT TO DO.
WE'RE ON IT, BOSS.

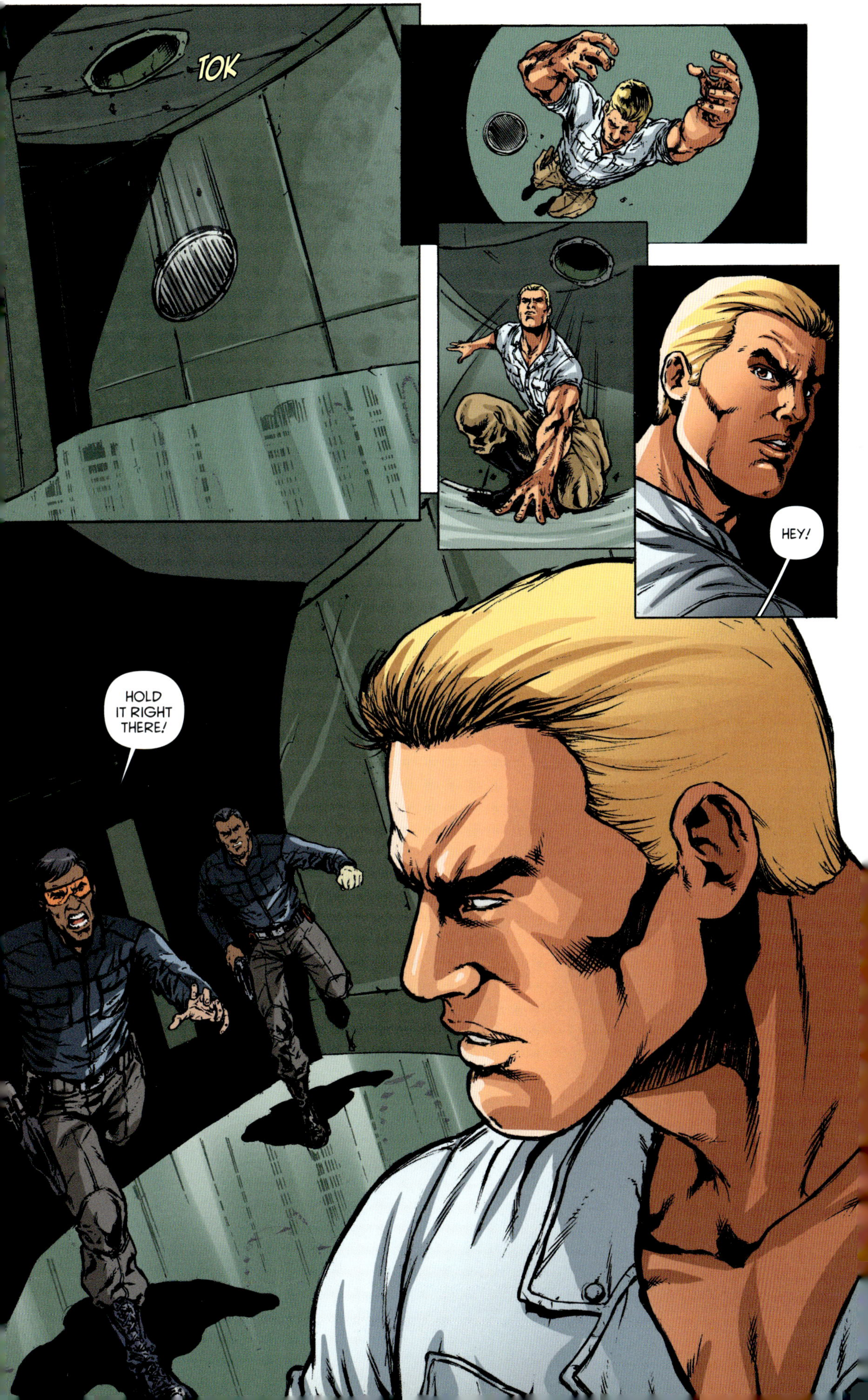
TOK
HEY!
HOLD IT RIGHT THERE!

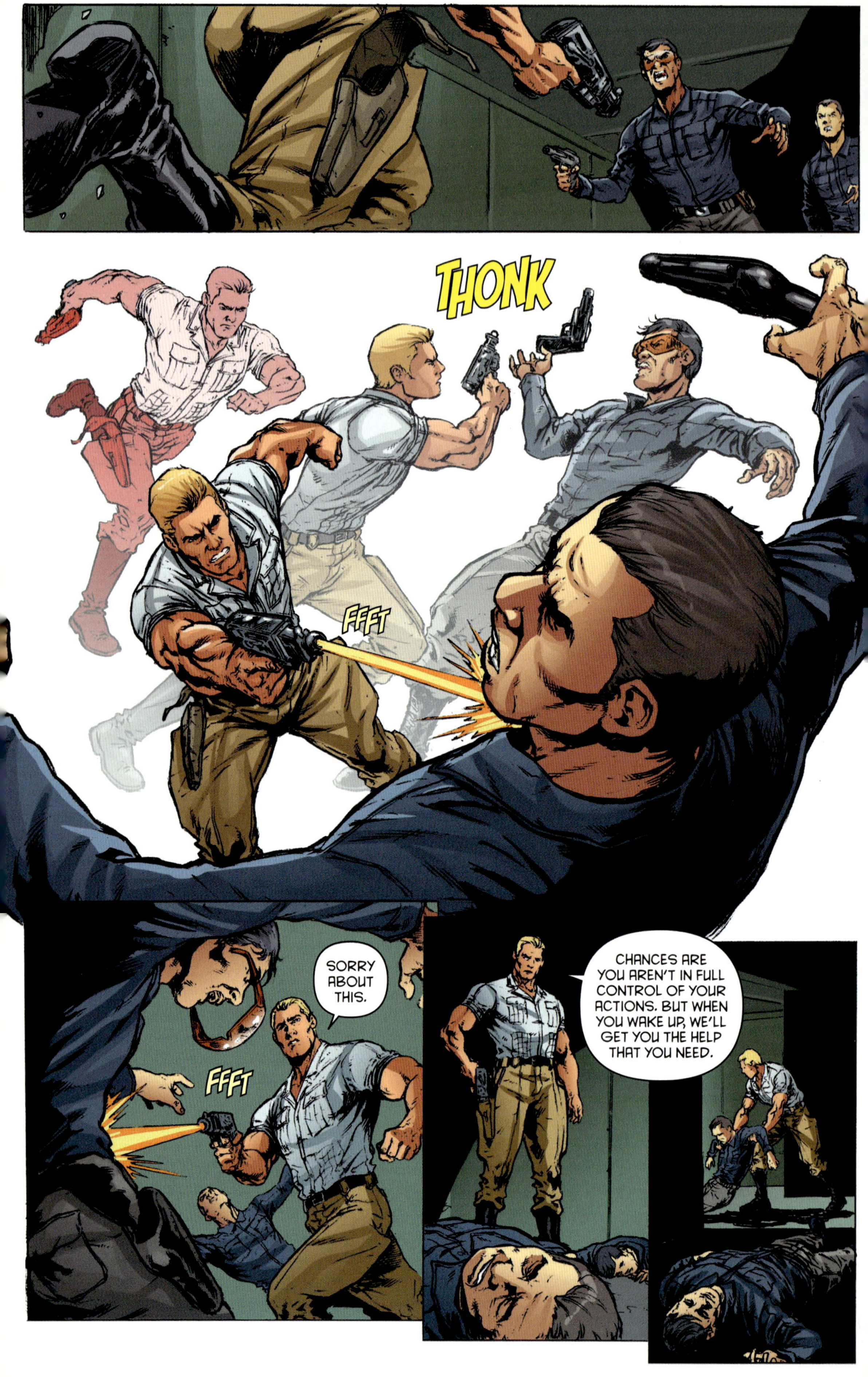
THONK
FFFT
SORRY ABOUT THIS.
FFFT
CHANCES ARE YOU AREN'T IN FULL CONTROL OF YOUR ACTIONS. BUT WHEN YOU WAKE UP, WE'LL GET YOU THE HELP THAT YOU NEED.

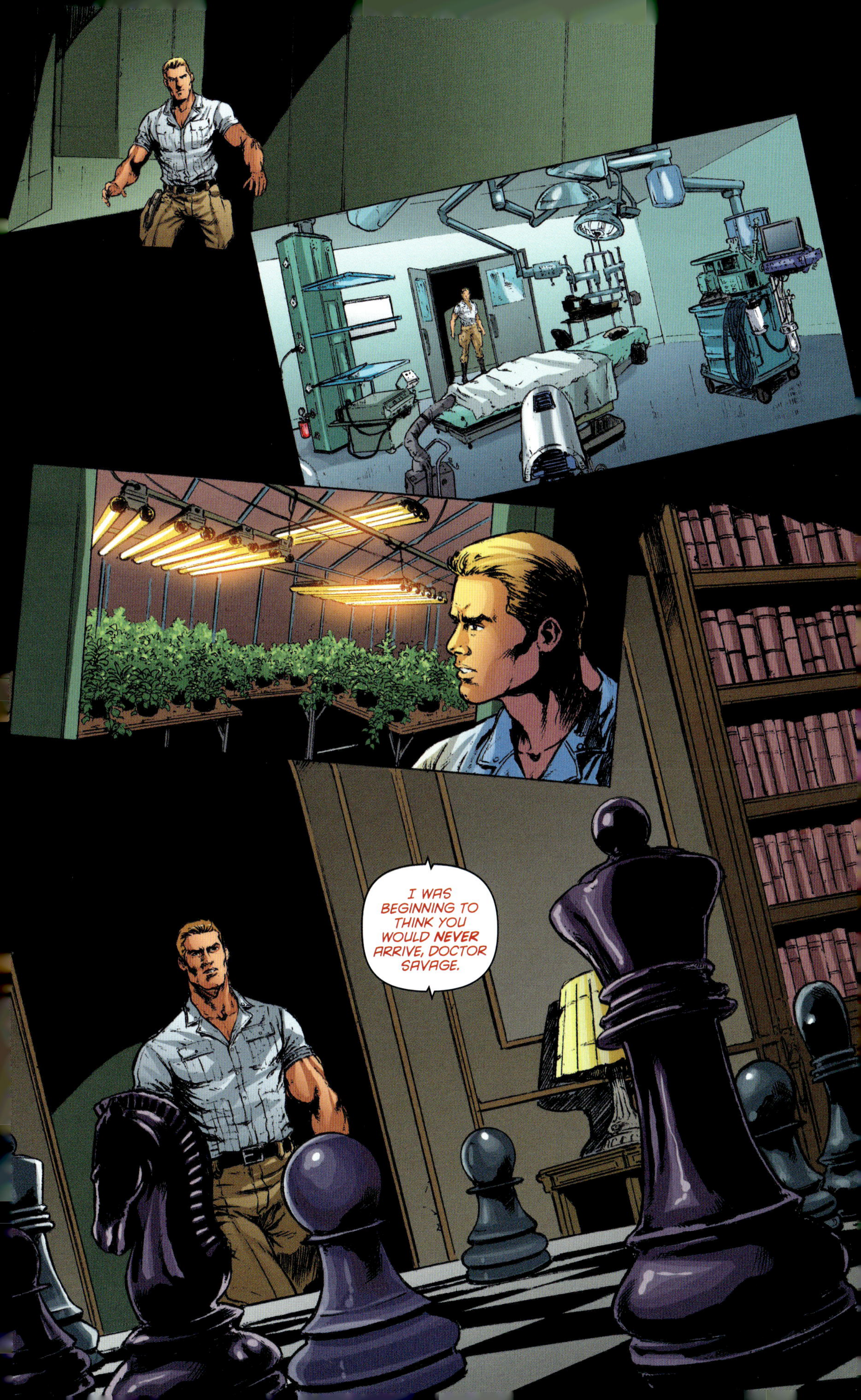
I WAS BEGINNING TO THINK YOU WOULD **NEVER** ARRIVE, DOCTOR SAVAGE.

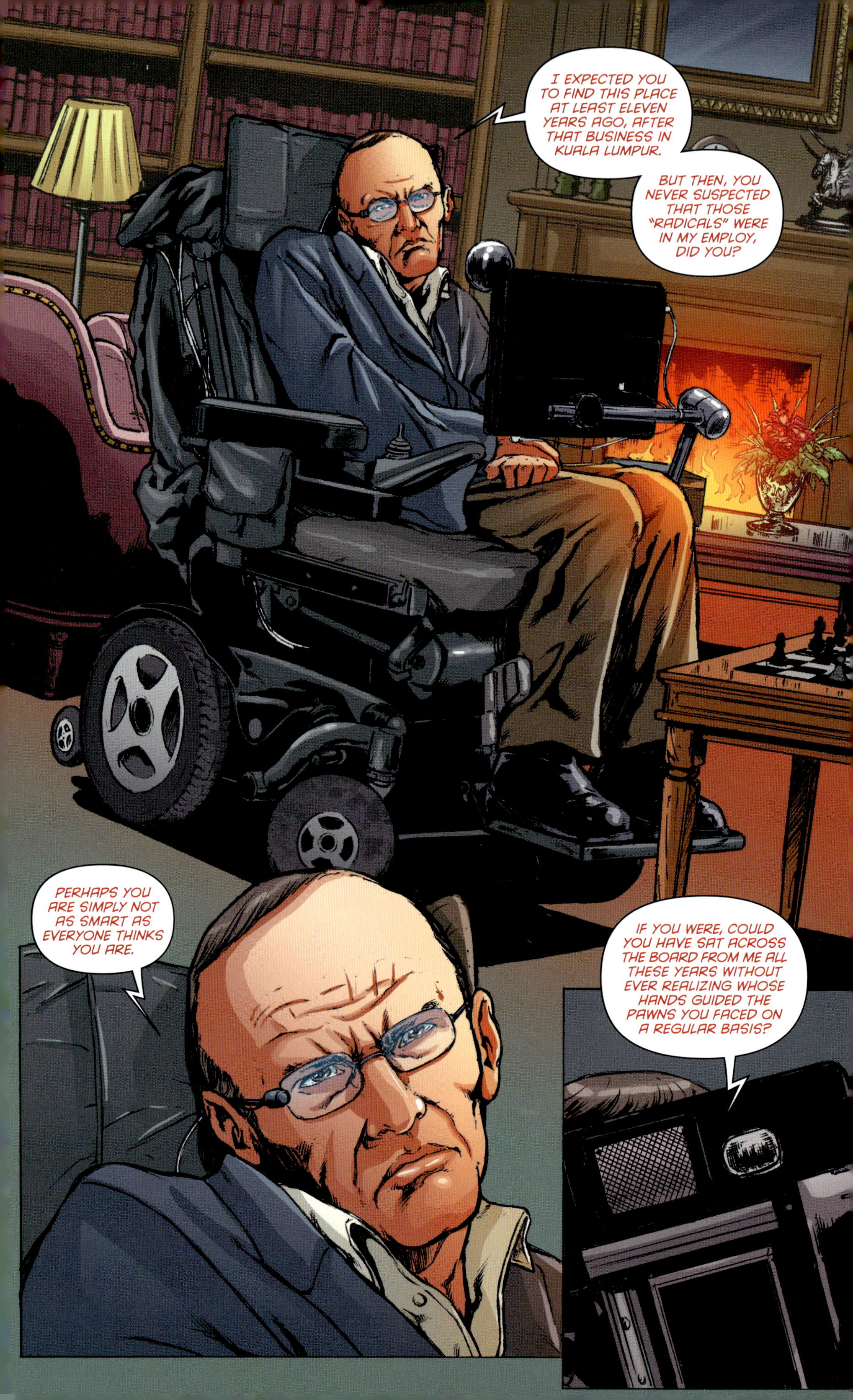
I EXPECTED YOU TO FIND THIS PLACE AT LEAST ELEVEN YEARS AGO, AFTER THAT BUSINESS IN KUALA LUMPUR.
BUT THEN, YOU NEVER SUSPECTED THAT THOSE "RADICALS" WERE IN MY EMPLOY, DID YOU?
PERHAPS YOU ARE SIMPLY NOT AS SMART AS EVERYONE THINKS YOU ARE.
IF YOU WERE, COULD YOU HAVE SAT ACROSS THE BOARD FROM ME ALL THESE YEARS WITHOUT EVER REALIZING WHOSE HANDS GUIDED THE PAWNS YOU FACED ON A REGULAR BASIS?

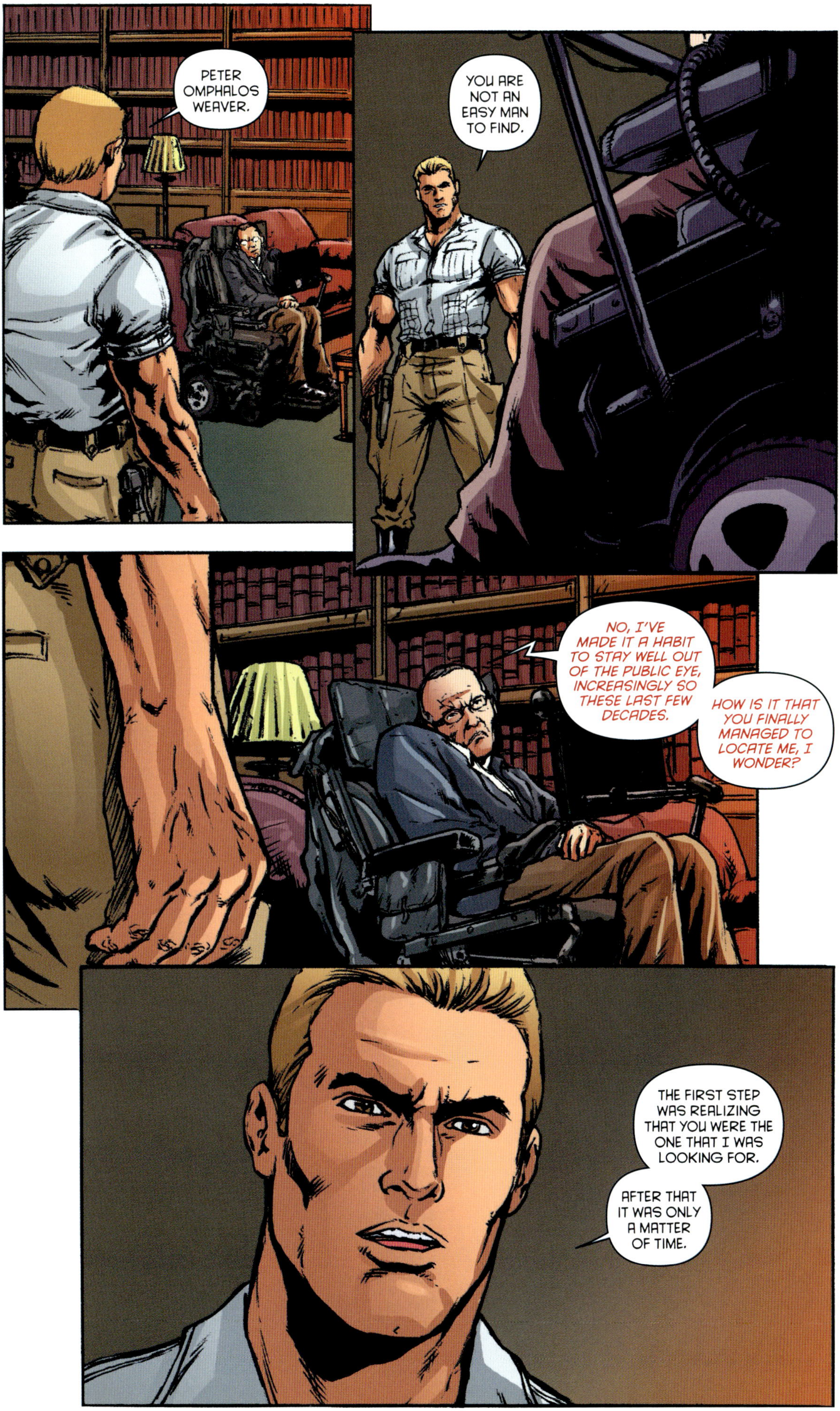
PETER OMPHALOS WEAVER.
YOU ARE NOT AN EASY MAN TO FIND.
NO, I'VE MADE IT A HABIT TO STAY WELL OUT OF THE PUBLIC EYE, INCREASINGLY SO THESE LAST FEW DECADES.
HOW IS IT THAT YOU FINALLY MANAGED TO LOCATE ME, I WONDER?
THE FIRST STEP WAS REALIZING THAT YOU WERE THE ONE THAT I WAS LOOKING FOR.
AFTER THAT IT WAS ONLY A MATTER OF TIME.

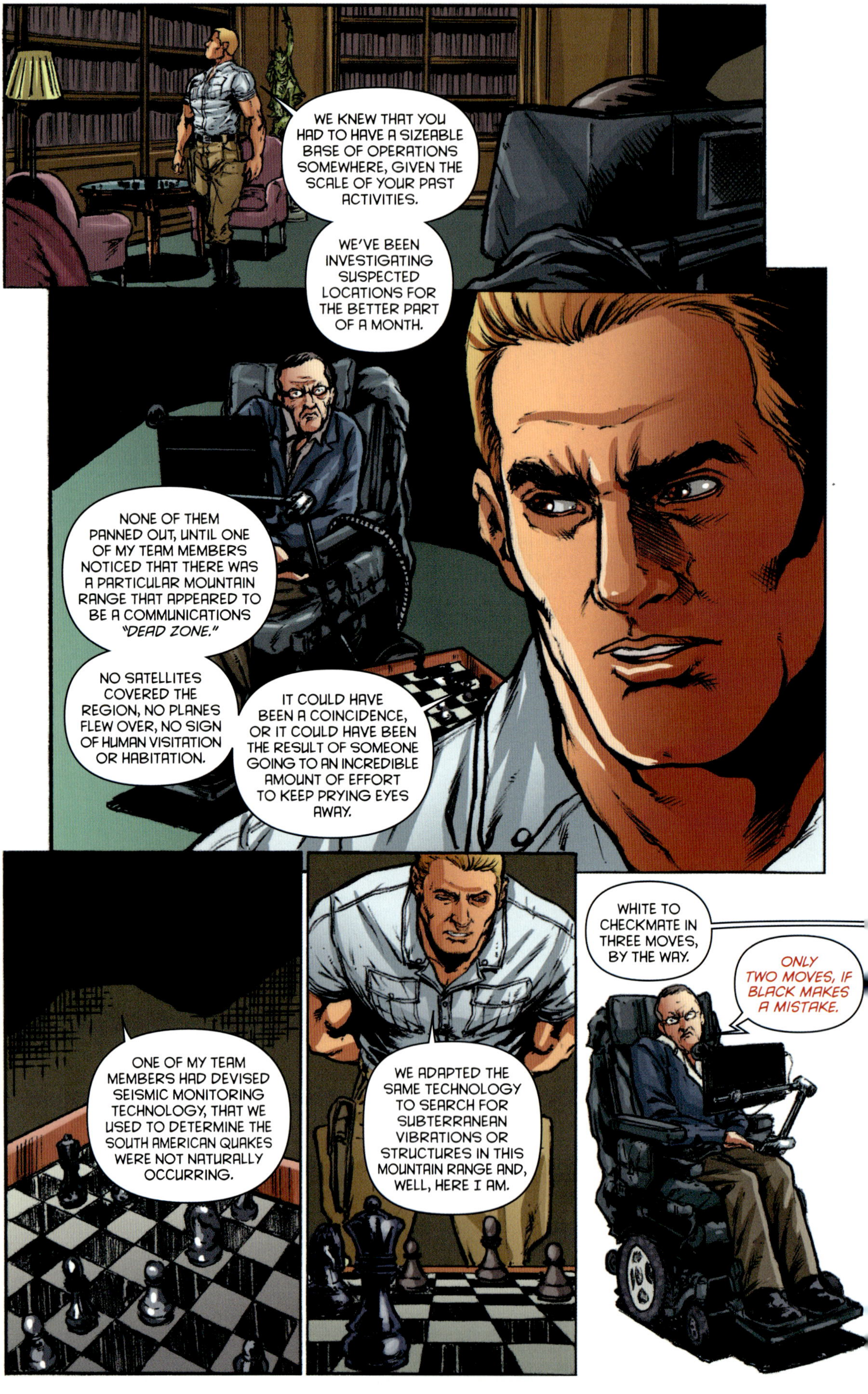
WE KNEW THAT YOU HAD TO HAVE A SIZEABLE BASE OF OPERATIONS SOMEWHERE, GIVEN THE SCALE OF YOUR PAST ACTIVITIES.
WE'VE BEEN INVESTIGATING SUSPECTED LOCATIONS FOR THE BETTER PART OF A MONTH.
NONE OF THEM PANNED OUT, UNTIL ONE OF MY TEAM MEMBERS NOTICED THAT THERE WAS A PARTICULAR MOUNTAIN RANGE THAT APPEARED TO BE A COMMUNICATIONS *"DEAD ZONE."*
NO SATELLITES COVERED THE REGION, NO PLANES FLEW OVER, NO SIGN OF HUMAN VISITATION OR HABITATION.
IT COULD HAVE BEEN A COINCIDENCE, OR IT COULD HAVE BEEN THE RESULT OF SOMEONE GOING TO AN INCREDIBLE AMOUNT OF EFFORT TO KEEP PRYING EYES AWAY.
ONE OF MY TEAM MEMBERS HAD DEVISED SEISMIC MONITORING TECHNOLOGY, THAT WE USED TO DETERMINE THE SOUTH AMERICAN QUAKES WERE NOT NATURALLY OCCURRING.
WE ADAPTED THE SAME TECHNOLOGY TO SEARCH FOR SUBTERRANEAN VIBRATIONS OR STRUCTURES IN THIS MOUNTAIN RANGE AND, WELL, HERE I AM.
WHITE TO CHECKMATE IN THREE MOVES, BY THE WAY.
ONLY TWO MOVES, IF BLACK MAKES A MISTAKE.

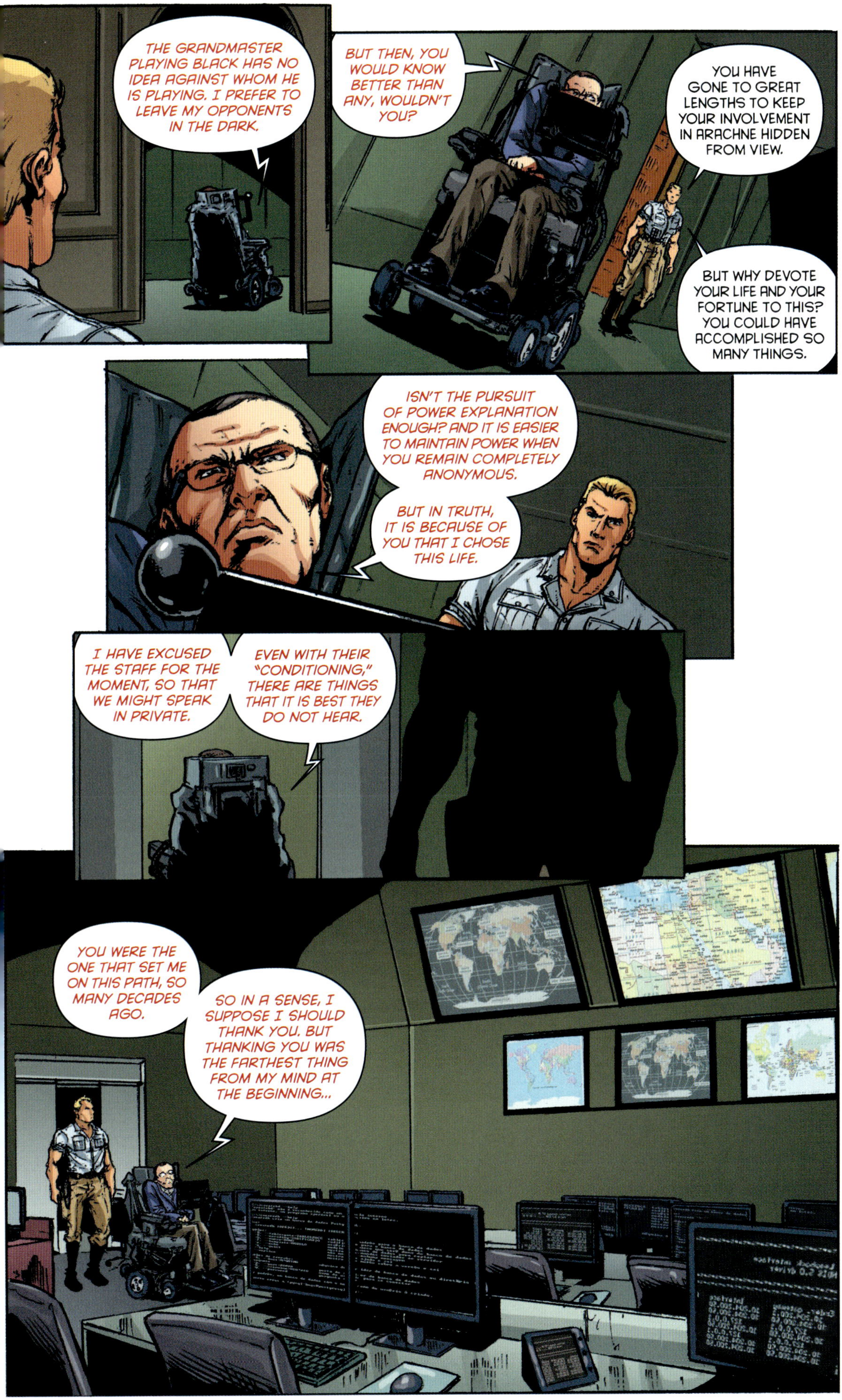
THE GRANDMASTER PLAYING BLACK HAS NO IDEA AGAINST WHOM HE IS PLAYING. I PREFER TO LEAVE MY OPPONENTS IN THE DARK.
BUT THEN, YOU WOULD KNOW BETTER THAN ANY, WOULDN'T YOU?
YOU HAVE GONE TO GREAT LENGTHS TO KEEP YOUR INVOLVEMENT IN ARACHNE HIDDEN FROM VIEW.
BUT WHY DEVOTE YOUR LIFE AND YOUR FORTUNE TO THIS? YOU COULD HAVE ACCOMPLISHED SO MANY THINGS.
ISN'T THE PURSUIT OF POWER EXPLANATION ENOUGH? AND IT IS EASIER TO MAINTAIN POWER WHEN YOU REMAIN COMPLETELY ANONYMOUS.
BUT IN TRUTH, IT IS BECAUSE OF YOU THAT I CHOSE THIS LIFE.
I HAVE EXCUSED THE STAFF FOR THE MOMENT, SO THAT WE MIGHT SPEAK IN PRIVATE.
EVEN WITH THEIR "CONDITIONING," THERE ARE THINGS THAT IT IS BEST THEY DO NOT HEAR.
YOU WERE THE ONE THAT SET ME ON THIS PATH, SO MANY DECADES AGO.
SO IN A SENSE, I SUPPOSE I SHOULD THANK YOU. BUT THANKING YOU WAS THE FARTHEST THING FROM MY MIND AT THE BEGINNING...

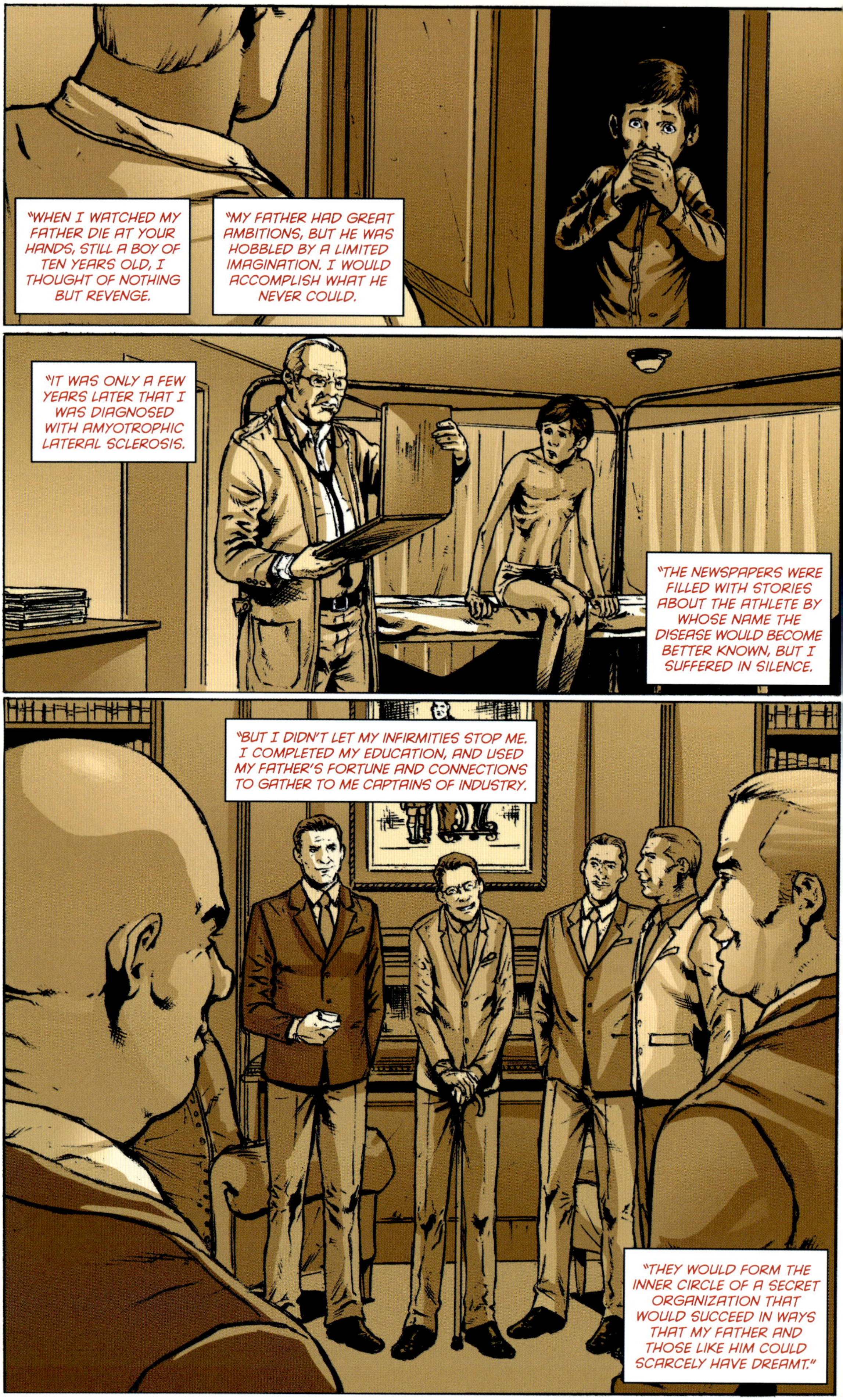
"WHEN I WATCHED MY FATHER DIE AT YOUR HANDS, STILL A BOY OF TEN YEARS OLD, I THOUGHT OF NOTHING BUT REVENGE.
"MY FATHER HAD GREAT AMBITIONS, BUT HE WAS HOBBLED BY A LIMITED IMAGINATION. I WOULD ACCOMPLISH WHAT HE NEVER COULD.
"IT WAS ONLY A FEW YEARS LATER THAT I WAS DIAGNOSED WITH AMYOTROPHIC LATERAL SCLEROSIS.
"THE NEWSPAPERS WERE FILLED WITH STORIES ABOUT THE ATHLETE BY WHOSE NAME THE DISEASE WOULD BECOME BETTER KNOWN, BUT I SUFFERED IN SILENCE.
"BUT I DIDN'T LET MY INFIRMITIES STOP ME. I COMPLETED MY EDUCATION, AND USED MY FATHER'S FORTUNE AND CONNECTIONS TO GATHER TO ME CAPTAINS OF INDUSTRY.
"THEY WOULD FORM THE INNER CIRCLE OF A SECRET ORGANIZATION THAT WOULD SUCCEED IN WAYS THAT MY FATHER AND THOSE LIKE HIM COULD SCARCELY HAVE DREAMT."

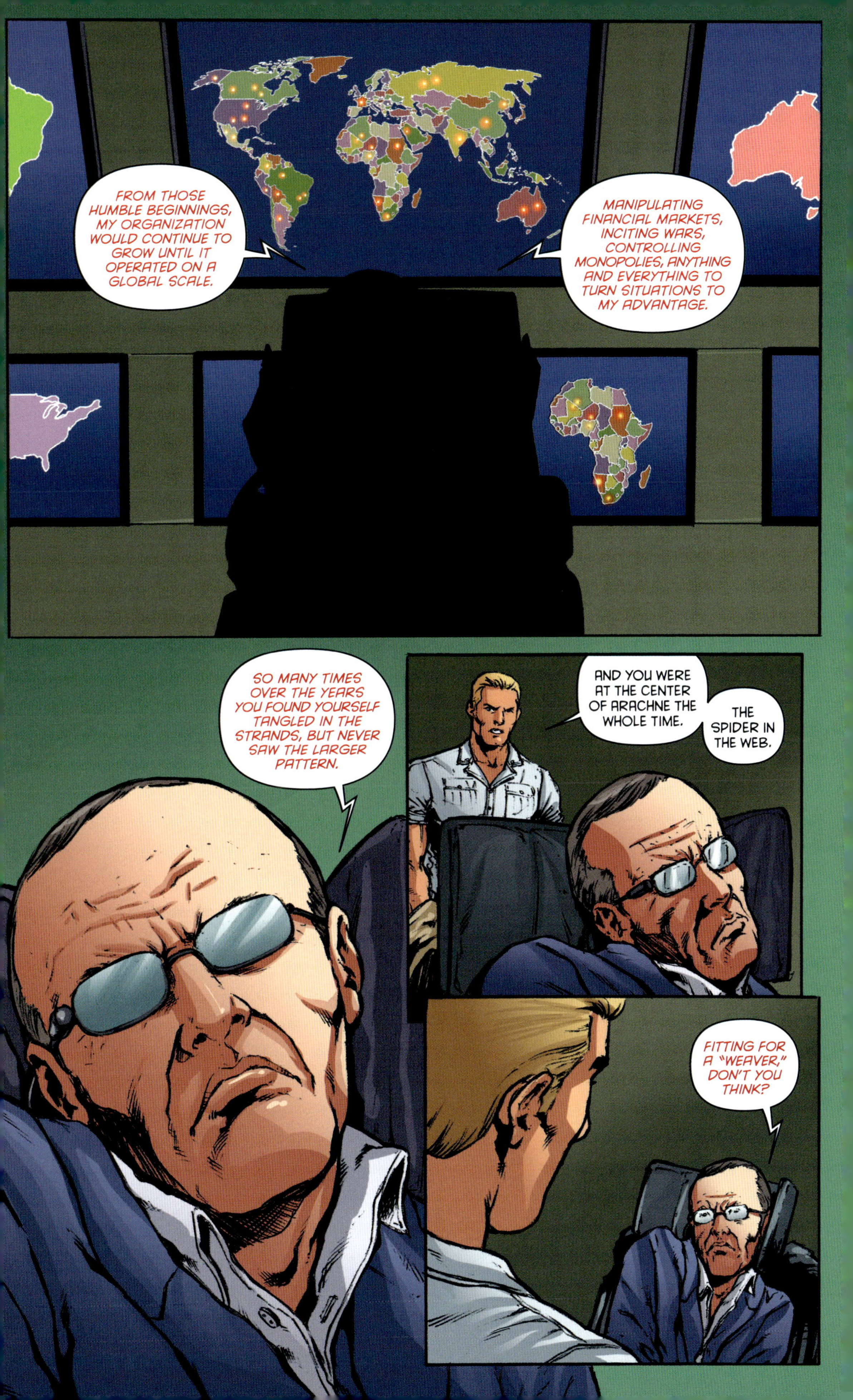
FROM THOSE HUMBLE BEGINNINGS, MY ORGANIZATION WOULD CONTINUE TO GROW UNTIL IT OPERATED ON A GLOBAL SCALE.
MANIPULATING FINANCIAL MARKETS, INCITING WARS, CONTROLLING MONOPOLIES, ANYTHING AND EVERYTHING TO TURN SITUATIONS TO MY ADVANTAGE.
SO MANY TIMES OVER THE YEARS YOU FOUND YOURSELF TANGLED IN THE STRANDS, BUT NEVER SAW THE LARGER PATTERN.
AND YOU WERE AT THE CENTER OF ARACHNE THE WHOLE TIME.
THE SPIDER IN THE WEB.
FITTING FOR A "WEAVER," DON'T YOU THINK?

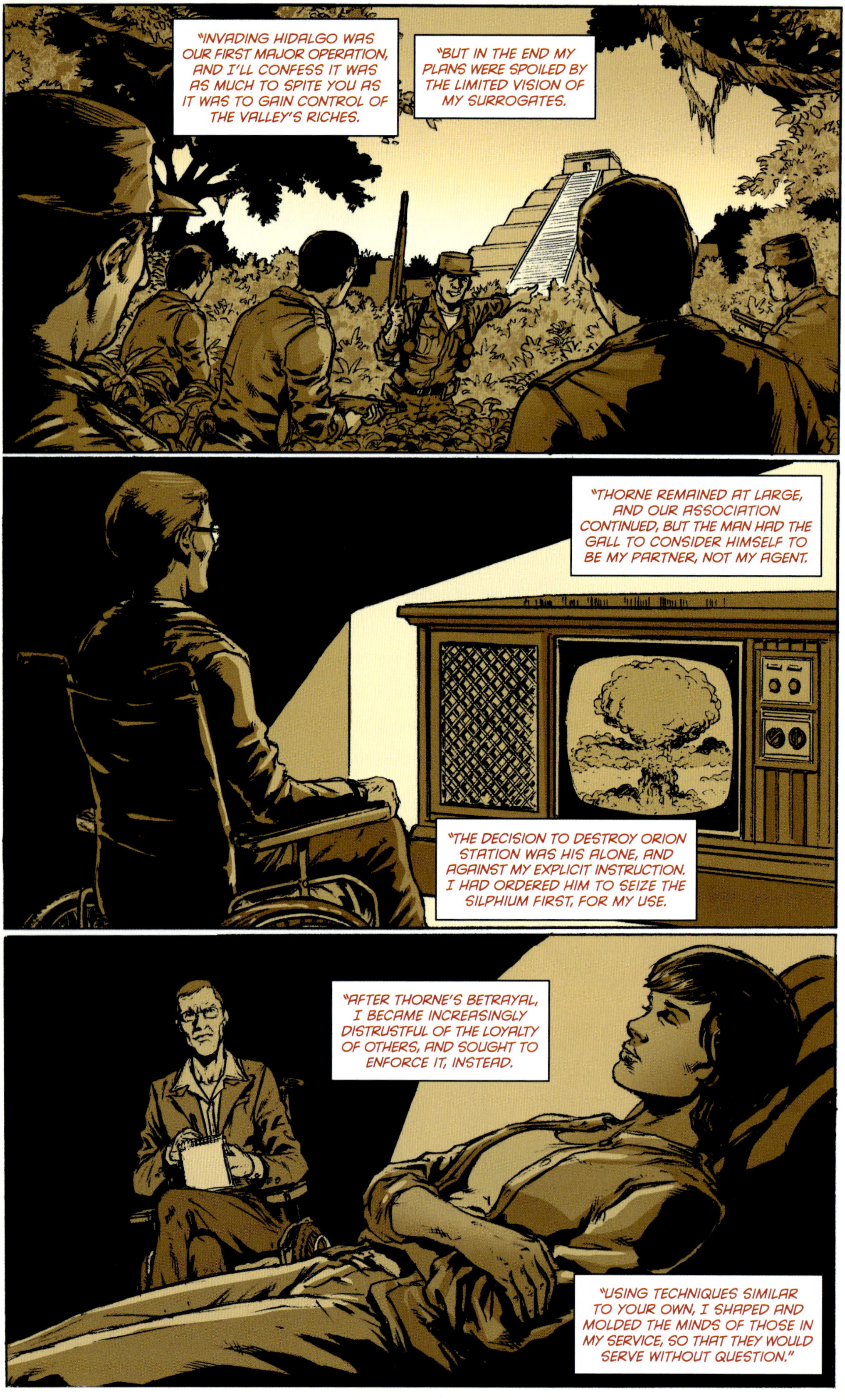
"INVADING HIDALGO WAS OUR FIRST MAJOR OPERATION, AND I'LL CONFESS IT WAS AS MUCH TO SPITE YOU AS IT WAS TO GAIN CONTROL OF THE VALLEY'S RICHES.
"BUT IN THE END MY PLANS WERE SPOILED BY THE LIMITED VISION OF MY SURROGATES.
"THORNE REMAINED AT LARGE, AND OUR ASSOCIATION CONTINUED, BUT THE MAN HAD THE GALL TO CONSIDER HIMSELF TO BE MY PARTNER, NOT MY AGENT.
"THE DECISION TO DESTROY ORION STATION WAS HIS ALONE, AND AGAINST MY EXPLICIT INSTRUCTION. I HAD ORDERED HIM TO SEIZE THE SILPHIUM FIRST, FOR MY USE.
"AFTER THORNE'S BETRAYAL, I BECAME INCREASINGLY DISTRUSTFUL OF THE LOYALTY OF OTHERS, AND SOUGHT TO ENFORCE IT, INSTEAD.
"USING TECHNIQUES SIMILAR TO YOUR OWN, I SHAPED AND MOLDED THE MINDS OF THOSE IN MY SERVICE, SO THAT THEY WOULD SERVE WITHOUT QUESTION."

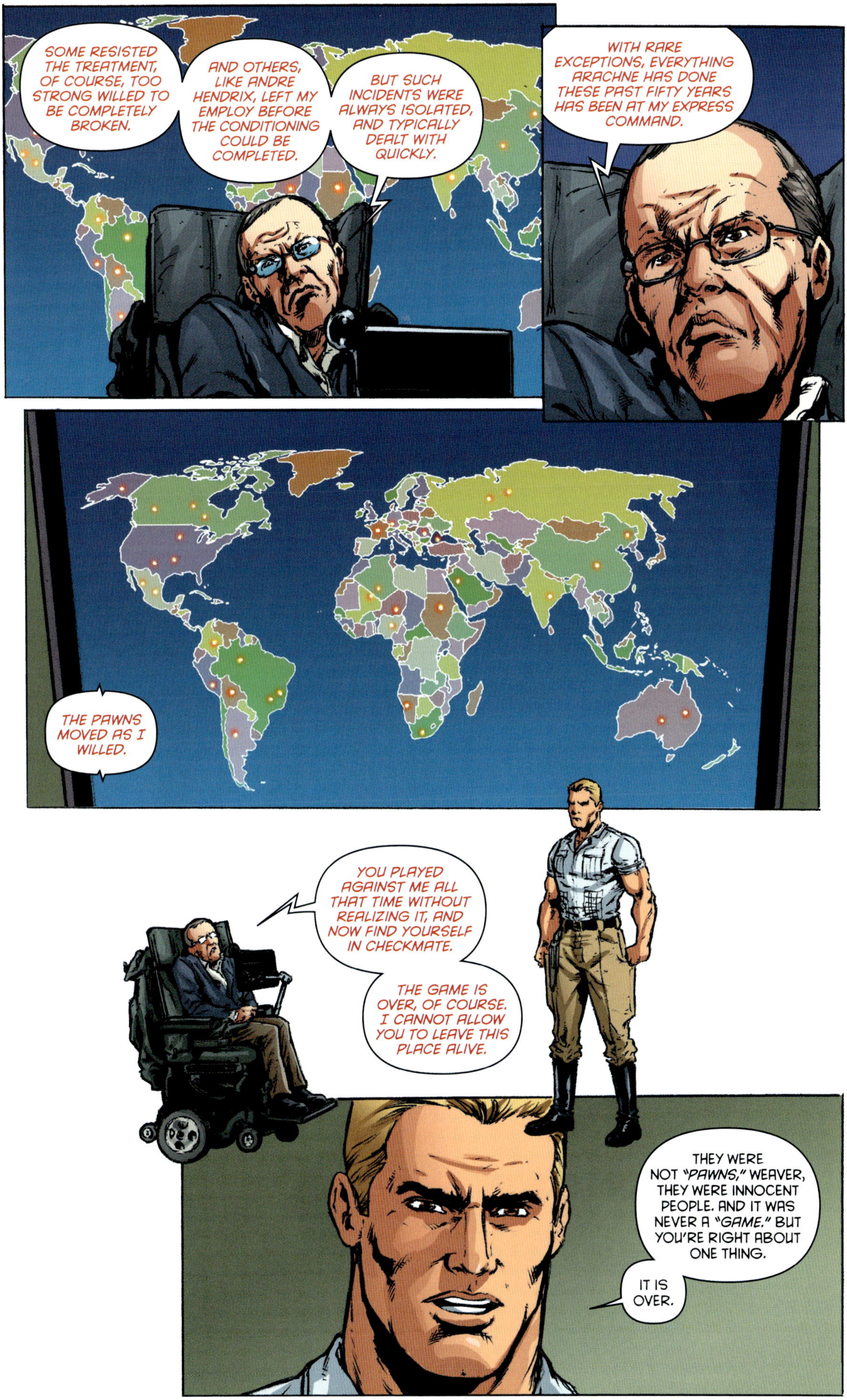
SOME RESISTED THE TREATMENT, OF COURSE, TOO STRONG WILLED TO BE COMPLETELY BROKEN.
AND OTHERS, LIKE ANDRE HENDRIX, LEFT MY EMPLOY BEFORE THE CONDITIONING COULD BE COMPLETED.
BUT SUCH INCIDENTS WERE ALWAYS ISOLATED, AND TYPICALLY DEALT WITH QUICKLY.
WITH RARE EXCEPTIONS, EVERYTHING ARACHNE HAS DONE THESE PAST FIFTY YEARS HAS BEEN AT MY EXPRESS COMMAND.
THE PAWNS MOVED AS I WILLED.
YOU PLAYED AGAINST ME ALL THAT TIME WITHOUT REALIZING IT, AND NOW FIND YOURSELF IN CHECKMATE.
THE GAME IS OVER, OF COURSE. I CANNOT ALLOW YOU TO LEAVE THIS PLACE ALIVE.
THEY WERE NOT "PAWNS," WEAVER, THEY WERE INNOCENT PEOPLE. AND IT WAS NEVER A "GAME." BUT YOU'RE RIGHT ABOUT ONE THING.
IT IS OVER.

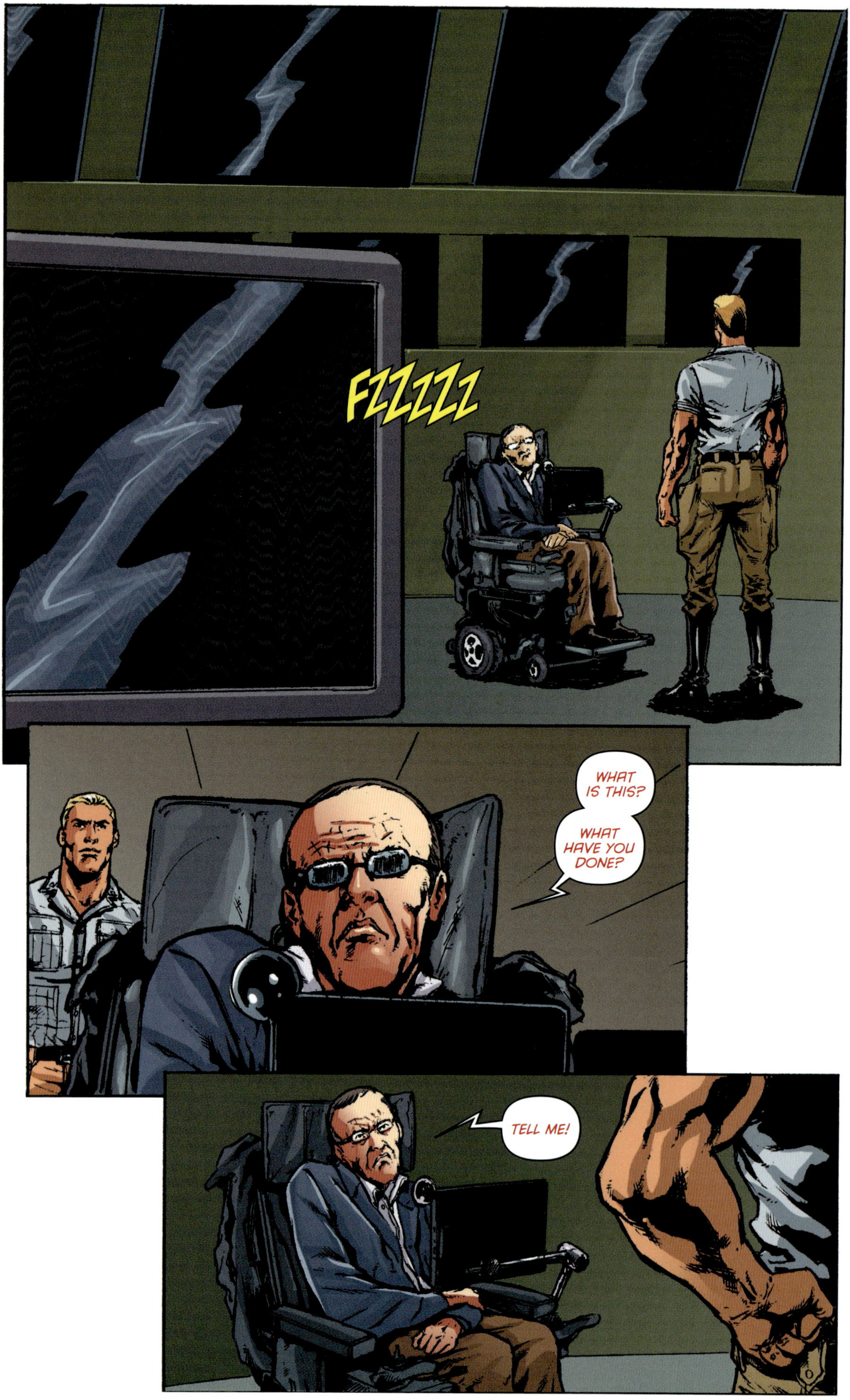
FZZZZz
WHAT IS THIS?
WHAT HAVE YOU DONE?
TELL ME!

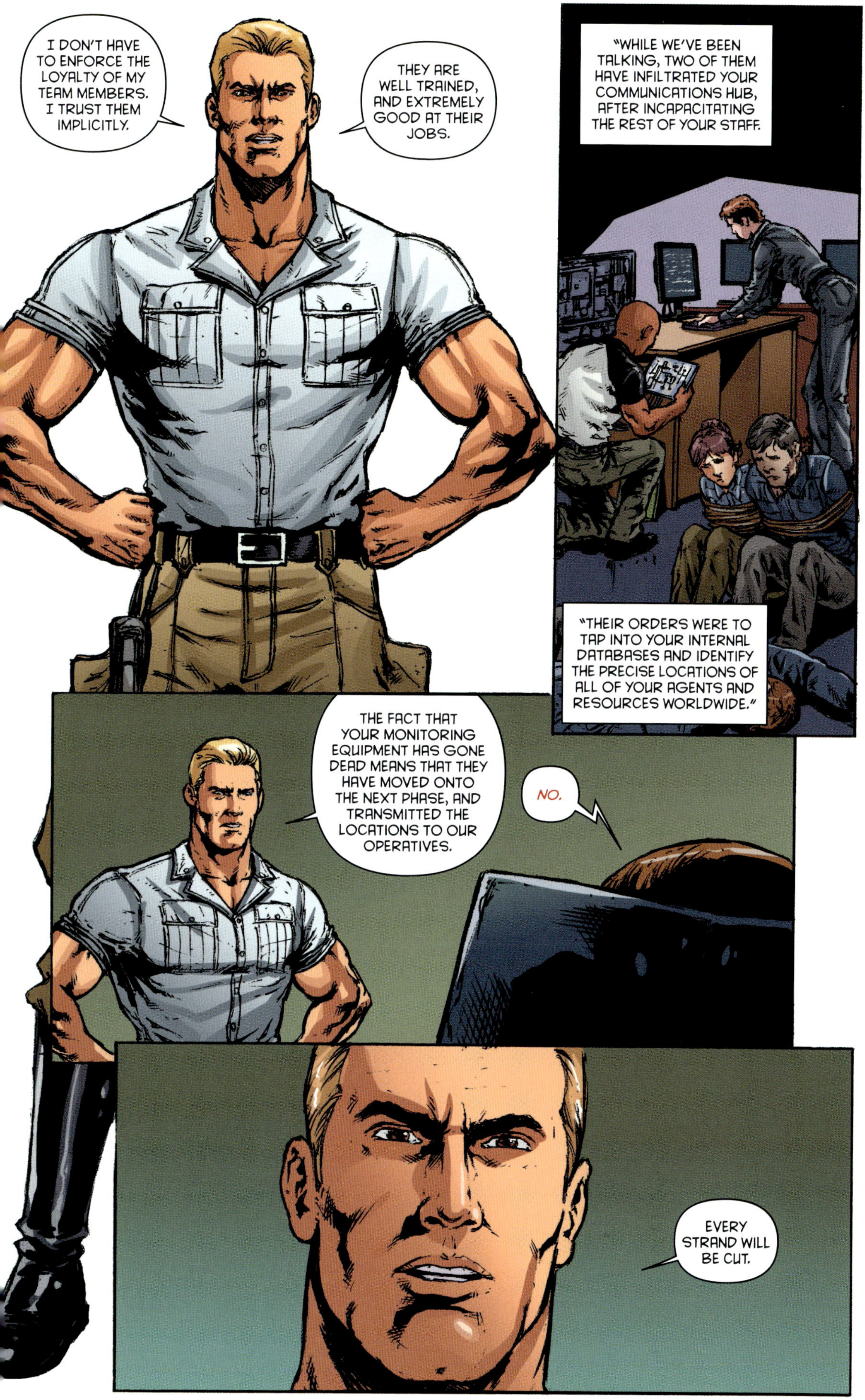
I DON'T HAVE TO ENFORCE THE LOYALTY OF MY TEAM MEMBERS. I TRUST THEM IMPLICITLY.
THEY ARE WELL TRAINED, AND EXTREMELY GOOD AT THEIR JOBS.
"WHILE WE'VE BEEN TALKING, TWO OF THEM HAVE INFILTRATED YOUR COMMUNICATIONS HUB, AFTER INCAPACITATING THE REST OF YOUR STAFF.
"THEIR ORDERS WERE TO TAP INTO YOUR INTERNAL DATABASES AND IDENTIFY THE PRECISE LOCATIONS OF ALL OF YOUR AGENTS AND RESOURCES WORLDWIDE."
THE FACT THAT YOUR MONITORING EQUIPMENT HAS GONE DEAD MEANS THAT THEY HAVE MOVED ONTO THE NEXT PHASE, AND TRANSMITTED THE LOCATIONS TO OUR OPERATIVES.
NO.
EVERY STRAND WILL BE CUT.

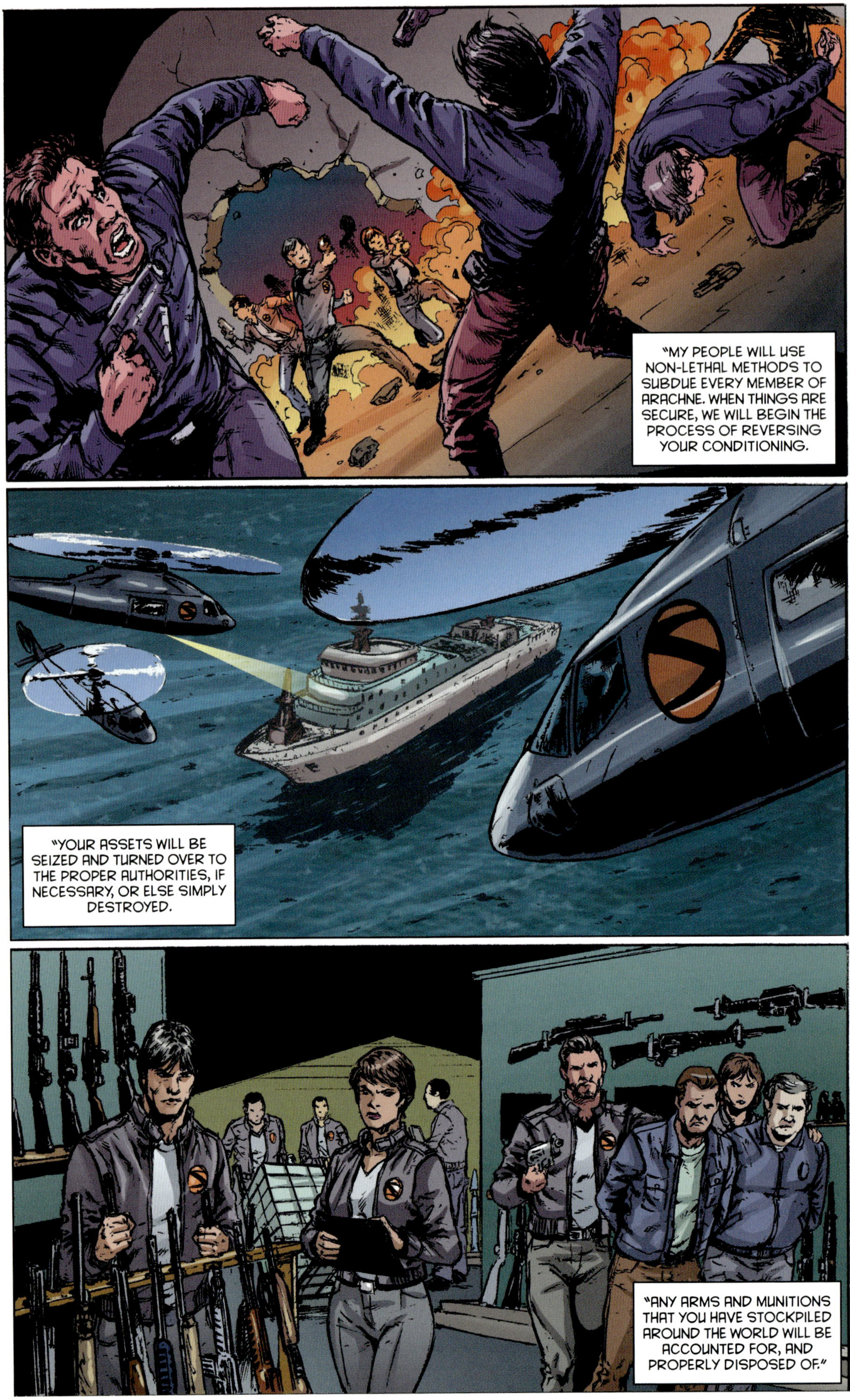
"MY PEOPLE WILL USE NON-LETHAL METHODS TO SUBDUE EVERY MEMBER OF ARACHNE. WHEN THINGS ARE SECURE, WE WILL BEGIN THE PROCESS OF REVERSING YOUR CONDITIONING.
"YOUR ASSETS WILL BE SEIZED AND TURNED OVER TO THE PROPER AUTHORITIES, IF NECESSARY, OR ELSE SIMPLY DESTROYED.
"ANY ARMS AND MUNITIONS THAT YOU HAVE STOCKPILED AROUND THE WORLD WILL BE ACCOUNTED FOR, AND PROPERLY DISPOSED OF."

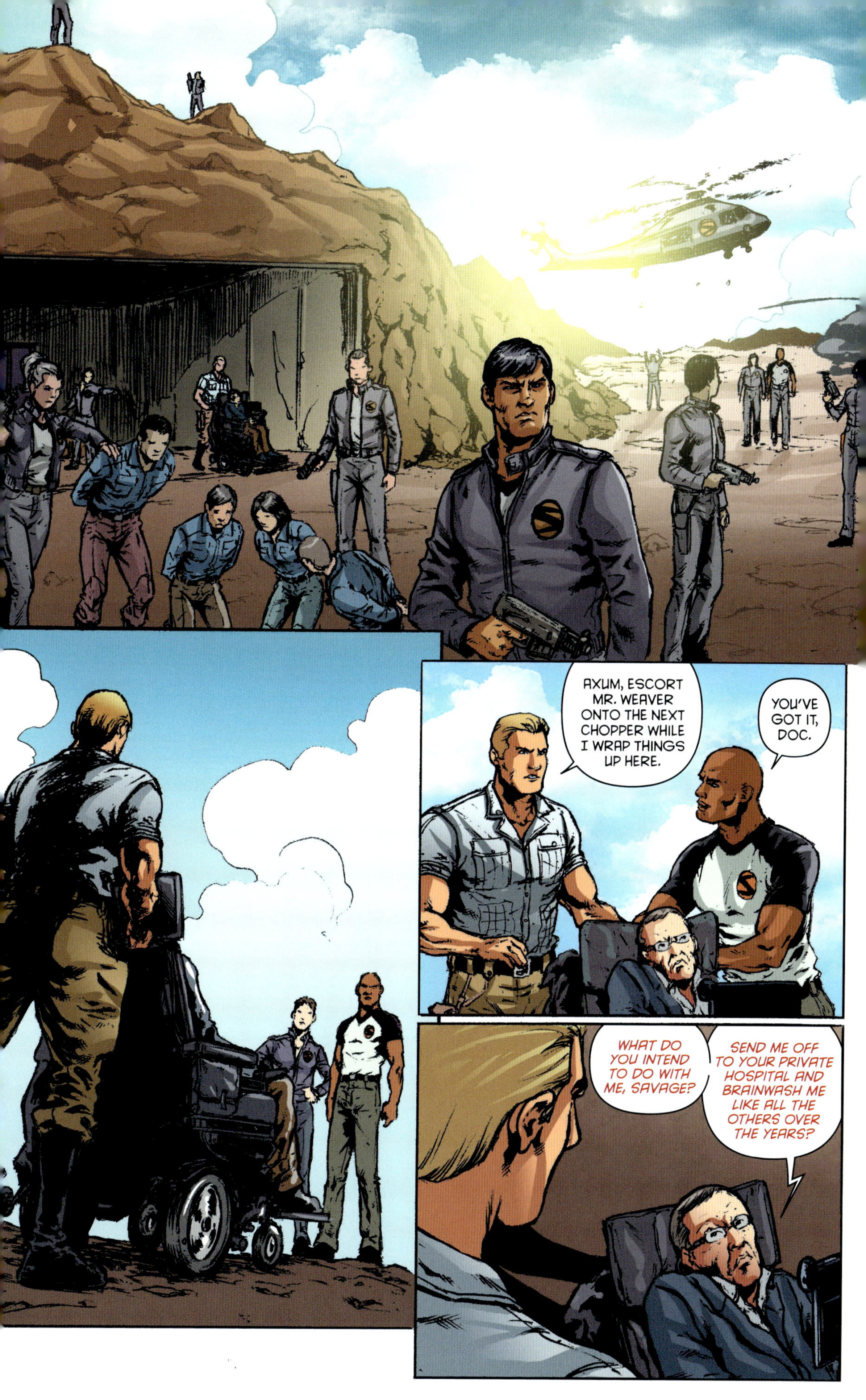
AXUM, ESCORT MR. WEAVER ONTO THE NEXT CHOPPER WHILE I WRAP THINGS UP HERE.
YOU'VE GOT IT, DOC.
WHAT DO YOU INTEND TO DO WITH ME, SAVAGE?
SEND ME OFF TO YOUR PRIVATE HOSPITAL AND BRAINWASH ME LIKE ALL THE OTHERS OVER THE YEARS?

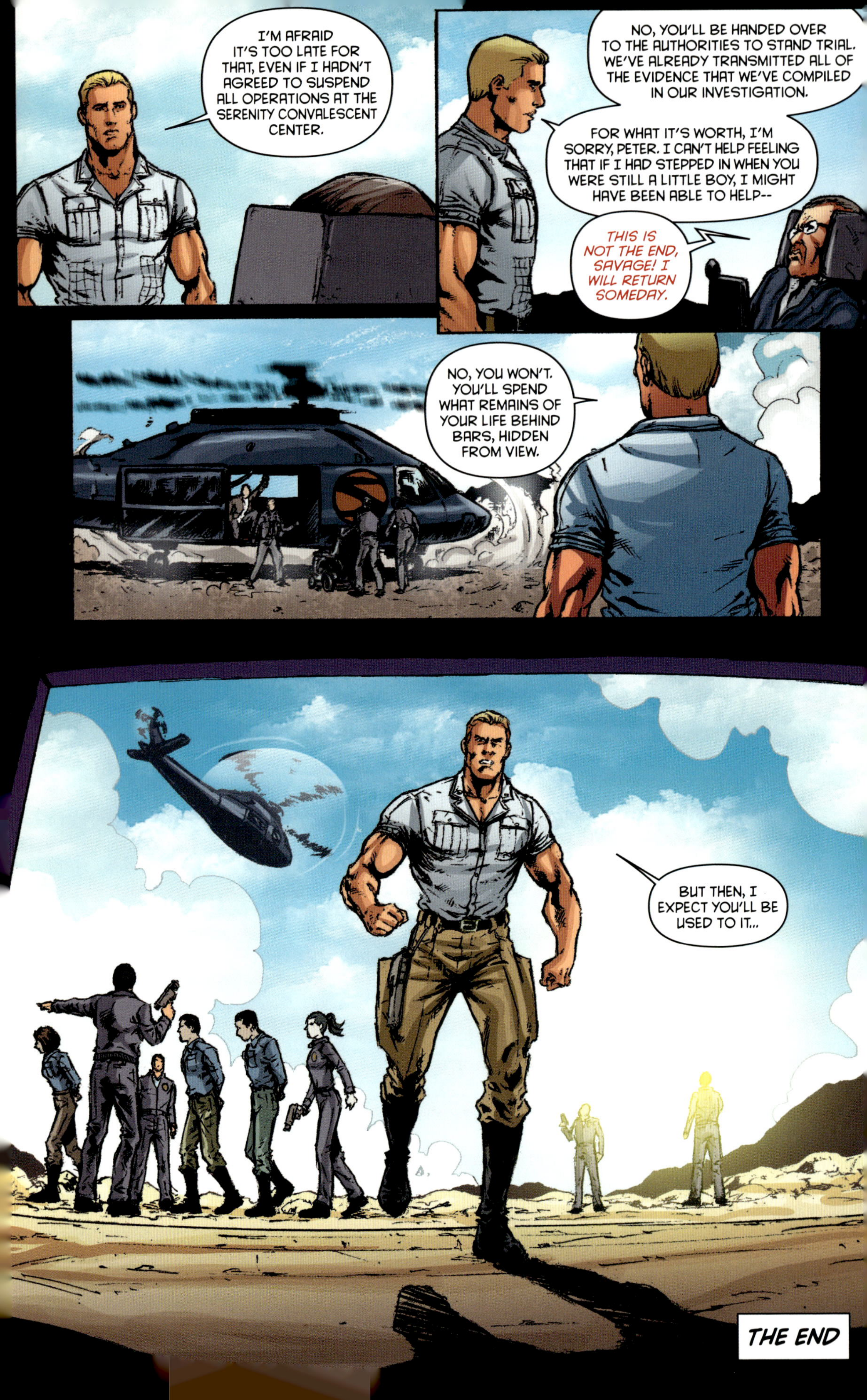

I'M AFRAID IT'S TOO LATE FOR THAT, EVEN IF I HADN'T AGREED TO SUSPEND ALL OPERATIONS AT THE SERENITY CONVALESCENT CENTER.
NO, YOU'LL BE HANDED OVER TO THE AUTHORITIES TO STAND TRIAL. WE'VE ALREADY TRANSMITTED ALL OF THE EVIDENCE THAT WE'VE COMPILED IN OUR INVESTIGATION.
FOR WHAT IT'S WORTH, I'M SORRY, PETER. I CAN'T HELP FEELING THAT IF I HAD STEPPED IN WHEN YOU WERE STILL A LITTLE BOY, I MIGHT HAVE BEEN ABLE TO HELP--
THIS IS NOT THE END, SAVAGE! I WILL RETURN SOMEDAY.
NO, YOU WON'T. YOU'LL SPEND WHAT REMAINS OF YOUR LIFE BEHIND BARS, HIDDEN FROM VIEW.
BUT THEN, I EXPECT YOU'LL BE USED TO IT...
THE END

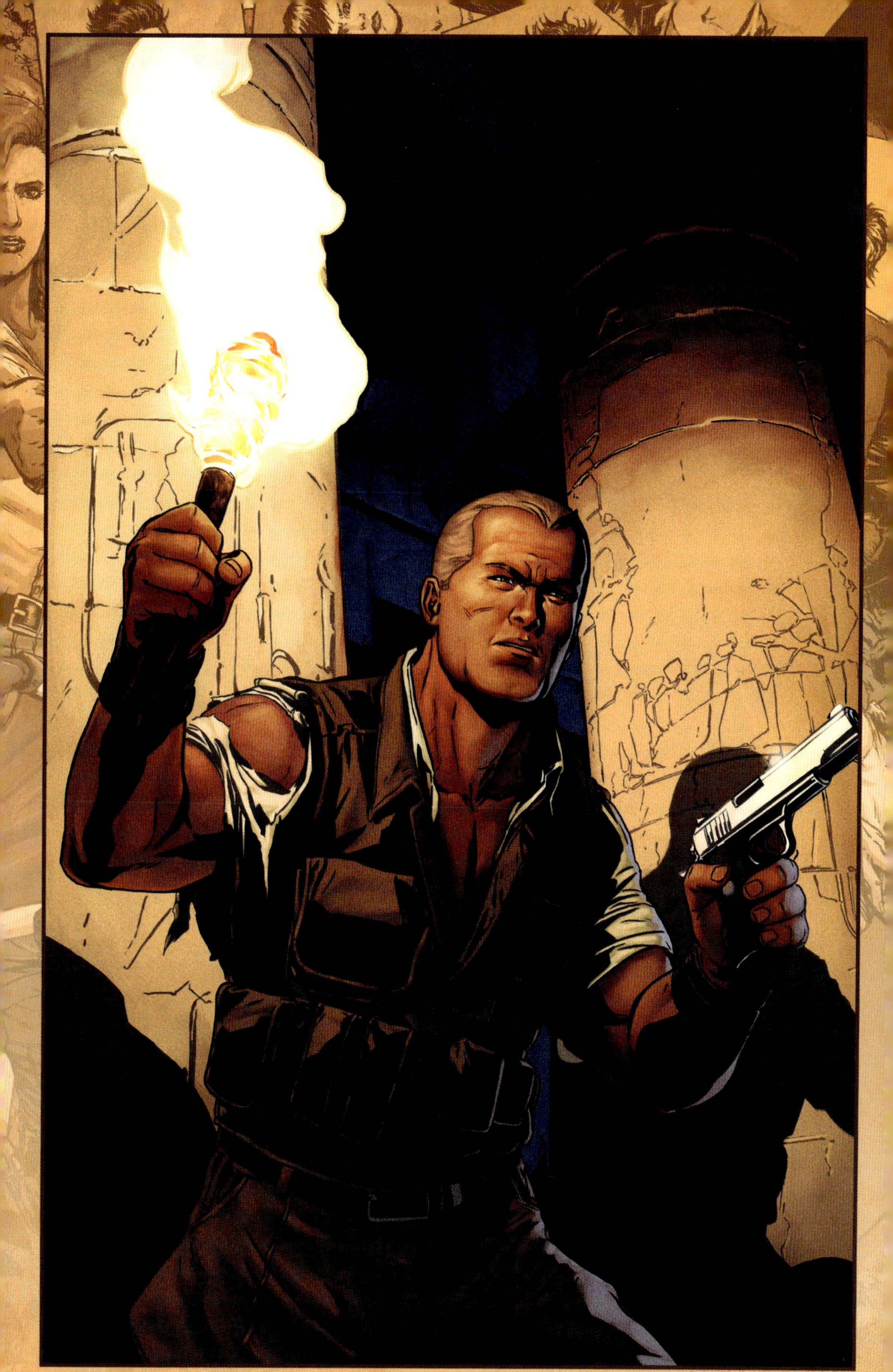

ISSUE #1 ALTERNATE COVER
art by MARC LAMING colors by LARA MARGARIDA

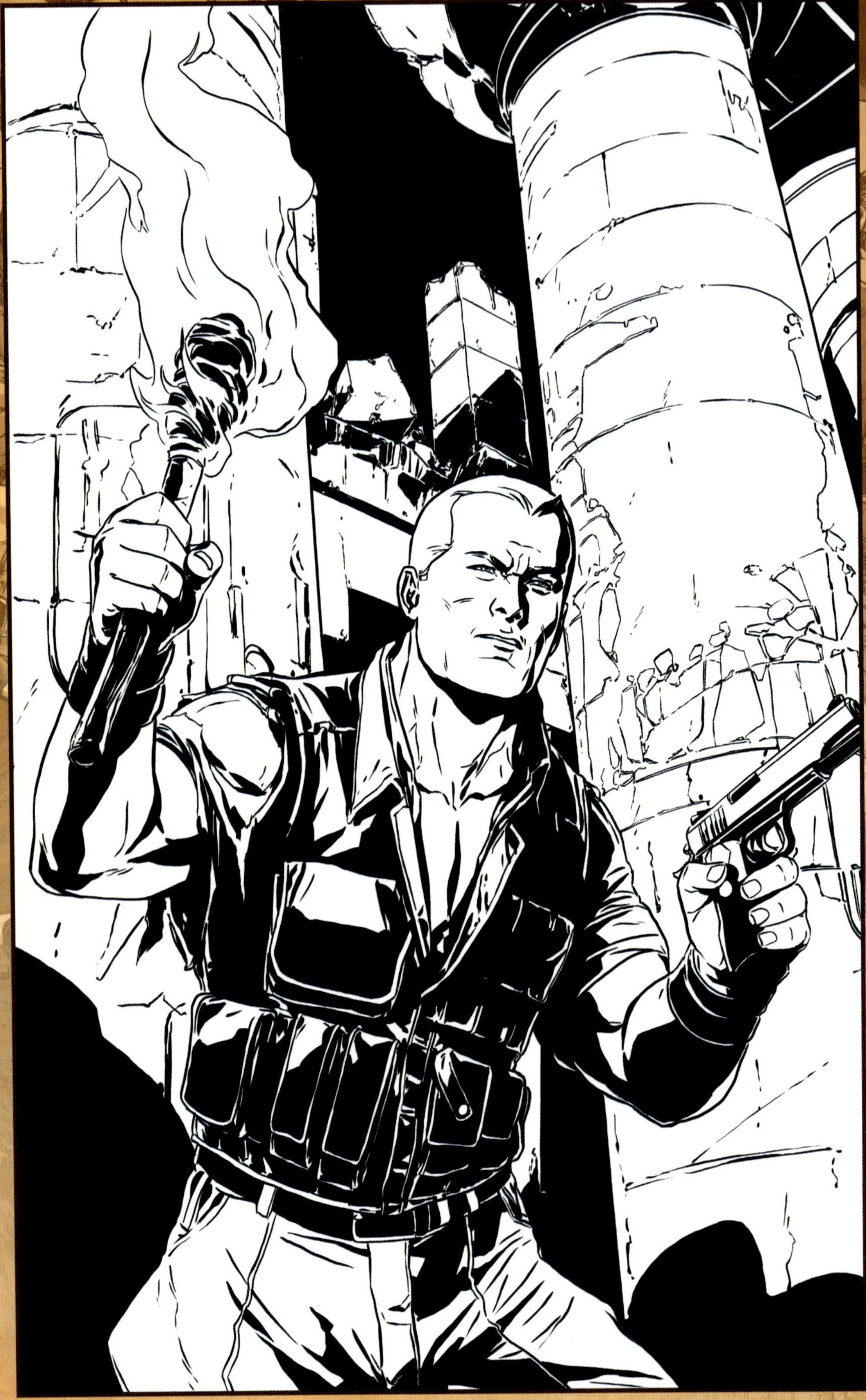

ISSUE **#1** ALTERNATE COVER LINE ART
by **MARC LAMING**

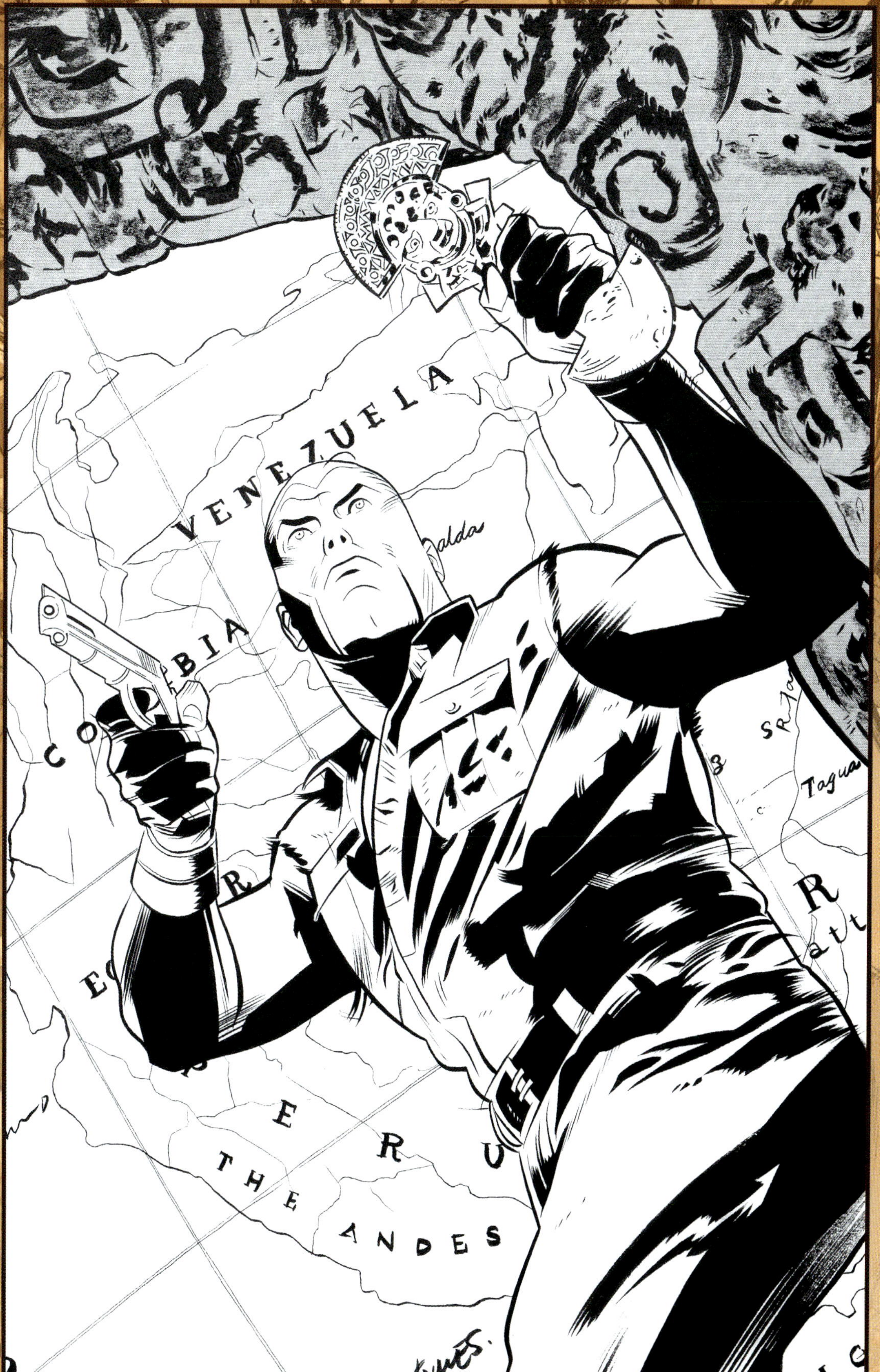
VENEZUELA
COLOMBIA
Caldas
ECUADOR
PERU
THE ANDES
R
SR
Tagua
EL
W. TORRES

ISSUE **#1** COVER LINE ART
by **WILFREDO TORRES**

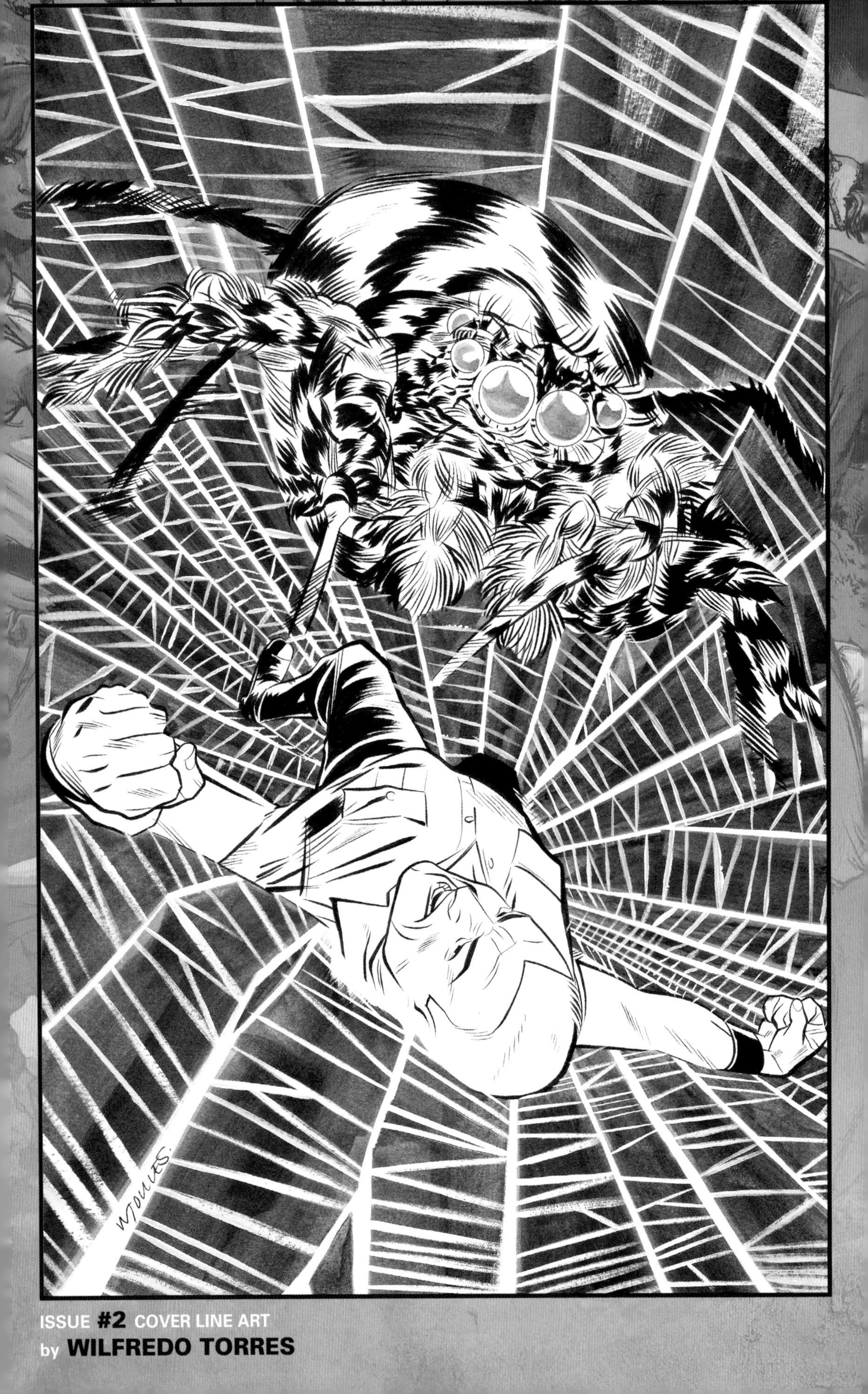

ISSUE #2 COVER LINE ART
by **WILFREDO TORRES**

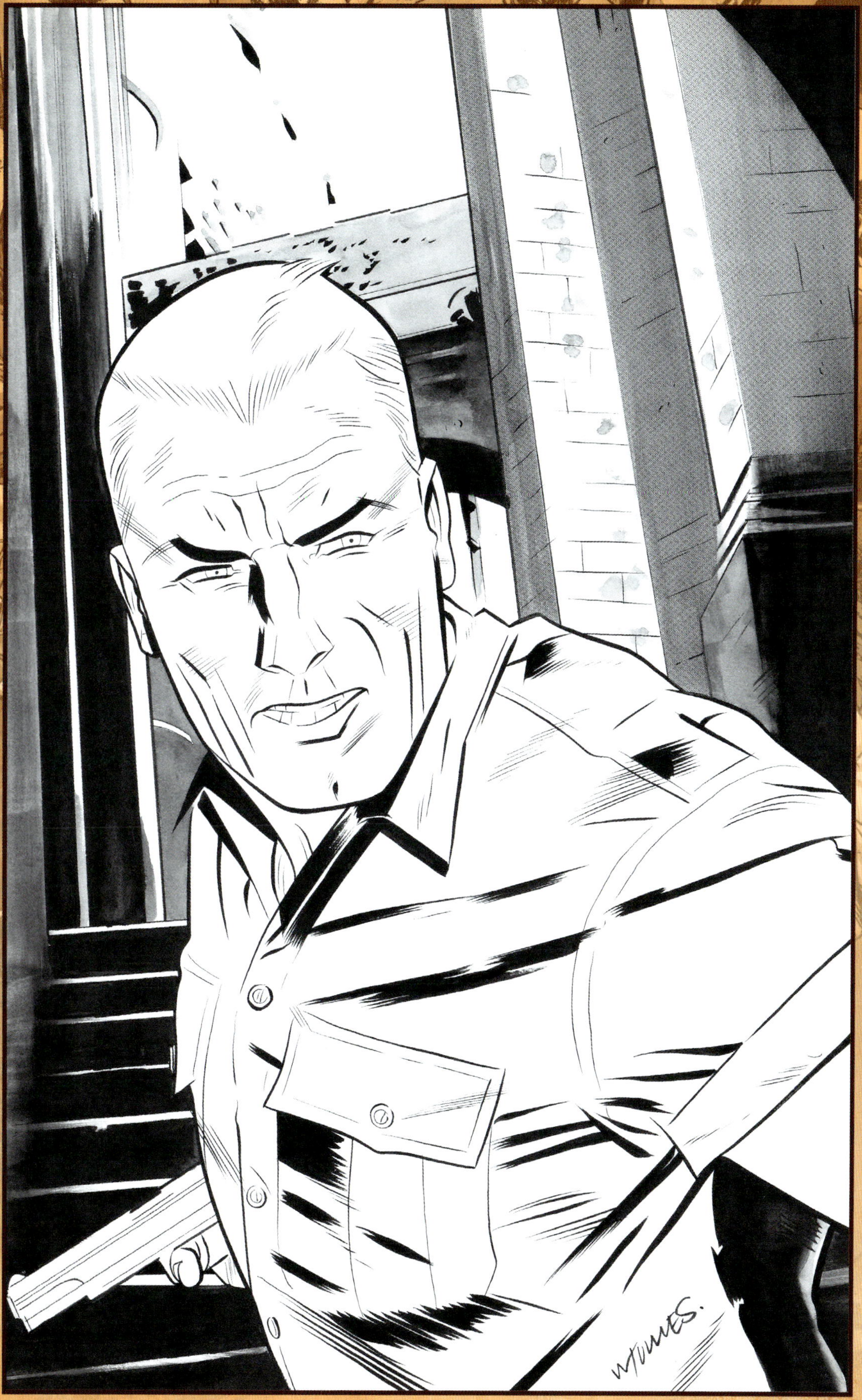

ISSUE **#3** COVER LINE ART
by **WILFREDO TORRES**

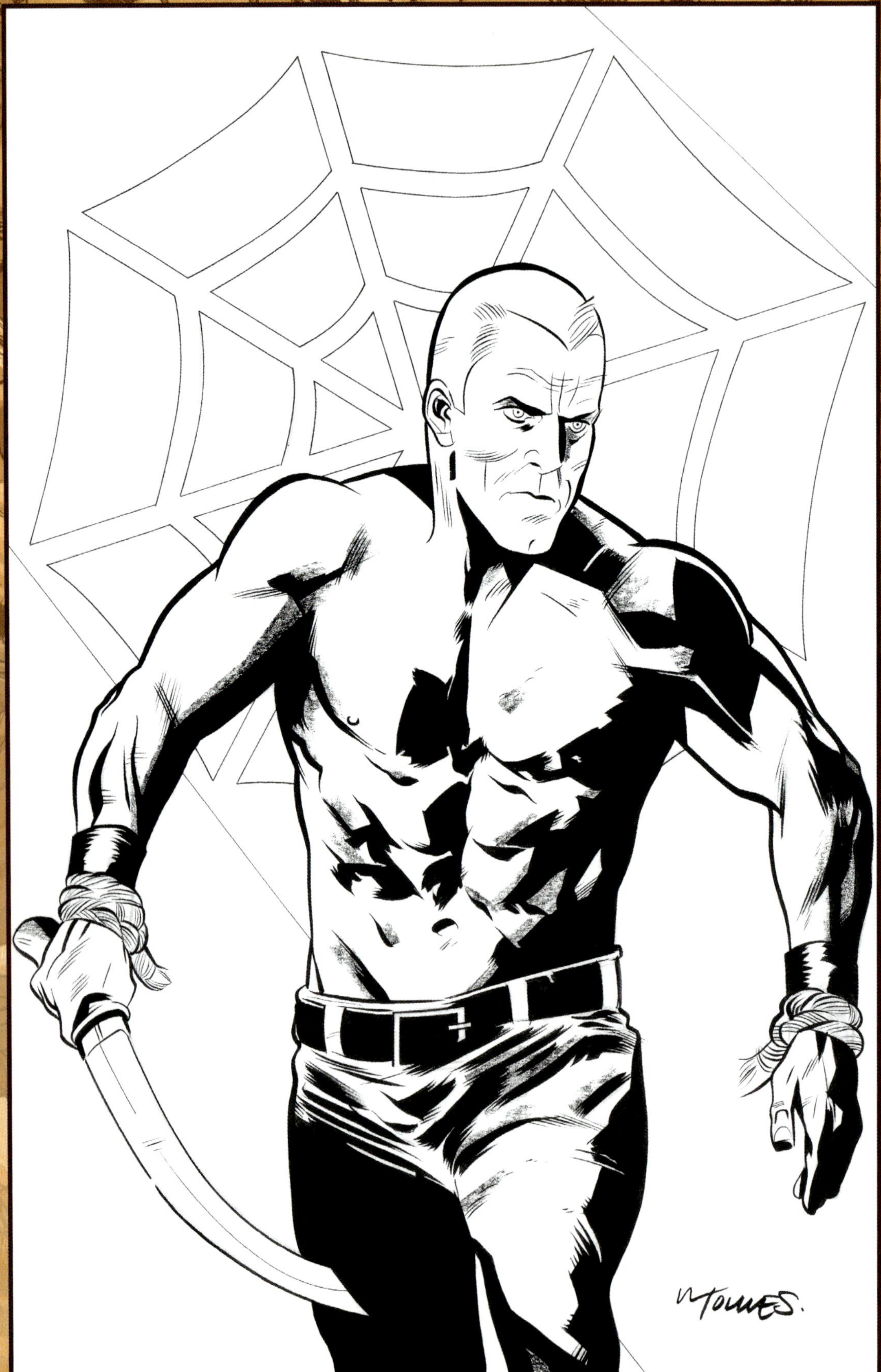
W TORRES.

ISSUE #4 COVER LINE ART
by WILFREDO TORRES

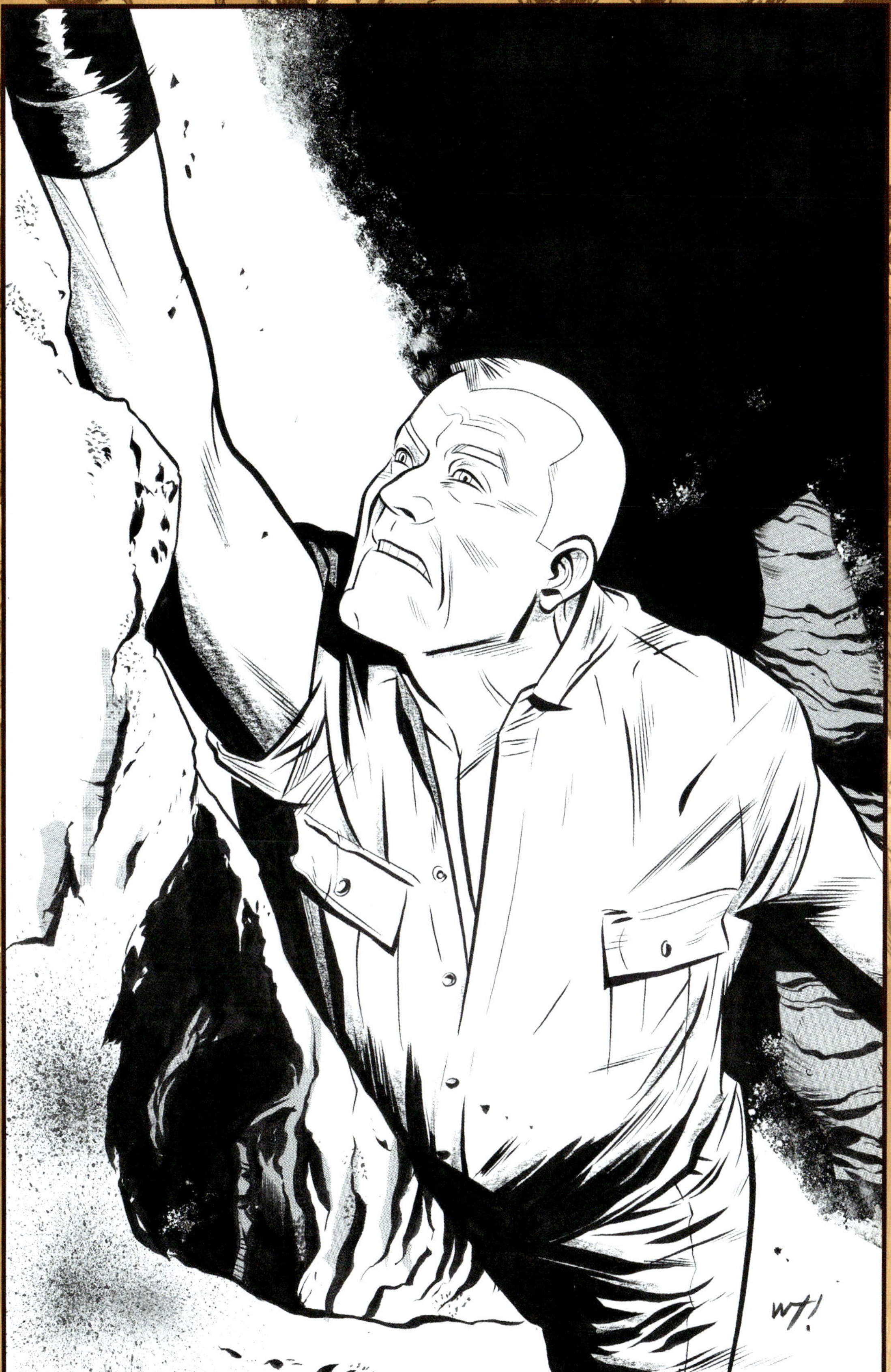
WT!

ISSUE #5 COVER LINE ART
by WILFREDO TORRES

THE MAN OF BRONZE RETURNS!

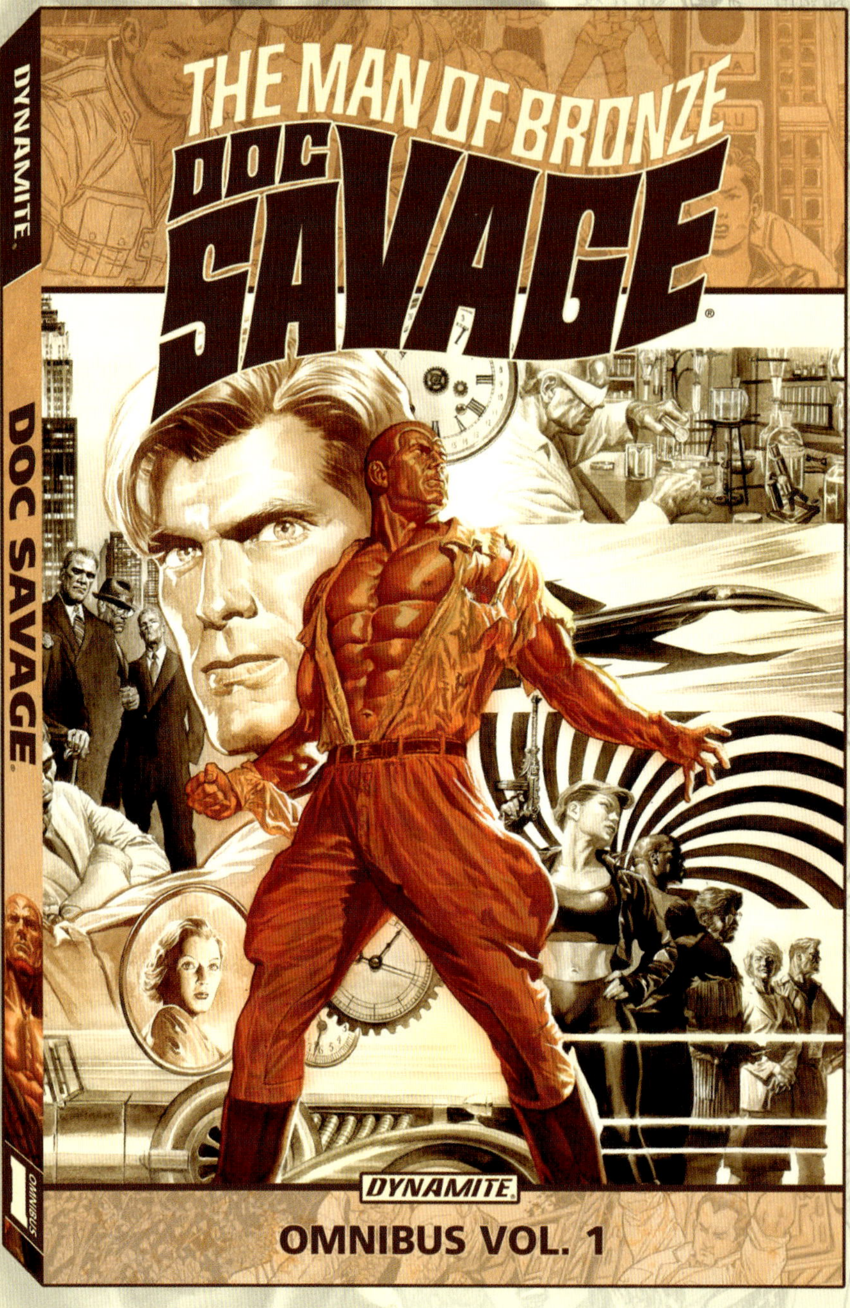
DYNAMITE
DOC SAVAGE
THE MAN OF BRONZE
DOC SAVAGE
DYNAMITE
OMNIBUS VOL. 1

DOC SAVAGE OMNIBUS VOLUME 1 TPB

COLLECTING ISSUES 1-8 PLUS THE DOC SAVAGE 2014 ANNUAL.

written by **CHRIS ROBERSON** and **SHANNON ERIC DENTON**

art by **BILQUIS EVELY** and **ROBERTO CASTRO**

cover by **ALEX ROSS**

IN STORES NOW!

DYNAMITE LEARN MORE ONLINE AT WWW.DYNAMITE.COM!

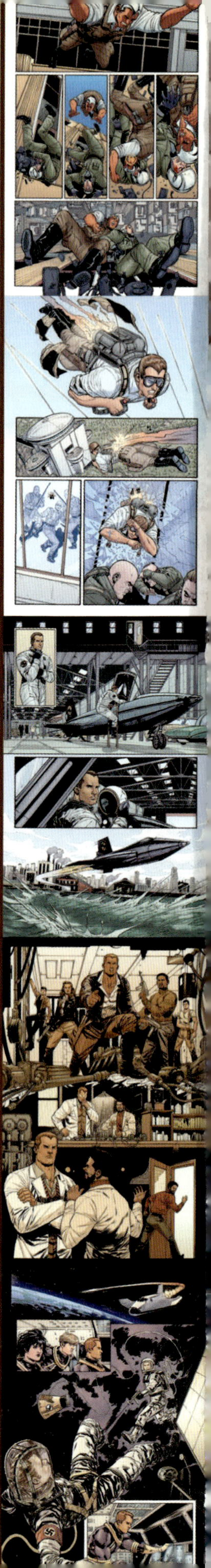